'Joyous, funny and full of warm, relatable characters, this is the queer Christmas romcom I've been waiting for'
**Laura Kay**

'A treat of a novel – cosy, Christmassy and wonderfully queer'
**Kate Davies**

'The perfect cosy Christmas read – sexy, sweet and smart'
**Kiran Millwood Hargrave**

'A thoroughly modern love story filled with joy, inappropriate Christmas jumpers and a daring reindeer rescue. I adored it'
**Tanya Byrne**

'An adorable Christmas novel filled with terrible schemes, a grand ball and one very horrible goose'
**Kat Dunn**

'Funny, sweet and emotionally satisfying . . . it's a festive delight!'
**Chloe Timms**

'Comforting Christmas chaos!'
**Amber Crewe**

'The joyous queer Christmas romcom you've been wishing for'
**Lily Lindon**

'Sweet, hot, and delightfully festive'
**Kate Dylan**

## About the Author

Lizzie Huxley-Jones is an autistic author and editor based in London.

They are the editor of *Stim*, an anthology of autistic authors and artists, which was published by Unbound in April 2020 to coincide with World Autism Awareness Week. They are also the author of the children's biography *Sir David Attenborough: A Life Story* (2020) and a contributor to the anthology *Allies: Real Talk About Showing Up, Screwing Up, And Trying Again* (2021).

They tweet too much and enjoy taking breaks to walk their dog Nerys.

# Make You Mine This Christmas

## Lizzie Huxley-Jones

HODDER

First published in Great Britain in 2022 by Hodder & Stoughton
An Hachette UK company

The authorised representative in the EEA is Hachette Ireland, 8 Castlecourt
Centre, Dublin 15, D15 XTP3, Ireland (email: info@hbgi.ie)

This paperback edition published in 2023

6

A CIP catalogue record for this title is available from the British Library

Paperback ISBN 978 1 399 70080 1
ebook ISBN 978 1 399 70081 8

Typeset in Plantin Light by Manipal Technologies Limited

Printed and bound in Great Britain by Clays Ltd, Elcograf S.p.A.

Hodder & Stoughton policy is to use papers that are natural,
renewable and recyclable products and made from wood grown in
sustainable forests. The logging and manufacturing processes are expected
to conform to the environmental regulations of the country of origin.

Hodder & Stoughton Ltd
Carmelite House
50 Victoria Embankment
London EC4Y 0DZ

www.hodder.co.uk

For Tim, the love of my life.

# Chapter One

To Haf Hughes, the best things about Christmas, in ascending order, are: all-you-can-eat mince pies, novelty jumpers, the fact you have a licence to be permanently too full and slightly pissed for the duration, and, most importantly, that there's no need to be a functioning person.

Which is why, while on the phone to her parents, she stumbles over the words, 'What do you mean you're going on holiday for Christmas?'

She hadn't even meant to ring them. The last few days at work had been so hectic that she barely felt awake. She'd finally crawled out of bed sometime around lunch, which had been happening more and more, and flopped down on the couch to watch *Gilmore Girls* for the tenth time. The only sense of time passing had been Netflix kindly asking if she was still watching. Twice. It was only as the season was nearing its regular Christmas episode that Haf had thought she could do the tiniest bit of life admin and ask her parents what train she should book home next week.

But in her half-asleep state, she'd hit the button to start a video call, and her mum had answered in record timing. Which had been, of course, completely typical because Haf was not looking the best version of herself. She's pretty sure that her mum recoiled when Haf appeared on screen, deep dark bags under her eyes, sallow skin and a hoodie barely hiding her dirty hair.

'Don't you remember, darling? I'm sure I told you.'

God, a functioning memory. Haf can't remember ever having one of those.

'I don't know,' she mumbles.

Her mum basks in the golden light of the nook – a room that was once Haf's bedroom but now has an admittedly very comfortable sofa bed, a small TV and lots of knitting supplies. In contrast, Haf's basically in the dark with the living-room curtains half-heartedly slung open, and only the wintry glow of *Gilmore Girls* providing any light.

'We just thought it would be a nice change. The travel agent in the village – you remember Emma? – she found a really nice hotel in Madeira, and we're going to spend Christmas Day on the beach. Flying out on Christmas Eve. All-inclusive, two weeks, just us two and the sun. We're so excited!'

'Just . . . you two?'

'Yes, just the two of us, darling. We've not had a Christmas just the two of us since before you were born. You *do* remember us talking about this, don't you?'

Haf mentally runs through the last few months – a blur of slogging away at work and staying late with the occasional half-paid-attention-to conversation with her parents, usually done while she was seeing to other essential life processes like eating or paying bills or – just that one time – while on the loo.

She comes up completely blank.

'Not really, Mum,' she admits. 'Things have been a little hectic.'

'Well, yes, I expect so with all your hard work and everything, but that's why we didn't think you'd be coming home. You've been *so* busy, and obviously we're very proud. We did tell you though. Didn't we, David?'

Half of her dad's face appears on screen. No matter how many tech demonstrations she's done in the past, her parents have never quite managed to position the camera so she can see both of them.

'We did, Mari. It was when we called you in October, when you wanted to know what a pension was.'

*Shit.* Haf must have forgotten, or not listened properly to start with. You think you'd remember something as important as Christmas plans, but Haf has forgotten all sorts of things over the last few months.

Both her parents, or the parts of their faces she can see, look a bit worried, so she picks the best option in front of her.

'Oh, yeah! Of course you did,' she says, her voice light with fake laughter. 'Silly old me. Brain's not plugged in today.'

'It's tired from all that thinking you've been doing.' Mum beams. 'We're really proud of you for working so hard the last few months.'

They didn't know the half of it.

'Thanks, guys.'

'I hope you're doing something nice too?' asks Dad.

*Nothing as nice as a two-week all-inclusive*, she thinks, trying and failing to not be bitter as orange pith.

'York is so lovely at Christmas, isn't it?' Mum says, though it's more a statement than an actual question.

'Well, yeah. Snowy. Lots of people doing their big Christmas-pressie shops. All the pubs have mulled wine on the go . . .'

A swirl of panic flickers in her stomach, but Haf ignores it and tries to focus on the pretence that she's not a total fuck-up.

But this panic has become a semi-regular feature, which she knows is likely not normal or healthy, but also seems to be part-and-parcel of being a certified adult . . . from what she can tell, anyway.

'Aren't you doing Christmas up there with Ambrose?'

'Oh, no. Ambrose's going home to their family. They're not staying here over Christmas,' she says, still trying to sound casual and slightly upbeat, as though she was actually really pleased for Ambrose to be celebrating with their family and not here.

Haf catches herself. Obviously, she's happy Ambrose has plans. She just wishes there was a backup, a plan B, a spare Christmas arrangement available to her right now.

But it's a whole desert of nothing.

And it's the 13th of December already, so there's basically zero time left; everyone who isn't a complete disaster will have sorted their plans weeks ago.

The chasm of a solo Christmas opens up before her.

'Are you upset? Oh dear, David, she's upset.'

Haf curses herself. Her parents have internal radars for negative emotions and are like bloodhounds specifically trained for lies. And it doesn't help that her face betrays every thought and feeling she ever has at the exact moment she has it.

'I said we should have double-checked with her, Mari,' mutters Dad, whose cheeks have gone bright pink under his beard.

'We did!' she hisses, turning the phone so that all Haf can see is the ceiling while Mum clearly berates him. After a moment, it flips back to showing her Mum's entire face bellowing, 'Are you upset, darling?' Haf's pretty sure this is supposed to be consoling rather than sounding like the voice of God as it echoes around the room.

'I'm—'

'Are you dating anyone? Maybe you can do something nice with them?'

'I—' she stammers, horrified that somehow this conversation is getting worse.

Haf decides the best thing she can do right now, which is admittedly not the most grown-up option, is to hang up. They'll just worry if they think she has nothing better to do. She'll ring them back later when she's decided what the hell she is doing, or at least come up with a better cover story.

After all, she might be desperate but she's not *quite* ready to beg her parents to take her on their romantic Christmas holiday.

'No! No, I'm absolutely fine!' she says, plastering on the biggest fake smile. 'I have a lot of plans, yes. Just working out which one to pick, ha ha. In fact, Ambrose and I are just off to a party thing, so I've gotta go! Oh, in fact, there they are! Gotta go! Call you soon! Love you, bye.'

As she hangs up, she cuts off her mum shouting goodbye.

Haf puts the phone face down on the coffee table just so she can't see any well-meaning follow-up messages, and unpauses *Gilmore Girls*.

'Bad news?'

Haf leaps out of her seat as Ambrose materialises in the living room, a sheet mask stuck on their face. 'Christ, warn a girl before you walk in with those on. I thought you were a ghost.'

'A sexy ghost, though, right? The kind you would want to be haunted by.' Ambrose glides down onto the couch, one perfectly shaped eyebrow raised, wrinkling the sheet. 'Didn't you just say to your mum I was here?'

'Oh, well. Yes. But that was a lie.'

'You don't usually lie to them. You're shit at it,' they say, taking the remote and pausing *Gilmore Girls*.

'They're going on holiday for Christmas,' Haf moans.

'Oh nice . . . or, not nice? Did they not tell you?'

'Apparently they did, and I completely forgot,' she says sulkily, pulling the blanket up to her face.

'Uh-oh.'

'Uh-oh, exactly. Of course this shitty year would end with me being alone for Christmas. Baby Jesus has it out for me, I swear.'

'Given you're a heathen, I don't think he'd care,' they say, wrapping an arm over the back of the couch and stroking the top of Haf's hoodie-covered head.

It hasn't been her year.

First, there was the break-up. She and Freddie had been together since university in Liverpool and had moved into a little house in the leafy suburbs where the proper adults lived, away from the streets lined with big five-bedroom houses full of undergraduates. Together they made a home, and it was, for a time. But then she moved, chasing a job that matched her degree, and Freddie had decided that actually he'd much rather be with someone who had their life together, like, for example, Jennifer, the woman he started dating the second Haf set foot on the train.

Second, the job that seemed great on paper was not actually the cushy, fun little role she'd hoped it would be. A communications position at a wildlife charity with fixed hours and a salary and no work on Christmas was a nice change from working in shops, even though she had liked the routine of retail a lot. Despite everyone and their mother wanting to 'go green', there were virtually no jobs and when she'd spotted the opening advertised online, she had no choice but to go for it. She'd pretty much got the job on the strength of her knowledge of Twitter and ability to write plausible copy. The thing she'd learned though was that while charities might be good, they're still a workplace, and bad jobs and bad managers who insist on micromanaging can happen anywhere. Her own nightmare micromanager insisted she account for every minute of her time without learning what she actually did, meaning her responsibilities piled up and up and up as the charity CEO insisted they needed to be present on every platform. The latest request had been for her to set up 'one of those ClickClocks'.

And now, because bad things happen in threes, she's facing a Christmas entirely alone.

'The one good thing that's happened this year has been you,' Haf whimpers to Ambrose.

'Obviously,' they say with a wolfish grin. 'I'm excellent.'

Through absolute sheer luck, a Twitter mutual had introduced them when Haf announced her impending move to York, as Ambrose was looking for someone to share their lovely two-bedroom terraced house. It's one of those perfect cottages that people envy – just near enough to the river to be aesthetically pleasing but not get flooded, and just a few streets from the good brunch places. It had only taken an evening of DMing about their favourite foods and wish lists of restaurants to visit for Ambrose to say Haf could move in. Haf is fairly sure her friendship with Ambrose is the most successful stable relationship she's ever had. They had even re-signed the lease for another year. Thank God for very online queer people.

Haf pulls uselessly at the toggles on her hoodie.

'Did you book your train home already?' Ambrose asks 'Do you need me to ring the customer service people and frighten them into giving you a refund? I love doing that.'

'No, luckily not.' The train tickets home to North Wales were always eye-wateringly expensive, no matter how far in advance she booked them.

'Well, now you can spend that on some posh Christmas food. We've got all the decorations up already at least.'

They decorated on the first day of December. Ambrose is strictly anti-tinsel, and Haf insists on fairy lights everywhere, but they'd managed to find a pleasant if slightly eclectic middle ground. The tiny yet convincingly fake tree was hung with Ambrose's beautiful gold and silver baubles in between Haf's assortment of weird ornaments that she had picked up over the years, the latest acquisition being a very shiny pink prawn holding a candy cane. They had filled the decorative fireplace with all their unused warmly scented candles, but quickly learned lighting them all at once in the hope it might look like a real fire was actually a hazard and the mixed scents made them both feel distinctly weird. Now they only light one at a time. Today's choice was cinnamon apple.

'I know, but also, I don't *want* that. I just want to be fed and not have to think about anything . . . I guess that's what my parents wanted too.'

Ambrose smiles gently, as though they'd been holding back pointing this out. 'It'll be okay.'

'Easy to say when you know your plans aren't going to change last minute.'

'You never know, Mum could surprise me and announce she's going on a cruise. In fact, I kind of wish she would.'

Haf fixes them with a dark look because that's the last thing in the world Ambrose's mother would ever do, and they both know it. Liew family Christmases are a big family affair, with aunties, uncles, cousins and all the grandparents piling into the family home. Ambrose has promised to take Haf home for their Lunar New Year celebrations, and as much as she wants to ask them to see if they can fit her in, she feels embarrassed. It's not the same when you haven't been specifically invited, and also Ambrose puts up with her all the rest of the year; they probably need a break.

'You're being a stroppy baby.'

'Well, you're not being nice enough in my hour of need,' Haf says, trying to ignore the whine in her voice.

Ambrose gets up, and a few minutes later returns with a mug of tea and the biscuit tin, and motions for Haf to drink some of the sickly sweet, strong tea. After a big sip, she says, 'All right, maybe I am being a bit of a stroppy baby.'

'The thing you're missing here – because you're too busy being an aforementioned stroppy baby – is that you now have the opportunity to have a perfect Christmas. You can do what you want, drink what you want, watch all the good films. You could make it your own perfect day – a nice hot bath, easy-cook Christmas food and all your favourite horrible pink wines. Heaven.'

This is a perfect example of where Ambrose and Haf differ. Ambrose isn't antisocial per se, but Haf is the only person they've successfully cohabited with for more than a few months. In a way, Ambrose is a cat. They like to be admired and see people on their terms, but also love their own company.

Haf, meanwhile, is a puppy. A very needy puppy that needs people, attention and lots of praise.

'A solo Christmas isn't really my thing,' she murmurs.

'Look, I'm leaving on Christmas Eve. I'll only be gone for a few days, and then we can do our own thing up here for Betwixtmas.'

'That's true . . .'

'Maybe this is a good thing? You've been rushing through the last year, just trying to keep going at your horrible little job with your dickhead boss, to the point that you literally forgot that your parents were going away for Christmas. Maybe having some quiet time in that lovely brain of yours would be a good thing for you.'

'That sounds like the exact opposite of what I want to do.'

'Need and want aren't always the same things. Anyway, let's forget about this. I think you *need* a distraction and some fun, and I *want* to go to a party tonight, so we are both going.'

Haf buries herself further into her blanket nest. 'I don't know if I want to go out after this, Ambrose,' she whines.

'We've not gone out and done anything fun or silly in months. I've watched you go from fun, excitable, spontaneous Haf, to . . . whoever this is. You've been worn down by spreadsheets and admin, and it's time to go to a party, have a good time and let the old Haf out to make a few silly decisions. Take an evening to stop worrying about all the big stuff, like your job or having your shit together.'

'How do you know I don't have plans already?' Haf puffs up her cheeks.

Ambrose says nothing, but silently points at *Gilmore Girls*, Haf's admittedly grubby hoodie and finishes by popping the air from her cheeks.

'And you know the best part?' they continue, ignoring her protests. 'It's a grown-up person party, which means that there'll be good snacks.'

'Snacks . . .' Haf says, glancing at Ambrose from the corner of her eye.

'Snacks. *Good* snacks. Middle-class, grown-up-people snacks. M&S party snacks.'

'I hate that you know me this well.'

'No, you don't, because then you wouldn't be invited to crash strangers' parties on the promise of a good buffet.'

Haf has always loved food, and thanks to learning from the brilliant and clever fat-positive babes online, she's now comfortable enough within her own body where she doesn't feel she ever has to hide that. There's no calling food *naughty* or talking about *walking it off* in her world. Ambrose is thin but has never made her feel like she needs to acknowledge the difference in their bodies when they talk about their shared love of food.

'Whose party is it?'

Ambrose waves their hand. 'I don't know. Someone from the psychology department, I think? I got invited by someone else who's going.'

'So we're, like, third-hand crashing?'

They shrug.

Haf wasn't sure she wanted to admit it, but maybe Ambrose was right. The last few months *had* been royally shit. Letting her hair down and trying out one of the many new lipsticks that are both too bright and too fun for work that she'd bought online on many a depressed Wednesday afternoon at the office but hadn't had the chance to wear could be good for her. If not, she can just fill up her purse with pork pies and get a cab home. At this juncture, she's not above this as a plan B.

'Fine. I'll go.'

'Excellent. It's a Christmas miracle.'

# Chapter Two

The best thing about crashing parties in midsize university towns is that there's a good chance you won't know many, if any, of the people there. This means that if you have no intention of behaving yourself or generally pretending to be a wholesome person, you don't have to. Most of the other partygoers won't remember you as more than the weird girl in the black fluffy coat, anyway. Or at least, that's what Haf hopes will happen.

Ambrose had rooted through Haf's wardrobe of, to their taste, questionable fashion and insisted she wore a dress they found in a sale as, according to them, Haf's tits would look very good in it. The dress was black velvet with structured shoulders and a deep V down the front. It was one of those rare, near-mythical finds in plus-size fashion – not floral, and no frills – and so Ambrose had insisted Haf buy it 'just in case'.

Complete with a brick-red lipstick and a bit of gold glitter across the apples of her cheeks, Haf not only feels a bit festive, but she feels hot. Especially so once she rubs the lipstick off her teeth.

Yes, she's facing a Christmas alone, which feels like her worst nightmare, but for now, she looks fit and is going to, hopefully, consume a considerable amount of booze and food.

Ambrose looks fantastic as always. Their blazer is scarlet red and embroidered with clouds, green butterflies, suns and dragon scales. They've paired it with a simple but secretly luxurious white silk shirt, high-waisted tailored black trousers and pointed boots. Haf thinks that they always look like a pop star – a compliment Ambrose likes to pretend they don't enjoy.

When they arrive just after eight thirty, half the guests are already on their way to being very drunk, sprawled around the living room, already deep into YouTube karaoke. Ambrose seems to recognise a few people and waves a polite hello but no one looks particularly familiar to Haf. She met a few of their co-workers and friends over the last year – all people from the university, usually a mix of admin staff like them, plus a few academics, and a couple of feral-looking PhD students that haven't seen sunlight or a full meal for weeks. Most people here seem to be nourished, probably have a babysitter with the kids at home, know how to properly drink whisky and have fun but still be an in-bed-by-eleven type of person. Real grown-ups.

Two guys in matching reindeer jumpers bellow along to a song that Haf swears is a very funky ode to Mrs Claus.

'Someone's getting some tonight,' Ambrose says archly, as a couple of women leap up from the couch to join them for the chorus.

Weirdly, no one comes to greet Ambrose or rushes over to say hello.

'Who invited you to this party, anyway?' Haf asks as they weave through groups of people in vaguely festive clothing.

Ambrose either doesn't hear or ignores her, probably the latter, but Haf chooses to allow it because it appears they've led her straight through the party to the kitchen, which is absolutely laden with food. An enormous buffet is spread across a long kitchen table, spilling over onto most of the counters.

'You're welcome,' they say.

'It's . . . it's beautiful.' Haf pretends to wipe a tear away, but is overcome enough that she almost does cry.

Whoever was throwing this party was not only an adult, but an adult willing to spend a not insignificant portion of their likely meagre academia salary on feeding a crowd. A true Christmas angel.

There's a whole tray of roasted gnocchi threaded onto cock-tail sticks, bookended with a sun-dried tomato, a little bit of spinach and a tiny ball of mozzarella. Little ramekins of sauces to dip them into dot the table. Freshly baked (or at least warmed-up) fancy breads steam slightly, next to an artfully laid-out charcuterie board, like the ones she's seen on Pinterest, plus pickles – both the condiment and the vegetables – and more kinds of cheese than Haf has ever seen outside of a supermarket counter. There's not one, but two baked Camemberts studded with garlic and rosemary, shining with sea-salt crystals. Little hot sausages rolled in grainy mustard and honey. Piles of mince pies – not just the standard ones with normal pastry but someone's added a batch of ones with puff pastry that are practically Eccles cakes.

Ambrose takes a reindeer-patterned paper plate from the stack, licking their lips as they look over the food, but then, as though they just remembered something important, drops it back onto the table.

'Erm, I've just got to go find someone,' they say, disappearing back into the crowd before Haf can object.

*When in Rome*, she thinks. She rescues the plate Ambrose abandoned. The plate is made of thin material and warps in her small hands. She respects the hosts' priorities of spending lots on expensive food but saving on cheap paper plates, right up until one of the gnocchi detaches itself from its cocktail stick, rolls off the side of the plate and lands with a plop on someone's very nice shiny shoe.

'Ohhh,' Haf groans, both for mucking up someone's shoe and the loss of a delicious potato treat.

'How very sad,' says the shoe's owner, who bends down to pick up the lost gnocchi.

Normally a five-second-rule kind of girl, Haf is about to retrieve the gnocchi from its rescuer but is struck by his bright eyes. They are the kind of blue you see in photos of Instagram influencers by the sea, almost too blue to be real. Startlingly so.

The colour distracts her so much she only notices he's popped it into the bin after the fact.

'May he rest in peace,' she says, worried that she's been gawking at this stranger, as though his blue eyes had hypnotised her like the snake from *Jungle Book*.

'We honour his sacrifice,' the man says, with a smile.

He's objectively, classically handsome. The kind that stops you in your tracks, even though – now she can look past his eyes – he's not Haf's type at all. Ambrose says that Haf's taste in men can be summarised as guys who might live like raccoons and are a bit grubby-hot, like Robert Pattinson now, or anyone from the Italian band that won Eurovision a few years ago. The women she found attractive couldn't be more different, though – suited, secretly dorky and possibly about to organise a heist. This guy is neither and instead has the clean-cut looks of the lead in a period drama.

'Nothing worse than a wasted potato,' says Haf.

'Really? I suppose I could think of a few things.'

'Oh sure, but at a jolly Christmas party?'

'I once saw someone try to serve raw chicken.'

'Raw chicken? Are you serious?'

'They said it was "rare". Sliced it up like sashimi.'

'Wow. I was thinking like mildly horrifying Christmas jumpers knitted by someone's granny, you know, like a snowman with a murderous edge to him. But that trumps everything. Who was hosting the party? A wild pack of dogs?'

'Close. My flatmate at uni.'

'Christ.'

'That's what I said.'

'I hope you threw it out.'

'The chicken or the flatmate?'

'Both.'

'That probably would have been the best idea. He also used to leave dirty pans under the sink.'

'How's there always one weirdo who does that in every flat? It's truly amazing.'

'Do you need help loading up?' he says, nodding towards her plate.

'Oh, would you mind?'

He turns his hands palms up and together, and Haf places the plate gently on them with reverence. His fingers are long and slender, almost girlish. Probably what you'd call pianist fingers if you were the type of person who could even think that phrase without thinking 'penis fingers'.

'Normally I wouldn't suggest such heresy as sharing a plate, but seeing as you're doing all the lifting work here, shall I put a few bits on for you?'

'Please,' he says with a soft lopsided smile.

Concerned about structural integrity and maximising snacks, Haf adds a little bit of everything good. She fashions a few olives and a cocktail sausage into a suggestible vignette, and the plate wobbles as he tries to stifle a giggle.

*Good*, thinks Haf. Someone who is game for saying funeral rites over carbs and will laugh at her terrible humour is exactly the sort of person she needs to be hanging out with in the absence of Ambrose, who has still not returned.

'Careful now,' she says. 'You're supposed to be the stable one.'

He goes completely rigid, like a Queen's Guard, as she adds the last few bits. It's a little overfilled.

As she finishes, a group of people swarm into the kitchen. Half of them head straight for the table, while the others cover every surface in cocktail supplies, following a YouTube video they keep pausing and rewinding. There's nowhere for them to comfortably stand and chat, and she kind of wants to talk to this nice tall man.

Two people come in through the back door, squeezing past Haf, and letting in a blast of icy Yorkshire night with them. In the tiny sweaty kitchen, it's a literal breath of fresh air. Haf peeks out the door and spies some chairs, a little firepit and some lights that might be fancy outdoor heaters like you get at nice pubs.

He joins her at the door. 'You want to go sit outside?'

'Yeah, it's boiling in here. We can bask under the lamps like big lizards.'

'I'll bring the food if you grab my coat.'

He tilts his head towards the coat hook, and they have a brief miming back and forth as Haf tries to guess which coat is his. It turns out to be a black long coat, with sharp lines and fine details. There's something vaguely architectural about it.

She slings his coat over her shoulder and grabs a few M&S gin-and-tonic tinnies that have been set out on one of the counters, stuffing them in the deep pockets of his coat. But before she can follow him outside, Ambrose waltzes into the kitchen, holding two empty glasses.

'Who's the new friend?' they say, squeezing around the cocktail makers to the sink.

'How did you see that from the other room?'

'I'm all-seeing. I know exactly what mischief you're up to at all times,' Ambrose says, rinsing the glasses under the tap. 'Anyway, good work. He's a snack, even if he's a bit clean for your taste. What's his name?'

'I don't know yet,' Haf says, trying to sound casual and mysterious.

Ambrose places their hands on Haf's shoulders and turns her to face them. 'You little minx.'

'I don't think it's quite that. I think just an opportunity to be a bit silly and have a little flirt, but that's it.'

'No? Not going to bring him home?'

'Nah, I don't think so.'

'Too clean.' They nod sagely. They get it. 'You're not leading him on though, are you?'

'Nah, pretty sure we're on the same page – unless his idea of flirting is watching me consume as much of a garlic-laden Camembert as possible.'

'You never know. There's a kink for everything and everyone.'

'Plus, I've got big pants on.'

'Precisely what I mean. Don't underestimate the sexiness of big pants,' Ambrose says with a deep seriousness. 'Anyway, I came to find you to tell you I'm leaving.'

'I've literally not seen you since we got here, which was only ten minutes ago. What have you been doing?'

There's a pause.

'*Who* have you been doing?'

Ambrose rolls their eyes. 'It's just Paco.'

Shrieking with glee, Haf peppers their arm with gentle excited punches. Ambrose has been low-key in love with Paco, the beautiful Brazilian postdoc from the education department, for months. Haf had clocked it was serious because Ambrose had mentioned his name in entirely positive contexts on three separate occasions, which for them was like gushing with praise.

'Is that who invited us?'

'Perhaps,' they say, raising their eyebrows.

'Aww, you brought me for emotional backup, didn't you?'

'No, I didn't. Shut up, I hate you,' they say, pouting.

Haf pulls them into a hug.

'Are you going to be all right here alone?'

'Of course. I've got my new tall friend, and if I get bored, I'll grab a taxi home.'

Ambrose thinks this over for a second and seems to decide they've been contrite for just long enough. Instead, they reach past Haf to a tote bag hanging from the back of a chair and bring out a nice bottle of Prosecco, a good two or three price levels up from what Haf usually drinks. They hold it out to her, an offering.

'Wow, thanks. Don't you want this?'

'No, it's to make up for being sneaky.'

'I'll allow it. Go have fun. Be safe. Text me,' Haf says, kissing them on the cheek. 'Love you.'

'Love you too.' Ambrose slinks off.

Armed with the bottle of Prosecco and G&T tinnies stuffed into every pocket, Haf decides to take the glasses Ambrose washed up with her, just in case they decide to be fancy enough to not swig it straight from the bottle.

As she heads out the back door, she spies the tote bag still slung over the back of the chair. It has a university logo on it, and she realises two things at once: one, Ambrose would not be caught dead using university promotional merchandise so this is definitely not theirs, and two, that means they forfeited a bottle they had obviously earmarked to steal for themselves. She's touched.

The cold air is refreshing after the thick heat of the tiny house, though Haf hopes the combined power of the lamps and her jacket are enough to prevent her boobs from icing over. *It smells like snow*, she thinks, and then questions whether a Christmas alone with more mid-noughties television is actually good for her.

Her new friend stands by the firepit warming his hands. The plate of food sits on a garden table between two chairs.

'Sorry about that. Was just saying goodbye to my friend,' she says, handing over his coat.

'Bloody hell,' he says at the sudden weight of it. 'It appears my jacket is full of cans.'

'That it is,' she says. 'Also got something a bit nicer for after, if we can stand the cold.'

She sets down the glasses and Prosecco on the floor, just out of accidental-kick range.

They each take a seat, basking in the heat from the fire.

He takes a couple of gin and tonics out from his pockets and hands her one. The drinks fizz as they pop them open, and he takes a sip.

'You get first dibs by the way,' she says, motioning the plate of food. 'Seeing as you did all the hard work.'

'Don't undersell your contribution. The curation was very important, especially the ad hoc artwork built into it. Very nice,' he says and pops a whole mini Scotch egg into his mouth.

Haf takes a slice of bread and dips it into the big scoop of melted Camembert. A whole roasted garlic clove peeks out from the top, which she scrapes up onto the bread with a finger. It's sweet and so strong on her tongue.

'So, my mystery friend, what brings you here?' says Haf, licking a trail of melted cheese off her thumb.

'To York, or this garden specifically?'

'Both.'

'I went to school with Sally.'

'Sally.'

'Sally.'

'And who is Sally?'

'Sally is the person who owns this house and is throwing the party?' he says slowly, like this is a fact Haf should very clearly know.

'Oh.'

'You've no idea who I'm talking about.'

'Not really, no. I'm afraid you've caught me out. I'm not only a gatecrasher, but I'm a second-tier gatecrasher. Maybe third. I've lost control of the maths.'

'As in, a less good one?'

'No, like, I was invited by someone else who was invited by someone who was *actually* invited, I think.'

'Like six degrees of separation but for party invitations?'

'Something like that. Anyway yes, I'm afraid I do not know Sally, but she is my new favourite person for providing all these treats.'

Luckily, he smiles. 'Well, she's a postdoc in the psychology department. Sleep science, in case that narrows it down.'

'Not even remotely.'

He laughs heartily.

'Oh God, is she your Mrs?'

'My . . . Mrs? No, she not. Sally's just a friend. But also, I don't think I'd ever call her that, even if she was.'

'Oh, he's a feminist, girlies!' Haf laughs, and he joins in. His laughter is warm and deep, coming right from the centre of his chest.

'To answer your question, I was up here for work, and Sally invited me, as she knew I was in town. I'm supposedly here to catch up, but I've not seen her in about half an hour.'

'It's kind of wild in there, isn't it?' Haf says as a roaring cheer sounds from the kitchen. She raises her can to them and drinks half of it in one go. 'Are you down in London normally?'

'How did you guess?' he asks, leaning back in the garden chair.

'You've got a London vibe about you, haven't you?.'

'Perhaps,' he laughs. 'Yes, I live in London. And yourself? Are you working at the university too?'

'God no, though I do live here, yeah,' Haf says, nibbling on a crispy gnocchi bite. 'I work for a charity in town. Wildlife conservation stuff, but I do all the comms, aka all the writing about the interesting stuff other people do.'

'As in save the badgers and all that?'

'Yeah, we've done a few badgers. Moths, ground-nesting birds, the occasional small mammal. Recently it's been a lot about fisheries and bees. It's truly all happening.'

'Sounds interesting.'

'I mean . . . yeah. Maybe.' That's definitely how she thought it would be. 'It's worthy, but I wish it were a bit more hands-on. I want to actually *do* something. What about you? Can you beat the conversational highs of fisheries management?'

As she turns back, she catches him grimace.

'That bad, huh?'

'I'm afraid it's considerably worse.'

'Go on then, you've got me curious.'

'I work in finance.'

'Oh dear.' Haf clutches her side in mock pain and cries out. 'You've got to warn a girl before you bring out the banking chat. It's potent stuff.'

He laughs. 'God, don't I know it.'

'So, you're a posh boy who lives in London and works in finance.'

'I know, I'm probably a cliché.'

'You're exactly every cliché about southern people I've ever heard. No offence.'

He laughs. 'None taken. I know what it sounds like.'

'Do you like it?' Haf asks, crunching on a carrot stick covered in unspecified yet delicious dip.

'It pays the bills.'

'That's more than I can say.'

The salary was a step up from the last shop she was at, but it's barely enough to get by in York even if she cycles everywhere. Whenever the temperature starts to drop, her dad sends her a twenty and an encouraging text to get the bus.

'You're telling me that mid-level charity work isn't lucrative? I'm shocked.'

'I know, right? Perhaps I'm doing something wrong. I need to launch a coup and take over one, get me an unscrupulous six-figure salary that people can whinge about. So are you up here for long?'

'Just overnight.'

'Pity.'

She doesn't mean to say it out loud, but apparently she has.

'Pity?' One of his eyebrows arches slightly, and there's a tiny smile playing the corner of his mouth. He takes another pair of tinnies out of his pockets and hands her a fresh one. 'Be truthful, it was my plate-carrying abilities, wasn't it?'

'Always nice to have local friends. Think of all the parties we could be stealing food from together,' Haf says, trying to be casual about it. 'Like Bonnie and Clyde but for vol-au-vents. Plus, you seem quite happy for me to make fun of you for being posh, which is always a quality I enjoy in posh people.'

The truth of it is, Haf doesn't want to admit that he's the first person since Ambrose that she's properly connected with, because that'll make her sound a little sad, maybe desperate.

But she's thinking it. The buzz between them reminds her of that night DMing Ambrose when she knew they were on the same level, that something good was going to come from them talking.

'Well, it's an honour to be your companion on this fair minus-four-degrees winter night.'

They both open their second cans at the same time, and clink them together in cheers.

'*Iechyd da.*'

'Bless you.'

'It's Welsh, you awful English wanker.' She laughs, kicking his foot with her own.

'I know, one of my flatmates at uni was Welsh.'

'God, I hope it wasn't the chicken-sushi one.'

'No, it wasn't.'

'Oh, all right. You're redeemed.'

They sit in comfortable silence, sipping their tins and watching the fire dance. The food dwindles and the cans empty, and Haf feels the gin softening the edges.

'There's so much sky here,' he says after a while. 'It's the thing I miss about home in the countryside. In London, it's all purply murk. No stars.'

She leans her head back to look up. It's a cold, clear night, and the sky is pitch black and glittered. 'I don't think I could hack that,' she says truthfully. 'I have been known to navigate myself home while drunk using the North Star.'

'Luckily we have a thing called the Night Tube that makes that less necessary.'

'Yeah, yeah,' she says.

Above her, something tied to one of the heat lamps catches her eye. Tied to the post with string is a small, sad-looking bunch of mistletoe. The sprigs don't so much hang as sag, and the berries are a little singed from being too close to the heat.

'Oh man,' laughs Haf, getting to her feet so she can inspect it closer. 'Look at this! It looks a little miserable, doesn't it?'

He joins her, wobbling slightly to his feet.

'Steady on, Bambi,' she laughs, taking his arm.

'Oh dear. It appears to be on the verge of death.'

'That's sad! It's so alone,' she says. 'Imagine being burned to death slowly on a fancy outdoor light. I hope it made someone kiss, at least. Imagine burning on a pyre for your job and you didn't even do it well,' Haf says, which turns into a nervous laugh as she realises she's not kissed anyone in months. Wait, was Freddie the last person she kissed? Because that would be incredibly depressing.

'I can imagine,' he mutters, 'unfortunately!'

It must be the booze, but both of them burst into slightly hysterical laughter.

'How much gin is in these?' he says, reading the side of the can. Or rather, he tries to, but mostly he just blinks really hard while looking at it.

'Look, I've got an idea,' Haf says, grasping his arm because suddenly she's closer to him than she realised, but that's fine because there's an arm here she can hold on to. 'You and I appear to be job disasters. The mistletoe' – she points up at it – 'might also be bad at its job. So we should send it off, make sure at least one of us has a good work day.'

'Are you suggesting that we grant it peace, by allowing it to fulfil its duty before it shuffles off this mortal coil . . . by kissing?' he asks with a soft laugh. The pink flush of his cheeks from the alcohol and fire seems to spread up to his ears, and she can see the edges of his confidence peeling away.

'Yes,' she half laughs, half shouts. 'I am!'

A dog barks in the distance and they fall apart into giggles and shushes again.

'So, we're in agreement then?' Haf asks once they're recovered.

'About what? Us being intoxicated?'

'I didn't say I was.'

'But you absolutely are. It's irrefutable.'

He's the kind of man who gets more verbose the tipsier he is. It's very endearing.

'I meant snogging to cheer up the mistletoe. Its final rites!'

They both giggle again at the silly idea, but fuck it, she thinks. *Ambrose told me to have fun, after all. I can make good choices for myself, probably.*

And before they can say anything else, she leans up to kiss him.

If the mistletoe needed a romantic kiss to thrive, well, it was going to be sorely disappointed.

They meet in a clash of teeth, noses bashing together. Haf laughs into his mouth, and they break into a fit of giggles, clutching against each other in the firelight. It is a truly, categorically shit kiss.

'Wow, I'm so sorry, that was probably the worst kiss I've ever done in my life,' she laughs, still clutching on to him lest she wobble into the firepit.

'The worst,' he says. He looks down at her face, and very gently touches her bottom lip with his thumb. 'Did I bite you? I'm a bit worried I bit you.'

'Ish okay,' she slurs, as he's still inspecting her lip.

And she's about to say it's so funny that they just launched a kiss on each other, and that they don't even know each other's names, and how silly everything is, when a voice interrupts everything.

'Oh my God. Toph?' cries a clipped, slightly nasal voice. 'Is that you?'

# Chapter Three

They're still standing in each other's arms as they're approached by two people, and Haf has to stop herself from leaping away from him, in case she falls straight into the firepit.

The woman who squealed is alarmingly tall and willowy. She's dressed in a thick tan wool jacket – the kind that looks a little like dressing gowns unless you are chic enough to pull them off – and brown leather riding boots. Her dark hair is styled so that there's a very soft curve to the ends, like it's a fur stole. It's a style composed of smatterings of 'Luxury Influencer' meshed with classic 'I Wear Pearls Unironically' in a way that really works.

Haf is so struck by this beautiful giant woman that she doesn't even realise that the guy she just kissed has dropped her arms and is moving over to greet the new arrival.

'Laurel? Hi. What are you doing here?'

'Kissing under the mistletoe, are we?' she asks with a raised eyebrow, arms folded as she neatly avoids his question.

'Look, it's not what you think,' Haf's mistletoe kiss says. He rubs the back of his neck with one hand, and his mouth curls in as he worries at his lips.

*Oh fuck*, thinks Haf, *did I just snog this beautiful giantess's man?*

He didn't say he was single, after all. Just that he wasn't dating Sally *specifically*. But it would be a weird flex to pretend you don't know anyone at a party just so you can have a kiss with a stranger under some singed mistletoe.

Especially given how it just played out. Hopefully, neither of them chipped a tooth.

He does seem more embarrassed than alarmed that he's been caught with another woman.

'Come on, Toph, you can't lie to me.' She pouts.

Not really the reaction of a scorned lover then. More like someone annoyed they've been left out of the gossip.

Also 'Toph'? Is that really his name? She imagines Ambrose popping up in her head to say that sounds more like a posh person sneezing than a name.

Behind the giant woman is a man drinking straight out of a bottle. His hair is such a pale wheat-blond it almost blends into his skin. There's an air of rich confidence about him. He's the kind of hench guy that's more square than person-shaped. A rugby man, almost certainly.

'You didn't even tell us you were coming up to Sal's do, Chrissy,' says the square man, who seems to also love nicknames. 'I knew you were up here for work, but I didn't think you were hanging about.'

'Chrissy' seems to fit him even worse, and he flinches at the use of it.

Christopher.

Christopher must be his name, and the full sharpness of it fits him much more than either of the two nicknames bestowed upon him by these mysterious interlopers.

Whoever *they* are.

Haf flashes her eyes at Christopher, hoping he might introduce her. Being the unexplained fourth wheel in a conversation is her own personal circle of hell at the best of times, but that plus having been caught engaged in the world's worst kiss really is taking it a bit far.

'Yes, well. It was quite last minute. I'm just here for work, and Sally said I should swing by. I didn't know you'd both be here too.'

'I should hope not, else I'd be very put out that you didn't drive up with us,' sniffs the giant woman, flicking a soft curl of hair over her shoulder. 'Anyway, come on, introduce us to your girlfriend, won't you?'

*Uh-oh.*

Girlfriend?

How on earth did they get that from a kiss that resulted in them laughing in each other's mouths? Unless, they didn't see that, and only saw the aftermath – standing in each other's arms in front of the fire, Christopher's thumb resting on her bottom lip. Oh . . . Oh dear. That's a very different vibe.

Next to her, Christopher has frozen and his pale-pinkish face starts to go a little green around the edges. 'I—'

But he's cut off by the giant woman, who takes Haf's hand in hers and brings her closer, clearly so she can get a better look at her. It's the kind of practised move that comes from knowing people want to know you, and always getting your way.

'I guess she'll have to do it herself,' she says. 'Hello, darling. I'm Laurel, and this is my Mark.'

Laurel peers down towards Haf like she's the most fascinating specimen she's ever encountered. Haf wonders if this is how show dogs feel at Crufts, or perhaps she is thinking about that because Laurel seems the right kind of posh to be a judge at a dog show. Maybe she'll win Best in Breed.

Haf gulps. 'Hiya, I'm Haf.'

'Half?' Laurel adds in a little too much of an L where one doesn't exist, one that most people don't even say in the word 'half'.

'Close!' she says, smiling a little too widely. 'Haf. Havvv. It's Welsh.'

'How charming. What does it mean?'

'Summer?' It becomes a question as she looks to Christopher for a little assistance, but he misses her plea, too busy looking like he wants the ground to swallow him up.

'Mark, isn't she so charming? How lovely, and *Welsh*,' she says, talking directly to Mark, who is paying barely any attention, presumably because they're not talking about him.

You can tell a lot about an English person depending on what bit of Wales they tell you they've been to. Most of the northerners that Haf met at uni would always yell about the now defunct borderline-dangerous indoor water park near to where Haf grew up. It contained both an indoor lightning show and a wave pool, which local legend claimed several children had been sucked into, never to return. It did, however, have an actually dangerous octopus slide that would defang you if you went down face first when the waves pulled back, so a whole bunch of kids in her year were missing their front teeth.

Instead, Laurel passionately tells her about the spa holiday she and Mark had at Portmeirion, a pastel-daubed fake Italy and former location of cult TV show, *The Prisoner,* which had the air of an abandoned theme park when Haf was a child but is now a luxury resort.

Haf nods along politely but is too busy trying to catch Christopher's attention to really listen to fancy-people anecdotes. What does he want her to do? The longer this conversation goes on, the longer the misunderstanding does, and while normally she would just set the record straight, there's something else going on here that she can't quite place.

'Toph, your parents will be delighted you're seeing someone new. Does Kit know? I bet she doesn't, you sneaky thing. I must tell Kit.'

'Laurel, please—'

'I'm so glad he's moved on to someone new,' Laurel says to Haf in a low, conspiratorial voice, but she's purposefully loud enough so all can hear her. 'I've been worried. I didn't think he was dating anyone, and we broke up ages ago now, but I'm so relieved to see he's with you because you're so lovely, and stunning.'

Oh fuck. She's his ex.

A memory flashes in Haf's mind. She'd got the train over to Liverpool to pick up the last of her things from Freddie, hopeful that maybe she could talk him round. She was right in the middle of an impassioned speech about why they should get back together, arms filled with her beloved knick-knacks, when Jennifer, the woman who had replaced her, came in, keys in hand.

In terms of all the worst ways to meet your ex's new partner, that was pretty up there. Ideally, you'd meet them while you were at a real high point in your life, like an event where she'd won a humanitarian award for being really good at Twitter. Instead, they met when she'd been crying so much that snot and tears had pooled on her top, turning it practically see-through. Typical, the one day you wear a white top, just to feel something new, and it reveals your soaked, falling-apart bra to your replacement. It was a strong contender for the most humiliating moment of her life, which was impressive considering how many she'd had.

And now, on Christopher's face she sees the look of sheer 'please end me now' that she recognises from herself. He looks grey, like an overcooked green bean. He's now the one in the see-through T-shirt, and Haf is the only one who can help.

If she can save one person from terminal embarrassment in front of an ex and their new partner, maybe it'll make her own hurt sting less . . .

What's one little lie, after all?

'Ha ha, well, no one needs to worry. We're both doing well and are very happy, aren't we, Christopher?'

The words are out of her mouth before she can think any more about it.

Christopher blinks very quickly. Confusion? Relief? Haf isn't sure, but she trots over to him and slides her arm around his waist, as though she's been doing it forever. He stiffens for a second but relaxes into it, wrapping an arm around her shoulders, holding her close to him.

There are good lies, and bad lies, and the kind of lies that are just . . . obscuring the truth, really, just a little. Sure, they haven't *actually* been dating, but they have been having a nice time all evening, and he seems reasonably well adjusted, or as much as any man who worries about mistletoe might be. Perhaps his family really doesn't need to worry. This is just a little light meddling to get him out of a sticky situation.

Laurel clasps her hands over her heart. 'You two are just adorable. How long has this been going on?'

'Oh, not long . . .' Haf says, looking up at Christopher with big Bambi eyes, hoping he'll take the hint to fill in the details to suit his timeline.

'A couple of months,' he says with a wobbly smile.

'And you met through Sal, I suppose,' Mark says, finally returning to the conversation. This is enough of a non-question statement that neither of them respond.

There's something she really doesn't like about this man. It's
a kind of instinctual primal reaction that she wants to kick him
in the back of the knees and run away. Christopher, beside her,
seems to wilt every time Mark throws his attention their way, and
somehow she feels deeply protective.

'Oh, they're so gooey-eyed, Mark. Isn't it divine?'

Mark gives a man-grunt in response that's supposed to convey
a yes.

At this, Haf decides it's time for them to escape.

'Actually, I'm really sorry to do this, but we were about to nip
off. He's got an early train, and I really wanted to take him out for
breakfast first,' Haf says in the sweetest, most doting voice she can
conjure. Luckily, it's very easy for her to be saccharine about a
fancy breakfast out. She loves breakfast.

She gently pulls at Christopher, and he reanimates. 'Yes, sorry.
We should head off, but it's been nice to unexpectedly bump into
you both.'

'Not going to open that here?' asks Mark, looking pointedly at
the unopened bottle of Prosecco and glasses by the fire.

*Fuck off, Mark*, she thinks intently, but picks up the bottle of
Prosecco from the floor, anyway. She's not leaving Ambrose's con-
traband for these people. They can afford their own stolen booze.

'Time just got away from us. Good seeing you, Mark,' Christopher says, giving him one of those one-shake handshakes.

'See you at Christmas, old boy,' he replies, clapping a hand to
Christopher's shoulder.

'Sorry, Laurel, I wish we could have caught up more,' he says.

It's very clear to Haf that he was lying out of his arse claiming
it was good to see Mark, but he does sound genuinely regretful to
have not caught up with Laurel.

Affectionately, Laurel rests a hand on his shoulder, a gesture
that seems more familiar than a hug or kiss could have. 'I'll see
you next week, anyway!'

Laurel practically has to bend at the waist to air-kiss Haf. 'It's been delightful to meet you.'

They politely back away, leaving Laurel and Mark under the mistletoe that got them into this mess.

Haf leads him by the hand through the thick, sweaty mass of truly drunken partygoers in a tiny house, and out into the fresh air of the street at the front. Away from the firepit and heaters, the ice in the air nips at her, but the adrenaline (and gin) coursing through her body helps keep it at bay, a little, but her boobs are definitely at risk of freezing over.

They drop hands, but she takes him by the arm to lead him through the winding suburban streets in the direction of home. After a few minutes, they reach the dark rushing of the river, lit by soft orange street lamps.

It takes a while for him to speak, and she gives him the space to, rather than demanding precisely what the fuck happened.

'Christ. Thanks for that,' he says eventually.

'You're welcome.'

'You didn't have to do it, though.'

'I know.'

'Why did you?'

'Honestly? You looked like you were about to expire on the spot. And, well, I've had my share of embarrassing moments in front of an ex and their new person. It sucks, and it seemed like I could help. She'd already decided we were a couple. Easy to play along, you know?'

'Perhaps. Where are we going anyway? I've no idea where we are,' he says, slowing down and finally taking in his surroundings.

'My house. I figured we could drink this bottle, or a coffee if you need it, and then you can get a cab back to your hotel.'

He pats her hand in agreement. 'That's . . . a great idea. Thank you.'

She loves going home by the river path. The fresh smell of plants mixes with the spray of rushing water, and it's lit just enough that it's safe to walk down at night and you can still see the stars. Behind them is the bright gold of town, York Minster peeking out in the distance, which Haf points out to him. Ahead is a curved, modern metal bridge lit in rainbow colours, an unintentional Pride flag lighting their way home.

They fall back into easy silence.

'You're kind of brilliant, you know?' he says, after a few minutes.

'Kind of? I'm wounded. You really know how to woo a girl,' she teases, and he flushes. 'Look at your little pink cheeks. It's far too easy for me to make you flustered. I think it's one of my favourite things about you, I've decided.'

'I'm so pleased my—'

'Englishness? Poshness? Stiff upper lip?'

'—amuses you so much. I just . . . I just want to make it clear that the last thing on my mind after all that is taking advantage of your hospitality or good nature.'

Haf tries not to laugh.

'What am I doing that's so funny now?'

'I don't know. You're just so . . . *nice*.'

'That does not sound like a compliment.'

'It is! Honestly, it is. I want to wrap you up in a blanket and keep you safe. Like a dormouse or something.'

'My ego is taking a battering tonight.'

'Look, sure you've just endured a mortifying interaction with your ex and her frankly shitty new boyfriend, but you've escaped with a brilliant fake girlfriend, aka me, on a night where I look like an absolute snack, if I do say so myself.'

'All very true points.'

'Thanking you,' she says. 'Anyway, I was just doing my bit for the other singles of the world. I would have killed for some hottie on my arm to show off in front of my ex.'

Neither of them moves to talk about their mutual heartbreaks, but it hangs in the air between them like a fine mist.

They cross the river via the bridge, which shakes as a cyclist passes them, but otherwise, it's quiet, apart from the back-and-forth calling between two owls.

'So, just to confirm. It's Christopher, yes? Or do you actually prefer Chrissy or Toph? Or should I make up my own? What about Ipher?'

'Please don't call me any of those,' he says with a chuckle, his eyes sparkling in the twilight. 'Christopher is fine.'

'Christopher,' she says, sounding it out as though she's speaking a spell into the night.

'And you're Haf.' He gets it right first time. 'Which isn't short for anything?'

'No, just Haf. And you can't do much with a three-letter name, luckily.'

'Oh, I don't know, I could call you H.'

'Like the guy from Steps?'

'Or the bomb. Hmm, perhaps not.'

They arrive home a few moments later. The house is dark, so Ambrose must still be out having fun with Paco. Good for them. Christopher takes his shoes off at the door, and she ushers them both towards the living room.

'Coffee or . . . ?' Haf waggles the bottle of Prosecco.

'Did you bring that to the party?'

'No, Ambrose gave it to me, which I think means they stole it from someone else.'

'So you second-degree crashed a party and also second-hand stole this?'

'Seems like it.'

'You're a complicated girl. We should probably drink it and destroy the evidence.'

'I'll make a criminal out of you yet, Christopher . . . ?'

'Calloway.'

'Sounds like a film star,' Haf says, taking two mugs from the kitchen cupboard for their Prosecco. She wants something stable to hold on to. Who needs to get out the fancy glasses when you just want to cosily sip fizz?

'I don't think I've ever had a mug of Prosecco before,' he says as she pours him a healthy serving.

'It's a night of new experiences! What shall we toast to? To . . . our two-month anniversary?' Haf holds out her mug to cheers, and Christopher clinks his gently against hers. 'I've got one stipulation for all this though, and you can tell I'm being serious because I'm bringing out the big words.'

'Go on,' he says.

'Just give me a really good backstory and dumping, will you? Come up with a fatal incompatibility so you can edit me out easily, but make me sound good, yeah? Else I'm worried Laurel the Giantess will hunt me down like a fox. She gives me those vibes. She's a horse girl, isn't she?'

'That she is.'

'Knew it. Do you still have feelings for her?' Haf asks, stretching her legs out so her heels rest on the edge of the coffee table.

Christopher sighs a deep, weary sigh.

'You don't have to answer,' Haf says, realising it was probably too big a tonal shift for someone unused to her style of hopping around topics in conversation.

'No, it's fine. I don't think so, no, but . . . I'm just in the middle of figuring things out. Not just relationship things. I mean, big things. Life things. And Laurel, she knows me so well, and she's like a bloodhound for this stuff. We've known each other since we were children, and we got together when I was fifteen and were together all through university. She always knows when something is off with me. Hopefully, your little performance helped her think it was just the whole break-up mess that's causing it.'

Haf takes a sip and the bubbles of Prosecco fizz in her nose.

'You know, Laurel's kind of terrifying in a way I deeply admire.'

'She'd love to hear that.'

'What about the square man?'

'The *square man*?' Christopher buckles with laughter.

'Don't even pretend that you don't see it.'

'Well, I try not to see much of Mark at all any more if I can help it,' he says, recovering.

'Wait, were you friends?'

He leans back against the couch and sighs another bone-weary sigh. 'Yes, we were at school together, and university too. We've known each other almost as long as I've known Laurel.'

'Oh God, he's not the chicken-sushi guy, is he?'

'I don't think Mark has cooked anything for himself in his life, so no.'

'Did he steal her off you?'

'Christ, you get to the point, don't you?'

'Side effect of living with the bluntest person in the world.' She shrugs apologetically. 'It's rubbed off.'

'He didn't steal her . . . necessarily.' He takes a sip from his mug. 'The first thing you need to know is that we started dating as teenagers. There was an attraction between us, obviously, and our parents were very pleased about it. But in the last few years, we were arguing a lot, mostly over pointless stuff. Miscommunications, mostly. Over the ten years we'd been together, we changed a lot as people, and I think the weight of who we used to be and what we were expecting us to become was too much. So we broke up, and then she started dating Mark. But I suppose I can't say that his constant obvious interest in her didn't expedite the process.'

'You mean he was after her when you were together?'

'I believe so.'

'Sneaky fucker.'

'Quite.'

'I *knew* I didn't like him!'

'You don't have to feel any way about him on my behalf.'

'I've decided that I do. Plus, you're way too nice about him. The universe needs the balance of me rightfully calling him a total arsehole if you're going to be so polite. Seems like a good new-friend duty.'

'To new friends,' Christopher says, clinking his mug against Haf's again.

'Gosh, my nose is aching,' she says, rubbing the bridge of it.

'We did collide with a bit of force.' He laughs.

'Do you think even terrible kisses count for mistletoe duties? I'm worried we goofed it.'

'Let's just say it does. And, err, just to be clear—'

Haf giggles at the sudden awkwardness. 'Don't worry, it was *just* a silly mistletoe kiss here too.'

'That makes me feel a bit better about it. Now I've sobered up, I was a bit worried I'd given you the wrong impression.'

'The only impression you gave me was that you're willing to go along with my silly schemes, which I like very much.'

'Well, then, that's good.'

*It's a pity he lives on the other side of the country,* she thinks. This had been such a weird night, but she feels so comfortable with him, and kind of protective too.

She'll be sad when he goes home.

And after that, what is there? Another few soul-draining weeks of work then a Christmas alone.

'Let's watch some shit telly, drink this, and get you off home to your old life,' she says, wanting to hold on to this moment as long as possible.

Some hours later, Haf wakes up on the couch, her mouth dry as sawdust.

She rubs sleep out of her eyes and finds Christopher is there too, her legs slung over his lap. They must have both fallen asleep before they could call a cab. His head has fallen back against the top of the sofa, and he snores very, very softly. Exactly like a dormouse.

She slides off him and the couch and takes the detritus from last night into the kitchen, flicking on the kettle as she passes.

It's dark outside, so she has no idea what time it is given they're in the darkest bit of winter. There's no clock in the kitchen and the microwave has resolutely been blinking *00:00* since she moved in. No phone in her bra either. She must have left it somewhere when they got home last night. Hopefully Christopher hasn't missed his train home.

She doesn't know how he takes his tea, so she makes two identical ones with milk and a hefty plonk of sugar, which they probably both need.

When she returns to the living room, Christopher is awake. And very, very pale. In his hand is his phone, which he seems to be scrolling back and forth on. A message thread is open on the screen, but she makes a point of trying not to read it.

'Everything all right?'

He doesn't answer, but nervously licks his lips.

'Not regretting any drunk texts, I hope?' she jokes, hoping to lighten the mood, but he looks just as grave still.

'I wish.'

'Cuppa?' she asks, putting it down on the coffee table in front of him. 'I didn't know how you liked it, so I just made it the same as mine.'

'Thank you.' He breaks his horrified scrolling to smile up at her.

'What's happened? Are you okay?' she asks softly, sitting down next to him.

'Err, well. Nothing *terrible* has happened. No sickness. No one's dead.'

He kind of looks like he wishes he was, though.

'Just, erm, a sticky situation.'

'Tell me.'

'It's embarrassing.'

'We fell asleep together on a couch fully dressed after I pretended to be your girlfriend in a fairly mortifying situation. How can this be worse?'

She curls up and shoves her icy feet under his thighs.

'Christ,' he says, as much to her icy feet as to whatever is bothering him. 'Well . . . How do I explain this? Remember Laurel?'

'How could I literally ever forget her?'

'Well, it seems that Laurel might have told some people about us.'

'About you and her?'

'About you and me.'

'Oh! But that's fine. We agreed you can just dump me dramatically off-screen, right?'

'Well . . . the situation has escalated somewhat.'

'Escalated?'

'Yes.'

'Christopher, do you always talk in riddles? It's like having a conversation with a wizard on a bridge.'

He does another sad-laugh, scrolls up on the phone and passes it to her. On screen is his family's group chat, named 'Those Calloways', and a message from his mother this morning.

**Mother:** We heard the wonderful news from Laurel! We're so pleased. You must bring her home next week. I'll update the shop so we've got enough food. Let me know what dates she'll be joining us from.
**Christopher:** You're inviting Laurel?
**Mother:** No, Christopher. Your girlfriend, Haf. Laurel says she's lovely – of course she'll come to the Howards' on Christmas Eve as well. You can both come up a few days before so we can get to know her.

'Uh-oh,' Haf says. 'Okay, so a bit trickier, I guess?'

'To say the least.'

'Can you not say yes, and then have me dump you like tomorrow?'

'Oh God, that would be even more pathetic.'

'Are they really that invested in your dating life?'

Christopher's eyes are very sad, suddenly. Not glassy, there's no tears, just . . . so tired. Like he's been through the mill with all this.

'Laurel and I broke up almost a year ago, and God . . . basically everyone thought we'd get married. We were high-school sweethearts. Our parents know each other well, so they'd quietly hoped we'd end up together, but it happened naturally when we were teenagers. So, when we broke up last year after ten years . . . It was like I had disappointed the whole family. Like I'd failed to keep her happy and that reflected on all of them.'

'Oh, Christopher,' Haf says, resting a hand on his forearm. 'That's unfair. It's not your responsibility.'

'Perhaps. Sometimes I just think they're worried I'm not going to produce an heir.'

'How *Downtown Abbey* of you.'

'You're not entirely wrong. They have all these plans for me and I just never seem to match up to what they want, and it's . . .'

'Exhausting.'

He murmurs in agreement.

'What are you going to do?'

'I don't know. If I tell them it was a misunderstanding with Laurel, everyone – and I mean *everyone* – we know is going to think I was just trying to make Laurel jealous and will think I'm completely pathetic.'

'But it was my doing?'

'They won't see it as you trying to help me out. I have only just managed to stop them trying to set me up with someone new. And they'd finally given up on all the check-ins. The "How are you doing now?"s. The "Aren't you over her yet?"s. Everything was just going back to normal and . . . I'm not sure I can deal with that right now . . . on top of . . . on top . . .'

Haf is about to tell him it'll be all right, when she realises her phone is buried inside the couch and is ringing. She wiggles around and retrieves it from the cushions, and sees it's her parents.

'Sorry, let me just get rid of them,' she says, patting his head as she passes.

She clutches the phone against her chest and scuttles back into the kitchen, cursing at the bite of cold tiles on her tight-clad feet.

'Haf?'

Haf curses her clumsy fingers for answering yet another video call with her parents, who, at this moment, are getting a close-up of her cleavage. She holds the phone up to her face and recoils a little at the sight of her smeared lipstick, panda eyes and through-a-hedge-backwards hair.

'Good morning to you too, dear,' says her mum dryly.

'Sorry, hi, parents.'

'Had a good time last night, did we?'

'Something like that. What time is it?'

'Oh, about nine.'

'And that's a normal time for you to be calling me? Wait is someone dead?'

'No one's dead.'

'Okay, well, that's a relief.'

She sets the phone against the toaster and pours herself a glass of orange juice in the hope that it makes her feel, if not look, slightly more human.

'Nine is a perfectly normal time to call my daughter,' says Mum, a little huffily.

'I dunno which daughter you're talking about, but it's not this one.' Haf is, of course, an only child.

'We're calling to see if you're all right, love,' says Dad, interrupting and defusing, as always.

'I'm fine, Dad, honestly,' she says, looking through the cupboards for anything that could constitute breakfast. The bag of bread only has the end slices left, truly the saddest kind of loaf there is. Maybe Christopher will agree to a McDonald's breakfast instead.

'Could you pay attention to us when we're speaking to you?' asks Mum.

'I'm just trying to wake up. You're the one who called at the arse crack of dawn without checking if I was hungover, dressed or even conscious. I'm zero for three over here.'

Ambrose swishes into the kitchen in their silk robe.

'I'm so hungover I might die. But not really, just like . . . a little bit.'

'Have you been home the whole time?' Haf whispers.

'Is that Ambrose?' Mum calls. 'Hello, Ambrose!'

Ambrose stands up straight and moves into view of the camera, waving at Haf's parents. 'Hello, Mr and Mrs Hughes. And no, I got a cab home about an hour ago. I have no desire to watch Paco work when I could be in my own bed.'

'Oh, don't they look so lovely? Ambrose always looks so well dressed,' I hear Mum say to Dad.

Ambrose takes one look at Haf's face and shakes their head. 'You're supposed to take your make-up off before sleep,' they whisper, rubbing a smudge of . . . something off Haf's face with a thumb. 'Anyway, who is the man having a breakdown on our couch?'

'Christopher. Don't you remember him? I told you we met last night.'

'Christopher . . . ?' they say, rubbing their eyes.

'Who's Christopher?' calls Dad. 'Are you still there, love?'

'Oh! Your *boyfriend*,' says Ambrose.

'You've got a boyfriend?' asks Mum.

'He's not really my boyfriend,' Haf hisses back to Ambrose.

'What do you mean not really?' they say, cocking their head.

'Fake boyfriend,' Haf mouths.

'Fake boyfriend?!' says Ambrose at full volume.

'Your boyfriend fainted?' asks Mum.

'No one's fainted, Mum,' Haf says, shooing Ambrose out of the kitchen. They head straight to Christopher, and Haf hopes that they're in the mood to play nice.

'If someone's fainted, elevate their legs and get some water and salts into them,' adds Dad.

'No one has fainted!'

'I'm sorry, darling, I think you're breaking up and we can't hear you. Is this Christopher your boyfriend? That's so nice to hear.'

Upon hearing his name bellowed through tinny phone speakers, Christopher looks up and their eyes meet through the open doorway.

Haf realises at this moment in time she has two choices. She could spend Christmas here, alone with her thoughts, *Gilmore Girls* and the candle-fire hazard. A solo Christmas where she has to watch people having their own lovely ones all over Instagram, while she tries to keep Ambrose's plants alive.

Or, she could keep playing the fake girlfriend. She could go to Christmas at the Calloways'. She could help him out, and not be alone.

'Yes, actually, he is my boyfriend. Sorry I haven't got around to telling you about him.'

'Oh how lovely!'

'Yes, and his mother invited me to their Christmas,' she says, not breaking eye contact with Christopher. Relief flashes across his face. In a lower voice, she adds, 'so you don't have to worry about me.'

Ambrose's eyebrows cycle through the full spectrum of confused, shocked and finally angry in the way that only best friends can be when they've worked out the exact breed of chaos you're enacting.

'What a relief, we were a bit worried when you hung up on us the other day.'

'Oh, yeah, we just hadn't confirmed any plans with his parents, so I didn't want to say. But we sorted that all out, so I'll go down next week and stay with them over the holidays.'

'Good idea, lovey, best not to jinx these things,' Mum whispers.

Ambrose storms over and holds up their phone to show me the notes app where they've written: *WE WILL TALK ABOUT THIS LATER.* They turn slowly, maintaining menacing eye contact, and stride upstairs yelling an exasperated, 'Aiyah!'

'Look, Mum. You don't have to worry. Everything's fine, but I need to get going. Christopher's got a train to catch.'

'All right, lovie, have a nice day,' she says. 'Love to Christopher!'

Haf hangs up and slinks back into the living room, collapsing back onto the couch. He barely winces when she shoves her feet back under his thighs.

'There we go. Problem solved. I'll come to your Christmas, get you through it with your family, and in return you're giving me something to do that's not just sitting here on my tod.'

'You don't need to do that, Haf.'

But it's a soft kind of no, a wanting hidden inside. His blue eyes shimmer with hope.

'I know. But you seem a bit like you need some help, and I'm officially the only person who can. So, it's simple really.'

'My family aren't easy, Haf,' he warns.

'Whose family is? You heard mine. We can look after each other. How long do you go home for?'

'Usually I stay until after Boxing Day. I was going to go on the twenty-first.'

'Okay, well I could do the same. That's like, what, six days? What's six days? That's not even a week. We can do that.'

'Haf, we've only just met. Are you always this willing to help strangers?'

'Only when they look as sad as you,' she teases. 'But really, I have nothing better to do – my parents are off to Madeira for a sun-soaked Christmas and I'm not invited, and I totally forgot about it so didn't make a plan. And Ambrose's going home to their family, and I don't want to just impose there. At least your mum invited me, even if she thinks I'm her future daughter-in-law. Really, you're doing me a favour.'

'I'm not so sure about that,' he says, staring into his cup as if looking for tea-leaf wisdom. He's not going to find much, unless the Yorkshire Tea bag split.

'Let me help. Come on, we got through Laurel thinking we're dating pretty smoothly. What's another few days of that?'

Christopher sighs and turns to Haf. He takes her hands in his, and for the first time this morning he looks content, happy almost.

'Okay,' he says.

# Chapter Four

Seven days later, as agreed, Haf arrives at King's Cross station, a little before lunchtime. Christmas music drifts through the air from some unknown source, and everything is lit in the glow of fairy lights strung across the balconies and doorways of shops. The roof is lit Santa red, which you think would be nudging towards horror-movie vibes, but it's warming, cosy and womb-like.

The station is full of people; rushing for trains, scrolling through their phones as they wait, sipping at overpriced coffee like it is precious nectar.

So many people have those chic little suitcases that stand upright and wheel along like they're gliding through the air. Haf watches them, transfixed, and very jealous.

Perhaps she should have bought something, or at least agreed to borrow Ambrose's spare wheely suitcase. The enormous and very grubby backpack on her back is one she bought for a university field trip that last got used when she moved house. It is, to say the least, far too big for a six-day trip. She had whacked a couple of people when she boarded the train at York and is now on constant alert, lest she take out some tiny granny with it. Hopefully, her clothes aren't too crumpled inside.

Nestled safely at the top is a gift box of all the best bits from Betty's – you can't really go wrong with Fat Rascal scones, and some nice tea and biscuits. Christopher had told her not to worry about buying things, that he'd organise everything, but she still felt like she should turn up with *something*.

**Haf:** I made it.
**Haf:** London, I am in you, etc.

**Christopher:** Excellent. See you in about an hour? If you cross over the street to St Pancras, the cafes and shops are nice, and the toilets are free.

**Haf:** You're speaking my language, Iphy

**Christopher:** Stop that

As he was already in town finishing up a few things at work, Christopher had agreed to meet her so they could travel back to Oxlea together. A huge relief to Haf. The last thing she wanted was to have to travel there alone. They haven't hashed out all the details of their fake relationship, as both of them have been too caught up in finishing work for the holidays, but the train journey home should be more than enough time. How complicated can it be?

It's a blue-sky bright sunny day outside. As she waits at the crossing, she nervously types out a message to Ambrose to tell them she arrived there safely.

All she gets back are two emojis – an earth and an asteroid.

Ambrose was in the middle of the classic 'I'm not angry, I'm just disappointed' stage of disapproval after realising that Haf had managed to wheedle her way out of a restful, sensible and thoughtful Christmas home alone by getting herself wrapped up in a virtual stranger's personal life. Haf had really tried to explain it the best she could, but the thing about best friends is that they can see right through your bullshit. And Ambrose practically had X-ray vision for it.

They had talked about it after Christopher had left for his train and Haf had slunk upstairs, changed into day pyjamas and crawled into Ambrose's bed alongside them.

'Haf, if you think this is completely normal behaviour, then you're either successfully kidding yourself, or you've finally officially lost it,' Ambrose had said, rubbing their temples to ward off both the hangover and the inevitable stress headache from the conversation to follow.

'I don't think it's normal, but like, what was I going to do? He needed my help. I wasn't going to just leave him to his family.'

Ambrose had fixed her with a hard stare. 'That's exactly what you should have done, you massive plum.'

'You were the one who told me to be my old self, let my hair down, or whatever. Make some impulsive decisions.'

'I meant have some fun, eat a bunch of fancy nibbles. Maybe snog a stranger. Not befriend said stranger and construct an elaborate lie to fool your families into thinking that you're both well-adjusted adults. Oh God, what have I done? This is my fault, isn't it?'

'It's not that bad.'

'Do you fancy him? Is that what this is about? Going for the old fake-dating-to-actual-lovers trope?'

'No, we're just friends. There's nothing romantic there. We just get each other, I think?'

'So, it's strictly platonic fake dating? Oh God, that's somehow *worse*.'

Naturally, Haf disagrees. It's much simpler this way.

And even when Christopher told her, repeatedly, she was welcome to back out, she said she wouldn't. It would work out fine. Sure, they'd have to do the odd peck and cuddle to keep up the ruse, but it's not like they'll be asked to strip naked and procreate in the middle of Christmas dinner.

Admittedly, Haf hadn't been the best friend to Ambrose. She hadn't even asked about Ambrose's date with Paco (which had been a very good time, and they were seeing him again in January) until a whole two days later, too caught up in her own drama. While Ambrose had been mostly ignoring her own presence, they'd been doing a lot of gooey-eyed giggling at their phone, which made Haf's chest ache – she just wanted to talk with them about it.

Ambrose wasn't actively freezing her out, she knew that. Their intense disapproval combined with a deep desire for Haf to sort herself out meant they truly just didn't know what to say, and didn't want to help in case it was a kind of encouragement. So instead, they kept the lebkuchen tin full. It was out of love, Haf knew. They'd come around eventually. Or she'd get herself into such a mess that even Ambrose couldn't hold out any longer.

After a quick free wee, Haf wanders down the beautifully decorated concourse of St Pancras station. There's a huge Christmas tree in the centre of the parade of shops, decorated with the same gold and red that hangs from the upper walkways. People swarm out from the Eurostar exit, and beneath the tree are dozens of little family reunions. Possible Christmas presents sparkle in shopfront windows – stationery, jumpers, cosy wellington boots and this season's toys just waiting to be bought and wrapped up for someone. Everything feels bright and loud and overwhelming, but in a good way. A kind of Christmas-specific sensory overload. It might just be a train station, but this is the first time all December that Haf has felt like it's Christmas.

Squeezed into one of the eaves, there's a bookshop. She's not a huge reader, and she absolutely hasn't read anything in months thanks to work, but maybe now's the time for a little treat. It would be nice to read something that isn't a dry scientific paper or her scheduled tweets in the charity's voice.

Plus, Christopher seems like the kind of guy who likes it when everyone hangs out quietly reading a book. Maybe all the Calloways do. She doesn't know what to expect. A book might be a good talking point at least, or an excuse.

She wanders in, and the bespectacled bookseller, who is busy filling up the gift bookmark pot on the counter, gives her a little hello nod. The shop is deceptively large, going much further back than she expected.

Christmas music plays here, as it does everywhere else, but it's a different album from outside. After a few seconds, she realises it's the duet by Ariana Grande and Kelly Clarkson from the 'make the yuletide gay' playlist that Ambrose has been playing on repeat all month.

**Haf:** I'm in a bookshop and they're playing Kelly & Ari. Miss you x

Ambrose replies only with a cowboy emoji, and after a few quiet moments:

**Ambrose:** Miss you too. A bit.

Even with a qualification, it's definitely better than the meteor, at least.

**Ambrose:** also err, I might have done a snarky poll after a glass of prosecco last night
**Ambrose:** soz x

Haf opens Twitter, navigating to Ambrose's page and barks with laughter.

**@ambroseliew** my friend is fake dating a man she just met for Christmas. is this the worst idea you've ever heard?
**Yes**: 99%
**No**: 1%
*301 votes*

She'll allow it. It's just a poll. At least it gave her a good laugh.

Admittedly, few books on the table displays are familiar to her. As she walks through, she spies a few classics that conjure thoughts of GCSE exams and BBC adaptations, but none of the displays of fresh fiction really grabs her attention. There's a chart of bestselling books on the wall, and she spies a new book by an author she read years ago on a summer holiday.

She takes the book from the shelf but it slips out of her clammy grasp, landing on the floor with a deafening thud. Bloody hardbacks. She mouths a sorry to the bookseller, who simply raises his eyebrows over his glasses and gives her a tiny shrug like 'What can you do?'

Typically, it has slid under the shelf, so Haf has to bend down to grapple for it. As she stands up, there's one of those horrible slow-motion moments where she realises she has hooked her enormous backpack onto the table behind her and also stood up far too quickly. There's a large bang as the table crashes back down, sending a whole display of books careening to the floor.

*Fuck.*

Haf carefully replaces the rescued hardback and shucks off her backpack and coat and leans them gently against a bare bit of wall.

The table is miraculously still standing, but around her is a landslide of books. On hands and knees, Haf gathers books into her arms. Most of them look undamaged, thank goodness. She ferries them from the floor into little piles on the table above her until she's got them all, and roughly clambers to her feet.

'You dropped this.'

She always thought the phrase was a cliché, but her heart actually does feel like it skips a beat as she looks up at the woman in front of her. Two books are cradled against her with one arm, as though she's trying to warm them up with her emerald green wool coat. Her other hand grips a sleek black walking stick with a curved handle like a question mark and a gold foot.

'And these two. And that one as well,' she says, pointing with her stick to one at her feet. She smiles with a sharp half-smile that you might at first glance think was fake, but it reaches her amber-brown eyes.

'Thank you,' Haf croaks, taking the stack from her and then rescuing the one from the floor. 'It's a bit of a catastrophe, isn't it? Hopefully, I'm not barred for damaging the stock . . . and the shop, I guess.'

Needing something to do with her hands, Haf starts putting the books into matching piles.

'Oh, I don't know, you're probably doing him a favour by offing some of his stock,' she whispers. She picks a paperback by one of those car guys off the telly, the kind of book that's aggressively For Men. 'This guy's a real arsehole. A good dent will probably improve the content. Or maybe they can send it back to be pulped, so no one has to read it. You might have done a great service to literature.'

Her voice is deep, slightly raspy and nearly whispered from cherry-red lips. Haf could wrap herself in the sound.

It's been a long time since she's flirted with another girl. She feels rusty, awkward, nervous.

Back when she was newly single, Ambrose and Haf had braved a regularly held queer meet-up at a nearby pub. But they'd both quickly realised neither of them liked regular commitments or organised fun, as nice as everyone was, so they never went back. There's one queer bar in town that she's never been to, and despite being a very online person, dating apps fill her with a very specific kind of dread – how do you market yourself to dates when you feel like a clam that got left out on the side too long a good 90 per cent of the time? At least her Twitter bubble is filled with awkward weirdos like her. You could meet *anyone* on a dating app. Normal, well-adjusted people. Terrifying.

'Certainly, can't make it worse,' Haf answers, hoping there hasn't been a huge gap of silence while she tried to remember how to flirt.

'Really, I think we'd be doing a public service to just kick it under the shelves. What do you think?' Her eyes sparkle with mischief and secrets.

'Ma'am, are you trying to peer-pressure me into committing a crime?'

She laughs, and it is music. 'Only a little one. Tiny, really.'

Haf glances over at the cashier, who looks entirely unbothered by their calamity. 'I think on this occasion, I'll be good and tidy up the mess I made with my enormous backpack.'

'Wow, you aren't kidding. Are you going on an expedition?' the stranger says, eyeing up Haf's luggage. 'North Pole, perhaps?'

'Something like that.'

Together, they manage to roughly reform the display of books, matching the other tables' pyramid layout with the biggest piles in the middle. Haf can't stop looking at her out of the corner of her eye. She's careful, straightening the edges with her delicate fingers and making sure the shiniest copies are at the top. Her rich dark hair falls forward over her face, like a river of dark bitter chocolate.

'Thanks for helping me. And I promise that when I do plan to engage in petty crime, I'll be sure to call on you.'

In reply, the woman winks. She *fucking winks*. A natural, no-squinting wink. Haf melts.

All the air has been sucked out of the room and only they exist. What do you say to someone who has just winked at you? But she said she'd call on her. Now would be the right time to ask for her number, but the words dry in Haf's mouth. This woman looks so beautiful, so put together. What does Haf have to offer but a gigantic backpack and the occasional awkward comeback?

The woman picks a book off the shelf and reads the back, and Haf feels a sense of loss, like she missed the moment to keep talking to her. What would it feel like to be touched by her? For this woman to appraise her, stroke her, whisper things against her ear. What would it be like to kiss those nearly smirking lips, to bite softly on the lower one?

*Snap out of it*, she thinks, taking a deep breath.

Nestled on the floor, she spies another lost book and reaches down to pick it up. The cover draws her in. A girl wearing an orange beret, staring into the distance. One arm leaning against a blank canvas, the other slung in the pocket of her grey coat. There's something so lovely about her that Haf can't stop looking at.

It's *Carol* by Patricia Highsmith, apparently. In all the chaos, she must have knocked it off the next table over, a display of 'The Best of LGBTQ* Fiction'. Even here, most books are new to her. She went through a phase at university of reading whatever she could get her hands on, usually battered copies found in charity shops, so there are lots of gaps in her knowledge. It's been one of those things that she's promised herself she'll spend time indulging in for . . . well, most of the last few years.

'Now that's a book.'

The stranger's attention is back on her, and the two women hold eye contact for a beat.

Unsure of what to do, Haf holds up the book.

'How good's my taste?'

'That depends,' she says, looking up with heavy-lidded eyes.

Haf gulps. *Holy shit.*

The stranger reaches forward, hooking her walking stick over one forearm, and takes the book from Haf's hands.

'Have you read this before?' She turns it over in her hands, smiling at it like an old friend.

'No. Oh wait, didn't they make a film of this? I swear everyone is always telling me to watch it.'

'You should read it.' She taps her red manicured nails on the cover.

'Yeah?'

'Yeah. Really, it's a romance, but it's written like a thriller. There's a bit of homophobia, bit of a shit husband, the usuals. But there is a happy-ever-after for the lesbians, probably the first in literature, which is nice.'

Haf takes the book back into her clammy hands, gripping onto it for dear life.

'Oh,' she says, all the air going from her throat. 'That makes a change.'

She's always struggled with this part, making it clear you're another queer woman. Most of the time she feels like an alien speaking human, and this feels like an expert level of communication that she's never sure she's managing. If only there was a hand signal, or that everyone still spoke Polari. It would be really useful if she had one of the enamel flag pins on her enormous rucksack, though pointing at it would likely be as awkward as what she's trying to do now.

'Is it set at Christmas?'

'A little bit, actually. That's how they meet. In a shop.'

Haf licks her bottom lip and bites down on it.

'The film is also very good, worth watching just for Cate Blanchett's wardrobe alone. And there's this scene where she's sitting on the floor and stands up so elegantly without using her hands . . . You'll get what I mean when you see it. It's almost erotic.'

Haf feels like she's going to pass out. Message received, apparently. She can't quite believe that she's managing it.

'Remember how to flirt! Remember how to flirt, you absolute disaster!' yells Ambrose's voice in her head. 'Ask her to watch it with you! Get her number!'

*I can do this*, she thinks.

She reaches for Party Haf – the brash confident version of herself that flirted with Christopher, the Haf who knows she's hot and brilliant. That Haf isn't completely separate from her, but she's a kind of the Big-Personality version of her. She's where Haf stores her bravery.

'Maybe—'

But before Haf can finish, the woman answers her phone.

'Hello? Oh yeah, hi. Everything okay?'

And with that she rushes away, out of the bookshop.

*Fuck.*

Haf stands clutching the copy of *Carol* in her hands and waits, but she doesn't come back. She's just . . . gone.

Haf missed her chance.

'Are you all right?' The bookseller appears at her side, hands deep in his cardigan pockets.

'I am absolutely not,' Haf whispers, watching the door.

'Sorry?'

'Oh! No I am fine, generally, ha ha,' she says too loudly. 'Um, can I buy this?'

He gives her a knowing, sympathetic look over the top of his glasses as he takes the copy of *Carol* that Haf has slightly warped with her tight grip. She follows him wordlessly to the counter, dragging the bag behind her.

'It's not often I get to see a meet-cute in here.'

Haf snaps out of her daze, a little embarrassed that her failure had a witness. 'I'd have thought train stations would be rife with it?'

'Less common than you'd think. Usually just business people looking for something to read on the train, or parents with gaggles of children. Making eyes over the queer books? Couldn't be more perfect.' He chuckles to himself before sighing contentedly. 'That's the kind of meet-cute you dream of, the kind of queer stories we deserve.'

Haf taps the payment through with her iPhone. 'Don't get too excited. I didn't get her number. Or even her name.'

His mouth hangs open. 'You're not serious? What about her Instagram? Twitter? TikTok? Anything?'

Haf shakes her head.

He tuts at her and sighs. 'Dear me.'

'I was . . . a mess,' she groans.

'I can't believe it. She looked like she was about to eat you up,' he says, typing something into the till. 'Maybe she'll come back?'

They both glance back to the door in hopeful unison, but she doesn't reappear.

Sighing, he passes her the book wrapped up in a paper bag, a complimentary bookmark sticking out from the pages.

'We've all been there. I took ten per cent off by the way.'

'Oh, I'm not a student.'

'I know, but you gave me five minutes of entertainment and an anecdote for forever.'

'Happy to help. You can call it "The Tale of the Useless Bisexual".'

She flips open the top of the rucksack, and gently places her book on top of the Betty's box, which appears to be miraculously undamaged. Secured, she carefully slings it back over her shoulders.

'Do you want to leave your number? In case she comes back?' he asks, eyes wide and chin resting in his hands.

'You think I should?'

'Yes. Absolutely. I mean, it's probably breaking some kind of data protection law, but I'll do it for love.'

Haf worries at her bottom lip. She could, but what if they didn't have anything in common? What if she didn't even come back for the number? Her number could live on the back of a receipt in this bookseller's pocket, abandoned and unlusted after.

'Or,' he says slowly, raising his eyebrows, 'do you have a pair of gloves? You could leave a glove.'

'Why would I leave a glove?' she asks.

'When you read the book, you'll get it.'

Sadly, she doesn't have any gloves, though she could leave her email. Perhaps, her Twitter or Instagram handle.

Her phone buzzes with a message from Christopher saying he's on his way and to meet her at the French café by the Christmas tree in about twenty minutes.

'No, it's okay. Just wasn't meant to be.'

Things were complicated enough right now with her fake boyfriend.

The bookseller seems to deflate. 'All right then. Have a merry Christmas. Enjoy the book.'

'You too. Thanks for this,' she says, meaning both the book and the solidarity. She waves goodbye and wobbles out of the shop to the café, past the enormous Christmas tree and another wave of fresh multilingual reunions by the Eurostar.

Haf drags her backpack through the tightly packed tables to a table in the corner that the waiter directs her to. The universe appears to be briefly on her side, because she doesn't bash anyone.

She orders a coffee, and takes the book out of her bag, unwrapping the paper. Waiting in a train station seems like the right time to read something new. But she just can't. She's too wrapped up in the failure of the moments that brought this book to her. She sets it face up on the table, and scrolls through Twitter instead.

**@thehafofit** Had a train station meet-cute and completely fumbled it lads. Womp womp.

This gets a few consolatory replies and even a pity like from Ambrose.

She loses herself in some mid-tier celebrity drama where she recognises no one's names, and Christopher appears just as she finishes her first coffee.

'Hello!' he says far too cheerily.

'Hi,' she says back in the same tone.

They share an awkward hug as they try to avoid knocking surrounding tables while compensating for the big height difference.

'How are you?' he asks.

Should she tell him? It might help explain why she's probably going to be even more socially wobbly for the next hour at least while she recovers herself.

But before she can answer, he continues on with, 'Shall we eat here before we go? They're not expecting us home until dinner, so we don't really need to rush.'

'Yes!' she says a little too eagerly. Food will be a good distraction. 'I'm starving.'

They eat platters of poached eggs with runny yolks and creamy mushrooms with soft bread with more coffees in tiny bowl cups.

It's all comfortable small talk as they both bemoan the last week and settle back into the ease between them that they felt that night. It wasn't just the booze, she's glad to find. Conversation flows easily, and she is genuinely very happy to see him, and it seems like the feeling is mutual.

It's time to focus on Christopher, she tells herself. *Yes, your pride is hurt. Yes, you missed out on something that felt real, but this man, right here, is the first person you've felt a deep, instant connection with since Ambrose. Time to get your head in the game.*

Christopher insists on paying, which is a relief. The train down and the much-needed final week of work coffees swallowed up a lot of her cash, and she's not being paid until the end of the month, which seems legitimately mean.

'Shall we go?' he asks, kindly taking the enormous bag from her. On him, it looks in proportion. 'We've got to get the Tube over to Paddington, and then we'll get a train from there. Hopefully, it won't be too busy.'

Haf glances down the concourse to the bookshop, checking on the faces of all the people they pass. There's no sign of her.

'Ready as I'll ever be.'

# Chapter Five

Christopher and Haf make it to Paddington unscathed. Mostly. There was a short fumble through the Tube entrance where Haf is pretty sure she very nearly got stuck in the gates, though Christopher insists she was absolutely fine. Paddington station is a whole different beast of a station: a deep cavernous tunnel where all the platforms snake off into the far distance.

When Christopher checks the train times on the departures board, Haf realises with embarrassment that she has no idea where in the country Oxlea even is, never mind what train they must get. She can picture Ambrose's disapproval, which is fair. Knowing where you're going with a near-stranger is probably the bare minimum, really.

Whenever there's a quiet moment, her mind slips back to the bookshop. The copy of *Carol* in her backpack feels like a beacon.

They have a little while to wait for the train, so Haf suggests they do a bunch of cute couples photos for their socials and for proof of them dating. A passer-by takes a photo of the two of them in front of a big Christmas tree, and Christopher snaps a quick photo of Haf donating to the charity box in front of the carol singers dressed in matching red velvet outfits, that make them look simultaneously like every member of the March family from the nineties version of *Little Women*.

She insists on a photo outside of the Paddington Bear shop, followed by one of them together next to the Paddington statute on the platform where their train is waiting.

'Do you have a big thing for Paddington? Or is it just fictional bears in general?' Christopher asks, hauling their bags onto the train.

'Oh my God, have you not seen *Paddington 2* – aka the greatest movie in the world? Paddington versus the industrial prison complex? Paddington is a radical!' Haf's voice gets a little bit shrieky because, truth be told, she really does have a big thing for Paddington.

'I have not.'

'We are watching it. I have it downloaded on my tablet for emergencies.'

'I didn't realise there were so many bear-based emergencies in your life.'

'Not many gay people in your life, are there?' she chuckles.

He flushes pink. 'There are.' He pouts.

The train is already humming with people going home for Christmas. They find their seats, but they're in the quiet carriage, which is full of people precariously balancing laptops on tiny tables as they try to finish up their work in time for the holidays. Normally, Haf would be very thankful for this. A normal train carriage can be such a barrage of random noise from phone calls and blown noses and crisp-eating, among many other horrible sounds that absolutely go through her. However, a carriage where you have to be quiet might not be the ideal site for discussing their plans.

Haf takes a few bits out of her gigantic rucksack, then slides into the window seat. The air con is on high to compensate for the amount of people in the train, so she keeps her coat for a lap blanket, while Christopher stows everything else above them.

He sits down and stretches his long legs out briefly, before having to tuck them in again as more people board.

'There,' she says, handing Christopher his phone. 'I made us by the tree your background, and mine is us in front of Paddington. Do you have an Instagram?'

'When did you take my phone? Did you pickpocket me?'

'Yeah, like thirty seconds ago when you were putting things away.'

'You're terrifying,' he says, narrowing his eyes at her.

'I work in socials, Christopher. I'm just efficient.'

'I don't have very much on my Instagram,' he admits.

'I saw.'

'Why are you asking if you already know? And why didn't you just post the photo for me?'

Haf shrugs. 'I wanted to ask your permission first.'

'Even though you stole the phone from me?'

She takes the phone back out of his hand and shows him the draft post she had whipped up. It's a square crop of the picture in front of the Christmas tree, and she's brightened the colours a bit. It's a good picture, and they look like a real couple, with his arm slung around her waist and her head tilted up to smile at him. Underneath the caption is, *Off home for Christmas*.

'Bloody hell, you are quick.'

'Fastest fingers in the West. Or East. Though now we're south . . .'

'You've not written very much.'

'You don't seem like a long-caption-and-multi-hashtag kind of guy.'

Haf peers over as Christopher makes a few edits, and sees he's added, *with my best girl*, followed by a snowflake emoji.

'Your best girl? You're going to make me cry. But also are you calling me a snowflake?'

'It's just a Christmassy emoji . . . Okay, I'll change it just to be safe.'

He swaps it for a Christmas tree to match the picture.

'Has no one ever called you a snowflake?'

'Not to my face.'

'There's still time,' she says, patting his hand.

As the train driver welcomes everyone on board, a final passenger gets onto their coach, squeezing past Christopher's legs, and settling on the table seat across the aisle from them. The man takes off his coat and hat with the exaggerated huffing of someone who has absolutely had enough. Laptop open, he begins typing furiously. His harried, furious-eyed look feels greatly at odds with his festive jumper, which features a knitted-on scarf you could store things in – his is currently hosting his water bottle. Haf makes a note to track one of these down on eBay after the holidays.

Her own Instagram feed hasn't been updated in a couple of months. The last few photos all variations on the red autumn leaves by various York backdrops – the Minster, a selfie from the Walls, the river, Betty's Halloween window display. She posts the Paddington photo too, with the caption, *Christmas with the best man in the world . . . Paddington Bear.*

'Hey,' he laughs. 'You don't need to keep it up on your profile, you know?'

'Of course I do. My parents think you're my new boyfriend, which suits me, as they will temporarily forget I'm a total train wreck, and as if your family isn't going to stalk me a bit on socials. Speak of the devil,' she says as a new comment from her mum appears under the photo: *Have a lovely time, he's very handsome!!!! Nice bear too.*

'I think you've got a fan,' she says. 'Oh, and I made my Twitter private, just to be safe. No one needs to see where I go to scream into the void.'

The man across the aisle coughs pointedly as the train starts to move, so Haf drops her voice to a whisper and hopes it's enough to not annoy anyone.

'Before I show you one of the greatest cinematic masterpieces of our time, we need to work out a few things. Our relationship history, our story, the practicalities of it all. What we're going to tell everyone when we get there. Speaking of, where are we going? I know Oxlea is the end destination but like . . .'

'You have no idea where we're going, do you?' He tries to hold back his smile, and a little wrinkle forms in one corner of his mouth.

'The South, obviously.' She can't explain why she hadn't looked up anything; something about leaving it all in Christopher's hands meant her brain had ticked it off the list of important things she had to think about.

'Obviously. But anything more specifically? County, perhaps?'

'Oh, yeah. Absolutely not. But it's not like you know where I'm from!' she says, opening the tab on her KeepCup to let some steam out.

'You're from Aberelwy in North Wales, right in the middle by the sea,' he says, as he places a napkin on the fold-down table on the back of the chair, pleased that he is, of course, 100 per cent correct.

'How did you know that?'

'When we watched *Gilmore Girls* the night we met, you said the town meeting reminded you of home.'

'Well, don't be too smug about it.' She pouts.

'I can and will be.' From a paper bag, he takes two chocolate-chip cookies and places them on the napkin. 'Forgiven?'

'Perhaps,' she says, breaking off a chunk with her fingers. 'So where are we going?'

'The Cotswolds.'

'Wait, isn't that like pure chocolate-box house territory?' Her voice rises a little too much, and the harried-looking person across the aisle gives her a pointed look over his glasses.

She mouths, 'Sorry,' and lowers her voice back to whispering. 'Okay, so dating a few months – that's what we told Laurel. How did we meet?'

'I think Laurel got the impression it was through Sally.'

'Okay, so *I* know I crashed her fancy little party, but give me your side.'

'Same school as us, but she was in my sister's year, so she's a bit older than Laurel and I. She's nice, the sort of person who likes to make all her friends be friends.'

'Okay, so let's stick with the truth that Ambrose took me to a party and we met there, and just make it a few months earlier.'

Christopher thinks for a moment. 'Let's say August, because I actually was up in Yorkshire for work.'

'Wow, four months. Go us. Let's say we went on a date then and we started going out. Lots of FaceTimes and that. Modern love. And then *this* party was the next time we were able to see each other, so we don't have to pretend we've been sneaking off to see each other or whatever. Also explains the lack of pics together.'

'Okay, that makes sense,' he says a little slowly, turning it over.

'It's easier if a lie has a grain of truth in it. That way it's far more convincing, like you can pull from things that actually happened,' she explains. 'It's not so much lying to your entire family, as bending the truth. Speaking of which, give me the cast list. Everyone's names and likes and who I need to impress most.'

She pauses for a second.

'It's definitely your mum, isn't it? You strike me as a mummy's boy.'

'I am not.' He huffs, affronted. He takes a piece of cookie and chews. After a moment he says, 'Mother—'

'Mother?!' Haf interrupts, with a snort. Another pointed cough sounds out, this time from someone else behind them.

'Yes, Mother,' he says, rolling his eyes. 'Her name is Esther. She's . . . Well, she's a bit of a . . . a character. She stayed at home when we were growing up, but she ran basically every committee in the county.'

'And your dad? Dads love me.'

'A bit of a man's man is my dad, Otto. He started his business – which is kind of like Airbnb for rich people and their multiple homes, I guess – a long time ago and it's still going. Branched out into other bits alongside it. He's good at innovating, I'll give him that. He's very keen I do well in work as I . . . err . . . expect he wants me to take over the company.'

'And you don't want that?' He pales a little, so she decides to skip over this for now. 'Is he a whisky man?'

Christopher nods.

'Excellent. I had a Cool Girl phase at uni and got really into whisky, which, it turns out, is very useful for talking to dads.'

It had absolutely worked with Freddie's dad, who had admittedly liked her much more than Freddie probably did. Whenever Freddie came back from a trip home, he'd bring a bottle of something nice for Haf that his dad had sent up.

'Okay, Esther and Otto Calloway. How cute. Siblings?'

'Just Kit.'

Haf's phone vibrates. Ambrose has sent a train emoji, followed by a question mark. She sends back a thumbs up, a pink heart and a sunflower, Ambrose's favourite. Two blue ticks appear, but nothing else follows.

'Everything all right?'

Haf puffs out her cheeks. 'Ambrose just thinks this is a bad idea.'

'Well, they're not wrong.'

They share a warm smile.

'I suppose if a friend of mine told me they were going to fake-date someone for Christmas, I'd probably kick off a bit too,' Haf admits.

'They sound like a good friend.'

'They are.' Apart from the Twitter roasting, she thinks, though she doesn't say this in case she worries him. 'We're very different, so sometimes we clash a bit, but it's good. I'm a puppy with separation anxiety who needs a lot of attention, so I get that I'm a bit annoying.'

'You'll be pleased to hear my parents have two dogs. No separation anxiety, though.'

'That's fine, I have enough for all of us. Go on, show me a picture then.'

Christopher's phone is filled with photos of two tan terriers with grey wiry bristles around their mouths. 'Stella and Luna,' he says. 'Border terriers. Probably the biggest personalities in that house, just about. Slip them a bit of bacon and you've got friends for life, though.'

'I love them,' Haf whispers. 'I've missed being around animals. Renting is so shit for that. I'm going to be unbearably clingy to them, just to warn you.'

'Taking the dogs out for a walk is also a good excuse to escape any situations that might arise.'

'Are you saying I should be prepared for some family drama?'

Christopher pauses a little too long. 'It's not going to be *Eastenders* or anything, just maybe a few comments. A disagreement or two, maybe.'

'Good to know. Also, you skipped your sister. Give me the details so I can get her on side.'

'Katharine, though most of her friends call her Kit. She's two years older than me, and an architect.'

'Wow, a grown-up.'

He laughs. 'Yes, pretty much.'

'Are you close?'

'We were, when we were younger. All our friends are basically the same people, hence Laurel and I. But architecture is kind of intense to qualify in, so she had less time for me, and then . . . you know.' He trails off. 'It's hard to feel close to the person your parents expect you to match up to.'

Before she can ask anything else, the harried man at the table across the aisle turns to them. 'Hi? Hello there. Chatty people? Can you both *please* be quiet?'

'I'm sorry,' Haf says, 'it's just a really important—'

'Look, I have so much work to do and all I can hear are you two discussing your weird schemes that I don't want to know anything about. I don't want to know that you're defrauding his family, or whatever it is you're doing. Please stop being *weird and loud.*'

From ahead of them, someone joins in with a meek, 'Yeah!'

'It's not that weird,' Haf protests before she can stop herself.

The man simply holds his hand up to his lips, and with the air of a teacher he simply says, 'Shush.'

A couple of half-hearted claps sound around them, and the man returns to his work, cheeks flushed with the success of telling someone off.

Mortified, Haf and Christopher sink down in their seats. She reaches for her tablet, and wordlessly hands him an earbud. Thank goodness for *Paddington 2*.

Exactly one hour and forty-four minutes later, Christopher and Haf both wipe tears away and pull the headphones out from their ears. Afraid of restoking the wrath of the passengers around them, Christopher simply nods at her as if to say, 'okay, you were right.'

Shortly after, the driver announces that the next stop will be Guildwick, which is their destination.

Once off the train, and free of the imposed silence, Haf lets out a loud yawn and stretch. 'Thank God, I can make noise again.'

'It's all right if you don't, you know,' Christopher teases, and she kicks at the air in his direction.

'Cheeky. Where now?'

'We'll get a taxi over. Everyone will be too busy to give us a lift and it'll be quicker this way.'

The station is the expected little chocolate-box kind of place. The buildings are all built in the same stone, and the bridge is painted in a fresh lick of green paint. It's like what she imagined the stations at home in Wales would look like if they were maintained, or if they hadn't been knocked down in favour of weird eighties monstrosities. There isn't even a ticket gate here, which feels quaint.

At the taxi rank outside, Christopher hauls their bags into the boot, and soon they're off. At a traffic light, a second taxi pulls alongside, and she sees the harried-looking man from the train and hides her face behind her hair.

'Are you ready to meet the family?' he asks.

'As I'll ever be!' She beams.

Haf's confidence that everything will go well lasts for almost the entire ride.

Right up until the car turns off the country roads that they've been whizzing along and begins to trundle down a small gravelly road that Christopher casually informs her is their private drive, at the end of which she spies a large sandstone-coloured house.

# Chapter Six

A private drive. A tree-lined private drive, at that. Who on earth has a private drive?

Well, Christopher's family apparently, but still. The only private drives Haf is used to are the ones for the farmers down the lane near where she grew up, and those are private more due to risk of potentially being run over by a tractor than rich-people confidentiality.

The taxi slows to a stop before she can finish taking in not only the private drive but the enormous house looming in front of her, and oh God, they have to get out now? Can she not stay in the car with the pleasantly silent taxi driver?

Apparently not.

Haf gulps as she stumbles out of the car. It even smells nice here. Everything is alarmingly neat in the garden, and the cars by the garage shine brightly in the sun. Her Doc Martens crunch almost too loudly on the gravel as they walk towards the shining green front door, decorated with a wreath of holly wrapped in plaid ribbons. The little potted hedges leading up to the front door have glittering gold lights in them, which are starting to twinkle as the light of the day drops.

Haf already feels too messy to be here.

Before she can open her mouth to say anything, the door opens inwards.

Standing inside a small porch area is Christopher's mother dressed in tailored trousers, a light cream shirt, and a long, flowing cardigan that is almost certainly cashmere.

'Darling, welcome home,' she cries, in a slightly raspy but distinctly clipped voice.

Despite being a good foot taller than her, she wraps her arms around Christopher's neck and pulls him down to her in a quick hug, ended with three firm pats on the back. It's motherly but restrained, like she has a set time that an appropriate hug should go on for.

'Hello, Mother,' he says, kissing her on the cheek as she releases him. 'Nice to see you.'

As Esther turns her attention to Haf, the similarities between Christopher and Esther, despite the height difference, become very clear. They have the same blueish undertone to their pale skin, offset by rosy pink cheeks. Christopher's long eyelashes must have come from someone else, but she recognises his smile on her. They share the same tone of light brown hair, but hers is styled in a gentle curl around her chin, revealing a flash of pearl earrings when she moves.

Esther holds Haf by the upper arms, a gesture that's not an actual hug, but carries affection in it. 'And, Haf, welcome to our home,' she says, her crow's feet dimpling with the force of her smile. The rasp of her crisp accent captures the V-sounding F in her name that English people never usually get right, which warms her heart.

'It's really lovely to meet you, Mrs Calloway,' Haf says, her mouth dry.

'Please, just call me Esther, my dear. It's so wonderful that Christopher brought you down to us for the holidays.'

There's a pregnant pause where Haf gets the distinct sense that Esther is evaluating her. Unsure what to do while still held by Esther, she raises a hand to pat her on the arm to return the gesture. But as she does, Esther moves forwards, and . . .

Oh God.

She's pretty sure that she just patted Christopher's mother's boob.

Esther has either not noticed or has the grace to not make a point of it as she opens the adjoining door from the porch to the rest of the house and ushers them in.

'Come in, come in. Let's go to the kitchen,' and she disappears around a corner.

*Please say I imagined it,* Haf wishes to the universe. *Please.*

The irony of being worried about saying the wrong thing then possibly fondling one of his parents at the first instance is not lost on her.

The warm air of the house filters into the porch, clove and cinnamon scented. It smells homely and a little fancy, like there's an expensive Christmas candle burning in every room.

'Everything okay?' Christopher whispers, leaning against the doorframe as Haf dumps her bag on the floor. 'You've gone a bit pale.'

'You didn't tell me you were posh,' she hisses, trying to forget that she might have just fondled his mother. There's only time for one crisis right now.

'We're not *that* posh,' he says, in a way that she knows is affected attempted humility, but comes across as completely clueless.

'Ugh, Christopher,' she says, rolling her eyes. 'Trust me, this is posh. Not just to me either. I think most people did not grow up in manor houses.'

'I wouldn't call it a manor . . .'

She shoots him a dead-eyed stare. 'Can you not hear it?'

'Hear what?'

'The comfortable sound of inherited wealth, Christopher,' she mutters, hoping his parents didn't overhear.

Maybe she should have known from his whole vibe, but pretty much all southern people sound the same to her (bar Essex – she watched enough *TOWIE* in her uni days to spot that one). Haf can never quite gauge whether clipped southern accents are someone who grew up with Radio 4 on in the house, minor gentry, or just from Surrey. Granted, someone could easily be all three, not that she'd be able to clock that either.

She'd thought he'd live in just a nice big house on a street in the fancy end of town or something. Instead, he apparently lives in a three-storey fancy house that has an extra bit of land just to conceal it from the riff-raff. Or at least random dog walkers.

'Are you coming through, darling?' calls his mother.

'Just a minute,' he shouts back.

Dazed, Haf awkwardly bends down to unlace her Doc Martens to leave them in the rack next to walking shoes almost as filthy as her boots. She probably should have cleaned them before this trip. Or ever.

Christopher bends down to help Haf with the knot in her shoelaces, and drops his voice to a whisper.

'I did try to warn you that my family were a lot.'

'I thought you meant they were inclined to passive aggressiveness. Not that you come from a line of former Etonians.'

He clearly is about to protest that none of them went to Eton, but thinks better of it and flattens his lips into a line.

'Should I have brought stuff to wear for dinner, like formalwear? I come from a pyjamas-all-day, watch-all-the-films-and-pass-out-slightly-pissed-Christmas-routine family, Christopher. My bag might be massive but the wardrobe options are not extensive enough to cover black tie.'

He pulls a face at this, but she presumes it's just horror from the state of her boots, which are admittedly a little worse for wear.

'Haf, honestly, it's okay. We're a pretty relaxed family. They won't care how you dress. And I'm sure you'd look adorable in all-day pyjamas.'

'Come on, I'm being serious,' she whines, nerves creeping into her voice, making it wobble slightly. As much as she is joking about it, this has thrown her.

'Sorry, I'm not trying to make fun of you,' he says, helping her up.

'I know, I know. It's just, I was thinking fancy picky teas, rather than formal dining and having to work out which fork for which course.'

'It'll be fine. They'll love you,' he says, touching her shoulder with such gentleness that all her worries attempt to evaporate, but then resettle like a heavy fog. 'And if you do struggle with the cutlery, I'll give you hints.'

Haf sticks her tongue out at him.

'Just give me a second, okay? I just need to . . . readjust my expectations.'

Can she even play a convincing fake girlfriend in this situation?

The thing she's struggling to explain, that she's never been able to explain, is that as brash and confident as she can be, it comes from a place of practice. She has a script that she sticks to. Compliment, offer to help out, ask about their interests; those are the three tenets of pleasing parents that she's relied on her whole life and it was a solid formula. But it also relied on a familiarity, shared cultural touchstones. Will she have anything in common with them? Sure, there's Christopher, but she can't talk about only him for the next four days or they'll think she's dangerously obsessed with him, rather than in want of a conversation topic. Granted, if she's absolutely awful and they hate her, that'll probably make fake-breaking up with her easier and his family would be really relieved about it.

She'll just have to get over it. There's no time for class anxiety this Christmas.

Haf takes a deep breath. *It'll be fine*, she tells herself. It'll have to be.

She looks up at Christopher and gives him a smile.

'You're doing great,' he says reassuringly.

She adds her coat to an empty hook, hoping she hasn't made a porch etiquette faux pas, on top of goosing his mother and being a peasant.

Christopher moves Haf's bag to the bottom of the old-looking bare wooden staircase – the sort of thing estate agents would list as a 'period feature'. The hallway is beautiful – all pea-green walls and a matching runner, contrasting with the darker wood of the floor and stairs. Everything is tasteful, but there's a sense of antiquity about the place. Haf is a bit worried she's going to break something.

'The dogs must be out, or they'd be all over you already,' he says, glancing at a dark wooden dresser standing near the door where they must keep the dog bits, as well as the keys and post.

He takes a small baggie of treats from the side and hands them to Haf. They smell like sheep.

'Thanks, but I don't need a snack. I'm still full from lunch.'

'Oh, ha ha,' he says. 'Just take them for when the dogs get here.'

'Clever idea. Then they'll love me most of all.'

'Something like that. Come on, the kitchen's just through here.'

The brightly lit kitchen is a handsome mishmash of country and modern aesthetics – white brick tiles line the walls above slate counters, and in the middle of the room stands a heavy oak butcher's block table next to a sleek kitchen island. It shouldn't work, but it does.

They join Esther, where she stands attending to a shiny copper pan on the hob.

'I thought you could do with a glass to warm you up,' she says.

Inside the pan is a batch of home-made mulled wine. As she stirs, bundles of spices and orange peel float to the surface before disappearing back into the dark. It smells divine.

'Yes please,' Haf says. 'Shall I get some cups?'

'Already done,' says Christopher, laying a couple of half-glazed stone-coloured ceramic mugs on the counter in front of her.

In the bright light from the large windows, Esther glows a little. Where Christopher is all languid movements, Esther is almost bird-like – aware of her surroundings, quick, elegant. Christopher's description of her had been scant at best, but she was expecting someone far more domineering than the quiet certainty in front of her. Perhaps that's just being someone's child; you always see them differently, as a parent first rather than a person in their own right. Intimacy and proximity always change things. To Haf, she just looks like a woman who knows what she likes.

Esther stirs the mulled wine in two full swirls, then ladles the dark liquid into two cups.

'How was the train journey? Pleasant, I hope?'

'Yes, thank you,' Haf says again, cursing herself silently for being a parrot. 'It wasn't too busy, and it was nice seeing all the decorations.'

'Did you get to see much of London?'

'Oh no, we just passed straight through. I've not been since I was a kid, actually.'

'Christopher, haven't you shown her all the sights yet?' Esther asks, a little affronted on behalf of Haf even though she's pretty sure they're nowhere near London now.

'It's on the cards,' he says, taking a cup from his mother. 'Is Father out with the dogs?'

'No, I think he's in the study,' she says, handing a cup to Haf. 'Your sister appeared about an hour before you and took them out straight away. She said she needed the fresh air.'

'Oh,' he says, surprised. 'I thought she wasn't coming down until the Howard party?'

Esther gives a delicate little shrug. 'You and I both. More fool us for expecting Kit to do anything other than exactly what she wants.'

Christopher laughs and smiles, and Haf gives a polite grin to agree, even though she has no idea if that's a fair characterisation or not.

'I suspect Laurel asked her to come down early,' Esther adds. 'Come, let's go sit by the fire.'

As they walk through the house, Haf clutches onto her cup for dear life. If she spills even a drop, she is going to be mortified. Haf has never drunk or eaten anything in her life without a spill or a dribble, at the very least.

As Esther walks, her slippers, designed to look like heels, clack pleasingly on the floors.

Haf pauses to take a quick swig of the mulled wine for courage – and so there's less in her cup that could spill everywhere. It feels like some of it went down the wrong way, and she coughs a little, before rushing after the Calloways.

The living room has the same colour scheme as the hallway – a rich-green sofa with two matching armchairs, and dark-wood bookcases stuffed with books – and a roaring fire in the centre of it all. Childhood photos line the mantelpiece, which she notes to noodle through later. A basket for the dogs slumps in front of the fire, surrounded by ragged toys and a very tired and slightly muddy woollen blanket.

A beautiful Christmas tree almost as tall as the high ceiling stands in front of the French windows, lit in soft golden light that reflects off the berry red baubles. Crystal snowflakes hang from the largest branches, and perched at the top is a gold sparkling star. It's the sort of literally-a-whole-tree Christmas tree Haf has seen in American Christmas films. Around the room, there are touches of seasonal décor too. There's no tinsel, just smatterings of red tartan that feel tasteful rather than fake Scottish.

She can see the dusk of winter outside, and a yawn escapes her. The fading dark feels so comforting from inside this cosy blanket of a room.

In an armchair, sits a man with a formidable moustache and perfectly round black glasses. The ankle of one foot is balanced on the other knee in the very masculine version of crossing your legs, and a large newspaper is spread over his lap. His hair is deep black, with only the faintest traces of silver.

'Ah! My boy!' he cries, folding the newspaper back along its original creases.

He leaps up enthusiastically, taking Christopher's hand and pulling him into a hug. It's one of those man hugs, where no one gets that close really and both slap each other's backs, but it's familial and sweet.

It's very clear where Christopher gets his height from; Otto is only a little shorter than him. Where Christopher is willowy, Otto is broad like a rugby player.

'Hi, Dad,' Christopher says as they step back to look at each other.

The tickle in her throat is still bothering her, so she tries to quietly tap against her chest with her knuckles while the men discuss the train from London.

'And this is Haf,' Esther says, directing Otto's attention over.

'Ah, Haf! Hello!' he says, or, rather, shouts. He's quite an ebullient man.

But when Haf opens her mouth to say hello, out comes an enormous hacking cough, the deafening sound reminiscent of a gun going off. Followed by another, and another.

*No, no, no, stop coughing!* Haf wills her lungs, which ache in response.

The wine in her cup slops ominously with the force of her coughing, and Christopher jumps to take the cup from her.

'Goodness,' cries Esther.

*This is a disaster*, she thinks, trying to free the bit of mulled wine in her windpipe. She bends over, hoping that gravity might intervene.

The last time she had a coughing fit, orange juice came out of her nose. The last thing she needs is a festive nasal evacuation right in the middle of the living room.

Thankfully, a few more coughs seem to sort it, and when she stands up, she catches her face in the mirror above the fire, slick and red as a tomato skin.

'Are you all right, my dear?' asks Otto, placing a hand on her back to steady her.

She nods wordlessly, trying to catch her breath.

'Oh, do you need a good whack?' Before she can say no, Otto hits her once in between her shoulders with one enormous bear-paw hand.

'Christ, Dad,' cries Christopher, catching her as she stumbles forward.

'Thanks,' she gasps, now completely winded as well.

'Are you all right? Do you need to sit down?' Christopher asks, taking her by the hand and leading her to the sofa.

'I'm fine,' she croaks, barely able to speak. Or breathe. But that's beside the point.

She stares into the fire, hoping it might swallow her whole so she can escape this excruciating moment.

'Was it the wine, or did you get a clove stuck in your throat . . . ?'

'Just some wine down the wrong way.'

'My spices are always well contained in their steeping bag, thank you, Christopher,' Esther says haughtily. 'Let me get you a glass of water, Haf.'

A few clacks later, Esther returns with a very cold, very fresh glass of water, which Haf sips at slowly.

Otto sinks back into his armchair, and Esther takes the other.

'So sorry, everyone,' Haf says after a few moments, finally able to breathe freely again.

'Let's try again, shall we?' Otto laughs, slapping his thigh with the joy of it all.

*At least I've entertained one of them,* she thinks.

'Tell us about yourself, Haf,' Otto asks, sliding his newspaper between the chair's arm and cushion.

'Yes, do,' agrees Esther, before shooting Otto a look that says, 'I've asked you not to store your papers in the couch for twenty years and you still do it.' He sheepishly removes it and drops it onto the coffee table.

*Okay, head in the game,* Haf thinks. *Get a hold of yourself.*

'Well, I'm from York. I mean, that's where I live now. I'm from Wales. North Wales, actually. By the sea, kind of. It's like a ten-minute drive, but it's closer than in York, ha ha,' she babbles. She takes a breath, urging herself to slow down. 'Anyway, yes, I moved to York at the start of the year, and it's very nice. And that's where I met Christopher, through Sally. Do you know Sally?'

Christopher puts a hand on her arm, that steadying touch again.

'Sorry, I was babbling, ha ha ha,' she laughs, wishing desperately she hadn't choked on her mulled wine so she could have something to hold on to.

'Sally Mayfield?' Esther asks Christopher, and he nods. 'Oh, she's a nice girl, was always very polite when she'd come round to play with Kit. Her mother and I were on the school PTA for a time.'

Haf nods politely at this, as what else can she say? She doesn't actually know Sally. She probably should have introduced herself before they ran out of the party, but never mind. Hopefully they won't run into her here either.

'And York is a lovely city.'

Phew, she thinks. Back on a topic they can talk about. 'It really is. I'm very lucky to live there.' Haf wishes she had time to see more of it, but work keeps her busy and then she's no spare energy to really do anything. Luckily, York is a nice city just to look at, anyway. 'Have you been?' she asks Esther.

'Yes, we have, but not for a long time. When was the last time we were up in Yorkshire, Otto?'

Otto's eyebrows and moustache all seem to waggle at once. 'When Christopher was at university. We stayed up in the little B&B on the moors, back when the girls were puppies. I wanted us to go for a long walk, but we weren't allowed,' he adds with a tease.

'First of all, dearest, we did not go walking because the trainer told us we shouldn't over walk the girls, as it is bad for the joints. And second, the last time you conned me into going for "just a walk" with you was some time in the eighties, and if I remember, you sold it as a short wander, which turned out to be an eight-hour hike uphill through rain.'

'It was bracing.'

'It was terrible. And I am not one to be tricked twice.'

'But you look rather fetching in a Barbour!'

'I'm sure I do, but I look much better in a very good and crucially warm restaurant with a glass of chilled wine in my hand.'

'Ah, is that a hint?' Otto gets to his feet and disappears off, presumably to get his wife a glass of wine.

'We did a lot of that in York, in the end.'

'Oh actually, I have something for you.' Haf trots out into the hallway to root through her bag. She sets the copy of *Carol* on the side table and takes out the box of goodies from Betty's. Thankfully, everything seems to have magically survived the journey, though the ribbon is a little askew and the box slightly dented, but not so badly to look ungiftable. She pads back into the living room and holds them out to Esther. 'They're from a really lovely bakery restaurant place that everyone goes to.'

'Oh gosh, of course we know Betty's,' Esther says. 'Otto is rather partial to a Fat Rascal. This is very kind of you, Haf. Thank you.'

She doesn't open the box, but places it on the coffee table gently.

*Score*, Haf thinks, relieved. One success.

Otto returns with a glass of pale white wine for Esther, and what looks like a whisky for himself. Excellent, that's another thing she can talk about later. *Okay, okay, this is back on track.*

'Is that a Betty's box I spy?' he asks, peering over his glasses.

'Haf brought them for us to enjoy.'

'Shall I get some plates?'

'Later, Otto. We're still getting to know her.'

'Yes, of course,' he says, a little chastened.

A sweet tooth, Haf thinks.

'So, what do you do for work, Haf?' asks Otto.

'I work in communications for a small charity. So, my job covers anything to do with words, and the social media too.'

'I don't really understand all that social media stuff,' says Otto somewhat dismissively. 'The holiday property side of the business has run on a paper version since we started – luxury catalogues, that sort of thing. But it's all about direct communication, face to face and all that. People like the personal touch, especially with the retirement homes – that's another branch. Everyone wants to know they're getting the best experience money can buy. Really give people the experience they want, that sort of thing. Social media feels far too impersonal for that to me.'

What Haf wants to point out is that 'social media' encapsulates multiple platforms, many of which have existed for well over a decade and are integral to many people's daily communications as well as businesses marketing strategies. And as for impersonal? It's pretty much how she's made and maintained all her friendships for way too long. But instead all she does is laugh awkwardly.

'For us, it's kind of like a live magazine, so people can read what we're up to.'

'And all Haf's work is about getting people to connect with nature, and it helps them with fundraising for conservation projects, like the Seeds for Bees fundraiser you did,' adds Christopher, and Haf's heart swells, because he's been reading.

'Oh, don't mind him, Haf. He's an absolute Luddite despite somehow running a successful business,' Esther says.

'Oh, I employ young people to do all that part for me. Maybe you can educate this old man, Haf?' Otto laughs. 'Is that your long-term career plan then?'

'Oh, well . . . no. I'm not sure, really. I did ecology at uni, so that's how I got into it, but it's the people and wildlife bit I like.'

'Must be hard to enjoy that part if you're behind a desk all the time,' Otto adds.

In flashes, Haf sees her sad little desk covered in papers, squeezed into a windowless corner in her sad little office surrounded by pictures of sad badgers and celebrities posing with dead fish.

Her throat tightens. She doesn't want to go back there.

Christopher pats her on the arm.

'It's not what I want forever, no,' she says, and then laughs awkwardly.

'Oh,' say both of Christopher's parents.

An awkward pause hangs in the air.

'If I can offer a little sage advice,' snuffs Otto. 'It's sensible to not give up on a good job just because the grass could be greener on the other side.'

Haf doesn't want to go into the specifics of how her job is draining the life out of her, so nods eagerly.

'Sure, but if it's making you miserable?' adds Christopher.

'It's a job, Christopher. It's not about happiness. It's about what puts food on the table, and if the money is good, then you stick it out. That's part of being an adult.'

Christopher winces. 'Money isn't everything, Dad,' he says firmly.

'Of course it is. Money is security, means you can buy the things you need, support your family,' he says, gesturing around at their home with his whisky glass. Even though Otto says this with a laugh, there's a seriousness underneath it all. This doesn't sound like a conversation that's been had just this once, either. 'I think it matters quite a lot.'

Determined to defuse whatever is happening, Haf pipes up. 'That's true, Otto, but I work for a charity, so the money is very bad,' she laughs.

This doesn't solicit the laughter she was hoping for, and instead Esther produces another 'Oh'.

Perhaps not the best thing to tell her rich fake boyfriend's parents, even as a distraction.

There's an awkward silence while everyone sips at their drinks, apart from Haf, who has not yet mustered the courage to pick up her mulled wine again, lest it bring on a coughing fit from sheer proximity.

*I'll take an awkward silence over arguing*, she thinks.

To her relief, the front door slams, rattling the windows in their frames and distracting everyone from their sulk.

'Oh, that'll be Kit back with the dogs,' says Otto.

Two scruffy terriers race into the living room, and head straight to Christopher, yapping and whining for attention. Their tails wag so hard with happiness that their little bodies turn comma shaped. Christopher clambers onto the floor to say hello, and they bounce around him, far too excited to be cuddled but still desperate to be touched.

Haf can kind of relate. Perhaps she's a terrier after all.

'All right, girls, calm down. I'm back,' he says, laughing as one of them jumps up and licks his glasses off his head. 'Come say hello, Haf.'

She joins him on the floor, cross-legged, and the dogs, who have almost entirely calmed down, realise someone new is here. They look at her with curiosity, tilting their heads as she says hello.

The slightly smaller one trots over and sniffs Haf's outstretched hand for a few moments, before licking it with a tiny pink tongue.

'That's Luna,' Christopher says. 'And this is Stella.'

'How can I tell them apart?' she asks, glancing between the two identical dogs.

'Luna has the greyer beard. Stella is podgier. They have the same parents, but they're from different litters. Luna is the older one.'

Stella joins Luna in sniffing Haf all over, until they successfully discover the bag of treats in her pocket, and begin gently pawing for her to give them over. She shifts to take two out of the bag, one in each hand, and presents them to the dogs who snaffle them up eagerly.

'Friends?' she asks, and the girls respond with a quick wag and big round eyes, hoping for more.

'They'll love you forever now.' Otto laughs, and clearly all is forgiven.

'All right, one more,' she says, getting the dogs to sit and give paw.

'Sorry I was so long. Is Christopher back?' shouts a voice from another room.

'We're all in here,' calls Esther.

'It's completely fucking Baltic out there.'

'Kit, don't say "fuck", it's vulgar,' admonishes Esther.

'In fairness, you just said it too,' she says, her voice getting closer.

'Stop being obstinate and come say hello to Christopher's girl-friend.'

As Kit walks into the room, unwinding the thick scarf around her neck, she locks eyes with Haf.

And a stone drops in Haf's stomach.

She would recognise that smile and that bitter-chocolate hair anywhere. In fact, she spent half of today looking everywhere for her.

Haf just didn't expect to find her here in Christopher's living room.

Kit is the girl from the bookshop.

# Chapter Seven

How can she be *his sister*?

What monumental coincidence and absolute fuckery has the universe thrown Haf's way? This is officially a completely cursed year.

It's definitely her. The dark eyes Haf's spent all day thinking of stare at her in confusion.

This is one thing too many. She wants to faint, be sick and run away, all at once. Or maybe not all at once, but at least one of the above seems like a better option than standing in this room looking at the first person she's felt anything for in like a year while standing next to the man she's supposed to be in love with and the parents she's trying to prove this love to.

'Hello?' Kit says, one dark eyebrow arched in a sleek curve. She looks from Haf to Christopher and back, another question unsaid.

'Kit, come say hello to Haf. She's Christopher's new girlfriend, remember?' says Esther, unfolding an arm in Haf's direction. 'I'm sure Laurel must have told you about meeting her.'

Haf's stomach flips as the bookshop girl, as *Kit*, meets her eyes. Again.

Her mouth is slightly ajar, a confused smirk in the corner of one lip.

Does she recognise her? Did that moment mean anything to her, like it did to Haf? Maybe Kit has people falling all over her in bookshops all the time. She's so beautiful that perhaps it happens all the time, and maybe it was simply another part of her day. Perhaps it didn't even register as a *moment* to her.

But there's a hesitation. A too-long pause after Esther's introduction that Haf doesn't think is just her own sense of time stretching out into slow motion due to a feeling of impending doom.

No smile grows, but she does walk towards Haf, dropping her scarf on the couch as she passes.

'Oh . . . Yes, I remember,' she says, her voice low, slightly barbed. Only a few hours ago, that rasp made Haf swoon. Now she's just terrified of what Kit's going to say next.

Fucking hell. *Please don't tell them I drooled all over you in the bookshop.*

But Kit just holds her hand out to shake.

A lifetime passes before Haf realises she needs to reach out and shake it, and gets to her feet, trying not to fall over as her legs threaten to turn to overcooked noodles.

As she takes Kit's hand, sparks soar through her body from her fingertips all the way up to her brain. All day she had been dreaming about what it would be like to touch her, and now that's come true, in front of Kit's whole family, under the shadow of a huge lie about who she is.

Their eyes lock on each other, and Haf bites down on her lip.

'It's so funny, but . . . You just look familiar to me, that's all. You must get that all the time, right? Just one of those faces,' says Kit, and there can be absolutely no doubt about it.

Kit *does* recognise her.

Her mouth completely dries up, but she pushes through, not wanting to make this moment even weirder than it already is. With a too-high silly voice, Haf manages to say, 'Yeah, maybe!'

Truthfully, the only person she's ever really compared to is Annie from *Shrill*, which she suspects is more about her body type than her actual face. All she can do is follow Kit's lead and pretend they've never met. But boy, does it feel awkward.

'It's nice to meet you,' Haf says in her sunniest voice.

Raising her eyebrow into a sharp arch, Kit drops her hand. Were they touching this whole time?

The dogs, clearly aware of the sexual tension above them, start whining very loudly. They probably think she's having some kind of medical emergency from all the physiological signs of being completely mortified and horny all at once. And Haf is out of treats to distract them.

Hopefully, the Calloways are not secretly experts in animal behaviour or the queer experience of realising everyone knows everyone, including your exes and people you wanted to kiss in bookshops.

Luckily, the rest of the humans appear completely oblivious.

'What's wrong with you girls today?' Christopher coos, slapping his thighs to call them over. The dogs turn their wiry little faces towards him for just a second, but quickly return to jittering around Haf's feet. 'Perhaps they just want some more snacks from you.'

As if in response to his obliviousness, Luna harrumphs and Stella sneezes.

'They must just be really excited about a new person being here,' offers Kit airily. 'You know, a completely new person they've never met before ever.'

If the floor could open up right now, that would be really great. Perhaps she could just immolate herself in the fireplace, or maybe she can walk out into the cold and never return, freezing to death like an old-time explorer.

Kit is not going to make this easy on her, that much is clear.

'It's good to see you, sis,' says Christopher, rising to greet her. It appears that Christopher has not noticed the sapphic drama in the living room, which is probably for the best. How the hell is she going to explain this to him?

The siblings have a moderately awkward hug that looks more like someone stacking two planks of wood closer together than a loving embrace. They exchange a little small talk about the train from London, which Haf completely misses because she's still considering all the ways she could extricate herself from this situation.

They look so different from each other. Where Christopher has the complexion of an English rose, Kit is dark like Otto – rich dark brown, almost-black hair and warm earth tones in their skin. She must have got the height from him too, as she's almost as tall as Christopher.

Maybe that's what inherited wealth gets you: height.

It's like she's in that horrible giant world from *The BFG* but instead of being terrifying, the giants are hot and wealthy. Right now, she feels more snozzcumber than Sophie . . .

She only snaps out of her mild panic spiral when Kit announces she's going for a lie-down before dinner and disappears upstairs.

*Thank God.*

If anything was going to put a wrinkle in their plans, it's this. It's having flirted very intensely with your fake boyfriend's sister over sapphic literature. Kit is a major fucking wrinkle.

The grandfather clock chimes the hour, the sound cutting through the room. *Saved by the bell*, thinks Haf.

'Time for dinner, perhaps?' asks Otto hopefully, his eyes almost identical to Stella and Luna's giant chocolate-drop eyes.

'It's a good job I've been cooking something up, isn't it?' Esther sighs in that teasing way that long-married-but-happy couples do.

'You're good to me.'

'Well, someone has to keep you fed. If I left it to you, we'd be having burnt soup.' She gives him a playful wink and glides from the room.

Christopher follows her, and in need of something to do, Haf kneels to play with the dogs again.

'Which room should I put Haf in?' she hears Christopher ask.

'Well, yours, dear. We're not running a convent.'

Why are they both so clueless? Why did they not think of this? Obviously they're going to have to share a bed.

Sharing a bed with the man you're fake dating in the same house as his sister that you would absolutely love to share a bed with, and accidentally sharing a couch after a drunken party feel like two very, very different things right now.

They've only been here an hour or so, and already things seem way less simple than they did when she agreed to it.

*Oh God, Ambrose was right. I am a massive plum.*

Christopher awkwardly returns to the living room and says, 'I'll show you to your room,' in the tone of a butler rather than her boyfriend, fake or not.

She follows him out, too nervous to even make a joke about his current resemblance to Lurch.

The copy of *Carol* is still on the sideboard where she left it when she got the Betty's box out. She can't just leave it there in the open, not now. It's gone from being a memory of a missed connection to a glaring symbol of lies and presumed infidelity and God knows what else Kit is thinking. Haf clutches it to her chest.

Christopher leads her up two flights of creaky stairs, carrying her backpack for her. 'We're on the top floor, I'm afraid,' he says.

Christopher's childhood bedroom looks over the back of the house, and through the window, all Haf can see are miles and miles of fields. The isolation seems even more oppressive.

Exhausted, Haf drops face down on to the bed.

Christopher closes the door with a soft click. 'Christ, sorry about this. I did not think she'd let us share a room. Laurel was in the spare room for years.'

'Yeah, but that was when you were teenagers, right?' she says, turning her face so he can hear her.

'And after that.'

'Huh. Maybe she just likes me better.'

'God, why is this so complicated?'

Haf bites back a rueful laugh because, boy, he has no idea. And how can she tell him? He looks like he's going to faint over the concept of them sharing a bed. How is he going to cope with knowing that only a few hours ago she was thinking about snogging his sister?

'We're both grown-ups. We can share a bed. This is fine,' she says, with more confidence than she feels. One thing has to be cleared up, or she's going to go completely potty. 'It'll be like, I dunno, camping.'

'Camping?' he asks incredulously. 'Have you ever *been* camping?'

'Yes, obviously,' she huffs. 'I grew up in Wales. What else are you supposed to do?'

'Most people don't share the bed when they camp.' He laughs, then blushes scarlet just as Haf realises that her experience of sharing a sleeping bag with Zahra from the year above, which was incidentally a strictly non-platonic activity, might not actually be a universal one.

'Forget about the camping. Point is, I'm all right with it. Are you?'

'Yes,' he says. 'Phew, well, okay. That's one thing sorted. Maybe we should have . . . agreed some ground rules about this fake dating.'

'Well, we would have if we'd had a chance to chat on the train.'

'Sorry about the quiet coach. I should have thought about that.'

'Never be sorry about the quiet coach,' she says seriously. 'What do you want to talk about?'

She rolls over and pats the bed next to her for him to lie down too, but he hesitates, his cheeks still flushed. 'Perhaps we should discuss, umm, elements such as physical touch and things like that.'

'I love that you talk like a thesaurus on the fritz when you're flustered. PDA, you mean?'

There's a brief pause where Christopher works out the acronym. 'Yes.'

She holds up a finger. 'First of all, we should probably agree on the occasional closed-mouth kiss, or people might not believe us.'

'No one's going to make us kiss, Haf. My family isn't that strange.'

'Err, hello? Did you forget how we got into this mess? Mistletoe? It's quite literally the season for public kissing.'

'Isn't that Valentine's Day?'

'Show me the plant that custom dictates you have to snog next to for Valentine's Day.'

'Okay, good point. All right, if we must.'

'If you *must*? Come on, you don't have to insult a girl. I'm not a toad! Plus, you've kissed me before.'

'You're not a toad,' he says hurriedly. He gives up and lies down next to her, though must practically be on the edge of the bed from the gap he leaves between them. 'I just . . . I don't really think of you that way, not really. And when we kissed, we were just a bit drunk and silly. I thought we were both on the same page.'

'We are, don't worry. And sure, I'm not gagging to snog you either, but we can do it. It's not going to change anything.'

'Okay,' he agrees quietly. 'Okay.'

'While we're on the topic' – here Christopher groans, desperate to be free of this conversation – 'hand holding and all that is fine, touching, I mean. I'll even allow a cheeky bum pat.'

'A what?' he asks, rolling to face her.

'You know, like if you're passing by me and want to just pat my bum. Like I'm a good horse.'

'I am absolutely not going to do that.'

'Shame,' pouts Haf. 'Even Ambrose does that to me.'

'I'm not comfortable . . . touching your bottom.'

'Your loss! It's a magnificent bottom.'

'Please, I beg you, stop talking about your bottom.'

'I can't guarantee a total moratorium, but I'll stop for now. By the way, I've just sort of launched myself on here, but do you have a side preference for sleeping?'

'I prefer the right.'

'Is that like, from when you look at the bed at the bottom, or when you're in it, like now? I never know which it's supposed to be.'

Christopher just points to the side he's already lying on.

'Works for me.'

Haf shuffles on her front like a worm and plonks down her phone and her now somewhat warped copy of *Carol* on the bed-side table. 'I'm going to get changed, I think. I feel all musty in these clothes.'

'Travelling always does that,' agrees Christopher. He takes his suitcase from the floor and sets it on top of his dresser, picking out a shirt. It's only when he's half-done unbuttoning the one he's wearing that he stops. 'Erm, should I—?'

'No, no, go ahead. I can admire the view.' He flushes again, and Haf adds, 'I mean out the window!'

'God, sorry. I need to relax.'

'You're doing fine. And anyway, I think it was more the almost dying and embarrassing myself in front of your parents that caused me to basically sweat through this layer of clothing.'

'Oh, you were fine.'

Haf snorts. 'You're being kind.'

Christopher gives her a small smile. 'I'm all done,' he says, and she turns to see him in a navy shirt, sleeves rolled up at his elbows. 'There's a little bathroom just down the hall. I'll let you freshen up and meet you downstairs?'

Truthfully, she does feel much better after a quick wash, spritz of perfume and a little spray of dry shampoo, so her hair doesn't look quite so flat. She passes what must be Kit's room as she goes between the bathroom and Christopher's bedroom and tries to keep walking completely normally. Yes, she could stop and knock on the door, and they could hash it out right now, but then she'd have to admit what's going on, or at the very least have a very awkward conversation. She's not ready for that yet.

Back in the bedroom, she decides to unpack her squashed clothes and hang them up so they have time to get unwrinkled (at least one thing needs to).

Buried deep in the bag, her hand brushes across something wrapped in paper. She pulls it out and sees on a little card is written, *A peace offering. Have a good time. Love you, you wally.*

Ambrose. They really do care.

Her eyes mist with tears as she peels back the paper. Inside is a Christmas jumper, bright cheery Santa red with jumping reindeers and Christmas decorations all over it. The wool is soft, not like the scratchy polyester novelty jumpers you find on Amazon. It's *nice*.

She'll call Ambrose after dinner, and make up with them properly. A little festive grovelling will go nicely with the jumper. Plus, it's like Ambrose's here with her now. Who needs a devil or angel on your shoulder when you have a sweater to conjure your most judgemental best friend?

*Okay, I can do this*, she thinks.

Haf slowly opens the bedroom door, worried she is going to bump into Kit up here, but thankfully her bedroom door is ajar. She makes it to the stairs and grips the stair rail. Peering downstairs, she kind of regrets agreeing with Christopher that she'll meet him down there. The first time she stayed with Freddie, he hadn't woken her up, and so she'd gone downstairs in pyjamas only to discover everyone fully dressed and sitting at the table reading papers. His parents didn't seem super impressed that she was still in her pyjamas, even if it was barely eight, having trampled all over a house rule she didn't even know existed. She feigned needing a glass of water before a shower and practically sprinted back upstairs. He had said it wasn't a big deal, but it was. Or at least, it felt like it. The worst thing about other people's families is that they think everything in their house is 'normal' and no one hands you the guidebook on the way in. You just have to guess.

So that's on her mind. And the pretending to be Christopher's girlfriend, convincingly. And Kit. And her raging crush on Kit. Just a few things.

Happy voices float up from downstairs as the Calloways laugh. It can't be that bad. Just a few steps. She's dressed this time, after all, and in a nice new jumper too. She takes a deep breath and walks down the stairs before she can worry about it any more.

In the hallway, Christopher passes, carrying serving platters from the kitchen.

'You look nice,' he says, gliding into what she presumes is the dining room with the practice of a waiter.

Esther and Otto are still in the kitchen, so she decides to play the good fake girlfriend and see if they need any help.

On the kitchen island are a few platters and jars of things to decant into ramekins. Whatever has been cooking in here smells divine.

It's so warm down here from all the cooking and the still-roaring fireplace in the living room that she slips off her sweater and wraps it round her waist. At least this way she won't get anything spilled on it.

'Can you take the last of the vegetables through, and Otto will follow with the meat, and then we're all ready to eat?' says Esther, her voice monotone as she reels off the instructions, making sure nothing has been missed.

From the counter, Haf takes the platter, concentrating very hard as she picks it up and walks with it in the direction of the dining room.

As she passes, Esther apparently remembers the gravy, springing to life and decanting a pan on the hob into a floral gravy boat.

In the dining room, Christopher directs Haf to put the platter down at one end of the table in its correct space.

Esther and Otto arrive just after her and, satisfied, Esther claps and tells everyone to sit down, opening a window to let in some fresh air before she takes her seat.

The Calloways must have reverted to the usual seating plan from when the kids were growing up. Otto and Esther naturally take the two ends and she wonders if they sit this far away from each other when it's just the two of them, a gulf of a table between them.

An extra seat has been put next to Christopher, which she presumes is for her.

She's not materialised yet, but Kit must be about to sit opposite, where she'll have the view of the gathering dark in the garden – perhaps being older meant she got to bag the best seat.

As Haf takes her seat, her hip bumps against the table, and the gravy boat, which Esther has just set down, ominously slops.

'Oh God, sorry,' she gasps, looking around for paper towels, but there's only beautiful cloth napkins, which she doesn't want to cover in gravy any more than the tablecloth.

'Don't worry, dear. I put a little dish under the boat, just in case of accidents like this.' Haf knows she must mean in general, but also it feels like a concession made specifically for her lack of spatial awareness, which . . . she doesn't know how to feel about, really. Luckily, the gravy slop didn't spill over the dish, so she has to be thankful for that at least.

Carrying a freshly opened bottle of red wine, Kit walks around the table, slowly filling everyone's crystal glasses. As she leans over to fill Otto's glass, Haf's eye is drawn to her cropped brown checked trousers. Even in winter, the gays love a bare ankle. It makes her giggle, but when Christopher tilts his head at her as if to ask what she's laughing at, she turns it into a cough. He's not told her much at all about Kit – how on earth could she explain that she's amusing herself thinking about queer coding without revealing exactly how she knows that?

'Do you want some?' Kit asks Haf, standing so close to her that Haf can smell the peppercorn spice of her perfume. 'It's a Pinot Noir, not too heavy.'

Unable to form a coherent reply, Haf simply nods.

God, she needs to stop acting like an absolute dork in front of the Calloways. At least in the bookshop, only the bookseller bore witness to her embarrassing behaviour.

Kit takes her seat and Haf realises she's going to have to stop studiously staring at her throughout this meal. What is the middle ground? Looking? She feels like she's forgotten how to just *look* at a person normally, which she's already bad at because, really, who even likes eye contact, anyway? Never mind looking without thinking about touching or kissing.

*Get your head in the game*, she tells herself, taking a hurried sip from the glass of water in front of her. She needs to do something that's not looking at Kit or thinking about looking at Kit, and oh God, she can hear herself and she sounds like she's lost it.

Act straight, that's what Ambrose would tell her to do. *Act like you've never fancied a girl in your life. Definitely not the one sitting opposite. Nope. Nope, nope.*

'Shall we raise a glass?' asks Otto, lifting his glass into the air.

They all cheers, but it's a polite, restrained one. Not the kind of cheers where everyone insists you must look deeply into everyone's eyes as your glasses clink together or it's bad luck, thankfully. Never mind Kit, that feels like too much sudden emotional intimacy with Christopher's parents.

As Otto gets up to carve the meat, Haf takes stock of the food in front of her. Esther has prepared a haunch of roast beef with a mustard crust, along with a pile of crispy roast potatoes, bright orange carrots and jewelled red cabbage. It's the kind of feast that they would sometimes have for Christmas Day dinner at home. There are Yorkshire puddings at the end of the table but it's not the single tray-bake monstrosity her mother would make for Christmas, but the perfectly shaped and surprisingly delicious individual ones that look like they've come from M&S.

Haf hasn't had a roast dinner in ages. They take so long, and she's not really got the attention span for cooking, not something that requires timings upon timings that all stack together so that everything is magically finished at once.

'This looks amazing, Esther, thank you,' Haf says, taking a plate with thin, rare slices of roast beef from Otto.

'It's Welsh,' she says with a smile, presumably meaning the beef.

Soon plates of sides are passed around, horseradish and red-currant sauces dolloped on plates, and gravy swirled on top. The food is genuinely delicious – she wasn't just sucking up to Esther. Perhaps that's how they can bond? It's probably not the best thing to hear, that her new potential daughter-in-law's cooking skills sound like they rival Otto's propensity to burn liquids, but maybe she can teach her? She files this away for later.

Christopher and Kit quickly revert to their small talk. It's kind of weird – they don't leap to sharing embarrassing stories or talk about mutual friends. It's all very polite. Given recent book-shop-based activities, maybe that's for the best.

'I didn't realise you were coming down early?' says Christopher to Kit. 'We could have caught the same train or something.'

'Me neither,' she says, slicing a roast potato in half. 'But we met our delivery deadline early, and I realised there was an opportunity for me to sneak off before someone tries to rope me into something else. I was going to do a few more bits in town, but Laurel rang me so I decided to hop on the next train home.'

Didn't Christopher say Kit and Laurel were best friends? Haf feels a tiny pang of guilt as she realises she's only started really paying attention to the tiny titbits she'd heard about his sister since she realised who she was. Before then she was content to just hopefully find a comfortable middle ground together.

Either way, she should probably still join in; it'll ingratiate her with the parents at least.

'What do you do?' Haf asks with an airy smile.

'She's a high-flying architect,' answers Otto proudly, but Kit cringes at the interruption.

'I don't know about high or flying, but yes. I'm an architect. I work at a small firm in London,' Kit answers in clipped tones.

'Woah,' says Haf, not really meaning to sound quite so wide-eyed, but she genuinely hasn't met an architect before. Her only frame of reference is moustachioed Tom Selleck in *Three Men and a Baby*, who she realises Otto bears a striking resemblance to.

Kit gives her a raised eyebrow as she takes a sip of wine.

'I mean, that's really cool. You must be really smart and have gone to school for a long time?'

'Yeah, I did it in about nine years—'

'Takes most people ten,' adds Esther smugly.

'You know, it's funny, Haf,' Kit begins, and for a brief moment, Haf is both thrilled to hear her name in Kit's mouth and terrified about what is going to follow. But instead, Kit looks pointedly at her parents in turn. 'I didn't know I was so good at throwing my voice. I mean, I knew I was good at it, but wow, I am practically a prodigy.'

Relieved, Haf laughs. 'Different voices, too,' she adds, and Kit gives her the smallest flash of a grin. Maybe Kit's had a change of heart and decided to go easy on her?

'Sorry, darling, we're just very proud of you,' concedes Esther.

Emboldened, Haf decides to ask her some more. 'So, as an architect, does that mean you essentially make a lot of buildings?'

'Something like that,' she says shortly. 'What about you?'

'Haf runs the communications for a wildlife charity,' Esther offers with a smile. This simultaneously makes Haf glow a little with pride that her fake mother-in-law paid attention to her, but also a quiet worry builds in a corner of her mind – what if Esther works them out?

'Hey, I didn't know you were a ventriloquist too,' says Kit, eyeing her mother. 'Socials and stuff?'

'Yeah, and a bit of scientific translation if I'm lucky. You know, like making dry science papers into normal, readable words.'

'Hmm, tough. You must be on all the time,' she says.

'Basically. Just in case something happens in the news or someone responds to a post at like eleven at night.'

Christopher gives her a gentle pat on the wrist, like a good boyfriend would do, and Haf sees Kit's eyes dart to his hand before jumping back to her own plate.

'Are you still at Miller and Miller?' Kit asks Christopher.

Haf realises this must be the name of the company he works at. Another thing she probably should have learned before now.

'Yes,' he says.

'Going okay?'

Christopher doesn't say anything, just tilts his head a little as though to say it's so-so.

'I can't believe you stayed,' says Kit.

Everyone is so hung up on Christopher and his job, Haf thinks. Though, perhaps that makes sense. Otto and Esther seem so enamoured with Kit's job. Do they feel that way about Christopher's? Was that what the tension was about?

Sensing this is a moment where she, as a good fake girlfriend, should gently stand up for him, Haf goes to speak but Kit barrels on past her.

'I thought Mark being promoted over you would have been the last straw,' Kit says flatly.

Christopher stiffens.

Mark? As in Mark the extremely cuboid rugby-man Mark? As in the one who stole his girlfriend . . .

'I didn't know you worked with him,' and the words are out of her mouth before she realises.

Everyone's eyes are on her, because, of course, she should know this. She looks to Christopher, hoping he might come up with something to save her.

'Yes, he's my sort of my line manager now, remember, darling?' he says, pointedly.

Perhaps not, she thinks. Well, best alternative option is to lean into the ditziness that they probably think is her entire personality by now.

'Oh, *Mark* Mark,' she says, trying to emphasise. 'I was thinking of, you know, the other Mark.'

'The other Mark? Do we know this other Mark?' asks Esther to Christopher.

'Oh, no, he's my' – she glances around wildly, and Kit's enormous scarf pops into her head – 'my knitting teacher. In York.'

'Does he work in finance too?'

'I don't know, ha ha ha,' Haf says, looking into her glass. 'I don't know why I said that, of course you wouldn't know him. Silly me! Must be the wine.'

'Mmm, well, perhaps that's enough for you then, dear,' says Esther.

Under the table, Haf gives Christopher's foot a little kick. She's so completely unprepared for all of this.

'God, I can't imagine having to work with that arsehole,' snarls Kit.

'Don't say "arsehole", Kit.' Esther sniffs.

'He is, though. All the Ratliff-Zouches are, you've met them.'

Otto nods silently in agreement.

'Don't you have to be nicer to him now Laurel is dating him?' asks Christopher.

'Not if I can help it,' she says, spearing an extra roast potato from the platter with her fork. 'She's a law unto herself.'

There's a moment where they catch each other's eyes across the table, and the gap between them seems to widen.

Kit lowers her voice and adds, 'I didn't tell her to break up with you for him, just so we're clear.'

'I didn't think you did,' mutters Christopher in a way that sounds not at all convincing.

'Let's not talk about all that business at the table,' warns Esther.

The chill from the fresh air – and let's face it, the icy conversation – brings up goosebumps on Haf's skin, so she decides it's time to don her nice jumper. After all, her plate is clean(ish) and she's drunk most of her wine, which Esther has clearly cut her off from, so all the major stain options are out of reach.

She wiggles awkwardly into it, which seems to distract the Calloways, as once her head pops through the neck hole, everyone has gone back to eating.

Except Kit.

Kit is staring at her, eyes wide and a smirk playing on her lips.

'What?' Haf mouths.

Widening her eyes, Kit nods towards Haf's chest.

There's nothing spilled on her. How could there be? She only just put it on. She does a tiny shrug at Kit, completely confused by what she's getting at.

'Your jumper,' Kit mouths.

Just to be safe, she checks her elbows to make sure she didn't lean on anything as she put it on, but there's nothing there either.

'What are you doing?' whispers Christopher to her.

Confused, she looks back to Kit, who is barely holding it together, lips clenched tight to hold in a laugh.

'What?' whispers Haf.

Esther, who doesn't even look up from slicing into her last bit of beef, simply says. 'Dear, I think she's trying to tell you that the reindeer on your jumper appear to be engaged in coitus.'

'In what?' asks Haf, pulling out the material to look at it.

'They're fucking!' cries Kit, who dissolves into such heavy laughter that she can barely get the 'ing' out before collapsing back into her chair.

'Kit, don't be vulgar.'

'Oh, wow, yes, Haf. They do appear to be . . . active,' says Christopher awkwardly.

He's not kidding. The reindeer are patterned across in stripes, and what she thought were frolics are considerably friendlier.

'Oh God,' she whispers.

*Swallow me whole, Earth! Just do it right now. A tiny sinkhole would be good, not for everyone, just me. Just right under this chair. Me and this fucking jumper.*

'I am so embarrassed. I'm so sorry,' she says. 'It was a gift from my housemate. I didn't realise.'

'A strange kind of gift,' says Esther.

'Yes, well, they're a strange kind of friend,' Haf says despairingly. 'I'll just take it off again.'

But as she slips her head down and pulls one arm out, she feels her fist connect with something distinctly fleshy, followed by a clatter.

'Oh God, the gravy!' cries Esther, and around her is a hive of activity as everyone, presumably, tries to mop up the gravy she just sent flying.

Jumper still stuck over her head, she mutters, 'I just punched you in the face, didn't I?'

'You did,' Christopher says, gently lifting the jumper off her face. 'You've got a good right hook.'

'I'm sorry,' she whispers, as she sees the red welt rise on his cheek.

The gravy is sopped up with the cloth serviettes, and order is relatively restored, apart from Kit, who is still uncontrollably giggling.

'Chaos really does follow in your wake, doesn't it?' laughs Otto.

'It seems like we're set for an exciting Christmas,' says Esther archly.

# Chapter Eight

The rest of the meal is thankfully uneventful, if a little chilly from taking her jumper back off again. It may be an inappropriate item to wear at a family dinner, but, boy, is it warm and cosy.

Once everyone has decided they've had enough, Haf hops up and begins clearing the table.

'I'll do the washing up,' she offers. She truly hates washing up, and realistically is completely rubbish at it, but right now she'll do anything to be on her own for a few moments.

Christopher gets up and helps her clear the plates, and as she's setting them down near the sink, everyone else comes in carrying more of the dirty dishes.

'You'll only need to do the glasses,' says Esther. 'Everything else will go in the dishwasher, but don't even bother trying to do that. Otto will just redo it, anyway.'

Fuck. She was hoping for a longer and considerably less delicate job than just washing the five glasses, but it's better than nothing.

'I'll come do that in a moment,' says Otto. 'Son, can you come help me with something on the computer? I am worried I've got one of those viruses.'

Christopher flashes her an apologetic look, before following his father out of the room.

In the dining room, there's just a few bits left. Now that the glasses are her job, she carefully takes them from each of the place settings, crossing them at the stem in one hand like she learned at the restaurant she worked at for like two weeks when she was a teenager.

'Be careful with them. They were my mother's,' says Esther as she passes her in the corridor.

Double fuck.

Luckily, Esther disappears, leaving Haf alone in the kitchen with the heirloom glasses and dirty dishes. It all feels a bit unintentional Cinderella.

Behind her, Kit puts the salt and pepper back in their places and swivels lids back on the sauce jars.

She can feel her when she's near, which is a weird thing to say, but it's true. Haf's not sure she's ever been so aware of someone else's body.

Haf runs the hot tap into a plugged sink, and makes far too many suds on the sponge, threatening to make everything slippery.

Kit appears at her side, a tea towel in one hand. 'I'll dry.'

So much for being alone. So much for avoiding being alone with Kit.

They don't speak as she washes the first glass, but Haf can feel the heat of her radiating across the gap.

'So,' Haf says eventually, focusing on removing Esther's lipstick from the rim. The glass looks expensive as well as potentially being some kind of heirloom, and she tries to concentrate desperately on not smashing it in the sink, but Kit is so close that her hands are shaking and her whole body feels like jelly. Electrified jelly.

'So.'

'Hi again.'

'Hello.'

She takes a deep breath. Maybe now's the time? Rip the plaster off, acknowledge the elephant in the room, point at the enormous raging horn she had for this woman only hours before.

Well, perhaps not the last bit.

Try to be normal.

'Thanks for the book recommendation,' she manages to croak out.

Somehow, the world doesn't end right at that moment, though it would have been nice if it did. Nothing really happens at all. If she was talking to Christopher, he'd stutter and flush, but Kit does neither of those things. She barely even reacts.

After a long pause, Kit speaks in a low voice.

'I did think it was perhaps too much of a coincidence for a brand-new copy to be on the hall table. Briefly wondered if Mum had accidentally found herself in a queer book club, or something. And you know, for a minute, I did think, what if this is the same book? It seemed like too much of a coincidence, but today seems to be full of coincidences.'

Her hand is outstretched expectantly, waiting for the first glass. Haf passes it, and their fingertips brush together, sending sparks of static through her.

'Yeah,' breathes Haf, taking another glass. 'It was definitely a surprise. I knew Christopher had, has a sister, obviously. But I didn't make the connection.'

'He hasn't shown you any photos, I suppose?'

Fuck, this seems like a mistake. There's obviously something going on between them, and to make it sound like they've never spoken about her in four months of their fake-dating timeline is not going to help that.

'No, it's more . . . I'm just bad at faces,' explains Haf.

This is actually true – she's never been able to translate a photograph to a real-life face. Another reason why online dating would have been a nightmare. Her dates would have to wear purple hats or red chrysanthemums for her to be able to find them, which might have killed the vibe a little. She even gets it a bit with people she's met – either never recognising them or always mistaking them for someone else. Really, it's a little impressive that she recognised Kit at all, but it also feels like there's just no one like her. Haf memorised her outline the moment they met. Plus, the flutters she gets in her chest whenever Kit is near are a dead giveaway.

Christopher obviously hadn't shown her photos of everyone, apart from the dogs. Perhaps another thing they should have thought about, mild face-blindness or no.

'Oh, that must be annoying.'

'It is.'

'I just thought . . .' Kit trails off for a second. 'We just don't talk a lot, that's all.'

Against the darkness outside, the mirror acts like a window, reflecting their faces back at them. Haf sees Kit lick her lips, concentrating a little too hard on buffing the second glass.

Four glasses to go, thinks Haf, taking the second from the side. Butterflies swirl in her stomach.

This is excruciating.

Kit's hair swishes as she turns slightly, putting the first dry glass straight into the cupboard. She smells like walking through a forest, hot coffee clasped in hand. Like the outside and possibility and comfort.

Get a grip, she tells herself.

'You said you're all done working for the holidays? It'll be nice to have a break, I expect.'

Kit snorts. 'There's always more work to be done, somehow. But yes, apart from checking my emails a few times, I'm off the hook until New Year's Day.'

'I know architects like make buildings and stuff, but is that like your day to day?'

'The emails or the "making buildings"?' she says, adding finger air quotes.

'That's a perfectly normal way to describe it.'

'I think the word you're looking for is "design",' she says, with a little smirk. 'There are lots of meetings and too much chatting up of stakeholders. Occasionally, I actually get to draw something which is nice.'

'And you like the drawing bit more?'

'And I like the drawing bit more.'

'Why are jobs never what you expect them to be?'

'Something-something capitalism?'

Haf hands this one over, and glass three slips a little in her sudsy hands, but she catches it without incident, thank goodness.

*This is going okay*, she thinks. A little bit of joking, a little getting to know each other better. She mentally runs through the list of questions she has in her head at all times for small talk to keep them on safe topics. Facts, not feelings. Anything that stops her from thinking about how close they are, and how much she would like to bridge the remaining distance.

'Do you have a lot of plans for the holidays? Seeing school friends or anything?'

Kit wrinkles her nose. 'I suspect Esther is going to rope me into getting things finished for the Christmas fête tomorrow. There's always a set of tasks she's set aside just for me that she'll surprise me with on the morning of.'

'What's the Christmas fête?'

'Christ,' Kit says, in a perfect imitation of Christopher, 'has my brother told you anything? He's absolutely useless.'

'I think it's a man thing.' Haf hands the clean glass to Kit, and takes another, which still has a ring of red wine in the bottom of it. She realises it must be hers, because there's also a slop of it down the outside.

'Wouldn't know,' scoffs Kit.

'Is it a big thing? The fête, I mean.'

'Oh yeah, quite big. A highlight of the Oxlea social calendar,' she says, affecting a posh voice. 'It's a charity event, usually raising money for supplies for the local primary school.'

'Your old school?'

Kit laughs. 'You'd think, but no. Esther sent us both off to private school all the way through, but this is an opportunity for her to "give back to the community".'

'You sound a little cynical about it all.'

'Only a smidge. Anyway, yes, it's a big deal with the mayor and all the school governors, and the local politicians usually show up, stuff like that. Esther organises it and, to be fair to her, it's always pretty good. I'll be at Laurel's quite a bit; I don't get to see her as much as I'd like when I'm working.'

'Have you guys been friends a long time?'

'Oh yeah, since we were tiny. I think Esther was quite keen on bringing the Howard and Calloway families together, if you know what I mean. If I'd been a boy, they probably would have married me off to her. Or if Laurel wasn't the straightest woman in the world, bless her.'

Kit finishes buffing the third glass and starts work on the fourth.

'There's the Howard family do as well, but that's about everything in terms of formal events. All the grandparents are elsewhere this year. Nonno is staying in Italy with my cousins. Granny and Grandpa, that's Esther's parents, have gone up to Scotland on a fancy holiday.'

'My parents too,' Haf says, 'but they picked Madeira.'

'Probably a better idea. Much warmer, at least. And the wine.'

The fifth glass is unarguably clean. Especially because Haf has been pretending to scrub at a stain that isn't there, like a horny Lady Macbeth wanting to prolong the moment. It feels like a truce, like they've found a comfortable middle ground together.

Maybe everything will be okay if they just stay here at the sink, engaged in polite conversation, washing wine glasses.

Conceding that she can't stretch this out any longer, Haf rinses it under the tap, but only a very thin stream of water comes out.

'What's up with this? Has the water pressure gone wonky?' she mutters, bending to look up at the faucet.

'That's the filtered water tap.'

'The . . . what?'

'You know, like the water jugs you put in the fridge that make tap water taste not like ass. But a tap.'

'That's a thing?'

'It's really not that unusual,' says Kit.

'Maybe for posh architects.'

They both laugh gently, and a quietness settles between them as Haf offers the final glass. Every moment must end.

'Just one thing,' Kit says, taking it from Haf, her red nails clinking softly against the glass.

'Yeah?'

She turns slightly towards Kit, hoping she's going to speak this truce into being, or maybe even give her a nice compliment.

But of course that's not what happens.

'If you're with my brother, perhaps don't flirt with strangers at train stations. It doesn't seem fair to him, even if it doesn't mean much to you to be flirting. He's sensitive, you know?'

Well, that didn't go as she expected. Haf knows her face must be scarlet now. 'Yeah,' she croaks out. 'You're right.'

'And then,' Kit says, setting down the dried glass in the cupboard and closing the door with a clack, 'you won't be leading anyone on either.'

Haf is completely and utterly mortified. 'Yeah. Of course.'

Kit is silent for a few moments, eyeing her up. 'Okay, that's all cleared up. I just had to say it, you know. Sisterly duty. Let's just put it behind us. Friends, yes?'

'Friends,' Haf says, nodding eagerly. 'Friends.'

'Okay. Good.' She nods back, and without another word, Kit leaves.

Rendered speechless, Haf stares at her reflection in the window, now alone. Kit's right, they just should put it behind them. It was just a crush, after all. A flirtation. She's a grown-up. Probably.

Friends.

Just friends.

Haf takes a few moments for herself and tidies up in the kitchen, wiping down the counter with the spray from under the sink. In such a large kitchen, she doesn't half feel like a maid, but at least she's doing this because she offered, and it gives her some time to come down from the intense highs and lows of the day.

Everyone else is in the front room with an after-dinner drink. Haf hangs in the doorway, quietly watching. All four Calloways are deep in their reading, be it the enormous newspaper slung across Otto's lap – the *Financial Times*, she thinks – or the recipe books in Esther's lap, which she flicks through with a long, delicate finger. Kit and Christopher occupy the couch, each reading a paperback book that they are basically folding in half while reading – a slightly horrifying shared habit.

Haf's treacherous copy of *Carol* is still upstairs on the bedside table. It feels like the absolute last thing she wants to read right now. It's not tainted, but it feels like an unexploded bomb.

The TV sits silent in the corner. At home, the TV wouldn't be turned off for basically the whole holiday, a constant background hum.

She should probably tell her parents that she got there safely, so she wiggles her phone out of the pocket of her pencil skirt and sends them a text. It feels wrong to use her phone in a room full of readers, even if none of them have noticed her lurking, so she puts it away as soon as the message sends. Something about the act feels like she's broadcasting inferiority to Esther and Otto, not that it wasn't already probably beaming like a neon sign on the Vegas strip. She needs something to do that makes her look smart, or useful. Ideally, she'd be teaching the dogs tricks, but both are curiously absent.

She approaches the couch from the back and Christopher looks up from his book and gives her a little smile.

Bells tinkle in the distance, and Christopher moves to get up.

'What is that?' whispers Haf, figuring that library rules are in play and everything that must be said must be whispered, if said at all.

'The dogs are ringing to go out for a wee. There's a bell hanging from the door that they hit when they want to go out.'

'Oh! I'll take them out,' she says. 'I'm already up after all. Do I need to put leads on or anything?'

'No, just keep an eye on them if you can,' he says.

*Perfect. If I cannot be academic, I will continue with being useful.*

Stella and Luna sit patiently on the back-door mat next to the garden clogs and some truly muddy wellies. Haf hazards a pair of clogs are almost her size, pulls on her naughty Christmas jumper, which she'd left in the kitchen, and slips out the back door with the dogs in tow. They disappear off into the darkness, though the security light on the back of the house clicks on after a few seconds, illuminating them like deer in headlights. They scamper about, sniffing around the lawn for the absolute right spot to pee.

Haf takes her phone out and video calls Ambrose.

Surprisingly, they answer in seconds.

'Evening,' they say, face covered in a sheet mask, the nose-flap hanging over the end of their nose like a curtain.

'Hi,' says Haf hesitantly. 'I didn't think you were going to answer.'

'I did consider not picking up, but then I remembered that you've been there for, what, six hours? That must mean several Haf-made disasters, and I thought that might be worth tuning in for.'

'Oh, cheers,' she hisses. 'It's not helped by this fucking jumper, by the way.'

'Oh, God, please tell me you didn't wear that in front of anyone.'

'Obviously I did!'

Ambrose drops the camera, so all Haf can see is the magnolia ceiling of their bedroom, but cackles sound from the speakers. 'You knob,' they wheeze. 'It has reindeer shagging on it!'

'I know that now!'

'Didn't you notice?'

'No, because when I unwrapped it, I was crying, as I was *touched by your gesture*, you absolute dickwad.'

'Oh, no,' they say, still laughing as they wipe a tear from their eye. 'I thought you'd, like, wear it in bed or something.'

'His mother pointed it out to me at the dinner table,' Haf moans. 'I was trying so hard to be a good fake daughter-in-law and it was just going wronger and wronger, and then that was an absolute reindeer turd on the top of it all.'

Stella and/or Luna bark in the distance, and something specifically non-dog rushes through the undergrowth near her.

'Okay, I do feel bad. But only like five per cent bad. I still can't believe you went. I could have strong armed Mum into letting you come home, though you'd have probably had to share a room with all my preteen nephews.'

Somehow a room full of Lynx Africa-wearing boys discovering their first pube would be preferable to the situation she finds herself in now, just about.

'Yeah, well, maybe I should have listened to you,' she sighs.

'Wait, what happened? Are you okay?' Everything in Ambrose's demeanour changes. They wipe the sheet mask from their face. 'I'm listening.' The love in this movement makes Haf want to cry. All she wants is to be talking this out together on their little couch in York.

'It's a long story.'

'Go on.'

'On the way here, at the train station . . . I met a really beautiful girl at the bookshop. She recommended me a book, *Carol*?'

'A sapphic classic, slick move.'

'And there was . . . this spark. Something I haven't felt in ages, and she was just so magnetic. I just wanted to talk to her forever. And she was so hot, Ambrose. Like I cannot impress on you how hot she was. But she had to leave, and the bookseller tried to get me to leave my number, and I chickened out.'

'Wise bookseller. Silly you. I saw your tweet about guffing it. Is that what's bothering you?'

'Not just that. Turns out I didn't need to worry about whether I'd see her again.'

'Oh yeah?' they say excitedly.

'Ambrose, she's Christopher's sister.'

There is a strained pause as they take this in. 'She is his sister?'

'Yes.'

'This fantasy girl who you fell in love at first sight with—'

'I wouldn't say love.'

'—is his sister.'

'Yes.'

'Who you are sharing a house with for Christmas?'

'Yes.'

Ambrose presses their lips together into a flat line and closes their eyes.

After a few moments, Haf says, 'Hello? Are you still there? You're not moving.'

'I'm just trying to think of the supportive emotional response you probably need, as opposed to all the things I want to say.'

'You can say those.'

'Oh no, no, no, no. I cannot say those. Mostly because they're not words as much as screeches of shock and laughter and karma's a bitch, et cetera, et cetera. Instead, I am going to opt for, "Wow that sounds super-duper hard for you in this horrible mess from the universe."'

'That doesn't sound like you're being serious.' Haf pouts.

'I am! I'm trying to be emotionally available!'

'Why?'

'A little self-improvement.' They take a breath, choosing their words. 'I am sorry you are now trapped in a house with this girl and dating her brother in an entirely avoidable impossible situation'

'*Fake* dating.'

'Are you going to leave?'

'No, I can't. I said I would help him out, and I want to.'

'Is facing Christmas alone *that bad*?' they ask gently.

'No, honestly, I am regretting not putting on my big-girl pants and doing the M&S order you suggested.'

'I am very wise.' Ambrose turns away briefly to shout something at an intruding preteen who Haf can hear in the distance.

'Everything okay at your end?'

'Yeah, my little cousins just keeping wanting to play *Fortnite*. Always fucking *Fortnite*. Give me *Mario Kart* – something I can beat their arses at. Not this. I might actually be old now, I'm realising. I hate it! Anyway, back to you. You're telling me you are choosing to stay in this absolute fuckery? And what? You're just going to pretend you don't want to smooch the face off his sister?'

Flashes of her lips as she laughed, as she smirked. The warmth of her as they stood at the sink. The way her hair shone in the lights.

'I think I'll be fine. We're leaving the day after Boxing Day, so it's only, what, five days and then we leave,' Haf says, telling herself as much as Ambrose. 'We can just be friends. It's probably just the horn, you know? It's not like I'm in love with her, I just fancy her a bit. I'll be fine.'

'I'm not sure what's the most ridiculous part of this. The fact that you think that you can stop yourself from flirting with her, or the fact you seem to think Christopher's not going to notice. I'm guessing you didn't tell him about this funny little coinkydink. How is he going to feel about it all?'

'He doesn't need to know because there's not going to be anything.'

'What if he picks up on your pining? Your big, gooey eyes? Your whole horny goblin vibes. That face of yours can't hide anything, especially not a crush.'

'God, I hope he doesn't work it out,' she mutters. 'But, like I said, if I keep focusing on us being friends, then the crush bit will die off. It'll be fine!'

Stella and Luna rush past her back inside.

'I should go. I just snuck out with the dogs.'

'Send pics. Of the dogs,' they say. 'And the sister.'

'I will.' She licks her lips. 'Will you . . . are we?'

'We're fine, and I will be your emotional support slash shouty mocking pocket pal, yes.'

'Thank you.'

'You're welcome.'

'I miss you.'

'I miss you too.'

# Chapter Nine

The glorious heat of the Calloway house hits Haf like a lullaby. She's exhausted from the weight of everything, and bed, or rather Christopher's bed, is calling to her.

The dogs trail her back into the living room, before slipping past to curl up in their basket in front of the fire.

'I think I'm going to go up to bed, if that's all right with everyone,' says Haf, poking her head into the room.

'Of course, dear. Are you well? It's still quite early,' says Esther. The big grandfather clock in the corner shows it's only eight thirty, somehow.

'Just tired from the journey!'

'And we've put you through the ringer,' says Otto, peering over his paper with a raised eyebrow.

'No, honestly. You've all been lovely. I'm just wiped out from all the excitement. Perhaps I'm a border terrier too,' she adds, as Stella begins snoring. Luna, in response, farts very loudly.

'Hopefully not,' chuckles Otto. 'We'll be stunk out.'

'I'll be up in a little while,' says Christopher.

Kit says nothing, but that's okay. Probably. It's not like she wants her to.

The upper floors of the house are significantly cooler. This is probably why everyone is curled up in the living room around the fire. She swears there's frost on the exposed wooden beams above her.

*Thank goodness for proper pyjamas*, she thinks, a sensible last-minute purchase after she realised all her current pyjamas had holes, stains or inappropriate slogans on them. She awkwardly clambers into the high bed and sinks down, dragging the soft covers up over her head so she can warm up quicker.

Her phone screen lights the dark, like she's a child reading by torchlight. Except most children, or hopefully any, would not be scrolling Twitter.

Ambrose's poll has gained more votes and replies. Apparently, people have a lot of thoughts about fake dating, and how no one with an ounce of sense would do that in real life.

Otherwise, her feed is full of people sharing festive photos from their family homes, from their childhood-made decorations to the makeshift beds that have been created for them in weird corners of the house.

For a moment, she thinks of sharing her own, but only Ambrose and her parents know where she is, really. Whenever her pocket pals asked her where she was going for Christmas, she just said very vaguely 'to a friend's', which isn't *technically* a lie. She just didn't want them to worry. Everyone's always worrying about her.

Plus, she doesn't want people to connect the poll to her.

It's strange being in Christopher's room without him. It's not a shrine to childhood – no Sonic bedsheets or lurid wallpaper. The walls are crisp white, and whatever bed he had as a child has been replaced with this beautiful sleigh one. Maybe snooping around his room will help with backstory, she tells herself as she sits up in the bed and looks around. An excavation of Christopher Calloway, so to speak. It's not like he's told her very much, anyway.

She wriggles out of the bed and goes over to a bookcase full of battered paperbacks of children's literature staples – *Redwall, The Subtle Knife* but none of the others, *The Hobbit*. A baby nerd, she thinks. On the bottom shelf is an enormous baking recipe book, which seems out of place.

In the drawer of his desk, she finds a few treasures. A pack of cards. A little bundle of birthday cards, tied up with a ribbon, which seems like an Esther touch. A Trebor mints tin is tucked into the corner, and Haf opens it, hoping she'll find a minty treat, but instead finds one very old hopeful condom, clearly acquired in his teenage years by the use-by date. She mentally notes to make fun of him for this later.

Somehow, she doesn't want to open his bedside table, as that feels like too much snooping – she might find in-date condoms, or his credit score, who knows! The one on her side seems fair game though, and in the drawers, there's very little except a couple of well-thumbed recipe books for children.

She pushes the drawer shut with her foot as Christopher wanders in. He smells like sugar and spices.

'Christ, it's cold up here.'

'Like a witch's tit, but don't worry, it's warm in here, dearest,' she says, waggling her eyebrows and hopping back under the covers. He eyes the bed with nervous distrust, like he's just seen a snake in there. Seizing the opportunity to tease him, Haf pats the duvet with a fiendish grin. 'Come on, get in. We can snuggle up.' She adds a little shoulder shimmy to really drive it home.

'This is already very weird. Stop trying to make it weirder.'

'I will not. Torturing you in private is my only relief from pretending to be the best girlfriend you've ever had, which as we've both seen I'm really terrible at—'

'You aren't.'

'I'm not great, but I'm trying.'

'You're definitely trying,' he drawls.

'Hey!' She pouts.

He sits down on top of the duvet and pulls a pair of brand-new cotton pyjamas, still in their wrapping, out from under the pillow. Esther must have put them there, she thinks. It's sweet.

'I didn't realise you were such a fantasy nerd,' she says, pointing at his bookcase.

It's Christopher's turn to pout, though it's not as dramatic and pronounced a look as Haf's, more like pinched lips. 'It's not nerdy to like *imaginative* things, Haf.'

'I bet you play D&D. Do you play D&D?'

'I'm not *that* nerdy.'

'Well, more fool you, it's very fun.'

'You play D&D?' he says, his eyebrows almost falling off his face with surprise.

'Sheilargh the Half-Orc is one of my greatest creations, I'll have you know. Our gang was a group of middle-aged adventurers who really liked to misbehave.'

'You continue to surprise me.'

'I'm very surprising. Are you reading much now?'

'Not really. I don't really have time for that,' he says, a little sadly.

'What were you reading downstairs?'

'*Earthsea.*'

'A classic.'

'Did you not want to join us downstairs and read for a bit? I saw you've got that book over there. What's it about, anyway?'

This is another crossroads moment. She could tell him about knowing Kit. *Hey funny story but I met your sister and wanted to snog her face off and she sexily encouraged me to buy this book, which is like the pinnacle of wlw literature?*

But he looks tired, and today has been enough of a revelation fest, she thinks.

'Oh, I'm not sure. I just liked the cover.'

'Fair enough,' he says, slinging his pyjamas over his shoulder. 'I'll get changed in the bathroom.'

'I can just shut my eyes.'

Christopher moves awkwardly.

'You don't trust me to not peek? I'm wounded!'

'It's not that. I'm just a bit . . . you know, shy about this stuff,' he says, before brushing past this with, 'And you would totally peek.'

'I would. Go on then, off with you.'

'I'm not a sheepdog,' he mutters as he leaves the room.

He's delicate, she thinks. It's sweet. Not many men have ever showed their fears to her. Most men seem obsessed with projecting some kind of horrifying masculinity. Freddie certainly did, so intent that he never have an emotion that they ended up never really talking about anything that mattered.

Christopher must trust her a lot.

And it would probably freak him out to mention Kit and her flirting in the bookshop. He doesn't need to know, it'll just worry him.

Haf puts her phone on airplane mode under her pillow, and snuggles back down under the duvet, pulling it over her head again.

A few minutes later, she hears Christopher come into the room, and he slides under the covers, trying not to disturb them. He brings a wave of fresh cold air, and the bright smell of minty toothpaste.

'Bloody hell,' mutters Haf. 'I'd just gotten it the right temperature under here.'

'It'll warm up in no time,' he says, shivering, his head still above the blanket.

'You can come all the way under, you know. It's much warmer.'

'I don't want to intrude.'

'It's fine – I'm inviting you, aren't I? It's like a sleepover.'

He wriggles down under the cover. 'Oh no, my feet are out.'

'Long-people problems.' Haf laughs as he rolls over and curls up into a little ball.

They're face to face now, and if this was any other situation, any other person, maybe this would be almost romantic.

'This feels very "there was only one bed".'

'Is that a thing?'

'Yeah, a romance trope, but don't worry. This is more like secret hideout planning time.'

'In bed?'

'A bed can be a hideout. A hidden base for planning and making confidential plans.'

He thinks about this for a moment. 'All right. Do I have to tell you some secrets now?'

'If you feel like it. Or you can ask me some. I feel like there's a lot of gaps.'

'All right,' he says, thinking quietly. 'Oh, actually. When did you move to York?'

Of course, he can't know this is a sensitive area, but he needs to know in case anyone asks. Haf bites her bottom lip.

'The start of this year. I was living in Liverpool with my ex, Freddie. I'd graduated and done nothing really with my degree, and, like . . . the world is burning, so I figured I should actually do something. And I found this job, so I applied for it and got it.'

'And he didn't move with you?'

'No, he's very settled there.' She pauses, licking her lips. 'Plus, he, err, pretty much already had a new girlfriend before I'd stepped on the train out, so . . .'

'I'm sorry.'

'It is what it is,' she says, trying to be carefree about it. As though she's processed it and got over it completely like a healthy person, rather than squashing it down and hoping she'd forgotten about it. 'What about you, finance man? Give me a few years. Like uni, where did you go to uni?'

'I went up to Oxford after school.'

'Did you? Well done. That makes sense though, with the whole posh vibes. Were you in any of those fancy clubs at Oxford, like a secret society or something? Do you have dirt on the future prime ministers?'

'No, luckily. Couldn't stand all that pomp and ceremony, to be honest. I was on the rugby team for a bit with Mark, but I kept to myself a lot.'

'I was on the fencing team for a bit.'

Christopher sits up in bed. 'Someone let you hold a *sword*?'

'Unbelievable, isn't it? I was terrible at it though. What happened after Oxford?'

'Graduated, went straight into working in investments. My job is a sort of mix between investment adviser and financial analyst.'

'Ohhh.'

There's a long pause, before Christopher asks, 'Are you okay?'

'Oh!' She snaps back. 'Sorry, I was trying to think about what that actually meant and then I kind of zoned out. Sorry. *Investment-finance* man, got it. You help rich people be richer, right?'

'Pretty much. And that's one of many reasons why I don't enjoy it.'

'And you and Laurel broke up last year after sneaky stinker Mark stole her. And now he's somehow your boss, or something?'

'Pretty much.'

'So we were both useless at university sports, have fairly recently had our hearts broken, and are both in jobs we dislike?'

'Almost like we were destined to meet.'

'Now you sound like a fantasy nerd.'

They lie there quietly in the dark. Haf is pretty sure Christopher is on the edge of sleep, when he whispers, 'Do you think this is working?'

'Our festive rouse?'

'Yeah.' He sounds so small, a boy again.

Haf reaches out to touch his cheek and just about makes it in the dark, though she's pretty sure she pokes him in the eye with her thumb. He's polite enough to not mention it.

'Do you feel happy? I mean, am I helping?'

'Happier than I would be alone.'

'Well then, that's good enough for me.'

He sighs deeply, and she can hear the curl of a smile when he says, 'Me too.'

# Chapter Ten

Several unusual noises in succession wake Haf the next morning. First, a bell – not a distant church bell, but something closer and more demanding. This is followed by the cackling squawks of a flock of geese, capped off with the howling woo-woo-wooooo barks of Stella and Luna.

As she wriggles up to sitting, Christopher bustles in with two steaming cups of tea.

'Thought caffeine might be needed.'

'You thought right. Bloody hell, are you one of those dreadfully perky morning people?' she says, realising he's fully dressed.

'Unfortunately,' he says, brushing some errant toast crumbs off his mustard cable-knit jumper. 'All of us are. Bar Kit.'

'Deal-breaker!' moans Haf, grabbing her phone from under the pillow. Her work alarm hasn't even gone off yet. 'If I'd known I was coming into the household of *active people*, I'd never have gone along with this. You're not going to make me go on a pre-breakfast hike, are you?'

'Hikes come after breakfast,' he says with a teasing wink.

'Christmas is in three days. Surely, surely that's holiday-mode time?' she murmurs.

He draws the curtains and wipes the window down with a cloth from the radiator that appears to only exist to wipe away condensation – this is the work of an adult person, thinks Haf. He opens the window to let fresh air in, and she dives back under the covers.

'Oh, you devil, close that!'

He rolls his eyes and shuts it. 'A bit of fresh air never hurt anyone.'

'Tell that to all the dead people on Everest.'

'Speaking of, I thought you might want to see the snow.'

Haf scrabbles out of the bed to the window. Christopher's right. A respectable blanket of snow covers everything. Ambrose had told her when she moved there that York always got a thick layer in winter, but it hadn't landed before she'd left and part of her was worried she had missed out. But here it is.

'We don't normally get it down here at Christmas, but the weatherperson said the country is covered. Even London, apparently.'

'We never got snow in Wales either. Too close to the sea,' she whispers, enraptured.

'Our first white Christmas, perhaps?' he says with a boyish smile.

The sunrise crests over the trees in the distance, brightening the sparkling white.

'Should I get up?'

'Sure, but no rush. I'm just helping Mother with some preparations. Just take your time, and I'll make you some breakfast when you join us?'

'How very boyfriendly of you.'

He beams, apparently very pleased to be useful and in the presence of snow, and practically skips out the door, closing it softly behind him.

She opens up Twitter and is briefly confused as to why her account is locked until she remembers doing it so the Calloways couldn't find her.

However, she might not have needed to worry so much about that, because it turns out Ambrose is running another poll.

**@ambroseliew** What would you do if you fancied your boyfriend's sister?

**Expire**: 42%
**Dump him for her**: 25%
**Other (explain)**: 33%
*359 votes*

There are a lot of comments discussing what they would do, and while she's tempted to scroll through them, part of her realises that might be a terrible idea. The fake dating was bad enough.

> **Haf:** Can you perhaps keep your roasting to WhatsApp please? I don't want anyone to find out. I didn't mind the first one so much, but I just don't want to risk it.
>
> **Ambrose:** oh please, who is going to work it out???
>
> **Ambrose:** let me have my fun
>
> **Haf:** Fine, keep it vague tho??
>
> **Haf:** I don't want people to realise it's about me bc we live together!!!
>
> **Ambrose:** also it's the sort of thing you'd do
>
> **Ambrose:** some good advice in the comments, especially this one

Ambrose forwards her a tweet.

> **@poopdoctor** @ambroseliew make them fight each other for my affection.

Haf sighs and flings the phone as far away from her as possible. *Let them have their fun,* she thinks. *Someone should be having fun.*

A couple of scalding hot sips of achingly sweet tea later, Haf slides off the mattress to her feet, grabbing her bathroom bag from the open suitcase on her side of the room.

*I should probably unpack that,* she thinks.

As she opens the bedroom door, the one opposite opens at the exact same time.

It's Kit. Unfortunately for Haf, she looks extremely cute, if very grumpy, in forest-green silk pyjamas. She grunts, and reaches up to smooth down her hair, which is standing up in big knots.

'Morning,' says Haf, swallowing her nerves and attempting to be cheery.

'Did I imagine it . . . or did someone ring a fucking bell?' she mumbles.

'No, I heard it too.'

'Ugh. I hate bells. Especially in my house. *Especially* in the morning.' Kit shrugs, yawns and groans all at once in a movement that says, 'I would rather not be awake, but I guess I am now.'

There's an awkward pause that Haf wants to fill. 'I'm just going to brush my teeth. I have a gross morning mouth.'

'Oh yeah, me too.'

The awkward pause returns, and all Haf can think to say is, 'Well, shall we?'

This is absolutely a ridiculous thing to say, as though they are going for a stroll not to use the bathroom, but in her half-asleep state, Kit seems unphased by this.

Kit wanders to the bathroom, leaving the door open, which Haf takes for an invitation. After rooting through the cabinet, Kit slumps down onto the closed toilet lid. In one hand is a glass of water, in her other two white tablets.

'Bad sleep?' Haf asks, taking out her toothbrush from the washbag.

Kit fumbles the pills into her mouth and takes a long, slow sip. 'I very rarely get a good one. Comes with the rest of it. Non-refreshing sleep.'

'Oh no, I'm sorry,' Haf gargles in between brushing her teeth, not really knowing what Kit means.

Kit takes another sip of water, then reaches up to the cabinet for a little jar of moisturiser. 'Sorry, you probably have no idea what I'm going on about.'

Haf waves her hand and gurgles out, 'You can tell me if you'd like to,' though it sounds more like, 'oohcahellmay.'

Kit laughs, while gently applying blobs of cream to her face. 'I have this thing called hypermobile Ehlers-Danlos Syndrome. It's why I use the walking stick. Basically, it makes all your tissues too stretchy, so my joints are really weak and pop out, or dislocate if they're feeling really spicy,' she says with a grin.

Haf laughs, and a little flurry of toothpaste snowfall floats in the air.

'It does a bunch of other stuff too, each thing more annoying than the last. The fatigue and bad sleep are the worst bits.' She taps the side of her head. 'Plus, sometimes I get this thing that is literally called "brain fog", so I can't think for shit some days either.'

Haf spits, rinses and dries her hands on a hand towel. 'That sounds rough.'

'It is. But I do a really good Y for "YMCA" though,' she says, her elbows overextending to make a very convincing Y shape.

'Well, I'd say it's all worth it then.'

'See, I knew you'd get it.'

Kit leans a hand against the back of the loo and pushes herself up to standing, groaning with the movement.

'Do you need a hand?'

'Nah, but thanks. Just need to warm . . . everything up a bit.'

'Well, the offer is open, for . . .'

'Getting off the loo?' Kit laughs, which sends Haf spluttering, unsure if she's being insensitive. Luckily, Kit adds, 'I will be sure to abuse your kindness as much as possible.'

The mystery bell rings again.

'You ever get the sense you're being summoned for something,' Kit mutters.

'Ventriloquism and now bell-ringing? The Calloways are a talented bunch.' Haf laughs.

A few splashes of water later, she feels a bit calmer. That was fine, a normal conversation almost. Only the tiniest teasing at the end, which could barely be considered flirting. And she hardly even noticed how cute Kit looked in her pyjamas.

*This will be fine! Friends!*

Haf drops her things back in the bedroom and gets dressed, not wanting a repeat of the incident at Freddie's family home. As Haf wanders downstairs, she hears Esther's voice, loud and commanding. She follows the sound of it down the hallway, towards the dining room.

'No, Aggy, surely we don't need any more carrots? . . . Well, what do you mean you underestimated the required carrot to reindeer ratio?' There's a pause, followed by several small stomps. 'I'll sort it.'

Haf pokes her head around the door to find Esther surrounded by what can only be described as – presumably organised – chaos. Boxes stack up against the wall, and the table is covered in lists, an open laptop, a very large cafetière of coffee and more boxes.

'Haf! Good morning, dear. I hope we didn't wake you with all the commotion.' In Esther's hand is the offending bell.

'Not at all,' she lies. 'Is this all for the village Christmas fair?'

'The fête, darling. The fête,' she corrects. Turning towards the kitchen, she suddenly takes a deep breath and in the direction of the door shouts, 'Otto? Did you pick up the carrots?'

Inside the boxes on the table are small pouches of wrapped white fabric.

'Oh, these are your spices from the mulled wine, right?' Haf asks, taking one of the muslin pouches out of the box. Each of them has a dried orange, cinnamon sticks, cloves and allspice wrapped up together. It smells heavenly.

'Yes, for the hot drinks stand. It's for charity, and we always raise more than you'd expect.'

'People love their mulled drinks.'

'Yes, and hopefully, we'll have no rogue cloves today,' she says, a little archly.

'Oh, it definitely wasn't the cloves.' Haf laughs awkwardly, replacing the pouch.

'I should hope not, or there'll be an incident.' She takes a deep breath again and bellows, 'OTTO!'

Esther has a powerful set of lungs on her. Haf is pretty sure the windows rattled in their frames, or perhaps they just cowered.

'Yes, Esther?' calls a muffled reply.

Both Haf and Esther turn around to see Otto outside, peering through the window, gardening gloves on his hands and terriers bustling at his feet.

'Don't yell at me, Otto. I'm not cattle,' she says, opening the window.

'I didn't say or mean to imply that you were cattle, dearest. What's troubling you?'

'I'm not troubled, I'm simply trying to ascertain whether you got the carrots.'

'The carrots?'

'Yes, did you get the *carrots*?'

'For the cattle?' Otto asks innocently.

Haf suppresses a laugh.

'Not for the cattle, the *reindeer*, Otto.'

'There's reindeer now? This is starting to sound like a real menagerie.'

'Otto, so help me, I will lock you outside and never let you in again if you keep testing me.'

'Right, right. I'm here, I'm listening, and I'm being very serious. The reindeer? You need carrots for reindeer?'

'Yes, Otto, that's what I said. Didn't I say that?' she says, suddenly turning to Haf.

'Yes, carrots!' squeaks Haf, who was not expecting to be called upon to testify.

'Carrots, Otto.'

'I didn't get any carrots, dear. I don't think you asked me to.'

'Are you positive?'

'I'm pretty sure.'

Esther takes a clipboard from the table and consults a list.

'Oh dear. I foolishly only asked Aggy Wimlott if she would, but she just rang me in a tizz because she thinks she's dramatically underestimated how many carrots we might need.'

'Are we about to be beset by a plague of reindeer?'

'Surely just nine?' asks Christopher, who wanders into the room holding a cup of coffee. 'Eight, if they're still excluding Rudolph.'

'Oh, don't you start too. I'm surrounded by impossible men.'

Esther's phone buzzes with another call.

'Hello, Mayor Clarke,' she says, all sweetness and calm. 'No, we haven't solved the carrot issue yet, but I'm on it.'

Despite being irritated by the men in her life and presented with logistical vegetable problems, Esther is clearly a woman who thrives on pressure.

'Wow, this is really escalating,' whispers Christopher conspiratorially.

'I'm getting out of here while I can,' says Otto. 'Good luck!' He trots around the corner out of sight.

Hanging up the phone, Esther joins them back by the window. 'Where did that man go?'

'Can we help you with the . . . carrots situation? It looks like you've got your hands full here. Maybe we can go get some more?' Haf asks.

Esther looks like the cat who got the cream. 'Thank you, Haf. It's very nice to see someone in this family wants to participate and help me in my hour of need.'

Haf's stomach does the tiniest flip at the word 'family'.

'I was helping this morning! And I thought you wanted me to do the gingerbread house?' protests Christopher.

'And you'll help even more by going to pick up some more carrots for me.'

'Mother, how many carrots can nine reindeer possibly eat in a single day? Be reasonable. Are we even allowed to feed them many? Surely, the reindeer . . .'

'Wranglers?' offers Haf.

'Right, surely the wranglers will bring food for them? There must be an upper limit of carrots they can eat. Or maybe we can't feed them carrots at all.'

'Like with ducks and bread,' Haf mutters.

'You can't feed ducks bread?' Christopher cries.

'Frozen peas are much better. Bread fills them up, causes malnutrition and makes them . . . poop everywhere,' she says, cautiously replacing the word 'shit' for something less rude.

'Dear God, my childhood was a lie . . . and possibly the cause of death for a number of ducks.'

Esther pointedly waits for them to finish their little back-and-forth.

'Don't question me, Christopher. We need them for the reindeer, but also for the snowmen. How are children going to build snowmen without carrot noses, Christopher?'

'There's not even that much snow, Mother.'

'Well then, they'll just have to be healthy snacks for the children. Just go do it.'

Esther hurriedly types out several messages on her phone, her manicured nails clacking on the plastic. 'There, I've sent you the details of the places you need to go.'

Christopher checks his phone. 'Mother, there's five places on here. Will any of them even be open this early?'

'The sooner you get going, the sooner you will find out,' she says, with a dismissive wave of her hand.

'Should I go with him?' asks Haf awkwardly.

'No. You can help me here.'

Christopher gives her an apologetic look and backs away from the centre of operations.

'Before we get going, I'm just going to grab a cup of tea, if that's all right?' asks Haf.

Esther gives her a distracted nod, so she takes the opportunity to follow Christopher.

In the hallway, he slips on his shoes. At the bottom of the stairs, looking slightly less tired than she did upstairs, is Kit.

'What mission are you on?' rasps Kit, now dressed in a slouchy grey knitted jumper and even slouchier jeans.

'Carrots.'

'Reindeer?'

'Exactly.'

Kit shakes her head, and in an alarmingly accurate impression of her mother, she says '"You know, Christopher, the village would never recover from a scandal of underfed reindeer."'

'"Katharine, Oxlea would forever be synonymous with hungry ungulates!"' Christopher replies in the same perfect mimic, and the pair of them fall about laughing. It's a perfect sibling moment. Haf hasn't seen them this relaxed with each other since they got here, and it kind of warms her heart.

'Don't you pair get cheeky now,' says Esther, startling Haf as she materialises behind them.

Sensing that if he doesn't leave now, he will be assigned extra tasks, Christopher rushes out the door without another word.

'I have a task specifically set aside for you,' she says, turning to Kit.

'For me?' asks Kit, pulling herself up to her feet. 'Oh no, what is it?'

'I need you to do the gingerbread house for the raffle.' Without another word, Esther turns and walks back to the dining room, leaving behind a very incredulous-looking Kit.

'Sorry, you want me to *make* a gingerbread house?' she asks, scrambling to her feet and leaning against the banister. 'One that's good enough for someone to win as a prize?'

'Yes, dear. That's what I said.'

'I have absolutely no idea how to do that.'

'Christopher made the dough last night, so all you have to do is assemble and decorate it. You're a clever girl, I'm sure you can work it out, and frankly there's no one else to do it.'

'No one is going to want a gingerbread house constructed by me. This is mad. Just wait for him to get home!'

'Katharine,' Esther says, turning to give her a serious and withering look. 'There is not enough time. Christopher is busy, and after all, you are an architect. We paid for you to go to one of the best architectural schools in the country. You work in one of the most renowned firms in the city. Surely, you can use your prodigious skills to build a simple house?'

It's such a slam dunk that it almost takes Haf's breath away. Kit, who clearly knows she's lost, still protests limply. 'Sure, but not out of biscuit, Esther,' she whines in the teenage cadence that returns once you've been under your parents' roof for a few hours.

'Don't "Esther" me. It's decided.' And in a movement designed to part crowds and shoo dogs, Esther walks towards them clapping her hands twice in quick succession. Esther ploughs into the kitchen, beckoning for them to follow with a wave of her hand without ever turning to check they're coming. It's obvious that they just would.

On the kitchen island are a couple of mounds of ginger-brown dough wrapped in cling film, plus several open cookbooks turned to pages with pictures of gingerbread houses, annotated with neatly written suggestions on Post-it notes.

'Mum, seriously. I'm tired. I need to have a rest if I'm going to be able to help later, and I haven't even eaten yet.'

Esther softens, placing a hand on Kit's cheek, her eyes searching Kit's face as if trying to locate the source of pain and eliminate it with a classic Esther Calloway stare.

'I can help,' pipes up Haf before she can even think about it.

Both Calloway women turn towards her, and it's eerie how similar their bullshit-searching look is.

'Have you ever made a gingerbread house before?' asks Kit.

'Not even once. I'm not even a very good baker. I've burned butterfly cakes before, ha ha . . . But two heads are better than one, right?'

'Good,' says Esther curtly, turning back down the hall. 'There are some croissants in the oven.'

# Chapter Eleven

'I don't think you really know what you've volunteered for.' Kit laughs ruefully as she flicks on the kettle like you might flick a really horrible bug.

'You sure you're up to this?' Haf asks gently, meaning both in terms of fatigue and the reality of working with Haf alone in a kitchen. Of course, that's only if she's feeling the tension between them as acutely as Haf is. Or maybe that's all in Haf's head.

'I'll be all right,' Kit says, taking two cups from the cupboard. 'Caffeine and painkillers will power me through. Plus, I'll delegate so you can do all the hard bits.'

'You heard me say I burn butterfly cakes, right?'

One of the recipes has been earmarked with a Post-it, notes scribbled in the corner. It seems to correspond to the dough in front of her.

'Crikey, there's a lot of maths involved here.' Haf grimaces and peers over the instructions. 'There's even a formula for angles and stuff. Shit. I can do statistics, but this might be beyond me.'

Kit snorts. 'Well, this is going to go well. I am shite at maths.'

Haf looks up at her slowly. 'Isn't maths like important for the whole making-buildings thing? You know, your job.'

'Yep.'

'Oh God, please let me know what buildings you've worked on so I'll be sure to never go near them.'

'Unfortunately, I worked on this extension,' Kit says, pointing at the whole room. 'Sorry to tell you. She's pretty study though. No collapses yet.'

Kit knocks on the wall with her knuckles, then pretends to startle at something going wrong, which makes Haf shriek. Naturally, Kit finds this hilarious and barks with laughter.

'That was mean.' Haf pouts.

'It was, but I'm making you a tea so that should make up for it, don't you think? Anyway, all the maths is done by computers. It's not like I'm wandering around building sites with an abacus or anything.'

Not only is there an alarming amount of maths required in the instructions, but Esther has compiled a resource of the various decorations they should attempt. Drizzled icing to look like snow, powdered sugar shaken over the top – this seems like an easy one, at least – plus wreaths and holly made out of green-dyed royal icing. This was going to be one sweet house.

'Let's divide and conquer,' says Haf as Kit sets down their steaming cuppas. 'I'll get us going and roll out the dough ready for baking. You handle the music.'

'Are you sure you're safe to operate an oven and move hot things around? No offence, but I saw what you did to the gravy yesterday. The mulled wine too.'

'You weren't even there for that one!'

'I hear things.' Kit says this in such an off-handed way that it makes Haf think of Esther.

'Oh, great.'

Haf *is* an unmitigated disaster in the kitchen, but Kit looks so tired. But then again, it's not for her to say what Kit should and shouldn't do. So that leaves fake confidence and lying her arse off, which seem to be her new hobby.

'I'll just concentrate really hard,' she says. 'It'll be fine!'

She turns on the oven to preheat, and in seconds, the terriers appear at her feet, sensing that food that might be imminent. 'How did you guys even get inside?' she mutters to the dogs, who are both doing big, deep sniffs.

'We will have to hope that's true,' concedes Kit, sitting down on a stool at the kitchen island. 'Someone entirely conscious is probably better than me, a half-asleep barely assembled meat sack, even if you apparently cannot cook. It's all on you, Hughes.'

It's embarrassing that this use of her surname makes her stomach flip.

Friends. They're just friends.

'How did you know that's my surname?'

'You're dating my brother. The least I could do was look you up. Google is free, and so is Facebook, unfortunately.'

'Oh?' she asks, trying to be casual. 'Did you find out anything interesting?'

Kit shrugs, and pulls out her phone. 'It's very trusting of you to let me control the music. What if what I choose is God awful?'

'I have a broad taste,' Haf says, hoping that the dismissal meant everything on her profile is sufficiently locked down. 'Though if it's really bad, I will judge you.'

'What if it's a playlist of all Britain's entries to Eurovision *after* 2013?'

Haf does a full body shudder. 'Dear God, that's a human rights violation.'

To her relief, flaccid attempts at Euro-pop doesn't play from the kitchen speakers. Instead, a jaunty guitar strikes up, joined by Dolly Parton. Thanks to Ambrose's love of the Christmas album, she's become quite the Parton connoisseur. As the chorus of 'Two Doors Down' – an absolute banger – starts, Haf joins in as she unwraps the thick, sweet dough from its cling film. It's still a little cool from being stored in the fridge overnight, but hopefully it'll roll out okay. The rolling pin is a terrifying marble affair that would definitely be the murder weapon in a cosy crime novel, and she can feel her biceps twinging as she lifts it.

The song builds, and she looks up from her dough to see Kit dancing. Kit plucks ingredients from packets to inspect them closer with a flourish, and bopping as she sketches decorative designs on a notepad. When she stops to think, her hands point into finger guns, tapping in the air to the beat. She is by no means a good dancer. Every movement is slightly off beat, and her waving arms never quite reach the ethereal elegance of a ballet dancer; the effect is a little bit flapping gosling, truth be told. But Haf can't tear her eyes away from this awkward, spiky girl.

Kit catches her watching, and her cheeks burn with embarrassment – what if she was paying too much attention? But rather than recoil or stop what she's doing out of embarrassment, Kit pulls a goofy face and does an arm wave, followed by a shoulder shimmy. With a burst of laughter, Haf copies her, the pair of them wiggling while waving baking instruments.

The key changes and the pair of them enthusiastically sing the, '*Oh oh ohhhh ohh, two doors down*' harmony, though neither of them are on-note. It's a glorious caterwaul.

They dance around the kitchen, laughing and singing and banging drum beats out on containers, and it all feels like the most natural thing in the world. All the pretence and awkwardness and history of the last twenty-four hours falls away, and they're just two girls dancing to Dolly.

This is friendship, right? The freedom to be silly together. They're comfortable, but everything is platonic. Friendship!

But soon the song is over, and Haf is a little sad their dancing is too.

'How's my taste?' Kit asks, turning down the volume on her phone as one of Dolly's more gospel, slower songs sounds out.

Haf tries to forget the last time she asked her that question.

'Dolly is always an impeccable choice,' she says quickly. 'But no Christmas music?'

'I have a very small window of tolerance for Christmas music,' Kit says, sipping her tea.

'Isn't this prime Christmas music time?'

'Sure, but I live and work in London, which means I've basically been accosted by Christmas music since the first of November. I'll listen voluntarily on Christmas Eve and Day.'

'Wow, I didn't realise your middle name was Ebenezer.'

Kit laughs a singular throaty 'ha'.

'Darlene Love deserves better than two days a year.' Haf sniffs as she returns to rolling out the dough. Her upper arms ache, and she's pretty sure a sheen of sweat is building on her forehead. 'Do you think this is thin enough?'

Appraising it with an architect's eye, Kit gets up so close that Haf thinks she's going to whip out a tape measure. 'That bit's too thick,' she says, directing Haf's rolling. Eventually, she nods with satisfaction.

With intense concentration and a fancy mechanical pencil, Kit draws templates onto baking paper. When she concentrates, she frowns, and the tiniest peek of pink tongue sticks out from the corner of her mouth.

Haf studiously concentrates on the cookbooks instead of Kit's lips.

'You think this will do?'

When she snaps back to attention, she sees that Kit has laid the cut templates onto the gingerbread and is holding out a butter knife.

Haf takes it and carefully cuts the walls and roof out of the dough. The butter knife is a little bit too blunt for the job, even though it's probably the safest option, what with the sticky dough and her greasy fingers and all her clumsiness. Transferring them onto the cookie sheet makes them warp and stretch a little, but she squishes them back into a rough semblance of the right shape.

Stella and Luna stand on their hind legs against the counter and thoroughly sniff at the slabs of gingerbread as Haf slides the trays into the oven.

'One job done,' says Haf, setting a timer for the cookies on her phone.

'You have a nice singing voice, by the way.' The compliment is genuine but there's a hesitation in Kit's voice.

'Thanks,' says Haf. 'We're both sopranos, Dolly and I, so it's the right range for me.'

They both nod like nodding dogs as the compliment hangs awkwardly in the air between them. *Friends can compliment each other*, she reminds herself. *It's not flirting.*

Before Haf can offer one back, Kit rushes to the back door.

'I'm just going to have a trot round the garden, it's too warm in here,' Kit says, stuffing her feet into a pair of garden clogs.

Despite the open back door, Stella and Luna stand on guard by the oven just in case.

Haf's phone buzzes with a message from Ambrose.

**Ambrose:** how is day 2 of operation Don't Smooch the Sister going

Haf sends back a grumpy-face emoji, but worried they will revert back to emoji-only communication, follows it up with a bit more.

**Haf:** We are making a gingerbread house for the fête
**Ambrose:** who let you bake? do they not know about the butterfly cakes??
**Haf:** Tried to warn them
**Ambrose:** i hope they didn't leave you unsupervised

Haf sighs and braces herself. Luna nudges her muzzle against Haf's calf, which she takes as emotional support, but could honestly be just a sneaky request for a treat now that all the Calloways are out of the room.

**Haf:** Kit's helping me

Ambrose sends back a string of letters that starts out *skskskskksksks* and keeps going for several lines.

**Ambrose:** you are fucked, my friend xoxo
**Haf:** Sod off >:(
**Haf:** We are just friends!!!!!

The timer goes off sooner than she expects – apparently ginger-bread needs very little cooking time at all.

She slides the trays out and sets them on a cork trivet.

The gingerbread has grown . . . a lot.

The moderately straight edges that Kit had crafted are now art déco curves, and there's a huge air bubble in a bit that she's pretty sure was supposed to be one of the walls. Hopefully, they can fix it once everything has cooled down.

It smells good, at least. Apparently, Christopher really knows how to make a gingerbread dough.

Her phone buzzes on the counter again, and she returns to their conversation to find Ambrose penning an essay.

**Ambrose:** baking together is probably inherently romantic

**Ambrose:** i bet you're making big, gooey eyes across the flour while listening to inappropriate pop songs about unrequited lesbian love

**Ambrose:** are we just friends or lovers, what is flirting, idk i'm just too gay, oooh oooh ohh

**Ambrose:** (these are the lyrics, i'll sing it you when you're home)

**Ambrose:** actually maybe you should keep going, this is very entertaining to me

**Haf:** It's Dolly Parton, actually!!!!

**Ambrose:** Oh no

**Ambrose:** Dolly is too powerful

**Ambrose:** Dolly is what human connections are formed around

**Ambrose:** were you dancing?

**Haf:** A bit

**Haf:** She dances like one of those whacky waving inflatable tube men

**Haf:** It was kind of cute

**Ambrose:** she's a dork??

**Ambrose:** a hot dork?

**Ambrose:** oh no no no.

**Ambrose:** ABORT ABORT

**Ambrose:** that's your kryptonite

**Ambrose:** I KNOW YOUR TYPE

**Ambrose:** goblin men and mean dorky women

**Ambrose:** get out of there!

**Haf:** I'M FINE

**Haf:** Go shoot something on Fortnite you menace

Ambrose sends back a string of emojis – a big red X, two girls standing together and a red lipstick smudge. A few seconds later, they send another big red X and a stop sign, just to be sure.

'All right, all right. I get the hint,' Haf says, slipping her phone back into her pocket.

'Dogs asking for treats?' Kit asks, closing the door behind her.

'Ha ha, yeah, I guess. These two know I'm the weakest link.'

As if on cue, Stella and Luna both give her a look that says, 'Please, I've never eaten anything in my life and I could be dying.'

'Nice try,' she tells them.

Kit gives the gingerbread an incredulous look as she passes to wash her hands in the sink. 'Huh. These look different . . . Are they supposed to be blobs?'

'Maybe we can slice them into the right shapes?'

'Maybe. Looks darker than the pictures too, doesn't it?' Kit prods the gingerbread slab closest to her, which is less a flat wall and more a series of small hills. 'It seems like there's going to be significant structural problems, whether or not we cut them back to the same shape.'

'Is this in your professional opinion?' Haf asks with a smirk. 'Are we going to have difficulties erecting them?' She snorts, tickled by her own dirty joke, and Kit gives her an exhausted look.

'Wow, I've never heard that one before,' she says, laying one of the paper templates over what looks like the matching section. Maybe they should have labelled them.

With a sharper knife, Kit slices away the warped edges, putting all spare bits into a little bowl. Haf steals a piece and nibbles on it. It's not the texture she was expecting. It's flavoured really nicely, but it's hard as a real wall and requires a worrying amount of jaw strength to bite into. And then, there's a bitter aftertaste, which she suspects might be because it's burned.

'Blergh, I hope no one is going to actually eat this,' she says, sticking her tongue out.

'The book says we've got to decorate the roof bit while it's warm,' says Kit, taking a handful of sliced almonds.

Pointy end first, she pushes it into the gingerbread, but nothing happens. The gingerbread doesn't give.

'Maybe it just needs a bit of encouragement,' Haf says, trying a slightly different, and yet similarly unyielding, spot. 'We literally just took it out? How quick did we have to be?'

Losing her cool, Kit tries to force one of the slices in and instead creates a rather big dent in the roof. 'Oh no. That doesn't seem structurally sound.'

'Wait!' cries Haf, leaning over to grab one of the reference pictures. 'How about we make some runny icing and glue them to the roof? Then it'll look a bit like a snowy roof.'

As Haf mixes up icing sugar and water in a bowl, plumes of sweet powder float into the air like smoke. A few flecks land in Kit's dark hair. She looks snow-dusted.

The packet is right in front of her . . . She could just grab some icing sugar and lob it at her.

But that sounds like *flirting* territory, doesn't it? Do friends throw sweet foods at each other in the hope they'll eventually touch? Do fake sisters-in-law?

It's all too complicated.

She goes back to the gloopy icing in her bowl that looks a little like PVA glue, which must be right.

With a small spatula, Kit spoons out small portions of icing and quickly puts the almonds in place.

'We'll just leave it to set, and get on with the rest of the decorating,' says Kit, confidence renewed.

Esther had left them some premade and coloured royal icing, so Kit and Haf get to work making decorations. Somehow, Haf ends up on door and window duty, neither of which are entirely straight, but she hopes that will be part of the charm.

Meanwhile, Kit intensely builds something out of marzipan. When it's done, she proudly sets it on the table, but Haf cannot work out what animal it's supposed to be. This reminds her of the time her little cousin Llew proudly gave her a piece of paper covered in an ominous blood-red squiggle, which, after some incorrect guesses he grumpily said was a portrait of her. This sad little monstrosity isn't quite so terrifying, but it is sagging a little, one leg giving way beneath it, but the setting icing manages to hold it together. It does look permanently exhausted though.

'Great!' Haf says with too much enthusiasm. 'Well done, very nice.'

Kit eyes her with suspicion. 'You don't know what it is, do you?' When Haf doesn't respond, she whines. 'I'm rubbish at animals.'

'No, it's very good. Absolutely lifelike. Maybe you should make another one.'

'Why?'

'Then you've got both Stella and Luna?'

'It's a reindeer!' huffs Kit.

This is like Llew all over again.

'Oh! Sorry, yes. *Of course it is.* I just got thrown by the ears. And lack of antlers.'

'Fine, it's a girl reindeer then.'

'They have antlers too.'

'All right, David Attenborough,' she says, sulkily rolling out some antlers to go on its head. Of course, these are far too big and the model far too set, and so Kit and Haf watch in silence as the new antlers just slide off the poor thing's head.

'We can say she's just moulted?' offers Haf.

'Yeah, from shock, having seen her own reflection for the first time.'

It's this proclamation, along with noticing how bug-eyed and angry it looks, that causes Haf to completely lose it.

'I know Esther was desperate, but do you think this was what she expected?' says Kit, laughing too. 'I made another thing too.'

In her hand is the world's worst-constructed snowman, made from two balls the exact same size, with nightmare eyes and an orange nose so big that it off-balances and the snowman falls on its face.

'How did you make something *more* horrible??' cries Haf, bent over laughing.

'What do you mean? It's clearly a work of art!'

'Put it in the Louvre!'

'Or the Tate Modern!'

'It'll scare the children.'

'We can only hope.'

After a few minutes of wheezing laughter, they recover, wiping tears away from their eyes.

'Come on, let's try to assemble it,' Haf says, confident the gingerbread is now firmed up. 'It can't get worse than this.'

Naturally, it does.

While Haf holds the sides up, Kit slathers in the icing to cement them together, but it just slops down the biscuit like melted ice cream.

'Let's just hold it a bit longer . . .' Kit says, pressing the sides together.

'Maybe it needs a little emotional support as well as structural.' Haf lowers her voice to a whisper. 'Wow, what a good house, you're doing really well at being a house.'

'Please don't make me laugh again, or I'm going to crush this.' Kit giggles as the corners on her side wobble.

'Okay, okay. Serious time.' Haf presses her lips into a flat line and scrunches her face into a deep frown.

'I can't look at you,' says Kit, staring at the floor. 'You make facial expressions like a cartoon character. And I don't think you've been serious for one minute in your whole life.'

'Maybe two. And a half. Possibly.'

'No more talking,' commands Kit.

This is, of course, exactly when Haf realises just how close they're standing to each other. Their hands wrap around the gingerbread house, fingertips only millimetres from each other.

'I think it's holding,' says Kit, taking her hands away. The walls, surprisingly, do hold. The stuck-on icing door and windows look a little soft from the heat of the biscuit and their hands. 'Just the roof to go.'

Kit gently lifts an almond covered roof tile from the baking tray, and with Haf's help, brings it to the rest of the house. But as soon as they tilt it ready to fix it on, the gloopy icing and almonds slide off in one enormous avalanche, all down the roof, their hands and over their little house.

'Oh, fuck!' shrieks Kit, setting it back on the tray where it promptly snaps in half.

The reindeer, having valiantly held on for as long as possible, finally gives way, falling onto its side.

'RIP,' says Kit solemnly, and they back into heaving laughter again.

To her surprise, Kit steadies herself against Haf, holding on to her arm. Their faces are only inches apart, and as the hysterical laughter softens between them, all that's left is a held look and heaving breaths.

Platonic. Friends. Don't look at her lips or think about how soft her hair is or how much you want to touch her or how good she smells. Fuck, she smells good. And that's just basic sexual chemistry, a very normal human response. Nothing romantic at all. Just hormones.

*Maybe Ambrose is right. I am a horny gremlin.*

She swears that, for just a second, Kit's eyes dart down to her lips. But she has to be wrong, because they're *just* friends.

This is fine.

'Bloody hell, what is that?'

They leap apart, and Haf has never been more relieved to be interrupted.

Christopher, who must have returned while they were laughing, stands next to them staring at their house in horror.

'It wasn't supposed to be a haunted house, you know.'

'It's quite clearly a festive gingerbread house . . . almost as ordered,' Haf says haughtily, suddenly feeling defensive over their monstrosity.

'Is it?' he says in disbelief. He picks up some of the offcuts and crumbles it between his fingers. Or rather, he tries to, but it is so hard it doesn't give away. 'You absolutely destroyed my lovely gingerbread. Did you nuke it?'

'We started it. Had a breakdown. Bon appétit,' says Kit, and Haf cackles gleefully at the reference to that celebrity baking competition show that was all over Twitter for months. 'You can thank Esther for thinking this was a good idea.'

'I *always* do it. I even made the dough. Why couldn't it wait?' He huffs.

'I think this was supposed to be a punishment for all of us teasing her.'

'And punishing whoever wins this monstrosity too, apparently.' With a cautious finger, he touches the gingerbread wall, only for his finger to go right through it, creating a sizeable hole. 'Oh dear.'

'More natural light at least.' Kit shrugs.

'It's kind of impressive that together you've created the worst gingerbread house to have ever existed. Has Mother seen this? Please tell me she hasn't seen this yet – I don't want to have missed that.'

As if on cue, Esther strides into the kitchen, takes once glance at the gingerbread house and stops in her tracks.

'What happened to it?'

'Nothing happened.'

'That's not what it's supposed to look like, Katharine. Something happened to it. A natural disaster. Floods? Earthquake? A plague of locusts, perhaps?'

'I think we were the natural disaster,' Haf whispers.

'What exactly am I going to do with this? It's supposed to be a house, not rubble,' Esther says, poking at the remaining mostly standing wall, which sags at her touch. She sighs deeply, and Haf is pretty sure she's counting down from ten, lest she absolutely lose her marbles at them.

'It's fine,' says Christopher, who is rooting through the fridge. 'Carrots have been obtained and delivered. Sensibly, I made extra dough – admittedly for us for a family-bonding activity, but I can whip it up in time for the fête, so you'll still have your Calloway gingerbread house for the raffle. Made by me, as it always should have been.' He adds the last bit pointedly.

'I just thought Haf wouldn't want to spend the whole day in the kitchen,' Esther says defensively. 'I'd have thought you'd want to see the sights.'

'I don't mind,' says Haf honestly. 'We can just hang out here and I can watch the master at work.'

Christopher beams at her, and she thinks of all the baking books in his childhood bedroom.

'You can taste test, and be on hot-drink duty,' he says.

Esther throws her hands up in the air. 'Fine, fine. I have to leave in twenty minutes, so can you just bring it straight down to the green when it's ready?'

Christopher gives Esther a little kiss on the forehead to say all is forgiven, and that, of course, he'll do that. In return, Esther gives him a little pat, then scuttles off to find her lists.

'Okay, well, now that we've all established that I'm not to be trusted with . . . any of this, I'm going to Laurel's before Esther can rope me into anything else. See you tonight,' Kit says, rushing off.

Haf wills herself not to follow Kit's escaping silhouette, and instead turns her attention to the technicolour mess before her.

'Shall we just bin this? I really don't think it's salvageable. Although, maybe this bit of wall is okay?' she says, but as she separates it from the house, it crumbles in her hands. 'Maybe not.'

It turns out Christopher is not just a bit good at baking. He's really, *really* good. All his gingerbread biscuits are even in thickness, with no weird warps or bubbles or holes, and when Haf steals a bit, it's completely delicious. Cinnamon and ginger and sweetness burst on her tongue.

'Oh my God, this is really good. I need you to make me this . . . biweekly, until the end of time.'

'Is that twice a week or every two weeks?'

'Omffff, just every day,' she says through another mouthful of biscuit.

While the biscuit cools, he makes decorations for the house. Candy canes and holly wreaths out of coloured icing, and he even whips up a little trio of gingerbread trees onto which he pipes white icing in Nordic patterns. His snowman not only looks not terrifying, but is pleasing to look at, even cute. He makes her a tiny baby snowman for her to nibble on; it tastes like a peppermint cream. A front door is constructed from red icing piped onto a

Nice biscuit with pretty scalloped edges he fished out from the tin by the kettle. The leftover peppermint icing from the snowmen is transformed into frosted window frames.

Christopher builds the gingerbread house with precision and care onto a square shiny cake base that she didn't even notice was among the equipment. In hindsight, this makes a lot more sense than just trying to build it on the countertop. Miraculously, all his pieces go together, and his icing – which there's apparently a ratio that you're supposed to follow to make it – is actually strong enough to hold all the pieces in place.

'You're really good at this,' she says when he's finished.

He stands up straight, dusting icing sugar from his apron, and she hands him a fresh cup of tea.

'Thank you,' he says, not meeting her eyes. There's a soft glow on his cheeks, which she thinks is from the praise rather than the heat of the kitchen. 'I've always liked it, and I suppose I'm all right at it.'

'All right?!'

'Quite good, then.'

'I'm not sure you know *how* good you are, Christopher. I'm not exaggerating.' She points at the bin. 'Do you remember what was here before? That wreckage? You literally saved Christmas.'

He laughs in his self-effacing way. 'Now that's definitely exaggerating.'

'No really, Christopher,' she says, hopping up on a kitchen stool. 'I follow baking people on Instagram who are less good than you and they've been on telly. Did you do any courses or anything?'

'As a teenager, I did a bit. And at uni. There was a baking society.'

'Oh my God . . . there must have been so much cake,' she says, thinking of a society of bakers making her every treat under the sun.

'So much cake. And *good* cake.'

Haf's stomach rumbles. 'I'm jealous. Why didn't you tell me about it before? All you talked about was rugby, which it sounds like you hated.'

He shrugs softly but offers no more.

'What else have you made?'

He takes out his phone and passes it to her. On the screen is an open pictures folder called Baking and inside are so many photos of beautiful and intricately designed cakes, biscuits, pies and all things baking. There are things in here that she knows are difficult to make, always coming up as the surprise technical challenge choice on *The Great British Bake Off*. Everything is precisely designed, and there are so many sweet little details.

'Did you make all these?'

He blushes, the tips of his ears going pink. 'Yes.'

'Holy heck, Christopher,' she breathes. 'Why do you work in finance when you can do this?'

'It's a nice hobby, but probably not one I think I could make money from.'

'Is that what you think, or what your parents say?' The air in the kitchen seems to freeze, along with Christopher. Her big mouth, she's always saying something too blunt. 'Sorry, I . . . that was over the line. I didn't—'

'No, you're right,' he says, sighing. 'That's exactly what they said.'

'You've talked to them about this before?'

'We should start assembling this all and then get over to the fête before Mother passes out from stress,' he says, looking at his watch.

'All right,' she concedes.

Conversation over. For now.

She's not going to leave this alone, not when he's this talented and obviously unhappy in . . . whatever his job his, damn it she can never remember.

Together, they fill the dishwasher and hand-wash the last little bits that would melt if they put them in the machine. The counters sparkle, and all the disaster bits are binned, much to the dogs' disappointment.

Just as they finish, Christopher disappears off and comes back with a lidded box.

'I just remembered something I thought you'd like.'

Christopher lifts off the lid, and out of it draws a bright-green velvet Santa hat. It's very obviously the work of a child – everything is wonky, and the furry edge is matted with eight different colours of glitter glue. At the end of the hat is a very badly sewn-on bell.

'Oh my God, did you just whip this up for me now?' she teases, as he plonks it onto her head. It fits remarkably well, probably because she has a tiny head.

He pulls out a second one in burnished-orange fabric. The pom-pom at the pointed tip of the hat has a smiley face drawn on in permanent marker, which she assumes is to make it look like a snowman. It is slightly too small for Christopher's head and stands up completely straight like a party hat. Probably from all the glitter glue – this one hasn't escaped it either.

'Kit and I made them when we were little. I thought we could get them out, as it's a special occasion.'

'Wow, they're so . . .'

'Terribly shit?'

'I was going to say nostalgically terrible, but okay,' Haf giggles.

'That's not much better.'

'This is the best thing I've ever been allowed to borrow. Do you think Kit'll mind?'

'Nah, I cleared it.'

'I'm honoured to wear a Calloway heirloom.'

Christopher fiddles with his hands, looking down. 'I probably owe you an apology.'

'What for?'

'I just . . . I find it hard to talk about all of this.'

'Being rich?' she says, and he flicks her on the nose.

'No, you pest. The . . . baking.'

'The not-finance.'

'Yes. That. Considering it's one of the many reasons I brought you here.'

'We don't have to talk about it right now, anyway. But I think we should,' she offers gently. 'Like, come on, who is going to get it more than ol' career-disaster McGee over here?'

'We can be disasters together.'

'It's a promise.' She proffers a pinkie, and he wraps his around hers.

'Come on, we elves have a delivery to make.'

# Chapter Twelve

The fête is in final preparation mode when Haf and Christopher arrive.

The roads around the green have been closed off, and little wooden huts like the ones in the Christmas market in York are lined up. They glow softly from all the fairy lights around them.

In the middle of it all is a very large Christmas tree, so large that she has no idea how they even got it here. People on ladders hang the final decorations and adjust the strung lights. Haf is pretty sure she can see Esther guiding them from the bottom, clipboard in hand.

As promised, there's a pen of very sweet-looking reindeer, happily munching away on carrots, bells and ribbons tied on their antlers. Haf squeals under her breath at the sight of them. There is no way she's missing out on stroking every single reindeer.

Just before they pull into the local car park, they pass a partially frozen duck pond, where two tiny children in full snowsuits throw peas enthusiastically for – or rather *at* – the ducks.

'Does your mum organise this every year?' asks Haf, her arms wrapped around the cake box that houses Christopher's stunning gingerbread house.

'Every year that I can remember,' says Christopher, driving his little red car into the parish church car park. It was his first car, apparently, and lives at home while he was at uni and now in London. Haf knows very little about cars, but this is way nicer than the first cars her friends at home had. It's nice being chauffeured around, especially with the heated seats.

Christopher gets out first and runs around the side of the car to take the cake box from her. This is, admittedly, a bit of a relief, as she had no idea how she was going to get out and not launch the gingerbread house skyward.

The sun is low in the sky, and Haf's breath mists in front of her. Even though Christopher said the fête won't officially start for another half an hour or so, the place is humming with people. Just ahead of them, she can see Esther's mulled-wine stall being set up, with gigantic tureens of hot drinks. The air is thick with the quintessential Christmas smell of roasting chestnuts, but there's also freshly popped popcorn and even the sweet ache of candyfloss.

As they walk down the promenade of wooden huts, people arrange their goods in cute displays, reams of wrapping paper and ribbons to hand ready for gift-wrapping.

A cluster of adults with an air of school teachers set up games for the children next to a big sign that says *Snowman Competition*. Haf spies a box of Calloway carrots next to donated scarves, hats, gathered sticks and clumps of coal, ready for everyone to decorate their snow people.

The air moves from sweet to meaty as they get closer to the hog roast. Haf's mouth waters, and she realises she hasn't eaten much today, other than gingerbread and decorations.

'I want to eat everything,' she whispers.

'Well, you can't eat this,' says Christopher, holding it back protectively.

'All I've eaten all day *is* that. I'm starving.'

'I promise to feed you once I've fulfilled my duty as a son.'

The Christmas tree looms large up ahead, somehow even bigger in person. On TV, she'd seen the Nordic Spruce that gets delivered to London every year, and she swears this is a solid rival to that.

Esther and Otto stand together just to the side of a stage that has been set up and decorated ready for the fête to open. Arms full of Christmas decorations, Otto is directed off to another part of the fête before they can say hello.

'Ah, my Christmas elves have arrived,' she says, looking up from her clipboard.

'I thought it would be a good occasion to bring them out,' says Christopher, shaking his head so the pom-poms on his hat dance.

'Very nostalgic of you. You know, we've got a stand to make them again this year. You could make a new one that's not rigid with glitter glue.'

'That's part of their appeal,' protests Haf. 'It's kind of impressive that my hair is getting stuck on it after all these years.'

Esther looks to the cake box. 'Please tell me this one is a prize someone might want to win?'

'If you'd let me do it first time, I could have saved you all that hassle,' says Christopher, smug that he's obviously right.

'Yes, yes,' she says, appraising it with a cursory glance. 'It's lovely, thank you. Can you set it down over there on the raffle table?'

Without another word, Christopher takes the gingerbread house away.

Is that it? Is that all she's going to say?

'He's so talented, isn't he?' she prods, after a moment. Even if he's not here to hear it, maybe it would be a good fake-girlfriend thing to share the pride.

'Very,' says Esther, but then she returns to her list, presumably ticking off the gingerbread house.

Part of her knows logically that Esther is just distracted, but Haf wants to grab her and say, 'No, go look at it properly. Look at what your talented, clever son can do! Tell him he's great.'

No wonder he doesn't talk about his baking.

As Christopher returns, Haf hears the jingle of bells in the distance and realises it's the reindeer.

'Do we have time to go see the reindeer before everything starts?' Haf asks.

'Yes, yes. Off you go,' says Esther, disappearing around the Christmas tree.

Trying to swallow her bristling, Haf gives Christopher a conciliatory smile.

'Come on then. I didn't go on the Great Carrot Mission for us to not then see these very well-fed reindeer.'

'Don't forget the snowmen too.'

Under a gabled roof decorated in holly and garlands stand five reindeer, corralled in by a white fence. Great big huffs of breath rise into the air around them, and everything smells like fresh, sweet hay. All the reindeer wear bridles and harnesses, embroidered with their names.

They're watched over by possibly the surliest man ever to wear a pair of novelty reindeer antlers, dressed in what she assumes is a regulation elf uniform – thin but very bright red velvet stitched into a jacket with large sleeves, bells fixed to the bottom of his lurid green trousers. The budget must have run out for fancy boots – he wears bog-standard country-person green wellies.

'Can I touch them?' she asks him, and he gives her a grunt in response and offers her a carrot. It takes her a moment to realise this is not for her but for the reindeer.

'One of the fabled Calloway carrots, I presume?' she whispers to Christopher. 'I feel honoured.'

She snaps the carrot in half, and all five of the reindeer look up at once. She's never been so close to a reindeer before. They're so beautiful, with their mottled brown and white coats, and their velvety noses and ears. Their large heads swivel towards the sound, and they start congregating around her, not taking their eyes off the carrot.

'God, they're as bad as the dogs.' Christopher laughs.

Unable to break it with her hands, Haf bites the carrot into chunks, and offers a little bit to each of them in turn.

'That's kind of disgusting,' says Christopher. 'It wasn't even washed.'

'What's a bit of soil?' She shrugs. 'Good for the immune system, probably.'

Christopher remains unconvinced.

The reindeer are much more polite than she expects, clearly used to this little routine as they wait in turn for their piece of carrot. The last reindeer takes the final chunk from her hand and leaves behind a trail of hot saliva.

'A bit of slobber too,' she adds, shaking it off her hand. 'What a treat.'

'Is that one called Pepsi? Doesn't seem like the most Christmassy name.'

'I suppose there's only so many times you can go through Santa's nine without getting bored with the names. That big one is called Alan.'

A big chunk of hay in the corner suddenly moves, and out stumbles a baby reindeer.

Haf makes a noise that can be only heard by dogs, or possibly reindeer, and drops down to her knees. The snow bites through her clothes but she doesn't care.

'What a lovely baby, oh you're so sweet!' she says, tickling its nose. On his tiny harness, is the word *Cupid*. 'Cupid, is that your name?' she asks him, and in response, he honks and wiggles his tail. 'I am never leaving. I love him. I would die for him.'

All around them, the sound of Christmas carols played on hand bells ring out.

'Ah, that's the sign things are starting. We should go get some mulled wine before it gets ransacked and leave the reindeer to the kids,' says Christopher, turning to the fête.

Dragging her attention from the reindeer, she feels Christopher stiffen next to her.

'Oh no,' whispers Christopher, as he stares into the crowd.

'What?' asks Haf, trying to follow his gaze.

'Sally is here.'

'Sally? As in party Sally?'

'Yes,' he bleats, and Haf grabs him by the arm, spinning them back round to face the reindeer in case Sally spots them. 'She must be home for Christmas.'

'Damn it, I hope she hasn't spoken to my family.'

'Hopefully. Okay, it'll be fine. We just need to avoid her, and keep her away from them. There's plenty of people here, that should be easy.'

'It's a small town,' he murmurs.

'Well, the other option is we somehow convince her she knows me, introduced us, and has been instrumental in our relationship. I'm not super familiar with the methods of false-memory implantation, I must admit, but it sounds tricky.'

'Thank goodness for that. You'd be a criminal mastermind.'

'Obviously. Okay, you've got to show me what she looks like. Though I am face-blind so it might not actually help that much. It'll give me her vibe, or at least her haircut. Hurry up.'

Christopher pulls out his phone and navigates to Facebook, where he pulls up Sally's profile. She has a very sensible long bob, a nice round face and really does look like she would throw a good buffet and set up her friends. If this were different circumstances, Haf thinks Sally would be a nice person to chat to – the kind of woman who seems very neat but now and then drops the rudest jokes.

'And where is she in relation to us?'

'Eight o'clock from you.'

'I'm sorry what?'

'Like on a clock. You know, the eight on the clock face?' Haf's face must be blank enough that Christopher sighs and says, 'Left and behind. In the bright orange coat.'

Doing a very unconvincing stretch-and-look-over-the-shoulder, Haf manages to spot her. 'We're lucky she decided to wear something visible from space. Let's just stay here until she's moved away, then we'll head to the wine.'

After a few tense moments, Sally heads back towards the stalls.

'Bye bye, best friends,' Haf whispers sadly to the reindeer, but all of their attention is on someone who has arrived with a bundle of fresh hay for them. Fickle creatures.

As they wander away, she spots a rogue carrot in the snow. It looks mostly clean, so she picks it up to give to the reindeer later. The pockets in her coat are the typical kind for women's clothing and are essentially non-functional, or at least not deep enough for carrots. And she didn't bring a bag at all, which was probably silly.

So, without another option, she does what any other sensible person with boobs in need of a pocket does. She slides it into her bra.

'I don't mean to be rude,' says Christopher after a few stunned seconds. 'But did you just put a carrot down your top?'

'Looking at my chest were you, Christopher?' she teases, and is absolutely delighted when his face lights up bright red. She cackles. 'Far too easy!'

'I walked right into that, didn't I?'

'Like a carrot into the bra.'

'I don't think that's a common turn of phrase.'

Haf shrugs and loops her arm around his. 'It is now.'

The fête is busier now, more people wrapped up tightly in knitwear, many of them accompanied by tiny children in the crocodile wellington boots that Haf thinks should absolutely be available for adults. A few families have started pushing around sludgy balls of snow ready for the snowman contest later.

At the mulled-wine stall, there's only a small queue. Instead of plastic cups, there are painted mugs that you can leave a deposit for or buy.

Haf picks up one with a finger-painted reindeer so wonky that it rivals Kit's marzipan attempt. 'I must have this one. It's a work of art. This could actually fetch a price! It is going home with me.'

'They're all painted by the kids from the primary school,' says the woman in a bright pink headscarf running the stall. She takes the mug delicately from Haf and fills it up with a glug of wine.

At the other end of the table is a box with the neat little bundles of spices from the Calloway dining room, which are for sale for a donation to the primary school. Everything is so wholesome and sweet, and Haf wants to spend her measly few remaining pounds on every home-made charity item she can find.

'Do you need help drinking it this time?' asks Christopher, taking his own mug – this one is covered in lurid-blue snowflakes that look like psychedelic spider webs.

Haf goes to swat him, but her fingers are so cold that the movement makes them ache. Gloves were, of course, another thing she forgot to pack.

'Thanks, fake boyfriend,' she says, as they move a little away from the stall towards the seating area.

'You're welcome,' he says. 'It's only a mug of Waitrose's own-brand wine jazzed up.'

'Don't knock Waitrose. Plus, I'm a cheap date and easy to please.'

Christopher looks at the time on his phone. 'The lights should all go on in fifteen minutes or so, that's kick-off. Mother always gives a little speech, so we should go over for that.'

Before they can decide, however, a very familiar voice calls their names.

Laurel strides over, arms wide, and wraps them both into a gigantic hug. Unsurprisingly, as well as being a giant woman, she gives very tight hugs. Laurel is wearing head-to-toe white, and terrified she's about to stain her clothes, Haf moves her cup of wine out of the way so quickly half of it slops over her hand. She hadn't expected this Christmas to involve quite so many spilled liquids, but there we have it.

'Hi, Laurel,' says Christopher, placing a polite kiss on her perfectly contoured cheeks.

'Hello!' says Haf. 'Nice to see you again.'

'Oh my God, look how adorable and Christmassy you both are!' she cries. Her perfectly manicured nails flick the bell at the end of Haf's hat, which sounds a very feeble chime. Maybe she should listen to Esther and make a new one; this is practically an antique.

'Be careful with that. It's basically an antique,' says Kit, who appears beside them, clutching a cup of hot cider in one hand. In the other, her black walking stick has been replaced with a bright red one wrapped with white ribbon, so it looks like a candy cane.

'You're looking very Christmassy too,' Haf says a bit too enthusiastically.

'Laurel's handiwork,' Kit says, turning it back and forth. 'I like it.'

*Calm down, Haf. Just act normal, if you can imagine what that's like.* 'Thanks for letting me wear the hat.'

'Did you see over there is a cute little stall where you can go decorate your own baubles?' Laurel says, pointing over from where they came . . . right at a familiar flash of Calippo orange. 'Why don't we go—'

'NO!' shout Christopher and Haf in union, before looking awkwardly at each other.

'Not right now, you just got here,' says Christopher, trying to rescue the moment.

'Yes, let's go later!' blabbers Haf, spilling more hot mulled wine onto her fingers. 'Let's catch up and drink this searing booze first.'

She tries to surreptitiously lick the wine off her hand, but Kit watches her with a baffled smile.

Laurel blinks a few times, but has the grace to move the conversation along.

'Come, come. Let's sit down,' says Laurel, ushering them towards a picnic table covered in thick tartan wool blankets, the kind you might buy from a National Trust shop.

Haf does a quick look around at the people milling about, but luckily, Sally and her orange coat appear to have moved on.

'What did you both get up to today? Haf, I heard you and Kit had a baking disaster.'

'Oh yes, turns out Kit and I should not be allowed near a kitchen. We had good fun, though. Sang a lot of Dolly.'

Kit's cheeks flush a little, but it must be the cold. And the wine.

'Kiiiit, you never sing with me.' She pouts. 'I want to sing Dolly. Let's go do karaoke.'

'No!' chorus the Calloways.

'Wow, do you guys not like joy?' asks Haf.

'They get competitive,' explains Laurel with a knowing look.

'About . . . . karaoke?' How can you be competitive?'

The Calloways eye each other like old rivals.

'*He* just doesn't want to be beaten again.'

'*She* just can't accept that it was a fluke that she won last time.'

'It was not a fluke, and you know it.'

While the siblings bicker, Haf looks to Laurel for an explanation.

'You know the one on the games-console things. It gives you a score at the end. It became . . . a source of conflict.' Laurel leans in and whispers conspiratorially. 'Truth be told, it just measures how accurately you can hold notes, and it's absolutely nothing to do with how well you can sing.'

'I was going to say, I've heard her sing. How bad must Christopher be for her to beat him?'

Laurel throws her head back and cackles.

'Oi,' snaps Kit.

Realising that anything else she says might be interpreted as siding with a Calloway sibling, she mimes zipping her mouth shut.

'Anyway, I meant normal karaoke with a booth and a champagne button,' says Laurel.

'A champagne button?' Haf whispers, her eyes wide. 'I want to go to that.'

Laurel nods sagely. 'When you're next in London, we can all go.'

'What have you been up to today, Laurel?' asks Christopher, moving the conversation away.

'It's been a busy one,' she says, and counts off the tasks on her fingers. 'I just finished scheduling my socials for Christmas week. There were a few photos I needed to sort this afternoon, and luckily Kit appeared out of nowhere. She's such a good photographer.'

Kit squirms at the praise. 'I'm know how to point and click. You just have a good camera.'

Laurel, of course, ignores this. 'Luckily, this morning I managed to corral Mummy to the spa, so she can have a relax before the big do.'

'Oh yeah, the party. Is it a big thing, then?' asks Haf, and at once, Kit and Laurel look at her with confused expressions.

'The Christmas Eve party? Yeah, it's pretty big,' says Kit. 'It's practically a ball. We go every year.'

Wait. A ball?!

'No one said anything about *a ball*,' Haf says, nerves creeping into her voice.

'It's not a ball,' Laurel says.

'How is not a ball?' Kit retorts.

'There's no prescribed dances. We're not in *Bridgerton*. Though we do have a string quartet this year . . . It's just a bit of an extravaganza.'

Haf is not sure how something can be 'a bit' of an extravaganza, but all she can think about is that this is absolutely, completely not what she planned for.

Laurel trails off as she watches Haf's face fall, and turns to Christopher with an exhausted look, the kind that comes from knowing someone for far, far too long. 'You didn't tell her to bring a dress, did you?'

Christopher blanches. 'Erm, it slipped my mind.'

'A dress? You mean like a ballgown or something?' Haf panics.

'Pretty much,' adds Kit. 'It's all formal wear.'

'Fuck. No, you didn't mention that, Christopher,' she whines. 'At most, I've packed for turkey-curry-supper level of party. I absolutely did not bring anything remotely *ball* suitable. What am I going to do? Turn up in my shagging-reindeer jumper and fluffy coat.'

Laurel, quite unsubtly, kicks Christopher under the table. 'You little turd. Was this to try and get out of coming?'

He doesn't even bother to lie.

'Christopher.' Haf groans. She wouldn't have minded if she was in on it, but this feels unfair, like he's hung her out to dry just to save himself.

'Useless man! Even if Haf doesn't have a dress, you know Esther would drag you there. It's for *charity*, Christopher. You can't be a big baby about it. This isn't about us.'

At this, Christopher flushes bright red under the furious gaze of the three women.

'S-s-sorry, Haf,' he stutters, finally. At least he looks apologetic. 'We can go shopping tomorrow. I still have presents to buy, anyway.'

Kit raises a finger. 'I'm sorry, what?'

'Oh my God, how was I with you for so long?' cries Laurel.

'Fuck's sake, there is no way I'm going to find something, Christopher.' Haf puts her head in her hands.

'It's okay, there's lots of time—'

'No, Christopher, you don't understand,' Haf says, her face glowing hot from the embarrassment of having to point out the fucking obvious. 'I wear plus size, Christopher. Have you ever been to a woman's shop on a normal British high street? Most top out at size sixteen. They never have anything in plus sizes, and if they do, it's like one enormous T-shirt dress and a too-frilly ditsy tea dress. That's it. The fancier shops won't even have that. I buy pretty much everything online, and nothing will get here in time.'

Christopher looks like he's about to shrivel up from sheer mortification.

'You are the worst,' hisses Kit, taking her turn to kick him under the table.

With a flick, Laurel picks up her gigantic phone and begins scrolling, counting under her breath. It's such a flourished move that everyone watches her in rapt silence. After a few moments, she looks up, beaming. 'Okay, perfect. I have the time. I'll do it.'

'Do what?' asks Kit.

'Haf, I'm going to make you a dress. If you come over first thing tomorrow, I'll get your measurements, we can go through my ideas, and I've got plenty of fabric that could work. I can do it.'

Haf is completely taken aback by this. She didn't even know Laurel could sew, and really, she doesn't even know Laurel at all. And yet here she is offering to sew her something for a party in less than forty-eight hours' time?

'Laurel, that's so kind, but you don't have to do that for me.'

'I know I don't have to,' Laurel says with such a confident air that Haf is in awe. 'I want to, and I have the time, now that

Kit helped me finish everything this afternoon. I never get the opportunity to work with a model. You'd be doing me a favour, Haf.'

'Don't you have a ball to plan?'

'Oh no, Mummy organises most of that, and luckily Christopher has just kindly volunteered himself to step in on my behalf for sorting out the last few bits.'

'Have I?'

'Yes,' she says, so sweetly it's kind of terrifying. She taps away at her phone.

'That's probably fair,' he concedes.

'I . . . I don't know what to say, but thank you,' Haf stammers, her head swimming.

Laurel's phone buzzes. 'Hi, Mummy.' She listens for a second, then hands the phone over to Christopher. He nods and agrees a few times, before saying goodbye and handing it back to Laurel.

'She says I have to come over now so she can walk me through everything. Are you all right with that? I'm sorry we won't be able to hang out here. Should we drop you home?'

'Don't be silly. Kit can show Haf around,' says Laurel simply.

'Oh, you don't have to,' Haf protests.

'No, Haf, you deserve to enjoy all the sights of an Oxlea Christmas. You looked like you were having such a good time until this one dropped the ball.' She chuckles briefly at this accidental pun. 'You two are great friends now, after all.'

If this were a movie, an enormous flashing danger sign would appear out of nowhere. Wandering around with her fake boyfriend being silly was a much more relaxed option. With Kit, she'll be spending the whole time ignoring her body screaming, *Kiss her!* while her brain tries very, very hard not to.

'I don't mind,' says Kit with a shrug. 'But I'm a bit tired, so we can't stay late if I'm going to drive us back. That okay?'

'Of course. I just want to see the reindeer again and go round the stalls.'

'That's doable.'

*Okay, that's not too bad,* she thinks. And hopefully they won't run into Sally.

'Perfect, we'll dash off after the lights,' says Laurel. 'Esther will murder us if we leave before that.'

Christmas music cuts through the sounds of the fête, followed by the voices of a full choir. They're singing 'Hark the Herald Angels Sing', and it feels like a summons. All at once, it feels like all the attendees turn and walk towards the Christmas tree. It's kind of magical – little kids bounce around excitedly and even the adults look rosy and happy.

'Come on, let's go show our faces,' says Kit, who leads the way through the gathering crowd towards the Christmas tree.

Christopher takes her by the arm as they walk. 'I'm sorry.'

'Mmm, you and I are going to have a talk about this later,' she murmurs. Somehow, Christopher manages to go paler, and she only feels about 5 per cent bad about it.

'We have bigger problems right now,' she whispers, pointing ahead of them. On the other side of the crowd stands Sally. 'We need to make sure that none of your family or Laurel bump into her, especially with us present.'

Christopher gulps.

They cluster together with Laurel and Kit. Up on the stage, a full choir performs, dressed in red velvet robes. Traditional song over, they switch to The Ronettes' 'Sleigh Ride', and the crowd bops along happily.

Behind the choir at the back of the stage stand Esther and Otto, along with a man who Haf presumes is Mayor Clarke from the gigantic gold necklace.

As the singing ends and the music fades out, everyone applauds and Esther steps up to the mic. 'Welcome, everyone, to this year's Oxlea Christmas Celebration!'

Once again, the crowd claps and cheers. Apparently, the people of Oxlea love a bit of enthusiastic participation.

'Thank you all for joining us to celebrate together. Remember, all your donations go towards the primary-school library budget, so dig deep and buy a few more mulled wines. There are donation boxes all around, so put in what you can. And if anyone wants to make a larger or longer-term donation, please come find me so we can talk.

'I am extremely passionate about literacy for all, and where this country is failing in getting books into children's hands, we in Oxlea are making a difference to a number of partner schools in our area. So, enjoy the festivities! And let there be light!'

And with that, the Christmas tree lights up in sparkling gold, candy red and silver. The light bounces off the ornaments, dappling light all around them. The star at the top of the tree turns out to be a giant light of its own and shines brightly. Around them, more and more strings of lights turn on until the whole green is a beautiful shining beacon. It is really stunning. Esther and all the other hard workers have done an amazing job.

As the choir bursts into 'Marshmallow World' – in Haf's opinion, another massively underrated bop – the whole crowd joins in, linking arms and waving their hands, mugs of wine and even the odd child. This is quite possibly the most Christmassy she's ever felt. A few songs and a lot more dancing later, the crowd starts to disperse off to buy hot food, judge snowmen and browse all the things for sale.

'We should get going,' says Laurel, linking arms with Christopher. 'It was so nice to see you again, Haf. I'm looking forward to getting to know you better tomorrow.'

She flashes a smile, and they're off through the crowd, Christopher waving a goodbye in the air behind them.

'She's kind of a whirlwind, isn't she?' Kit says with affection.

'I can't believe she's going to make me a dress. I just . . . That's such a lot to do for a person you just met! Even if she says it's me doing her a favour, which I'm not buying.'

'Laurel loves to do the unexpected,' Kit says. 'And she really does care about people. She's got a big heart under all the influencer aesthetic. Sorry, this is probably a bit weird for you, isn't it?'

'What is?' Haf asks, scanning the crowd ahead.

'Your boyfriend and his ex?' Kit prompts, just as a flash of orange peeks through the crowd up ahead.

'Oh!' shouts Haf, stopping in her tracks. Kit spins towards her, a concerned look on her face, but crucially is now facing the opposite way from Sally, who is ambling towards them.

'What?' cries Kit.

'Your shoelace!' Haf says a little too loudly and drops to her knees to untie Kit's lace. 'I didn't want you to trip.'

'Oh, I didn't realise it had come loose,' Kit mutters. 'Thanks for that.'

'No problem!' Haf says, fiddling with the knot.

Truthfully, it hasn't loosened at all, and Haf tugs at it with numb fingers in the hope that she's giving a good impression of someone who might be tying a knot. She can't even tie her own shoes at the best of times; Ambrose is forever doing it for her.

'And no, it's totally fine!' she says, looking up at Kit from her feet. 'I know they're friends.'

'Mmm, sort of,' Kit murmurs as Haf clambers back to her feet, wondering if maybe she should be acting more worried. What would a real girlfriend do? Is it a bit too Cool Girl of her to be calm about it?

Haf doesn't have much time to ponder this because, typically, Sally must have been waylaid along the path, as she's now only a few steps away from them.

'Wow! Look at these!' Haf shrieks, pulling Kit over to a stall.

It's a stand with rows of beautifully knitted gloves and scarves run by a tiny squat lady covered head to toe in her own creations.

'Oh, these are nice,' Kit says as Haf points out a thick green scarf that matches her coat. 'Are you going to get something?'

The stallholder looks hopefully up at them, but keeps her lips pressed together in a polite smile. If Haf was being sensible, she would spend the last few pounds in her sad bank account on a pair of Fair Isle red and white gloves that catch her eye, but instead she shoves her hands deeper into her coat pockets.

'I don't get paid until after Christmas,' she sighs.

'Urgh, the worst.'

'Do you have a website?' she asks the seller, who tells her about the various places she can buy her wares and hands her a business card.

Kit is still eyeing the green scarf, and slips off a glove to touch it. 'You should get it,' encourages Haf. 'It looks soft.'

'Yeah, actually, I will,' she says, and luckily, is busy getting her card out and paying as Sally walks past them, sauntering off into the distance.

Haf watches her vanish and breathes a sigh of relief.

'How do I look?' Her attention snaps back to Kit, who has wrapped the scarf around her face so that the tip of her nose peeks out over it.

There are so many words she wants to say, but instead Haf goes for a safe and enthusiastic 'Great!' with a thumbs up to seal the deal.

'Come on, let's get some food in you,' says Kit. 'I can hear your stomach gurgling all the way from here.'

Another time, Haf might have been embarrassed to know her stomach could be heard through a thick scarf, but she's too flooded with relief to care.

An enormous floury bap stuffed with melt-in-your-mouth roasted pork slathered in apple sauce later, and Haf feels a little restored. Kit too.

'What do you want to do now we've fed you?' Kit asks. 'There's the snowman contest, which they'll probably judge soon before all the kids fall asleep. Then a bit of shopping, and you can drink some more mulled wine? Do you want the last of my mulled cider, actually? I don't *think* it's booze, but honestly, I can't tell when it's hot,' Kit says and offers her cup out to Haf.

There's a lipstick mark on the rim, and Haf can't drag her brain from it. Those cherry-red lips in their wry smile . . . Why does mulled alcohol go to her head so quickly?

'I—' she begins, feeling completely star-struck.

'Don't worry, I'll just tip it out,' Kit says, emptying it into the snow.

'Sorry, I think I've probably had enough already. Let's just mooch, shall we?' she manages after a moment.

Kit nods, and they both wander off through the fête.

Everything is kind of perfect. At one of the stalls, Kit buys some home-made fudge, and Haf buys a tiny jar of local honey for

Ambrose, who likes to swirl it into their tea. There are stalls filled with stunning pottery and paintings and cakes, so many cakes.

They reach the snowmen contest, where all the little snow people are assembled in a row, all slightly different. Most of them are the usual generic snowman, but there's some kind of snow-monster, possibly a yeti, and someone has obviously whacked a pair of boobs supported by a lacy bra onto the front of one of them. The children stand hopefully by their creations as the mayor inspects them all. Esther watches on, garlands in hand to crown the winners. She gives Kit and Haf a little wave when she spots them.

All is perfect and well and Christmassy.

But then she spots a flash of orange. Sally is back and heading right towards them. Haf curses herself for not paying attention, too distracted by the nice time she was having with Kit.

'Wow, look at this one, Kit! It's a very, very good snowman,' she says loudly, hoping to drag her attention.

Kit naturally just gives her a slightly confused but amused look, but continues to glance around.

'No really, Kit. Come admire the creativity of these children.' Desperation is creeping into her voice almost as quickly as Sally is approaching.

'I didn't realise you cared so much about snow. Or children.' Kit laughs, joining her in front of one that really isn't very creative. It's just a bog-standard snowman, and not even a very big one at that. 'Oh hey, is that Sally?'

Haf has to bite her tongue to stop herself from swearing loudly in front of a large group of children.

'Oh yeah, ha ha,' she says airily.

Not only has Kit spotted Sally, but Esther and Sally are waving at each other across the field of snowmen, and Haf knows it's only a matter of time before any of the women start up a conversation and then everyone will realise she doesn't even know Sally, she just crashed her party and then all of this will totally fall apart.

A wave of startled cries swells towards them, and Haf turns to see the surly reindeer keeper rushing through the crowd. His face is bright red, and his eyes wild with alarm. He rushes up to Esther and takes the loudhailer from her hand and turns back to the crowd.

'The reindeer! The reindeer is out!' he pants.

People nervously look round, parents picking up young children into their arms.

'I didn't have "be stampeded any second by a herd of marauding carrot-hungry reindeer" on my lists of things I wanted to do tonight,' says Kit.

'Everyone, please calm down,' says Esther, taking the loudhailer back from him. And then, aside to the man, she says, 'This is not yours to snatch.'

'They're still in their pen?!' shouts back someone. The crowd turns at once to see all five of the big reindeer in their pen, completely nonplussed and munching away on hay.

The surly reindeer man signals for the loudhailer, and Esther reluctantly tilts it towards him.

'The little one,' he says, catching his breath. 'The little one got out. Someone stole him!'

# Chapter Thirteen

The atmosphere of the fête changes immediately.

The reindeer keeper rushes back off to the pen to make sure that no more reindeer escape or are stolen. Though stealing an adult reindeer seems like a much more difficult prospect.

Esther starts making phone calls, and the mayor does the same, the snowmen contest forgotten. A few of the children start crying, though Haf isn't quite sure if that's because Cupid is missing, or because their snowmen weren't fairly judged. At least it's cold enough that they won't melt.

'Who would steal a baby reindeer?' Kit mutters.

'Did you not see him, Kit? He was extremely cute. Like . . . really cute. And small.'

'Maybe he just slipped out?'

'I'm not sure that's better,' Haf says, nibbling at her lower lip.

'You're worried about him, aren't you?' Kit softens.

'Cupid. His name was Cupid,' corrects Haf. 'We've got to help find him.'

'Okay, sure. Let's do it.'

Haf tries to ignore the flutter in her chest at Kit's simple agreement.

'I'm trying to think where a baby reindeer would go, you know, if he got out rather than was stolen. In uni, we did a bunch of animal-behaviour stuff, but not very much on reindeer.'

'That's surprising,' Kit says dryly, and Haf pulls a tongue at her, but is thankful for the lightness. 'Hierarchy-of-needs stuff, right?'

'He already had warmth and comfort. So maybe what he wanted was food. Maybe they ran out of food while everyone was talking, and he snuck out?'

At that exact moment, a caterwaul sounds around them as a blur that might possibly be Cupid the preteen reindeer barrels right through several of the contest snowmen, stealing their carrots as he goes.

'Oh my God!' Kit laughs.

'Quick! Let's go after him,' Haf says.

'Go, I can't run. I'll catch up with you. You're the reindeer detective.'

Luckily for her, and unluckily for everyone else, Cupid is easy to follow from the chaos he leaves in his wake. After demolishing all the carrots from the snowmen, he races down the centre of the fête, knocking over tables and chairs (and many small children) as he goes.

'Cupid, stop!' she yells after him, as though he might recognise her or even know his own name, but honestly, at this point, she's desperate.

'He went that way!' cries one of the cake vendors, who is now covered in whatever they were selling.

'Thank you!' she yells.

She turns a corner and finds herself next to the raffle stand, Christopher's gingerbread house still pristine in its cake box.

A wave of cries speed towards her, and she realises that Cupid is headed straight for the raffle prizes, which are perched on top of a very flimsy-looking table.

'No!' she yells as Cupid barrels into a leg, sending all the prizes skyborne.

Including the gingerbread house.

She can't let it be destroyed. Not after all the hard work Christopher put into it.

But Cupid is so close that maybe she could grab him.

House or reindeer?

Haf runs, leaps and somehow, in the greatest luck of her whole life, she catches the gingerbread house in mid-air and lands, stumbling to her knees. Inside the box, the gingerbread house is completely intact and when she stands to put it somewhere safe, Haf comes face to face with the man from the quiet carriage, who is apparently in charge of the raffle stand.

'You!' they shout in unison.

'I—' she begins, but he cuts her off with a 'I don't want to know!', waving his hands about wildly. 'Don't tell me anything else!'

'Look after this and keep it safe,' she says, shoving it into his arms. 'Did anyone see where the reindeer went?'

Mayor Clarke, who appears to be hiding under the collapsed raffle table, points towards the stage. 'He went that way!'

Haf races off, following the mayor's directions. Up ahead, there's a huge crash and the lights on the Christmas tree flicker, and then start to fall.

He's run *through* the Christmas tree.

And apparently, taken the bottom-most layer of lights out with him.

Currently very thankful for that month she did Couch to 5k, Haf pivots and runs right round the tree. On the other side, she finds Esther yelling after Cupid, who is now wrapped in string lights like a feather boa.

'Put those back!' Esther yells after him, as though he might suddenly obey her.

'I'll grab him, don't worry!' Haf shouts as she passes.

Clearly fed up with everyone chasing him, and wanting to get away from all the chaos he has caused, Cupid changes course and runs into the dark.

Haf keeps running, following what she hopes is the sound of the wired lights against the ground. She runs past one abandoned string of lights, and then another. He's left a trail in his wake. Haf realises that she's running back towards where Christopher parked the car. But Cupid is nowhere to be seen. There are no more fairy lights, and it's so much darker over here, away from the fête.

'Haf!' Kit is calling for her, but she can't see where from. Haf spins around slowly, and spots Kit waving from the edge of the duck pond.

Running purely on adrenaline and the remains of the wine, Haf ploughs on through the snow to Kit's side.

'Did you find him?' she pants.

Kit points out into the centre of the lake. 'He's there!'

In the middle of the duck pond is an island with a bright red duck house decorated in holly and a wreath. And shivering next to it is a half-soaked, dishevelled Cupid.

'Oh thank God, he stopped,' Haf cries.

'How are we going to get him? Do you think we can coax him to swim back?'

'He looks pretty scared. Maybe we've tired him out enough that he'll let us come to him.'

'Yeah, but how? I don't think there are any paddle boats here. Where's the guy who is supposed to be looking after them?'

A big hiss cuts through the air, dragging their attention to the ice on the pond. Advancing towards Cupid is one very furious-looking goose, white feathers so puffed out that they almost stand on end. It is somehow the biggest goose that Haf has ever seen, even though she lives in York, which is basically the goose capital of England, if not the whole of Britain. She's found geese in her garden, barring the office doorway, even blocking her path, and she's managed to escape them every time. But that's because she almost always has some food to lob in the other direction to distract them.

The baby reindeer has no snacks. And so there's a good chance that the baby reindeer is about to get goosed.

Several ducks look on, concerned, but drift away on the water as the goose gets closer. They appear to know better than to stay near an angry goose.

Everyone else is still dealing with Cupid's chaos or is searching on the other side of the fête by the reindeer pen. No one can see them when it's so much darker over here, and even if they shout for someone else to come, that goose is practically on top of Cupid.

There's only one thing to be done.

'Should I go find someone?' Kit begins, but Haf cuts her off by handing her the antique Christmas hat.

'I'm going in,' she says, marching down the muddy bank towards the water.

'What?!. No! Don't be ridiculous!' Kit yells. 'You'll freeze!'

'I'll be quick!' Haf shouts back, not turning in case Kit catches up with her.

As she scrambles down the bank to the icy water, the mud gives way suddenly and she crashes straight in, up to her knees.

'Fuck my life!' she screeches at the chill and the shock of the fall.

Behind her, Kit is yelling her name.

'I'm all right!' she calls back, striding forward with teeth gritted.

The duck pond is much deeper than she expected, licking over her knees as she wades slowly. The mud in the bottom of the pond is as thick as pudding, and the plants keep wrapping around her boots. It is a struggle, but she must keep going, because if she stops, the goose will attack either her or Cupid, or they will all just freeze in this silly little pond.

The ducks swim up to her, quacking with concern and probably a bit of amusement that some enormous wally has walked into their home.

Up ahead, the goose's hissing gets louder, and it pads along the ice towards them.

'Yeah, yeah, I hear you, dickhead. Just leave us alone and we'll be out of here in a moment.'

The ducks, who realise she has nothing to offer them, start to back away. She wonders what it says about her that the ducks seem more capable of sensible decisions than she is.

The little reindeer makes a sad little noise, something between a mew and a honk.

'Oh my God, there's someone in the lake!' she hears someone shout behind her, and she risks a glance over her shoulder to see a crowd gathering.

'It's Haf! She's found the reindeer,' she hears Kit shout back.

'Someone call the fire brigade? The RNLI?' Another voice shouts, unsure which emergency service is correct for someone voluntarily walking into an ice-cold pond.

'Keep going! It would be really embarrassing if you froze out there!' Kit yells.

Over her head, Haf puts up her middle finger, and she hears a few gasps, realising there's probably children behind her too.

'Sorry!' she yells back and catches the sound of Kit laughing in the air.

As she turns back to the mission at hand, she realises the goose is closer than she thought. It perches right on the edge of the ice, stretching its neck and nasty little beak out as far as it will go.

Haf likes pretty much every animal going, but this might be the goose that breaks the camel's back.

As she gets closer, it hisses at her and flaps its huge wings.

'Fuck off,' she barks at the goose, hoping it will go away.

On the upside, it now seems no longer interested in Cupid. The downside is that it's ready to murder Haf instead.

Wiggling her foot free, Haf takes another quick step forward, arms stretched out for Cupid, who has been watching this whole farce with what can only be the reindeer equivalent of great concern.

Will he even let her pick him up? He's much bigger than she remembers, now that she's closer to him. And those tiny antlers are almost certainly going to give her a black eye.

'Come on, Cupie. It's me, your old friend Haf. The one with the carrots. Let's get out of this nightmare, come on,' she coos.

Haf takes one last stride forward, Cupid almost within reach, but as she does, the horrible goose leaps forward and grasps her arm in its beak. The entire act shocks her so much that she doesn't make a single noise, and simply keels over, landing arse first in the duck pond. The disgusting water goes practically up to her chin.

A wave of cries goes up from the crowd, followed by several people yelling her name.

Arse suctioned firmly to the mud, Haf rolls herself upwards and staggers to her feet in a kind of rough doggy paddle.

To her surprise, the crowd cheers.

And the sound is followed by a series of very loud thuds.

An army of children has assembled on the bank and are throwing snowballs right at the goose. They all have terrific aim – a credit to the Oxlea school district's physical education programme – and soon the goose is dodging and swerving out of the way of huge chunks of snow. To her relief, it begins to back away across the ice, and to the bank furthest away from the frozen artillery regiment, hissing and honking as it goes.

Soaked to the bone, Haf reaches out again for the baby reindeer.

Unsurprisingly, Cupid doesn't see a rescuer in front of him as much as a veritable swamp monster, and so doesn't seem particularly inclined to leap into her arms.

'Come on, babe. Let's get out of here,' she pleads. 'I'm freezing my tits off.'

At her words, Cupid begins sniffing, scenting the air. He stretches out his long neck and sniffs right in the direction of her boobs.

By some kind of miracle, and well-constructed underwiring, the carrot she found before is still wedged in her bra.

'You want this?' she says, taking it out to show him. Her ice-cold fingers against her warm skin make her shriek. In a flash Cupid has taken it from her hand and she sweeps him up into her arms. His little tail wiggles with delight as he happily munches away.

Together, they wade slowly back as the fête attendees start to clap and cheer. His back legs drag a little in the water, and he keeps kicking his feet up to keep them dry, and whacking Haf directly in the stomach as he goes.

'Just a bit longer, mate, come on.'

As well as not accounting for how big he is, Haf had not considered how heavy he was and how little carrying of living animals she's done.

Her soaked body is screeching at her to give up, to drop the reindeer, to leg it out of here, or to just expire so she won't have to feel any of the above any more.

'Come on, you're almost there,' Kit shouts from the bank, antique Santa hat jauntily placed on her head. 'Just focus on me!'

So Haf does. Eyes on Kit, she takes one step at a time. Cupid, who is now done with his carrot, begins to honk happily, rubbing his head against her shoulder. She takes this as a sign of encouragement too.

They're almost at the bank, and so many arms stretch out towards them.

She pulls her foot up in the shallows with an enormous glug, and falters, the foot underwater sliding and she's certain she's about to fall over, crashing both her and reindeer into the muck.

But someone grabs her, and she's steady. She lets out a huge breath and opens her eyes, to find Kit in the water with her.

'Last few steps,' she says, steadying them both with her walking stick against the bank. 'You're almost done.'

'Who'd have thought wading through a mucky pond with a baby reindeer in your arms would be hard, eh?' Haf jokes through gritted teeth.

'What a trio we make.' Kit laughs, pulling her along. 'Clumsy, chaos and the structurally unstable.'

'Which is which?'

'That's the beauty of it – those could apply to any of us.'

Otto steadies Haf as she climbs up the bank. Cupid, now back on dry land, desperately wants to get down, but she absolutely cannot let go of him now. Not yet. Not after being savaged by a goose and possibly contracting trench foot.

He turns to help Kit out, who slips in the mud and splashes back into the pool with a very loud sharp, 'FUCK!'

An older lady mutters something about the language of youth these days, which is overshadowed by Kit climbing out and hissing, 'Fuuuuuck,' once again at the sight of her completely sodden, muck-soaked boots.

Around them, the onlookers cheer and whoop and clap. Haf feels like a hero, albeit a soggy one that you shouldn't stand too close to because she's pretty sure she smells absolutely disgusting. Adrenaline fading and cold setting in, she starts to shiver and is very thankful for the warm little body of the reindeer.

'Someone go get some blankets!' Esther yells, and a bunch of people scurry off. A coat is wrapped around her shoulders, and she's guided back towards the fête.

Everything is still a bit chaotic, but most of Cupid's antics have been rectified. Several people eye him warily. Most just give her proud smiles or thumbs up. She even gets a few 'good on you's.

Haf and Kit (and Cupid) are guided to the picnic tables near the mulled-wine stand, and as they sit down, people with blankets materialise and practically cocoon them in wool. Despite all the layers, she's still shivering.

It's not long before the reindeer man appears, having been looking in the exact opposite end of Oxlea's green.

'Oh my God, thank you,' he cries, sagging with relief. 'Thank you so much for finding him.'

Realising he's finally going home, Cupid does a big carroty huff of hot air in Haf's face and nuzzles his nose against her chin.

'Looks like you've adopted a reindeer,' Kit says, tickling his velvety nose.

Haf sighs. 'No, I'm afraid you'll have to go home now, Cupie,' says Haf. She squeezes him tightly, plants a kiss on his damp forehead and passes him over to the reindeer keeper. 'Bye bye, little pal.'

Cupid honks a little goodbye, and as the man carries him away, she can see his tiny tail wiggling.

It's then, when everything is finally over, that she completely crashes. Tears spring to her eyes, and she has to bite down on her lip to stop herself from bawling in the middle of this crowd of mostly strangers.

'Hey,' Kit whispers. 'It's okay. You saved the day, and he's safe now.'

Sniffing, Haf does a very wobbly nod.

'Is the gingerbread house okay?'

'Our one? That was definitely not okay.'

'No,' she sniffs. 'Christopher's one. I saved it from Cupid.'

'I'll find out, I promise. But first we need to get you home.' Kit looks down at the muck that is starting to solidify on Haf's clothes. 'And washed.'

# Chapter Fourteen

Turns out, it's a terrible idea to wade into a duck pond in the middle of winter. Even though the donated blankets sopped up the excess, Haf is still soaked. Luckily, the drive home isn't very long and Kit blasts all the heaters.

They pull up in front of the Calloway house, and when she turns the ignition off, Kit's whole body sags.

A little warmer now, if still very damp, Haf scurries around the car and opens the door for her.

'Do you want a hand?' she says, offering one from her blankety outer layer.

'God, yeah. Thanks,' Kit says, taking her hand and pulling herself up to standing. Under her eyes, the skin is dark, and Haf feels guilty for keeping her out in the snow on a wild reindeer chase when clearly Kit needed to come home and rest.

'Come on, we'd better get in and warm up. And wipe some of the crap off me,' she says, locking the car behind her.

'Not actual crap, I hope?'

'It *was* a duck pond. A prime place for duck-poo accumulation.'

'Oh God . . . Do I smell of poo?!'

Kit theatrically sniffs her. 'Just reindeer and . . . a touch of frozen dickhead.'

'Oh, ha ha.'

The front door rattles a little as Stella and Luna jump up against it from the inside, whining as they go. When Kit unlocks the door, they rush out, circling both women and jumping up and down around them.

Once they're all in the porch with the door closed, the dogs stop bouncing around. Instead, with deep concern, they sniff at Haf and Kit's dirty clothes as if to say, 'Just what the heck were you up to without us?'

Taking off the muck-covered Doc Martens is a frankly disgusting task, and Haf pogoes about to avoid having to touch them with her hands any more than she needs to. Not that her hands are particularly clean, either.

Kit pulls a large blue Ikea bag out from a tote bag of bags hanging from the coat hooks. 'Throw all your stuff in there and we'll either wash it all or nuke it. Your choice.'

'Even the shoes? Feels wrong to put shoes on clothes.'

'I think they're about as disgusting as the rest of you,' she says, to which Haf protests with a harrumph. 'I mean your clothes. Plus, Esther will have a coronary if either of us goes into that house covered in duck shit, so come on. Strip.'

To her horror, Kit just starts undoing her jeans.

Haf's face is on fire, and she turns away so quickly that she almost slides into the door. 'I'm not looking!' she shouts.

'Fine, but come on, get yours off too. And the blanket mound. I'll shut my eyes.'

There are plenty of circumstances when Haf wouldn't think twice about stripping off her clothes, but usually that doesn't involve stripping in front of the woman she's trying to convince herself she doesn't have a crush on while standing in her fake in-laws' front porch.

She takes a deep breath and just gets on with it.

'I'm keeping my underwear on.'

'Obviously,' Kit mutters.

'Was it obvious? You told me to strip.' Haf sulks as she peels her disgusting jumper off over her head.

Haf opens her eyes to put everything in the bag, which she keeps her eyes firmly fixed on and tries to ignore the fact that Kit is also standing in front of her in her underwear, looking intently at the bag.

'Do you want me to carry that through?' she offers with a gulp.

'We'll take it together,' says Kit, taking a handle. 'Your blankets are heavy.'

Together, they drag it through the house, down a corridor off the kitchen. There's a couple of doors here, and one leads into a compact laundry room. They release the bag in front of the washing machine, and in the confines of this small room, Haf realises that everything really does reek.

Including her.

'You go upstairs and use the shower on our floor. I'll clean up in Esther's en suite, and then get the fire going,' Kit says, padding back through the house.

Without another word, Haf obeys.

They both wander up the stairs, and Haf stares intently at the steps.

Calvin Klein. They were a black matching Calvin Klein set.

Before her horrible brain can think any more about Kit being half-naked in front of her, Kit disappears into a room on the first floor. Haf continues upstairs, waddling and willing her aching, frozen legs up. She can't give up, because just collapsing here in her pants would probably be the worst scenario, somehow.

The hot shower is a welcome relief, even if her skin is so cold that it almost burns when she gets in. She was too tired to dig out the shower stuff from Christopher's room, and knew if she saw the bed, she'd just clamber in and go to sleep, so she picks up a fancy bottle from the side and squeezes out a big blob. Unsure if her hair was wet or pooed on, she decides to wash it too, just to be safe.

At least she smells better now, for definite.

It takes her two attempts to get out because on the first go, the house is so cold that she goes back in and turns the water on to heat herself back up.

Eventually, she wanders back downstairs, dressed in clean pyjamas, hair still wrapped in a towel because God knows whether Christopher would have a hairdryer.

To her relief, Kit has got the fire going in the living room. She and the dogs are curled up in a nest of cushions and (clean) blankets in front of the fire. Stella lies on her back, belly warm and pink. Kit lies with her head propped up by a cushion, Luna curled up against her chest. Her eyes are closed, but she's gently massaging Luna's ears.

It's such a sweet moment that Haf wants to stand in the doorway and watch quietly, committing this softness to memory.

But the house is too damn cold.

'You lifesaver,' she says, walking in. 'Need anything?'

'I'm good right now. Come join us,' Kit murmurs, sleepily patting the covers.

Too tired for grace, Haf flops down and buries herself in the nest. There's an underlayer of a duvet that Kit must have dragged from somewhere.

Sensing the opportunity for fussing, Stella wriggles herself over. Haf strokes her soft warm belly, and when she gets the right spot, the dog's little foot kicks.

'Look at you. You're practically the patron saint of small mammals,' says Kit.

'What about you?' she replies, nodding towards Luna who is now snoring deeply. 'You could be too.'

'I don't think I'm as dedicated as you are.'

'Hmm, okay. Is that my official title? Do I get bonuses, like days off?'

'It should be. And I don't think saints get days off. Come to think of it, most of them are dead.'

'The ultimate day off?'

'Dark,' laughs Kit. 'You're no Ferris Bueller.'

'Thank the saints for that.'

'Do you want some wine?' Kit asks, indicating a bottle and two glasses on the step in front of the fireplace. 'I know something hot is probably better when we've got so cold, but this Malbec is the first thing I grabbed.'

'God, yes,' says Haf. 'I'll take anything that's wine and drinkable.'

'A real connoisseur then.' Kit laughs. She slops a good amount into both glasses and passes one to Haf. 'Cheers.'

'*Iechyd da*' Haf says.

'Is that Welsh?'

She nods. 'It means cheers. *Yeah*, then you've got to get a nice guttural sound for the *chi*, and then *dar*.'

Kit sounds out a plausible version of her own and looks very pleased with herself.

Their glasses clink together, sparkling in the flame light. Haf takes a sip, and it's delicious, much nicer than the heavy cheap red wine she occasionally drank at uni. That always gave her head-aches, in addition to the general hangover.

'You surprised me today,' Kit says after a while. 'I don't know many people who'd willingly wade into a bog in the middle of winter to rescue a reindeer that probably didn't really need res-cuing.'

'He was scared! You're going to make a *baby* swim in frozen waters?'

Kit takes a sip of her wine, her lips curved into a smirk.

'Stop teasing me.' Haf huffs.

'You just make it very easy.'

Haf unwraps her hair from the towel, letting it hang in loose, damp curls which she periodically scrunches with the towel. She's pretty sure whatever she scrubbed her head with is not going to be curly-hair friendly and she is going to end up with a megaton of frizz that she can hopefully fix in the morning. Perhaps she'll get lucky and find out duck shit has secret nutritious hair-curling powers.

'Anyway, it was just a duck pond. It's not the grossest thing I've waded into.'

'Really?' Kit eyes her with surprise. 'What other foul places have you waded into?'

'Well, my degree is in ecology, which to be honest meant a lot of standing around in very cold places doing surveys on what animals and plants are there,' Haf explains, taking another sip of wine. 'On one trip, we all had to collect a cube of anoxic mud – so like, no oxygen in it at all – and see what animals were inside it. And honestly, the poopy duck pond had nothing on that.'

Pondering this for a moment, Kit says, 'So you just counted a lot of animals?'

'Yep. I'm really good at it, look.' She points to Stella, then Luna. 'One, two. And two humans, if you want to be technical about it.'

Kit laughs throatily. 'And are you still counting animals for work?'

'God, I wish. And it's more complicated than that, Miss Makes-Buildings.'

'I'm sure it is!'

'Anyway, no. I hoped I'd be able to go out and do a bit, even just so I could write about it, but it's all like writing stuff to convince various people to give us money so we can do more stuff. Like, "Hey assuage your guilt and give us some cash, yeah?"'

'Wow, I never thought I'd hear you be cynical about anything,' Kit says, a little shocked.

'Really? Why's that?'

'You're just so . . . earnest.'

'Wow. Thanks?'

'It's a nice thing, really. I don't mean it in a bad way.'

'Well, now you've absolutely convinced me. Do you not get a lot of that in architecture? I'd have thought you'd all be jizzing yourself over bricks, or something.'

Kit snorts with laughter. '*Jizzing ourselves?!*'

'Yeah, you know. "Ooh, that's a lovely bit of wall. Look at that light."'

From her blanket pile comes even more giggles, and Kit must take a moment to calm down before she can speak again.

'To answer your original question—'

'Not about the jizzing?'

'No, no more jizzing talk please. Anyway . . .' She blows out her cheeks as if to reset herself. 'No, there's not a lot of earnestness in private architecture. There's a lot of overworked people making expensive apartments for people in London that are bought for investment and barely occupied, which ultimately just function to drive up the price of everything else around them.'

'Wow. Are we playing cynicism Top Trumps now?'

'Is it cynicism when it's just so obviously happening? I think it's fine to be realistic about the limitations of what we do for work.' Kit sighs. She pushes herself up to sitting and wiggles round so that she's leaning against the couch, as though being serious demanded that she be a bit more upright. 'Don't get me wrong, I love it, or some of it. I love designing a permanent place for someone to live, or a really beautiful workplace that anyone can use and enjoy. But there's bits of it I don't love, and even am a bit morally conflicted on. That's before you even add in working full-time as a disabled woman.' Kit drains the last of the glass of wine. 'Sorry, you probably don't want to hear about that.'

'Sure I do,' Haf says, shifting round to face her.

Kit taps her fingers against the glass, a strand of hair behind her ear.

'Look, I'll put on my very best listening face,' Haf says, pressing her fists against her cheeks and widening her eyes and smile into the most enthusiastic face she can make.

'Please, stop,' Kit laughs. 'Whatever you're trying to do is horrible!'

'What? What do you mean?'

'That face!'

Haf raises her eyebrows and makes her eyes even wider.

'What face? This is just my rapt face.'

'I hate it!' Kit laughs. 'Please no more listening-face. Maybe just don't look at me.'

'All right, all right,' she concedes.

Haf shifts back round to face the fire and leans back against the couch as well, giving the muscles in her back a much-needed break. The wine is helping, as did the hot shower, but stiffness is setting in, especially in the muscles she didn't even know she had.

Beside her, Kit fidgets with her hair as she works out where to start. 'The thing is, sometimes people see the walking stick before me. It's not always easy to work out how someone is going to react, which is a lot of mental energy with new people.'

'I can relate to that,' Haf says, before realising she just interrupted. 'Sorry, go on.'

'Some people are just like "Oh hey, a cool walking stick, okay."
Others start wondering why I'm using one when I'm a young person, which means they ask a bunch of questions like "Why are
you using that?" or "Did you break your leg?" and then they get
all shirty when I tell them I'm disabled, like I offended them. And
sometimes that means that they talk down to me, like I'm a child.'

'I can't imagine anyone talking down to you,' Haf mutters. 'Not
that I don't believe they do, from what you say. I just mean, I can't
believe they'd do that to you specifically, seeing as you're, you
know . . . terrifying.'

'That's sweet of you.'

'I truly mean it.'

'I bet,' she says with a wolfish grin. 'And yet still, I get fucked
around a lot or they misunderstand, though sometimes I can't
help but feel they're doing that wilfully. Like how is it complicated to understand going to the office unnecessarily wipes me
out, and I will do better and more work at home, where I can
look after myself, rather than satisfying someone's desire for pre-
senteeism?'

'Do they just presume you're slacking off or something?'

'Yeah, even though I'm handing in the work.'

'That . . . doesn't even make sense.'

'Tell me about it. The amount of energy I have to waste fighting
for a bit of adjustment and then explaining that I am still working
is ridiculous.'

'Especially because you must already be exhausted, like all the
time? I've known you like forty-eight hours and I feel like I've
worked that out.'

'I appreciate that, by the way.'

Haf shrugs. 'It shouldn't be a big deal to meet someone where
they're at.'

'Hmm,' Kit says. 'Quite. Anyway, all this makes a person pretty
tenacious, or it did for me. I'll never let them squash me out when
I deserve to be there and supported at the same time, irrespective
of the good work I do. And the good PR for them.'

'Ugh, seriously?'

'Seriously. Which is fucking bullshit, because they should do that anyway, because I'm good. I'm really fucking good.'

'I can imagine,' Haf says softly. 'You know . . . I really admire you. I wish I could stand up for myself more. It's not the same thing but . . .'

'No, go on. Tell me about it,' Kit encourages.

'I just . . . I feel like there's nothing left of me after work. I'm just doing so much and they won't hire anyone to help—'

'And I bet like they're acting like it's your fault you're not keeping up.'

'Exactly! Like, maybe part of it *is* me. Maybe I'm not suited to it. But I feel so ground down that I can't even work it out.'

'What does Christopher say about it? I figure out of everyone he probably gets what it's like to work for a place that's eating away at you.'

'Yeah, what's up with that?' she mutters. 'Why doesn't he just quit?'

'You tell me.' Kit sighs. 'I know he doesn't tell you much about important things like Christmas traditions and major events you might have to attend, but surely you've talked about that?'

Talking to Kit has been so easy that Haf has to remind herself that she's supposed to be his girlfriend. 'Err, only a little. He holds a lot in, doesn't he?' she says.

'That's the Calloway way. What would you do if you didn't work there any more? Can you afford to just quit?'

'That would require them to pay me a decent wage,' she laughs. 'It's not just that, though . . . It's more like I don't trust myself to make good decisions. Like, whenever I pick something, make a firm decision, it seems like the right thing in the moment. But so often it feels like things don't pan out the way I expect. I just don't trust my judgement. Better the devil you know, right? I mean, I *did* just get into a pond in the middle of winter.'

It all spills out of her so fast she can barely catch her breath. Everything she's been holding in threatens to unleash right now, probably in part thanks to the glass of wine she apparently already finished. It's like she can't get enough air and her heart is leaping— but then Kit is there, facing her and her hand on her knee.

'Breathe slowly. Follow me,' she commands, and every cell in Haf's body obeys, matching Kit's long deep breaths.

They're so close. So very close that Haf can smell the remnants of the deep oud perfume Kit wears, imprinted in the wool of her jumper.

Kit watches her breathing, and Haf has to drag her eyes away from her, over and over. It's like looking at the sun; she's going to get burned if she looks too long.

'I'm okay,' she says eventually, even though she's not really okay for a very different reason – Kit's hand is on her leg.

'We don't have to talk about it any more, but I will say one thing. You might be a bit, how would you say it? Esther would say "socially unpolished"—'

'Wow, thanks.'

'—but people seem to respond to you. When you came out from the swamp, Esther put *her coat* on you. I'm her kid, and I'm pretty sure she wouldn't do that for me.'

Haf scrunches up her face. 'I don't think she likes me more than you. Even if you do seem to spend all your time annoying her by "being vulgar".'

'Perhaps not,' Kit laughs. 'But she trusts you, or she thinks she can rely on you. I don't know. There's something open about you that people respond to, so maybe you should be doing something with people, rather than behind a screen?'

There's probably some element of truth to this, but this conversation makes her feel deeply strange. She doesn't want to break the trust of Esther, and while she's not sure Kit necessarily trusts her, it still makes her feel unmoored to know she's lying to them all. The lie is an itchy second skin.

'You're a people person, even if you're a bit wonky about it.'

'Hey!' she protests.

'I didn't say it was a bad thing,' laughs Kit. 'It's just very different from me. I'm not the warmest of people at first meeting. Can you imagine children listening to me telling them to pick up trash? They'd kick me in the back of the knee and run off.'

'I'm sure there's at least a few children desperate for a bit of cold authority. You know, future civil servants, cult members and that.'

'Fucking hell.' Kit laughs, swatting at her. 'So you're saying only the children primed for a bit of brainwashing would listen to me? That's a more damning indictment of my character than anything else I've heard.'

'I was trying to gas you up!' Haf shrieks as Kit whacks her squarely in the face with a cushion. 'I thought you'd love to know you'd make a great dictator!'

She takes a cushion from the pile, much to Stella's annoyance, and bats it gently at Kit, who cackles in her face. 'Is that all you've got?'

Chaos unleashes as Kit and Haf scrabble for more cushions to lob at each other, giggling like children. For all Kit's sarcasm and coolness, it turns out she is also very silly. The dancing in the kitchen should have been a giveaway, but here Kit is scrabbling about and hiding behind furniture, very into this pillow fight.

'You'll never win!' She cackles from behind an armchair. 'I know where all the pillows are.'

And on cue, a tiny embroidered decorative pillow whizzes just past Haf's head.

'I have the power of sneakiness on my side,' Haf says, edging slowly around the couch.

'Sneaky? Have you heard yourself? You are a very loud person.'

Luckily, Kit is looking the other way, and Haf creeps closer to her. Just as Haf goes to take a proper swing, Kit spins round and clamps the cushion between her hands like she's squashing a bug. The move shocks Haf so much that she barely notices as Kit yanks it out from her hands and lobs it across the room, where it lands with a soft thud.

They kneel facing each other, and Kit is so close to her that she can practically taste the wine on Kit's breath.

'Aha! And now you're unarmed. What are you going to do now, huh?'

Haf can think of so many things.

In another universe, Haf would reach out and kiss her. Pull Kit into her arms and press their wine-stained mouths together. Or maybe, she would push a loose strand of hair back behind her ear, and kiss the newly bare skin where jaw meets neck.

Or she could push her down onto the floor, straddle her.

Truthfully, Haf wants to bottle this moment, along with their dancing in the kitchen. This freeness, this complete silliness between them. What would it be like to have a million moments like this? A quiet forever of domesticity and silly jokes. Of poorly assembled gingerbread houses, and of lovingly given painkillers washed down with mugs of tea. A lifetime of dancing in the kitchen.

They *could* be really good friends.

But is that all she wants?

Is it all Kit wants?

Their eyes lock, and her lips part, just slightly.

Kit is so close to her. All they do is breathe.

The fire crackles, and so does the tension between them.

Is this it? Is this the moment where she throws it all away, throws away all the lies and subterfuge just for a kiss?

Kit's eyes dart to her lips, and Haf feels hypnotised, unable to move, and honestly, she does not want to.

It feels like if she doesn't kiss Kit right now, the world might end.

And that's when the front door slams shut.

The dogs leap to their feet, awoken from their slumber, and rush, barking, to the front door. The yaps are so loud in the quiet Kit and Haf had built, the quiet of their own private universe.

In a flash, Kit is on her feet and walking to the front door to greet Otto and Esther who have returned home.

Everything feels blurry. Not from the wine, but that isn't helping. She feels whiplashed.

Haf gets to her feet awkwardly, but her mind is still swirling.

Was Kit thinking about kissing me?

Dazed, she walks to the hallway to greet Esther and Otto. Catching her eyes, Kit rushes off to the kitchen, calling back, 'I'll go make tea for you both.'

There's a split second as she passes where their eyes meet, and Kit looks away quickly. It's a message. *You got the wrong idea. This isn't happening. Move on.* Haf feels sick.

'How was the end of the fête?' she asks, desperate to force her mind onto something else. Anything else.

'Once the reindeer debacle was dealt with, everything went as planned. Naturally,' says Esther, unwinding a scarf from her neck. She hangs it over the back of the chair by the hall telephone.

'You did very well, my dear,' says Otto, who kisses her on the cheek.

It's such a tender, delicate moment that Haf feels like she's intruded on their intimacy, on a lifetime of knowing each other and bending together.

'How are you doing, dear? You must be tired after your death-defying adventures.' Esther laughs, but it's not unkind. Maybe Kit was right. Perhaps Esther does like her, at least a little bit.

'Oh yes, I'm fine now. Just tired.'

'Good, I'm glad Kit looked after you. Is Christopher not back yet?'

Her heart plummets into her stomach. She hasn't even thought about him. Didn't even text him to tell him what happened, or that she's safe. He didn't even cross her mind when she was about to kiss Kit. Fuck, she's the worst person alive.

'No, he's still at Laurel's, I think,' she croaks.

'I'm sure he'll be back any moment.'

'Yeah, I'm sure. I'll give him a text to make sure he's not stuck in the snow. But I'm just going to go off to bed,' Haf says, giving a little wave of the hand. 'Long day!'

'Yes, goodnight, dear,' Otto says with a broad smile.

Her muscles protest as she trudges upstairs. Haf slumps down onto the bed. A fox barks in the distance, and the telltale twit-twoo of two owls echoes through the dark.

She must stop thinking about what could have happened. For the first part, she probably was imagining it, or misread the signals. Maybe it was the wine clouding her judgement.

But the thing is, deep in her heart, she knows that it doesn't matter. Because what just happened has proved something to her.

She wants Kit.

There's no denying it. This crush has spiralled out of control, and suppressing her thoughts and feelings did nothing. She can't pretend she wants them to be just friends, can't pretend it's just a physical attraction.

A crush is just want – lust and the spark of attraction and hunger. And she does want, oh boy, does she *want*.

But the problem that's dawning on her is that she doesn't just want Kit that way; she's starting to feel things. Yearning, needful feelings that are deep and scary and real.

She wants more than just the wanting. She *feels* more than just the wanting.

And she has no idea what to do about it.

# Chapter Fifteen

Despite worrying that they would talk about the events of the evening in bed, Christopher got home late and fell asleep with barely a word to Haf. It had only taken him a few minutes to nod off. Not that she minds; she didn't exactly want to tell him about what happened, or might have almost happened, between her and Kit. She doesn't want to admit that she nearly jeopardised everything. Or that she might possibly, definitely have feelings for Kit.

So over breakfast, she had regaled him with the saga of rescuing Cupid, quietly side-stepping around everything that happened after.

Everything seems normal between them, even though the guilt is eating away at her like rust on metal. In her pocket, Ambrose's check-in texts are unanswered. Haf can't face talking to them right now either.

Christopher drives them both over to Laurel's early. It turns out the Howard house is practically a stately home, dwarfing the Calloway house, which she previously thought was some kind of manor. This could be a castle.

Laurel greets them at the front door, in expensive-looking matching yoga wear under a long, loose open cardigan. All of it is white.

'Haf, darling! The great reindeer rescuer! Let's get you a dress!'

The white theme extends into the house, the foyer decorated with white marble and gold. Cut flowers provide a splash of colour, but still in a tasteful and pastel range.

Everything smells so nice here, like vanilla and fresh citrus, as well as the heady floral scents from the bouquets.

'Now, before we get started, Toph, I think Mummy is in the kitchen, so go right through.'

Christopher lurks nervously in the doorway, as though he couldn't cross the threshold into the room without permission.

'I think she wants you to help her do some final decoration checks, seeing as you're so tall. Hope that's okay?'

This strikes Haf as a slightly mad thing to say given that she's pretty sure Laurel and Christopher are very nearly the same height.

'Mummy is tiny, so is Daddy,' Laurel explains as Christopher disappears off with a wave of the hand. 'God knows where my leggy genes came from. Normally, I do it but I'm glad to get out of it and do some actual design work. Plus they love him. I bet your parents do too.'

It takes Haf a few too many beats to realise she's supposed to be in fake girlfriend mode. 'Oh, they haven't met him properly yet. Wales is pretty far from everywhere and you can't get through Wales without going into England for a little bit so . . .' She trails off, laughing nervously.

'They'll love him when they do,' says Laurel with a kind smile. 'You two have such great chemistry, and I know Kit's absolutely—' She cuts herself off quickly. 'We'll get to work in the sewing room. Come on,' she says, leading her up a grand curved staircase.

When Haf thinks of a sewing room, she thinks of her converted bedroom back home. A tiny and very stuffed cosy room, with haberdashery hidden in Danish cookie tins.

Laurel's sewing room is naturally very different from this.

Rails of clothes line the walls, along with shelves and shelves of folders labelled with things like *Patterns – Spring 2021* and *lingerie*. A sewing machine plus another more terrifying kind of possible torture device with lots of threads and pointy arms sit together on a very wide desk with one extremely fancy desk chair on wheels behind, presumably to roll between them. Several body forms stand with paper grafted onto them – dramatically cut bodices and sweeping pleated trains.

'Wow, this is amazing,' says Haf.

'Thank you. It's a work in progress,' says Laurel.

Haf walks to the rack of clothes and looks through them. There's all sorts of clothes here – lots of dresses in all kinds, of fabrics and styles, tailored trousers and matching suit jackets, even jeans. On the other side of the room, there's a section that appears to just be athleisure wear, just like the set Laurel is wearing.

'Wait, did you make all of this?' she asks, hoping she sounds more impressed than surprised.

'Oh yeah, this is an old prototype,' she says, gesturing to the outfit she's wearing. 'It took a little time, but I've finessed the design a little since then – it needed more support in the boobs and the leggings needed redrafting, not enough give in the seams. You'll see when I bend down, they pull a bit too much.'

'They are amazing. You could sell those. I'd buy them, especially if they could restrain these lads,' she says, pointing at her chest.

'That's the plan, one day maybe,' she says, wandering to the desk where there are pencils, paper and chalk strewn everywhere. 'Anyway, I picked out some pattern ideas from what I already had drafted, but I can mix and match and adjust and hopefully we can find something you like. I hope you don't think I'm presumptuous, but I guessed that you were probably wearing about a size twenty?'

Laurel is, of course, absolutely correct.

'That's a cool and slightly terrifying skill,' Haf says, impressed.

'I know.' She snorts. 'I can do bra size at three paces too.'

Haf covers her chest with her hands, and they both laugh.

'Anyway, I can grade the pattern to your measurements but it's always a good start to know a rough dress size.'

Laurel beckons her over to her computer where she's made a mood board of images of girls wearing dresses. But not just any girls; they're all fat. And they all look killer.

'I wanted to pick models who were similar shapes to you, so you could get a good idea of what the shape might look like on you.'

'Wow, thank you,' says Haf. 'That's really thoughtful. The thing I hate most is when they only ever show you what it looks like on . . .'

'Skinny people like me. God, don't I know it. As a designer I find it utterly reductive. The average size in the UK is a sixteen, for fuck's sake. Imagine not catering to all those fabulous fit people.'

'Okay, it's official. I like you.'

Laurel beams.

All the dresses are dramatic and beautiful. 'God, I don't know where to start. They're all so beautiful. Normally for things like this I usually ask my flatmate Ambrose to help me decide. They have a great sense of style.'

'Wait . . . You don't mean,' Laurel says, pulling up her Instagram and turning it to Haf. On the screen is Ambrose, lots of little Ambroses in different outfits, leaning against beautiful York backgrounds and looking effortlessly fashionable.

'Oh yeah, that's them. Ambrose Liew.'

Laurel screeches. It's quite alarming, and Haf is just about to ask her if she's okay, when Laurel starts speaking at high speed. 'I can't believe you not only know but *live* with Ambrose! They are like one of my style icons! I am obsessed with their take on androgyny and femininity and changing up the game on what people expect non-binary people to wear!' She is so excited and fangirly that Haf can't help but like her more. Every time she meets Laurel, it feels like she finds a whole new piece of her.

'Oh my God, please make them be my friend,' she says with complete seriousness.

Of course, Haf logically knew that Ambrose was kind of a big deal in the influencer fashion world. PR packages regularly arrived at the house, and they sometimes did photoshoots together along the river – luckily her parents had bought her a nice camera years ago for birdwatching and field work, and it came in useful when Ambrose needed to shoot something quickly.

Obviously, she knew Ambrose was cool. After all, that's pretty much why she couldn't really believe that they were friends. It was kind of nice to know other people realised how cool they were too.

'Erm, we could just ring them?' Haf says. 'Get their opinion and you can talk to them.'

'Oh my God. We can't!' Laurel blanches, and then coyly adds, 'Can we?'

'I'm going to call them,' she says, stepping out the room. Haf swears she hears Laurel mutter something about changing her clothes.

'What have you done now?'

'Nothing! I've done nothing! Also normal people usually answer with "hello" by the way.'

'Sweetie, I'm not going to take advice on normality from you. So, what did you do?'

Haf huffs. 'Nothing!'

Ambrose interrupts this with a barking, 'Ha!'

'Look, I'm going to introduce you to someone but I need you to behave, you know. Be on book, so to speak.'

'What are you talking about?'

'You know, the scheme . . .' she hisses.

'Oh, don't blow the fake-dating cover. Got it.'

'I'm putting you on video, so be good.'

Ambrose appears on screen, dressed in a chic black coat.

'Where are you?' Haf asks. 'Are you outside?'

'Ugh. I am, can you believe it? Joanne insisted I take the cousins out for a bit of exercise, so I pointed them at the playground and hoped for the best. Luckily, I have a double espresso.'

'Aren't they teenagers? Isn't that too old for a playground?'

'Probably. Either way, they're racing to see how many times they can slide down the slide in ten minutes so who am I to judge?'

Haf walks back into the room where Laurel runs her fingers through her hair and adjusts her outfit, brushing off lint that doesn't exist. Haf sits down on a little velvet couch and Laurel joins her, so both of them are on screen. Unfortunately, Ambrose is busy yelling something at their rampaging cousins.

'Hello, Ambrose. I love your style, I follow you on Insta,' says Laurel, giving a little wave as Ambrose turns back to the phone.

'Oh hey, you're Laurel Howard, right?'

Blushing, Laurel flicks her hair over her shoulder. 'That's me.'

'Nice to meet you. What are you doing with this dork? I accidentally let her out of her cage and now she's on a rampage in the South.'

All at once Laurel and Haf say, 'I'm making her a dress!' and, 'She's making me a dress.'

They giggle, and Haf continues. 'Laurel is *very kindly* making me a dress for the Christmas party, which has turned out to be a literal ball, and as ever, I wanted your advice.'

'Because you can't dress yourself.'

'I can. A bit. Sometimes. This is just beyond my usual.'

'Okay, show me the goods.'

Haf tilts her phone camera down to her boobs.

'Why do you always do that?' Ambrose laughs.

Haf cackles at her own joke and hands the phone over to Laurel, who walks Ambrose through her design ideas. The topic quickly turns to recent designs from the catwalk or couture, and Haf is completely lost. Instead, she just runs her hand along all the fabric samples that are laid out on the table.

She needs to talk to Ambrose about what happened with Kit, but that will have to wait until later. Kit was rather conspicuously missing all morning, up and out the house with Esther before Haf was even awake. She knew she was probably being oversensitive, or worrying too much, but it felt purposeful. Like Kit was avoiding her. After all, she said she wasn't an early riser.

The conversation soon slows down as Laurel holds different ideas up to the camera, and Ambrose makes very loud 'hmmm' thinking noises.

'Show me the first one again?'

Laurel complies, and for a while, Ambrose is silent. They close their eyes and there's a slight humming coming from the speakers.

'What's happening?' whispers Laurel.

'They're thinking. Or they're probably going to say something super blunt and are trying to be nicer.'

'Oh, great.'

After a much longer stretch of time than Haf was expecting, Ambrose's eyes open and they lean forward.

'Okay, so I really like the bottom half of that first one, and I like the idea of creating a little capelet that was in idea . . . three? But overall, it's just . . .' They pause, clearly trying to find the polite way of saying it for Laurel's benefit. 'I'm not sure how else to say this, but I think all these options are very heterosexual.'

Ambrose and Haf fall apart laughing, and Laurel makes a sudden loud, 'Oh!'

'Oh?' asks Haf.

'Oh, I just didn't realise you were queer. It makes sense that Kit likes you, I mean. You know,' Laurel stumbles over her words. 'Anyway, I see it now. Yes, it's a bit too "I'm going to marry my extremely straight husband in my extremely heterosexual but slightly kooky wedding", isn't it? You want something with a little more of an edge?'

'You can find it. I've seen your feed; I know you can do it,' Ambrose says.

Laurel clutches at her chest, shocked at the compliment that has snuck in among the criticism.

'Just as long as you don't lean so far as something like that God awful Peg-the-Patriarchy bullet vest. Just like . . . a bit of sauce to it.'

'What if . . . ?' Laurel says, but trails off, handing the phone back to Haf. She grabs a notebook and starts sketching, creating a miniature Haf outline on paper, surrounded by a halo of floaty material, plus a deep plunging neckline.

'What about this?'

'Wow, she's going to need some serious tit holders if you're going to pull that off.'

Ambrose is not wrong.

'I have some ideas on how to construct it. It'll be clever . . .'

Their conversation flies over Haf's head again, but she takes the paper dress in her hands and says, 'I like this.'

'It's settled then!' says Laurel, rushing to the other side of the room. From a drawer, she pulls out an armful of black gauzy material, which she brings over to Haf and shakes out. It sparkles in the light, and as Laurel holds it up against her body, Haf can see that it's subtly patterned with stars. But not just stars, it's the constellations of the night sky.

'With that pattern and this fabric, it's going to be very Alexander McQueen. Plus, what's queerer than astrology?' Ambrose says with a wink.

'Isn't this technically astronomy?' asks Laurel.

'Who cares, I love it,' Haf says breathlessly, taking the fabric in her hands. 'But . . . umm. This fabric must be really expensive and your time and it's like literally tomorrow. I don't know if I can afford—'

Laurel stills her with a hand on her shoulder. 'You're giving me an opportunity to create something beautiful with a fabric that has been sitting in that drawer for years, and I get to show everyone I know how good a designer I am? Seriously, this isn't purely altruistic. I just ask that you'll let me take some photos when you're all dolled up.'

'Okay,' she says.

'This is going to be so hot. Laurel, DM me updates, I wanna see them. Haf, call me later, you dodo.'

Ambrose disappears from the screen, and Laurel does a deep breath out. 'Wow, they're so cool.'

'They're something all right.'

'Now, look, darling, I hope this isn't awkward, but the best measurements will be if you whip everything off and stand there in your underwear. Bra can stay, but I might ask you to do a few for me without it if needs be. Is that okay with you?'

At this point, Haf doesn't think she can really object to stripping off in front of Laurel, and so she does. Luckily, it's not as cold as the Calloway house, and Laurel works quickly, whipping around her with a measuring tape before swapping to pinning strips of calico fabric together on her body.

'Are you looking forward to the party tomorrow night, then?' Haf asks her, needing to spark up a bit of conversation so she might be able to ignore the fact that Laurel is extremely close to her mostly naked body.

'Oh, yeah, it will be great, once it happens.' She sings a little laugh. 'The build-up is always a lot. Takes a few months, as Mummy always wants to change the theming and food and music.'

'I bet it'll be nice to finally enjoy it.'

'Absolutely. It's nice to have something else to think about,' she says, leaning back to admire her work. 'Luckily, I've got a little time to do my full hair and relaxation routine tonight, as Mark's meeting some friends in the pub.'

'Did he not want to go to the fête?' Haf asks slowly. This is dangerous ground in fake-girlfriend world, but also in reality-Haf world, because in both of those, she vehemently dislikes him, but she should probably take an interest. It just makes her wonder even more why Laurel and Christopher fell apart. He's a much better person than Mark, after all. And they seem to get on okay now.

'No. Not really his thing,' she says quickly. 'Plus, it gave me some more time with Kit. And obviously it worked out well with me finding out you didn't have a dress. What a mischief Christopher is.'

'They love to test us.'

'Oh, don't I know it.'

After a while, Laurel seems satisfied, and unpins all the bits of fabric from her. Christopher arrives at the same instant, pointedly not looking at Haf as she puts her clothes back on.

'All going well?'

'Perfectly,' says Laurel distractedly. 'You both can go if you're done helping Mummy. I've got to get working.' She says this with a little wiggle of glee.

So absorbed in her work, Haf's not even sure Laurel hears them say goodbye.

'Did you get everything done?' Haf asks as they wander back down the stairs. 'I thought you'd be way longer if you were going to the venue.'

'It's happening here. They've got a ballroom through there,' he says offhandedly, as though it's not absolutely ridiculous for someone to have a *ballroom* in their house.

'Wow, okay. I'm really not in Kansas any more,' she says. 'Shall we go do your Christmas shopping then? I can be useful, or at least present.'

Christopher beams and holds the car door open for her. 'After you.'

As they drive along, she watches the snowy world go by and inevitably pulls up Twitter. Ambrose's latest poll is perhaps a little too specific for comfort, but she lets it slide as they were useful with Laurel. Plus, it's kind of true.

**@ambroseliew** isn't it awkward when your fake-bf's ex-gf is making you a dress that makes your tits look banging enough to make his sister fall in love with you

**what?:** 98%
**also what?:** 2%
*423 votes*

Half an hour later, they're wandering down the high street of Hazelmoor, a pretty little market town not too far from Oxlea. It kind of reminds her of some parts of York – all cobbled streets that curl around buildings that lean into each other. Nothing is shabby but beautifully old, and decorated in full Christmas glory.

'I honestly can't believe that you have left this all to the last minute,' says Haf, stepping out of the way of a tiny woman carrying more shopping bags than a person her size should be able to.

'It's not last minute. That would be tomorrow,' he says, ushering her into a tiny but heavily floral-scented boutique.

'Urgh, you're such a man.' Haf sighs.

She picks up a bath bomb from a basket display and sniffs it, leaving a tiny dusting of bomb on the tip of her nose. Christopher smiles and wipes it away with a gloved thumb.

'Correct, I am a man. You've found me out,' he says, smiling, but quickly falters like a malfunctioned factory robot, holding out two bottles of bath oil in front of him. 'But . . . I'm not like *a man,* all the time. Like a bloke. You wouldn't call me a lad. I'm not blokey. Am I? Christ.'

'Are you having some sort of crisis of masculinity right now?'

'Maybe a little one,' he says, sagging. 'Which smells best?'

Haf takes the bottles from his hands, sniffs them both and puts one in the wicker shopping basket she has slung over one arm.

'You're not fucking intolerable, if that's what you mean,' she says, shuddering at the memories of all the blokey stag-dos she's been caught up in back in York. For some reason, people seem to love having stag and hen parties in the little city, and so most summer evenings involve finding the places where they won't be.

'What I'm saying is you guys aren't like pressured into making everything perfect as early as possible, and you get away with it, which is infuriating, though to be honest, you probably only get away with it because all the women are doing the hard Christmas prep.'

The shopkeeper behind them lets out a shocked pfft gasp, then quickly busies herself behind the counter to hide her red face.

'Look, now you're making me go off on a feminist rant in a nice boutique. No one wants this.'

'True. And fine, you're right. I am suitably chastened and promise to do better next year,' he says, attempting to play into the jokiness, but he's being so sincere that it makes Haf's heart ache a little. 'That's my Christmas wish sorted.'

'Christmas wish?'

'Yeah, like, when you make a wish on a star before Santa comes? We usually go out and pick one using the telescope, but some-times if it's cloudy we'll just wish on a star on top of the tree. The wish is the important bit.'

Haf clasps her heart. 'I'm sorry, what is this incredibly darling childhood anecdote you're ambushing me with?'

'Everyone does a Christmas wish, don't they?'

Haf looks to the shop assistant, who seems to have recovered, and they shrug, clearly not familiar with Christmas wishes either.

'I think it might just be a Calloway thing. I'm obsessed. Is this ritual time specific?'

'We usually do it at midnight on Christmas Eve, or the equivalent of that when we were little. Laurel—' He pauses to clear his throat. 'Laurel and I used to do it at the party.'

'Well, we can find a star to wish on, just for you,' she says, reaching up to tweak him on the nose.

Christopher picks out a couple of items – plus the bath bomb Haf nosed – and passes them over to the shop assistant to pay. Haf winces as the price racks up on the till, but Christopher hands over his card without a blink.

'It's on me, remember? I dragged you down here. I'm not going to ask you to pay for everyone's presents too.'

'Thank God,' she sighs.

The air is frigid as they step outside, the sun hanging really low in the sky, even though it's barely three o'clock.

Haf buys them takeaway hot chocolates from a stand on the street – hers flavoured with peppermint, his topped with an enormous hillock of whipped cream – which warm them up as they continue to browse.

The rest of their shopping goes surprisingly quickly. At a tiny antique bookseller, Christopher collects a prewrapped parcel for his dad – apparently an old and moderately rare edition of his favourite book, *The Hound of the Baskervilles*. Haf picks out a handmade bookmark made from old maps to go with it.

For Kit, Christopher had already picked out some bath salts from the fancy boutique – good for her aching muscles, he explains – and then they go to a fancy little clothes shop that has brands Haf doesn't recognise. For Esther, he chooses a grey cashmere scarf, and a pair of expensive but very cosy-looking slippers with firm soles for Kit.

'I read that they're good for stability,' he says. 'Hopefully, they'll be really comfortable.'

'Is that everyone?' Haf asks as they step back onto the street.

'I think so.'

'Good. Let's go have a drink, yeah?'

'I'm driving?'

'Is there not a pub near your house we can stumble to?'

'Yes, but it's kind of a farmers' pub,' he says with reluctance. 'Definitely an old man's kind of place. One guy nursing a Guinness for two hours and not saying a word.'

'Perfect, those are my favourite kind, and then no one will bother us. I think we need a break from' – she waves in the air around her – 'all this fake-dating stuff.'

'Me too.'

They drive home and park the car, dropping off the presents inside. No one else is home, so they wander off to the pub through the snow. There's been another little flurry of snow this afternoon, so the trees are all freshly dusted.

The pub is exactly as described. Haf spots two dilapidated armchairs by the roaring fire and goes to investigate.

'Not you again,' moans a familiar voice.

It's Quiet Carriage Man, or perhaps Raffle Man. Now Old Man Pub Man, but either way he still looks exhausted, slumped in one of the armchairs.

'Hello,' Haf says brightly, but he cuts her off.

'No, I don't want to know. I don't want to know about your schemes or what reindeer you're chasing.'

'I just wanted to say thank you for looking after the gingerbread house for me.'

'You're welcome.' He awkwardly runs a hand through his curly black hair and gets to his feet. 'You know what? Take my seat. I'll just leave!'

'Oh, okay?' Haf says, feeling a little bad but ultimately relieved. As he puts his glass on the bar, she calls, 'See you again soon!'

'I hope not!' he cries and slams the pub door shut.

'Christ, what was that all about?' asks Christopher, passing her a cup of mulled cider.

'He was the guy who told us off on the train. I keep bumping into him. He saved the gingerbread house from Cupid's rampage.'

'The one who overheard all the fake-dating stuff?' Christopher says, paling.

'Yeah, but every time I see him, he just freaks out, so it's probably fine. I don't think he'll tell anyone.'

'Wait, was he also running the raffle? I wondered why the person on the stand was being so weird.'

They curl up in the chairs and soon are well on their way to being a little drunk. It turns out that this pub's version of mulled cider is practically rocket fuel, and after one cup – which Haf initially swigged like tea – they are both giggling like teenagers.

'I know we said we wanted to get away from all that stuff,' says Christopher, 'but I'm glad you're here and it's all working out.'

'Me too,' she says. Emboldened by the booze, she adds, 'You know, there's another funny coincidence that I can't get my head around.'

'What's that?' he mumbles.

'I've met Kit before.'

'What do you mean?' he asks sleepily.

'On the way here, we met in St Pancras before you got there, and we flirted and I was going to ask for her number and then she disappeared off and . . .'

Haf trails off as Christopher sits up.

'You mean, Kit recognised you?'

'Yeah, but it's okay. She just gave me shit for flirting. It's all fine.'

But Christopher is not acting like it's fine. 'What if she tells my parents? Then everyone will think I'm an absolute laughing stock, having to strong-arm someone into pretending to date me—'

'Christopher, you didn't strong-arm me into anything. I agreed to this. It's just a weird coincidence. It doesn't matter.'

He says nothing for what feels like a huge stretch of time.

'Please say something, Christopher,' she croaks.

'Why didn't you tell me this two days ago when we got here?'

'I . . . I didn't know how to talk about it, and I didn't want to upset you. I didn't want to make things more complicated—'

'Well, apparently they already are!'

'Christopher, come on. Just listen to me,' she pleads.

He's just about to speak, and she hopes with all her heart that he's going to say okay, it's all okay, and we are a team, it'll work out.

But instead, someone steps between them. A very large, rectangle-shaped man.

Mark.

'Here's the man of the hour,' he says, pulling over a stool.

'What are you doing here, Mark?' asks Christopher, too tired for niceties.

'Just having a drink with some of the boys from school,' Mark says, gesturing to a corner with his pint. Across the pub, Haf can see a table full of more rectangle men in almost matching shirts rolled up at the forearms. They look like the cast of *Made in Chelsea* on a weekend away.

'Oh, that's nice,' he says blandly. 'We were actually in the middle of a conversation.'

'I'm sure Haf doesn't mind me joining you for a moment,' he says with all the good nature of an eel.

'Sure,' she says, torn between wanting to get rid of Mark and avoiding the rest of that conversation with Christopher. 'Hello, Mark, how are you?'

'I'm very well, thank you. Enjoying the holidays, and this one has earned a good break, haven't you, Chrissy?'

Christopher gives him a weak nod.

'I heard Laurel is making a dress for you,' he says with a strange, almost leering look. Haf feels naked under his gaze. 'Didn't think to bring anything black tie with you?'

'Why would I own black tie?' she drawls.

'Why *wouldn't* you? Standard outfit, is it not? What are you going to wear to your functions at the Oxford and Cambridge club?'

Haf wanted to ask what a private members' club even was, as it's the sort of thing she's heard of but not been to. But that was probably a question that answered itself: if you didn't know what it was, then it wasn't for you.

'I'm not a member,' says Christopher.

'Why not?' asks Mark, a little affronted.

'It's just a bit, you know . . .'

'Exclusive,' adds Haf.

'I don't think the Oxford and Cambridge club is that exclusive.'

'Isn't it literally a club only for people who went to the top two universities in the UK, who are disproportionately sourced from private schools?' says Haf boldly.

She swears that across the way, Christopher gives her a little smile.

'Well, I—' Mark splutters, and this seems to be just enough of an interruption for Christopher to take over.

He gets to his feet, rubbing the back of his neck with his hands. 'Look, we've got to get back home. We'll see you at the party tomorrow,' he says.

'All right then,' says Mark, striding back to his table of clones.

Haf gathers her things and follows Christopher out the door. He's striding through the snow, so she has to trot to keep up with him.

'Jesus, he's such a toad,' Haf mutters as she catches up with Christopher. 'I can't believe you have to work with him.'

'Don't remind me,' he sighs. 'You got a nice riposte on him there though, so well done. Got us out of there, at least.'

He's distant still, a little weary, but they've got a little while to walk, so Haf decides to try her apology again.

'I'm really sorry, Christopher. I didn't mean to make things more complicated for you. It's just a weird coincidence that she was your sister. And now we're all stuck in the same house together . . .'

Christopher holds up a hand to stop her babbling.

'Haf, I just . . . I can't talk about this right now. My head is spinning, from this and the drink, and . . . I just think it would be better if we go home.'

Haf says nothing else, because what is there to say? He doesn't seem angry, he didn't shout, and yet she feels like a reprimanded child.

They get back to the Calloway house, and Christopher immediately takes the dogs out for a long walk, without asking her to come along.

There's no sign of Kit, or their parents either.

She can't believe that she has found herself in a situation where her fake boyfriend and the woman she might be falling for are currently occupying the same house and neither are speaking to her.

And that's before she even thinks about the fact her fake boyfriend's real ex-girlfriend is literally making her a dress and possibly also trying to be her real-life friend?

As if on cue, her phone buzzes with a photo of the dress in progress, Laurel giving a thumbs up at the camera.

She sends back a heart emoji.

*What a fucking state my life is,* she thinks.

Overcome with exhaustion, Haf sinks down into the covers and sends a pleading message off to Ambrose, but before she can hit send, she falls asleep.

# Chapter Sixteen

The Howard house has been transformed into a magical Christmas wonderland. The hedges that line the private road are woven with soft golden lights to match the glowing warmth of the house ahead.

All the cars are directed to a yard at the side of the house. Haf was almost expecting there to be a valet – not that she could imagine Otto yielding his sports car to a teenager with a recent qualification. He had insisted on driving so they could arrive in style. Christopher is up in the front, and Esther sits primly in the back with Haf, who tries to control the spill of fabric from taking over the whole seat.

Through the dark, Haf can see stables in the distance and the occasional happy clop of a horse. Maybe she can sneak off later and make a friend, if she needs a break from the unending awkward drama she's mired in.

Pretty much as soon as he woke up, Christopher had been summoned for a work emergency that held him up in Otto's den making frustrated phone calls for the best part of the day. Apparently, no one really cared that it was Christmas Eve, or that anyone was on booked holiday.

At one point, she had snuck in to bring him a cuppa and a plate of biscuits, sliding them onto the table while he was in the middle of a Zoom meeting. On screen, she spied Mark looking a bit worse for wear, sipping at an enormous coffee. As she had turned to slink away, Christopher had reached out and gently taken her wrist in his hand, giving it a little thank-you squeeze.

He'd just said he needed a little time to process it, and she couldn't deny him that. But she hated existing in this weird limbo of not being able to just talk it all out with him.

The day had been a weird, quiet one for her. Kit was still conspicuously absent, though there were signs that she'd been home at some point – empty packets of painkillers, a mug with a dark lipstick stain.

In the end, she'd spent most of the day reading *Carol* quietly in the living room. That's basically what Ambrose had suggested she do with her Christmas anyway, and despite the weird tense emotional atmosphere that only she and Christopher were aware of (or rather, she hoped that was true) it was kind of relaxing.

She hadn't heard from Ambrose all day, not that she'd prodded them for support either. The most non-Calloway socialising she could manage was liking a few cute photos on Twitter, and that was completely one-sided.

In the middle of the afternoon, a courier had arrived with an enormous box addressed to Haf Hughes. Inside, wrapped in tissue paper, was her dress. She had tried it on in the bedroom upstairs and cried. It was perfect and fit her like a glove. Laurel's talent was clear, not only from the delicate sewing but from the fact that her boobs felt very secure inside the bodice of the dress. The constellations caught in the light, and as she turned, the circle of the skirt flared out like a sigh.

The text she sent to Laurel was more a string of letters and exclamation marks than formed words, and she sent a grainy mirror selfie, which was followed up with Laurel's own overcome wordless reply.

Just as she was thinking she didn't want to ever take the dress off, a knock had sounded on the door, and Esther had walked in, and told her she was beautiful. Boy, did she need to hear that today.

Of course, now Esther is equally resplendent in a deep-red wrap dress and delicate gold heels.

Underneath her dress, Haf wears her reliable black heels – the ones she wore when she met Christopher. She had been tempted to wear the Doc Martens, as no one would see them under the floor-length dress, but she suspected that might be a little much for even her to pull off. Not to mention, they were still covered in duck poop.

Ever the gentlemen, Otto and Christopher open the doors for Esther and Haf.

Standing there, holding the door open for her, Christopher is a picture of handsomeness. That clean, period-piece beauty is accentuated by his sleek black suit and the tiny black velvet dickie bow he wears that should make him look like a total dork, but somehow works.

They probably make a very beautiful pair together, both dressed like the night sky.

'Shall we?' cries Otto, keen to get the festivities started. He looks like a professor from a movie in his tweed suit, a little flash of red to match his wife's dress in his pocket square and tie.

To her surprise, Christopher holds out her arm to take. But of course he would. Even if he were furious, he'd still be chivalrous. Christopher is endlessly polite and good and kind.

The steps that lead up to the front door have been covered by a dark red carpet. Otto knocks on the door with a flourish, and a man dressed in black and white opens it wide, greeting them. A dainty woman steps forward with a tray of champagne flutes filled with sparkling gold. Haf and the Calloways all take one, and cheer, clinking their glasses softly together.

'Just a sip for me,' Otto says, replacing the glass after a taste and a toast. 'Now, my dear, I believe there's dancing to be done.'

Esther giggles, which is truly a sound Haf did not expect to ever hear, and they whisk away down the corridor towards the party.

Christopher leads her after them, following the growing sound of strings and merriment through the house. Through an open and very grand door, there is a literal ballroom. Enormous crystal chandeliers hang from a ceiling painted like the Sistine Chapel. Tables and chairs line the wall, plus there's serving tables piled with food and a bar set up at one end. Huge windows, fringed with thick dark velvet curtains that hang to the floor, reveal the dark outside. There's a staircase that leads to an upper level, where people stand drinking and watching the dancers. There's something Versailles about it all; a glorious riot of excess.

Couples dance in the centre of the room to the music, and Esther and Otto are already out there, dancing together in a moment all their own.

It's like a ball from movies, from her dreams. But it's real, and she's there. It's kind of impossible to believe.

'Okay,' she whispers. 'I take back all the rich jokes I made about you, because you're positively a pauper compared to this, right?'

Christopher laughs. 'Very much so.'

'Crikey. And I thought your Brita-filter tap gave me class anxiety. They're all going to think I'm Eliza Doolittle.'

'Hang what they think,' he says, laughing as the strings strike up a rendition of 'Last Christmas'. 'Shall we dance, milady?'

And right then, it feels like everything might be okay between them. Obviously, they still need to talk, but for now, there's dancing.

'Let's, m' . . . . m'lad?'

'I think it's probably, good sir.'

'Look, you're teaching me something new already. I told you, it's practically *Pygmalion* in here.'

He leads her towards the other dancers, and they stand for a moment, her hand on his shoulder, the other in his hand. 'Do you mind if I lead?'

'Look at you, Mr Equalitarian,' she laughs. 'Get going or I'll stand on your feet.'

It's a miracle. Christopher and Haf dance together like long-term partners, their bodies naturally working together. When Christopher goes to spin her, her body reacts instinctively, and the fabric of her dress billows out beautifully. Behind them, they hear some admiring gasps.

It's trust, she thinks. And love.

They might not be in *love*, but they love each other. They've weathered so much together already that she knows their friendship is one for a lifetime. A lifetime of being silly on dance floors.

Haf is so happy, right in this moment with him. All the complications of their fake Christmas fall away, and it feels real. Not the romance part, but the happiness, the celebration, the being together.

They trot through the jaunty rendition of 'Christmas Wrapping' and only decide to stop for a break and a breath when the quartet take a break too. More drinks and food are brought out to placate the dancers.

'Come on, we've got a buffet to ransack.' She laughs, tugging at his arm.

'What rude vignettes are you going to create for me this time?'

'That would be spoiling it!'

There's a little queue, so they hang back while the older guests take their time being served by staff. They can wait. They have time. They have all the time in the world.

But her bliss is short-lived, because they're joined by Mark.

'Chrissy, my man. Good job on that meeting today. Sorry to drag you in on the holidays, but needs must.'

'No worries, hopefully everything is sorted now,' says Christopher stiffly.

'Capitalism never sleeps,' Haf mutters.

'And *Half*, nice to see you again,' he says, and he wobbles slightly as he goes in for, what she realises in horror is, a kiss on the cheek.

He smells like a distillery. He wasn't this drunk last night, even when he was interrupting their chat.

'Ha ha, nice to see you again too,' she says, flashing her eyes to Christopher.

Laurel's boyfriend is absolutely wasted at her family's charity holiday party, and it's barely eight o'clock.

'Where's Laurel? I'd love to thank her in person for my dress.'

'I dunno.' He shrugs, taking a deep sip of whatever concoction he's drinking.

'Maybe you've had enough of that, pal,' says Christopher jovially, reaching to take the glass from him, but Mark turns away at the last second.

'Hey look!' he says, wobbling and pointing up at the ceiling. 'It's mistletoe! We're all under the mistletoe.'

Out of instinct, Haf clings to Christopher's side, lest Mark try to snog her.

'Go on then,' he says, swaying.

'Go on what, Mark?' Christopher asks.

'Kiss! KISS!' he bellows, and a few people's heads turn towards them. 'If you're so in love and so over *my girlfriend*' – he spits this so hard that actual saliva comes flying from his mouth – 'or are you still trying to get with her?' He pokes a finger hard against Christopher's chest.

'I know you were helping her the other night. "Helping",' he says, adding finger quotes.

'We were with Samira and Paul the whole time, Mark. We traded me helping her parents out for her making Haf's dress. Everything is above board, and I'm not trying to steal your girlfriend. There's nothing nefarious going on.'

'Nefarious!' Mark says, laughing. 'Oh, nefarious, he says!'

Christopher looks exhausted. This isn't just his old friend, or the new boyfriend of his ex, but a colleague. She doesn't know how to handle this.

'Mark, listen to me. I'm not after your girlfriend. Not this time, or the last time you accused me of it.'

'Well, then.' He sways. 'Prove it.' Mark points a wobbly finger up to the mistletoe.

An actual crowd has formed around them, keen to wonder what all the fuss is, and why this cuboid human is yelling about mistletoe.

But across the sea of heads, Haf spies Laurel, who looks like she wants the ground to swallow her whole.

There is one way that Haf can put a stop to this and save Laurel this huge fucking embarrassment.

'Oh, for fuck's sake,' hisses Haf, and she grabs Christopher by the lapels on his jacket, pulling him into a hard kiss.

Christopher cottons on fast for someone who was so nervous about their rules around PDA, and as they kiss, he dips her low to the floor. The cape of her dress spreading out beneath them like an oil slick.

Objectively, it's a good kiss. Aesthetically convincing, a little stylish. In keeping with their dancing, perhaps.

She doesn't feel anything though, no sparks or friction, which is kind of a relief to her. If she's going to snog her fake boyfriend, there better be no more emotional complications.

As they come up for air, a few people awkwardly clap. They both laugh awkwardly, and she wipes off a smudge of her red lipstick from the corner of his mouth.

At the back of the crowd, clutching a plate of food, she catches the eyes of Quiet Carriage Man. She gives him a little wave, and he sighs, his wiry body crumpling with the exhaustion of never escaping her. He waves back a slightly sarcastic wave and hurries away.

'Satisfied?' Haf asks Mark, taking his arm. 'Come on. Why don't we go out for some air?'

'I don't want some fucking air,' he slurs.

'A cheeky smoke then?'

'Oh all right,' he relents, letting her lead him back to the front of the house.

Christopher follows, his arms out wide to grab Mark lest he keel over.

The crowd of onlookers disperse quickly as the band strikes up again, and as she steers this mass of a man down the corridor back to the front door, Laurel appears at their side.

They steer Mark into a chair in an alcove just off the main entrance, and Laurel asks one of the staff members to call a car to take him home. Haf wonders if they should stay with him, but within seconds he's deep in loud-snoring sleep.

'I'll keep an eye on him,' says Christopher. 'He can get a little fighty when he wakes up.'

*God, what a turd of a man,* she thinks as she joins Laurel in the atrium where she is pacing and fiddling with her own stunning dress, a waterfall of silver silk that makes her look like an ice sculpture.

'Oh God, thank you for that,' Laurel breathes. 'He's been a complete *toad* all evening.'

'It's okay. I think he was just spoiling for a fight.'

'Feels like he always is,' she says, nibbling a nail.

Reaching up, Haf takes Laurel's hand in hers to stop her chewing.

'Laurel, can I ask you something?'

She nods eagerly.

'Why are you with him? Do you even like him?'

Laurel nervously licks her lips. 'I did, at the start. I think. Truth be told, I've wanted to break up with him for a while, but it's the holidays! How do you break up with someone at Christmas?! It just feels so mean . . .'

'The kindest time to break up with someone is as soon as you decide to,' says Haf, parroting a relationship columnist's advice she heard years ago. 'Not that he deserves your kindness, but also you deserve to not have to deal with him.'

'I know, I know.' She sighs. 'You're right. He's just been such a . . . such a . . .'

'Arsehole.'

'Yes! Arsehole. Especially around Christopher, and I feel awful for not noticing it all before.'

'Infatuation does weird things to us.'

'Rebounds too. Thank you, I really needed to get that out,' she says, pulling Haf into a hug.

'It was the least I could do after you made me this,' says Haf, twirling about as Laurel releases her.

Clearly something in Laurel's brain switches from crisis mode to business mode, and she appraises her work. She walks around Haf, making her turn this way and that to admire how the dress moves.

'Wow, I really did a good job, didn't I?'

'An amazing job. A near psychic-level design job, I'd say. I can't believe you did this just off my measurements. It's perfect, Laurel. You're really talented.'

She flushes at the compliment. 'No, I . . .' she begins, and before she can downplay her work, Haf stops her.

'No, listen to you. You made something amazing, and you did a really kind thing for me. I'll never forget that.'

Laurel wafts her hand at her face and looks up at the ceiling. 'Hush, you'll make me cry.'

'You should, because have you seen how good my tits look?'

'I thought it would be rude to comment, but really. Wowzers!' She laughs, the tears dried now.

From his seat in the alcove, a semi-conscious Mark does an extremely loud burp that echoes around the atrium, and a fart. Haf doesn't even hold herself back from rolling her eyes. Laurel is so much better than this man.

'Have you shown Ambrose yet?' Laurel asks, trying to feign casualness but her nerves are clear from her fidgeting fingers.

'Let's send them some photos now?' Haf says, opening up her WhatsApp.

In the chat box, is her drafted message from last night, which she hurriedly deletes and hopes Laurel didn't see because she's pretty sure she wrote something about wanting to kiss Kit. The last thing they need is someone else finding out – the ever-present Quiet Carriage Man is bad enough.

Instead, she fires off, *Photos incoming x* and the ticks go blue immediately. Has Ambrose been waiting to hear from her?

Laurel positions Haf on the stairs, so the cape slinks behind her. She takes several photos, which they send the best of to Ambrose, who immediately texts back a string of AAAAAAs, which goes on for several lines followed by, *I am dead.*

'I think they like it,' Haf laughs, showing Laurel.

'Do you think . . . Would you mind if I . . . ?'

'Go on, say it,' she says, nudging her.

'Can I put it on my feed? I want to show what I'm doing, and I think . . . This is just such a good photo. I think the engagement right at this moment would be perfect, as so many people are at home, and—'

'You don't have to explain it to me! I'm merely the body. You're the artist! Tell everyone what a shit-hot designer you are.'

Her heart swells as Laurel gives her the warmest smile and her fingers flash across the screen. She barely needs to edit the photo, as the light is so good in here, and within seconds of posting, her phone starts vibrating with people messaging her.

'Thank you. Can you believe that's the first thing I've said was my own creation on there? I've never been brave enough to share things I've made.'

'That's ridiculous! You should be screaming how talented you are from the rooftops. I know I will. I already am. Hey, does this staircase go all the way up to the roof? I've got screaming to do,' she shouts the last part to the doorman, and Laurel hushes her with a giggle.

'Haf. You're a very kind person. I think,' she says slowly, 'I owe you an apology too. Things spiralled so fast with me telling the family. I thought I was just messaging Kit, but I'd had a few too many to drink at Sally's, and Mark was being . . . well . . . Mark, and it turned out I was replying to the group chat for organising the ball, so Christopher's mum and my parents found out immediately. It was definitely not my intention! I hope you don't feel roped into all of this?'

Given the situation, Haf tries not to laugh. It is sweet of her to apologise, though.

'Oh no, honestly. I totally get it. Family stuff spreads like wildfire. I know you wouldn't have done anything malicious.'

Truthfully, she probably owes Laurel an apology for reducing her to The Ex, the Posh Girl, the Horse Girl. She could have missed out on knowing this cool person.

'Thank God,' says Laurel with relief. 'I've been hoping to apologise for ages, and I nearly did when we were doing the dress, but I just didn't want to make it awkward. And the rest of the time, there were always other people around, and I worried . . . they would think I was trying to scare you off or something.'

'That's fine. I get it. This stuff is complicated.'

'It is.'

'Is it helpful to know I find you a bit terrifying, but in like a good way? Not in like an ex-way, but more like a wow-this-girl-has-her-shit together way.'

Laurel laughs, and it's a high twinkling sound like crystal. 'That is nice to know.'

Something flashes across her face as she looks from Haf to Christopher and Mark. 'I'm going to go find Kit and check on the party, if that's okay?'

'Yes, yes, go host,' Haf says.

Laurel turns to walk back to the party, but pauses a second, looking back at Haf. 'You should go talk to Kit.'

And with that, she's gone before Haf can process what she might be saying, what she might know.

The car arrives, and Mark wakes up just enough for them to squeeze him in. Christopher slips the driver a couple of twenties for the hassle of having to deal with him in this state and Haf hopes that he won't barf all over this nice man's car.

As they walk back to the ball, the thought that Haf has been trying to squash all evening rises now that Laurel mentioned her. After all, where *is* Kit? She must have been here all day, hiding out at Laurel's. What did she tell her about all this?

All night, she's been lying to herself that she's not been looking for Kit in the crowd, not listening out for her throaty laugh or looking for a swish of bitter-chocolate hair.

Relieved that he's free of babysitting duties, Christopher disappears off to go to the bathroom. Back in the ballroom, Haf takes a new glass of Champagne from a tray and wanders up the steps to the upper level of the ballroom so she can watch the dancers below.

The musicians have returned to their instruments, refreshed from their break, and begin to play a beautiful arrangement of 'O Holy Night'. The music swells around her, and the lights glitter, and it feels like the whole crowd parts to reveal her.

Kit.

Haf's breath catches in her throat. She's so beautiful, positively radiant in a flowing dark jade dress that falls off her strong shoulders, accessorised with a gold matt walking stick with a curved handle. She stands with a couple of people around their age that Haf doesn't recognise, school friends, perhaps. And when she laughs, the sound is lost in the music and the sound of the crowd, but Haf knows the sound by heart.

And then Kit looks up.

Their eyes meet, and it's like the rest of the world falls away, and it's only the two of them in the whole universe, never mind the ballroom.

The little half-smile curves on her red lips, and she nods her head at Haf's dress. In return, Haf swishes it and laughs.

Kit raises a glass in cheers, and Haf raises hers in return, and mouths, 'Happy Christmas Eve.'

The spell is broken as Laurel appears next to Kit, and they all animatedly chatter, catching up on the last year of gossip and stories and life.

When Haf goes home for Christmas, her school friends have a standing arrangement to meet in the pub where they spent lunch-times playing pool in during high school. Even if they don't keep in touch all year, they'll be there still, even with new partners and new babies. Doing that in a literal ball in your literal childhood home is just another life. Another world.

Christopher finds her, and they return to the dance floor, spinning through arrangements of pop songs. They even swap with his parents, Otto gently swaying her to 'Underneath the Christmas Tree' while Esther and Christopher bop around them happily, both laughing and caught up in the reverie.

The hours slip by, dancing broken up with finally getting a plateful of food from the buffet. As the night they met, Christopher holds the plate and Haf loads them up with food, even though a member of staff offers to fill it up for them. Thin little toasts with rare beef and a dollop of creamy horseradish sauce. Smoked salmon blinis by the dozen, and ones topped with what she's pretty sure is caviar. She has never eaten caviar, or even seen it in real life, and so she absolutely wants to eat it, just so she can say she has. There are little cones of whipped blue cheese and fig jam that look a little like savoury ice-cream cones, and tiny ched-dar tartlets. Next to those are grilled prawns and bacon-wrapped scallops on long sticks, arranged around little bowls of sauces to dip them in. And at one end is a display of pastel macarons, which Haf plans to empty, given half the chance.

They take up a table in a corner with their one laden plate.

'I'm sad you didn't make me a rude picture,' Christopher comments.

'Yes, I did,' says Haf, pointing at a pile of meat and olives she's fashioned to look like a vulva.

'Oh good God,' he laughs.

'Slightly concerning that you can't find the clitoris even when it's on a plate,' she teases, and he swats at her with a scallop lollipop. Waving food in her general direction is a mistake, of course, and she bites the end off it.

'Christ,' he says, looking at the ragged end of it. 'I'm quite glad you're not really my girlfriend now.'

They tease and laugh and play with their food like children until Laurel joins them, slumping at the table.

'Cheese and rice, running a party is always so exhausting. My feet are completely rancid in these shoes.'

'I'm sorry, did you just say "cheese and rice"?' Haf says, looking at Christopher for backup.

'It's the polite way of "taking the Lord's name", according to my auntie who insists I don't blaspheme in her presence. And she's been here all day prepping for the party, so now obviously I can't stop saying it.' Laurel sighs, rolling her ankles gently.

'Go barefoot?' suggests Haf.

'And subject the guests to her stinky feet?' Christopher teases.

'Don't be rude,' Haf says, tapping him with an empty lollipop stick.

'No, truly, he's right. My feet are awful. Too much squeezing into tiny little designer shoes,' she says, with a dramatic sigh.

'Life is so hard when you have to be so beautiful all the time,' Christopher consoles.

If Haf was really his girlfriend, she might feel a pinch at him calling Laurel beautiful, but Haf doesn't. It's lovely that they can be so kind to each other, after all the hurt.

'You're dangerously close to getting a feminist rant about beauty standards for women,' Laurel mutters.

'Yeah,' says Haf, wanting to back her up.

'Please don't. I get enough of those from Kit.'

'Speaking of, I haven't seen her for a while,' says Laurel, shoving a mini cheese tart into her mouth whole. 'Have you seen her?'

Christopher shakes his head. 'I've barely seen her all night.'

'She's sneaky like that,' Laurel says.

Realising she hasn't had a wee since they go there, Haf leaves Laurel and Christopher laughing in her wake. The affection is still there, so obvious between them, almost a kind of nostalgia for what once was.

The bathroom is alarmingly elegant, and she's half tempted to nick the soaps like it's a fancy hotel, but manages to snap herself out of it before someone spies her.

Kit is still nowhere to be seen. Her absence is an ache to Haf, one that she's sure will only be cured by finding her. But also, she should probably look for her in case she's not feeling well. No other reason.

Haf makes her way back upstairs to see if she can spot her in the crowd again. But on this upper floor, she spies an open door that leads outside.

And there, she finds Kit, leaning against the balustrade as she gazes into the night. She is so impossibly beautiful. Her dress pools around her like green light.

*Courage, Haf*, she thinks. *You've got to speak to her, clear the air.* Set this all right again. Maybe it'll be easier now that things with her and Laurel are clearer, and that she and Christopher are okay again. This is the last hurdle before she can reach the finish line of a nice Christmas.

Her shoes clack against the stone balcony, startling Kit from her reverie. She turns towards Haf, her eyes brightly reflecting the light from inside the house.

'Hi,' Haf says.

'Hi.'

She turns back to the view, and Haf joins her at the edge. Their breath fogs around them in the icy air. Everything is lit gold, and the twinkle lights remind her of fireflies.

'Laurel was wondering where you were, so I offered to come find you,' she explains. 'I wanted to make sure you were okay, you know, just in case.'

Kit looks back at her with soft eyes and a sigh. 'Well, you found me. I was thinking of trying to steal a cigarette off someone, but everyone seems to be vaping or smoking a cigar.'

Haf opens her purse, and inside is a packet with only one cig-arette remaining, and her lucky pink lighter that has somehow lasted years. 'It's your lucky night, I guess.'

She and Ambrose often shared a single cigarette on a night out, and she had decided to bring the last one with her for a bit of luck, or some much-needed nicotine if things got really hairy. She always liked to have a backup reason to escape a room.

The flame from the lighter illuminates the soft lines of Kit's face.

'Thanks,' she says, exhaling a cloud into the night air. 'I know it's gross. I smoked like a chimney through uni. Everyone did. And sometimes I just crave one.'

'Me too. The escape and a little break from everything is nice too.'

Kit hmms an agreement.

'Your dress is lovely,' Haf says, trying not to say all the bigger, more meaningful, and much more dangerous words that dance on her tongue.

'Thanks,' she says, holding her cigarette away from it so she can swirl the emerald green fabric around her. 'It's silk chiffon.'

'It suits you. The dress, but the colour too.'

'It brings out your eyes,' she wants to say, but that feels like dangerous territory.

'I don't normally wear dresses, really, but Laurel insisted I try this one. She claims it's something she was sent by a brand, but I'm pretty sure she bought it for me after she saw me looking at it on Instagram a while ago.' She pauses. 'Or actually, thinking about it, she probably emailed them and outright asked for it. That would be just like her.'

She does a small adoring laugh as she rubs the fabric between her fingers and smiles. 'It's definitely not something I could afford otherwise. Newly qualified architects do well, let's be real, but not *this* well for just a Christmas party.'

'That's a really thoughtful gift,' says Haf distractedly, searching for pleasantries, because her mind is racing. In the moonlight, Kit is dazzling and Haf can't stop thinking about what it would be like to slip the straps from Kit's shoulders, to kiss her bare collarbone. Apparently, since she realised she's falling for this woman, her brain has opened the floodgates on all her desperate swooning thoughts and desires. She wishes it would shut up.

'That's Laurel. She just really cares about her people. Not everyone, but the people who matter to her, you know? Probably why she made you that dress.'

Kit holds the cigarette towards Haf, and she takes it. A rose of dark brown lipstick dots the end, and she adds her own scarlet colour over the top as she takes a drag.

'I didn't think I was quite that important yet. It was just, you know, mutually beneficial.'

'Mmm, I'm sure that's what she said. And yes, probably there was an element of that, but I think she likes you too,' Kit says, turning around so her back curves against the balustrade as she looks up at the stars. 'She was so excited when she told me about you and Christopher, really she was. It's just a pity it all went wonky, and she accidentally told everyone we know.'

'Yeah, she just explained what happened to me downstairs. We had a moment after I had to wrangle Mark out the ball.'

'God, he's such a piece of shit,' Kit snarls as she takes the cigarette back from her, breathing another long drag. The paper is almost all burned up, and all that remains is the stub covered in their mouths. 'Talk about a rebound guy to end all rebound guys.'

'You really don't like him, huh?'

'Of course not, he's a prick. I don't think she really likes him that much either, but it is a rebound. I guess that doesn't matter too much.'

While Haf wonders whether she should tell Kit that Laurel is finally on that same page, Kit ploughs ahead like a train off the tracks.

'When you rebound, you just want someone, anyone, who is so diametrically opposed to who you were with before that you forget all the normal shit that matters to you. The blinkers are on, like she's a racehorse just gunning it.'

Haf's mouth falls open clumsily, unsure what to say.

'Oh, don't worry, I've told her all this,' Kit says. She stands up straight, stretches her long arms out above her head like she's trying to get taller. 'But sometimes people aren't ready to listen. You have to give them time.'

'Maybe she will be now,' Haf ventures cautiously. 'Ambrose and I are like that, and being upfront and honest just make things easier long term, even if it's hard in the moment.'

To her surprise, Kit snickers.

But it's not the warm throaty laugh she's used to. It's bitter.

'Honesty? *Honesty*. Of all people, I think you need to reassess your relationship with honesty.'

Haf bristles, and Kit stamps out the end of the cigarette under her foot with such force that it could be Haf's own heart.

'As nice as you appear to be, you might also be the biggest liar I've ever met,' she scoffs.

'That's not fair,' Haf whispers half-heartedly, standing up to face Kit.

'Fairness? Honesty?' Kit laughs again. 'I think my brother deserves some of both of those, but you seem completely incapable of mastering either concept.'

Hot tears prick in the corner of her eyes, but Haf bites down hard on her lip. She will not cry, even though she really, really wants to.

It's not like Christopher is being honest with anyone either, but that's not her story to tell. So, she says nothing, glad that she's sober, or mostly so.

She expects Kit to leave, but she doesn't. They stand facing each other on the balcony, completely alone and in silence. As if they're waiting for the other to say anything else.

Eventually, Kit softly chuckles, but it's a strangely sad sound.

'It's just so . . . So . . . Completely fucking ironic. Or typical, I guess. Sod's law, isn't that basically what Alanis was singing about?' Her eyes are glued to the floor, the shine in them growing with tears.

After a few more beats of silence, Haf rallies herself and asks, 'What is?'

'Architecture school was just so intense. For years and years, you're just juggling so many deadlines and probably even a real job too,' Kit says, now looking out into the dark. 'There's no time to meet anyone, apart from the occasional supply-closet hook-up, and when you factor queerness into everything, it just makes the pool so small. I can't tell you how many straight girls I've kissed out of sheer relief to be touched.'

A thick tear breaks off the sharp ridge of her cheekbone.

'And the first person I meet, the first person who comes along that I think could be something . . . is dating my brother.'

'Oh, Kit,' she murmurs.

'I knew I should have gone back to the bookshop, but Laurel called me, and I chickened out. And I can't help but think if I did, something would have changed. But it wouldn't have, because you are still dating Christopher. It's all so fucking stupid.'

'It's not.'

'And I feel completely ridiculous saying this to you, because I don't even know if . . . I don't even know if you even feel any-where near what I do. And I'm probably just being presumptuous and imagining things that aren't there and getting mad at you for something you haven't even done.' She takes a deep breath and slows her voice down. 'But I thought . . . in front of the fire, I thought . . .'

'I feel the same,' Haf gasps, the words spilling out of her now. Her heart races as Kit's eyes turn to her. 'You didn't imagine it. I felt . . . I feel the same way. It's not just you. And I can't ignore it any more.'

Speaking the words to Christopher, and that almost-kiss in front of the fireplace, have unleashed all these huge feelings and she absolutely can't hold them back any more. Not now she knows that Kit feels the same. Not now she knows that all these moments that meant something to her mean something to Kit too. That other universe was real all along.

They're closer now, their bodies magnetised to each other. The heat of Kit's body radiates across the space towards her.

'We can't,' says Kit, her mouth an angry slash. 'We can't. I can't.'

'I know. I know that.'

'But I want to.'

Haf begins to speak, but before she can explain anything, or stop all this, Kit is kissing her. Her cold hands cup Haf's face, and Haf melts. This is all she wanted, and she can't believe it's happening. She could die in this moment.

Kit's mouth opens to her, hungry for more, and their kiss is filled with the pent-up longing of the last few days. Those lips, those wry, smiling lips, kiss her with such longing.

Haf slides her hands up her back, pulling Kit's body against her like their survival in the cold night depends on it. Their heartbeats beat against each other, desperate to mesh.

Below them, the string quartet strikes up again and Haf could swear she is dreaming.

It's a kiss made of magic and stardust, and the world around them explodes. It's a beautiful disaster and she doesn't want it to end.

They break apart slowly, smaller kisses that beg for more. Just another kiss to stay in this world of their own.

But as they finally break apart, they are hit with the reality of what they've done.

Kit's hand goes to her kiss-bruised mouth. 'Fuck. Oh fuck. I have to go.'

Gathering her dress in her hands, Kit runs back inside, slamming the door behind her.

After a moment of shock, Haf touches her lips with her frozen fingers. It really did happen; she didn't imagine it. They kissed, and Kit really does want her in the same way she wants her. She can't let her leave like this.

The heat of the ball is a welcome relief as she launches herself down the stairs, hoping she doesn't fall down them. She can't possibly stop. Because every moment that gathers between the start of the kiss and now is going to fill with regret and anger. Kit is going to close herself off. She can feel it.

Haf squeezes her way through the dance floor, dodging around couples dancing happily.

'Kit!' she calls, but her voice is swallowed by the cacophony of the merry dancing crowd. The sound swims in her head and she is dizzy with it.

There's a flash of green in the distance and she pushes past the revellers. Racing away is Kit, fleeing the ball like Cinderella at the stroke of midnight.

Ahead, Kit bursts through the front door, much to the surprise of the doorman, who, seeing Haf following, holds it open.

'Kit, please!' she yells from where she stands at the top of the stairs.

Everything is illuminated by the golden light from the house that melds with the blue moonlight, like it's covered in a layer of pearl. In the middle of the garden stands Kit, her green dress dyed silver in the dark.

Haf runs to her, and as she gets closer, Kit finally turns. She looks so desperately sad.

'Kit,' she breathes. 'Don't leave.'

'I can't stay, not now. I shouldn't have . . . *We* shouldn't have done that.' Angry sobs rack her body. 'Fuck!'

'I know,' Haf whispers, walking towards her with arms open like she's approaching a dangerous creature. 'I know, but let's just talk. Please?'

'I think you should stay away from me,' Kit hisses. 'You have to stay away.'

Her eyes and body soften.

'Please, stay away,' she whispers. 'I can't— I can't trust myself.'

A surprised shriek sounds through the air, and Kit and Haf turn to see Laurel and Christopher standing very closely together. Like they were just kissing.

What the hell is going on?

'Are you two all right?' asks Christopher, straightening his suit jacket.

Her stomach roils. He's not her boyfriend, obviously, but she feels like she betrayed him. 'Is anything wrong?'

'No, nothing,' she says hurriedly.

'Something *is* wrong, Christopher,' Kit sniffs angrily, wiping her tears away with the back of her hand.

'Kit, wait, please,' Haf begs.

She just wants a moment to explain to Christopher before it all comes out. To apologise. To admit that even though she tried to keep away from Kit, tried to push everything down, she failed. And this failure has compromised everything they've been doing. The whole fucking point of all of this.

But she's too slow. Kit charges over and it all spills out.

'We kissed. I kissed her. Your horrible sister kissed your lying girlfriend,' she spits.

'Oh!' cries Laurel.

At this, it's almost as though Kit realises that Laurel has been there the whole time.

'Wait, what are you two doing?' Kit snaps, and Laurel moves her hand to her mouth to cover her very smeared lipstick.

Which is also all over Christopher.

'Were you two out here kissing?!' Kit shrieks.

'Uh-oh,' Haf mutters.

'Only a bit,' laughs Laurel, who is clearly a bit drunk. 'We came to see the horses and then, you know, one thing led to another! Ha ha ha!'

Kit's whole body flushes.

'What the fuck is wrong with us all?' she yells. 'For fuck's sake, Christopher, I just kissed your girlfriend! While you were apparently busy cheating with your ex!'

'Kit,' says Christopher softly, approaching her like a wild animal. 'She's not my girlfriend.'

What is he doing?

'Christopher, you don't have to do this,' Haf whispers.

'I would hope not after all this,' Kit says, another round of hot angry, shameful tears rushing down her face. 'Apparently we're all just *horrible people.*'

'No, Kit listen to me,' he says in that same soft voice that makes Kit look up at him for the first time. And with that, Christopher blows everything up.

'Haf was never my girlfriend. It's all a lie.'

# Chapter Seventeen

Time stands still as Kit looks slowly from Haf to Christopher and back again.

'What do you mean, it's all a lie?'

The flow of tears ceases, drying against Kit's skin, except for one large drop that hangs on to her lip for dear life. Kit blows it away with a huff.

'Exactly that, Kit. We're not together.'

Her mouth hangs open. 'You're not dating?'

'No,' they chorus.

'Kit, they've never been dating,' says Laurel too loudly, and starts shushing herself.

'You knew?!'

'Yes. Didn't you?'

'Obviously not! Why didn't you tell me?'

'I just thought you knew! Especially after you told me all that stuff about how you had feelings—'

'Please! Stop! Talking!'

'Wait, how did you know, Laurel?' Haf interjects.

'Ambrose's Twitter polls confirmed it.' Haf makes a mental note to definitely murder Ambrose. 'And also it was kind of obvious, darling. He can't lie to me. I sniff everything out!'

'She got it out of me this evening,' he concedes.

'It's all very funny, really!' laughs Laurel. 'I only thought they were together because I saw them kiss under some mistletoe.'

'I'm sorry, what?'

'We . . . We did have a drunken snog, though it was more like a peck. A very bad one. There was some mistletoe, and it was all . . . burned up, and we felt bad for it,' Haf explains. 'We did it for the mistletoe.'

'For what?' Kit snaps, brow furrowed. 'For *mistletoe*?'

'Well, now that I say it out loud, it does sound a bit weird.'

'Yes, we kissed at Sally's party, which Laurel saw, but she presumed we were together,' Christopher explains in a way that makes it sound much more normal than Haf's meandering.

'Yeah, and I felt so bad for him being caught snogging by his ex and fucking Mark that I just went along with it, and then we stole some Prosecco and ran away.'

'Then I fell asleep on your couch,' adds Christopher for some reason.

'And then I accidentally told everyone,' says Laurel brightly.

'Precisely,' says Christopher.

'Wait, so who even are you then?' Kit spins towards Haf.

'Everything I've told you about myself is true,' she says this with emphasis on you. 'Just not the Christopher timeline of it.'

'This is all . . .' Kit mutters. 'I have no fucking idea what it is, but we need to go home so I can shout at you some more without half of Oxlea thinking we are re-enacting an episode of *Eastenders*, or something.'

'I'll go ask the doorman to order us a car,' says Christopher. 'As long as you two are not going to murder each other.'

'I can wait,' Kit snaps.

'We'll be fine,' says Haf. 'Can you get my coat too? My tits are going to fall off.'

'Must you always tell me about your tits?' he mutters, walking off. With an apologetic look, Laurel trots off after him.

Alone again, it's deathly silent. This is somehow worse than Kit swearing or crying. But she doesn't say or do anything. She just stares out into nothing, gaze unfocused and lost in her own thoughts as her brain reprocesses the memories of the last few days.

'Kit—' Haf begins, but Kit silences her with a hand.

'No. No more talking until we get home and I can raid Dad's whisky cabinet. This is . . .' She shakes her head, unable to continue.

Her unfinished sentence hangs in the air between them like their breath.

So they say no more, standing near each other in the frigid air.

In the distance, Haf hears a whinny and wishes she could disappear off to the stables, perhaps ride away like a heroine in a historical fantasy novel.

Soon, Christopher returns with the coats, and a car arrives pretty much immediately – the Howards must have had some waiting for guests.

'I told our parents that we're leaving early,' he says when they're all in the car. 'Apparently our generation don't have any stamina, which is a horrifying phrase, the more I think about it.'

It feels wrong to laugh, and so Haf just offers a weak smile.

The driver must think some kind of family tragedy has occurred, and Christopher slips him a note as they all pile out of the car. Haf is relieved that he seems to have a wallet full of twenties on hand and ready to appease freaked-out drivers.

The dogs are extremely excited that they are home, and squeal and bounce around Kit as she strides through the house to let them outside for a wee. No one follows her, she probably needs a break from them both.

With horror, Haf notices the clock in the hallway says it's only just gone half ten. After everything that happened, Haf could have sworn it was about three in the morning, or maybe that was just the whole fleeing-the-ball thing. It certainly feels that way.

Instead, Haf follows Christopher into the living room, where he gets the fire going. Clearly, he needs to be doing something with his hands to shed himself of anxiety, but in the literal and emotional chill Haf is relieved either way.

Returning in a gust of cold air, Kit heads straight to the wooden drinks trolley and pulls out an expensive-looking bottle. The amber liquid sloshes in its large tumbler.

Haf and Christopher glance at each other, but no one speaks. The only sound comes from Stella and Luna as they wander back in and curl up in their usual spot in front of the fire.

Eventually, Kit throws herself into the armchair that Otto usually occupies and takes a deep breath, followed by a sip of whisky.

'Okay, I'm ready,' she announces.

'Ready?' asks Christopher, who stands up, dusting ash from his hands.

'Ready for you both to explain what the fuck is up with this hare-brained scheme.'

'It's not *hare-brained*.'

'All right then, how about *fucking ridiculous?*'

Haf wants to tell them to settle down but getting in the way of siblings snapping at each other probably is an overstep.

'What I want to know,' says Kit slowly, 'is why? Why not just like fake break-up with her, or even say no to Esther?'

'It's not so easy saying no to Mother.'

'I say no to her all the time.'

'And yet you still ended up making that horror show of a gingerbread house.'

'Fair point. But that was baking something silly, not like . . . cosplaying my life.'

'I just,' Christopher begins, wiping his face with his hand. 'I just didn't want to have to deal with the inevitable set-ups that Mother told me she was planning, and I wanted something to talk about with them that wasn't my job, or the company, or anything.'

'So she's just a conversation piece to you?' Kit gestures her glass towards Haf.

'That's a little reductive.'

'Not really, from what you've said. You just said this whole fake-dating thing was so Esther wouldn't set you up with anyone else, and so the parents wouldn't hassle you about your work life.'

Christopher says nothing, but flushes beetroot red.

Kit's mouth becomes a hard line. 'Christopher, do you not think it's entirely batshit that you constructed this mess just so that you didn't have to have a conversation with them?'

'It's . . . it's . . .' he stumbles, rubbing the back of his neck. His nervous habit.

'Let me guess, you haven't told them you hate your job either?' Christopher looks down at his socks. 'Why? What are you so afraid of?'

'Come on, Kit, we both know Dad's been wanting me to go work for his company since I was a teenager. I can't exactly say, "Sorry, Dad I'm quitting this job, but I don't want to work with you either" because it means I'm rejecting all that, everything he built for us, and I just—'

'Yes, he built it for us but that doesn't mean you have to,' she says, a softness creeping in. 'It's not up to you to take over his company. This isn't fucking old-school primogeniture, Christopher. You're not the next in line for the throne.'

'That's easy for you to say.'

'Is it?' she laughs. 'Pray tell why you think that? Go on, I'm curious.'

'You've always banged your own drum, and they respected you for that. You're your own person. You've always been.'

A smirk appears in the corner of her mouth, which turns into a laugh of disbelief. 'Are you actually serious?'

'Of course I'm serious!'

'Christopher, I had to be like that because otherwise Esther would have wrapped me up in cotton wool and not let me do anything, ever. It's not because I wanted to be like that, it's because I had to. Can you imagine what my life would look like if they had got their way and kept me here in Oxlea instead of letting me go out into the world?'

'Mmm. Fair point,' he murmurs. 'There probably would have been significantly more murder.'

'More murder?' Haf squeaks.

'There's been no murder.' Kit huffs.

'She wasn't trying to jail you though, Kit,' Christopher says weakly.

'Is that what you remember?' Kit asks with a deep tiredness.

He does a kind of combination nod-shrug, a little guilty for his recollection obviously not lining up with hers.

'Well, no offence, bud,' she laughs. 'But you were a thirteen-year-old boy. Of course, you didn't notice what was going on;

you were too busy trying to get into Laurel's knickers. A running theme, apparently.'

Shocked, Haf falls apart laughing. Christopher's flush is practically crimson now, but he's smiling at least.

'Thanks for that. As if this conversation wasn't already completely mortifying.'

'It's all your own making, kiddo,' says Kit, shaking her head. 'But really, it's okay. I don't blame you for not knowing what was going on. We both know I'm hardly an open book at the best of times, never mind when I was a dickhead fifteen-year-old.'

'I'm sorry though, for not paying attention,' he says. 'And for not being there now. Maybe it was okay to be oblivious as a teenager, but I'm not one any more.'

'Ostensibly,' she teases. 'This whole fake-dating thing feels very emotionally teenage, don't you think?'

Luna yawns, as if in agreement.

'But.' She sighs. 'Saying all that, I can imagine that meant the parents put more pressure on you, especially if Otto was determined one of us inherit the business.'

'Why do you say that?' Christopher asks.

'I don't think they'd trust me with it. They don't think I'm well enough to be working,' she says softly. 'Do you know how many times Esther has essentially suggested that I retire early?'

In her impression of Esther's voice, she continues, 'You know, Katharine, when you and your partner have children, you could be the stay-at-home parent. Wouldn't that be better for you than working full-time? Katharine, have you ever considered asking to go part-time at your work? Katharine, I read this article about people who'd changed careers to do something from home and it really seems to be like such a fascinating idea. Katharine, why don't you quit and move back home?'

'Eesh, that's a lot,' Haf says.

'It is. And if I try to be generous, which let it be known is very difficult for me right now, I can imagine that probably added more to your plate.' Christopher tries to speak but she stops him. 'I'm not apologising, but acknowledging that things are different for us.'

'What do you *actually* want to do, Christopher?' Haf asks. 'The baking?'

And perhaps because it's late, or because he's so tired and worn out, Christopher answers truthfully. 'Yes. I want to go to patisserie school, do my training, and work up to owning my own bakery.'

'You should tell them that's what you want, and then go do it,' says Kit. 'You've got the money saved, I'm sure. And you own that little flat.' As Christopher shakes his head, Kit gets up and sits next to him on the sofa. 'You can't live your life doing what you think they might want you to do. You've got to live your life for yourself. No fake girlfriends and careers you hate.'

'It's probably too late for me to retrain.'

'Christopher, you're twenty-seven. You're hardly on your death bed. And if you were, that would be a perfect reason to chase your dream,' says Kit.

He sighs wearily.

He's not there yet. Haf can feel it in her bones. But maybe, with their help, he could be. 'Maybe this is a conversation for after Christmas?' Haf says. 'Or daylight?'

Kit gives her a little nod of agreement.

That's one thing finally talked about.

She's dreading the next part, and what will inevitably come after.

'So, we should probably talk about what's going to happen now.'

'What do you mean?' asks Kit.

'The secret's out, isn't it?' shrugs Haf. 'Or half out? I dunno. Where are we going with all this?'

Kit gets up from the couch and refills her glass.

'You know, you could offer us one of those,' Haf points out, though doesn't get up to get her own.

'Whisky isn't for liars,' Kit says, sticking her tongue out at them both, but she does take two more glasses from the cart and fills them. She hands a glass to each of them and returns to her seat.

'Considering the circumstances, and that we're already four days deep into this lie, I will agree to go along with it on a few conditions.'

'Really!?' cries Haf at the same time Christopher hopefully whispers, 'Really?'

'No matter how much you deserve to be found out, I am not going to be the one to drop that bombshell. I'm not the biggest Christmas fan, but I also am inclined to pick the easiest road and just go along with this mess. Plus, can you imagine what Esther would be like if she found out?'

'Thank you, Kit,' breathes Christopher, and Haf could swear he's about to keel over in sheer relief.

'Don't thank me yet. You haven't heard my conditions.'

'Go on then,' Haf urges.

'Condition one,' she begins, pointing at Christopher. 'In January, you have to tell the parents you're quitting. You can come up with a plan, show them how it's going to work and what your aims are, so it's like a business case. I'll help you with it.'

Christopher blanches. There's something distinctly rabbit-in-the-headlights about his eyes.

'Kit,' Haf says softly, shaking her head. 'Give him time. I don't think either of us can ultimatum him into this.'

'He needs a push.'

'Yes, but not off a cliff.'

Kit rolls her eyes.

'Can I think about it?' he whispers, and Haf's heart swells with pride. 'I just . . . I'm not saying I won't. You're right about needing to present it to them, and I think it'll help me too. I haven't let myself think about it before, and that's not going to help.'

'Okay,' agrees Kit. 'No deadline. Just a commitment that you're working on it. And I'll help.'

'Deal,' he says, and they shake hands.

'I can't believe you haggled me down from my first condition,' Kit mutters before taking another sip.

'What's condition two?'

'I'm working on it.'

'I'm not sure you're in the position to demand quite so much when you kissed my girlfriend,' he sniffs, a tiny grin on his lips.

'Yeah, your *fake* girlfriend. I don't think that counts.'

'You didn't know that at the time,' Haf points out.

'Hang on. Why are you mad at me and not your fake girl-friend over here?' Kit says with a smirk. 'She was busy putting it about!'

'Hmm. That's a good point,' he says, arching an eyebrow as he turns to Haf. It's now, as they both give her the same look, that Haf finally sees the sibling resemblance.

'Hey, hey, I thought we were having a beautiful moment of sibling reconciliation,' Haf protests. 'And I was not *putting it* about. You'd know if I was putting it about.'

'What a terrifying proposition,' says Christopher.

'How did I not realise you guys weren't dating? You have the sexual chemistry of a pair of salt-and-pepper shakers.'

'Also, to be fair to Haf, I did actually know that she knew you already and that she had feelings for you.'

'What? Really? And you were just fine with that?'

'He was not fine about it,' Haf scoffs.

'She's right. I was in quite a tizzy over it.'

'A tizzy?' Haf practically chokes on her whisky from laughter.

'Yes, a tizzy. That's a fine word. And I was only feeling that way because you forgot to tell me straight away.'

'When did she tell you?'

'Last night.'

Kit gives her a knowing look.

'Look, it was only because I didn't want you to like throw me out or something. And I was trying really hard to repress everything. You know, just keep it all inside until I just die.'

'Your combined lack of sense is absolutely horrifying to me,' drawls Kit. 'You two are more alike than I thought – emotionally stunted and horrendously repressed.'

'Says you,' Haf quips. 'And *you* were the one who kissed me.'

Kit makes a series of angry little noises but is interrupted as Christopher laughs. It's body-shaking, near-hysterical laughter. Relieved laughter.

'Oh dear, Christmas madness has set in,' Haf says, shaking her head.

'No, I'm just,' he says, wiping a tear from his eye. 'What are the chances that you fell in love with each other?'

Both Kit and Haf go various shades of red at the word 'love'. They both start to mumble protests, but he holds up a hand to silence them. 'You know what I mean. It's kind of lovely.'

'That's alarmingly grown-up of you,' says Kit. 'I swear you were twelve a blink ago.'

Christopher rolls his eyes playfully, a perfect copy of Kit just a few moments before. He gets to his feet, waking the dogs, who look up at him, waiting for the moment he says it's bedtime.

But instead, what he says is this.

'I just want to say one thing. I know the circumstances in which you met each other are hardly . . . ideal.'

'That's one word for it,' Kit scoffs.

'But I see the way you look at each other. You obviously care about one another. Kit, don't let Haf take the fall for helping me be a coward.'

And with that, he walks upstairs, followed by the dogs.

The silence he leaves behind hangs heavy over them.

And now that he's got up from the couch, Haf is distinctly aware that it's just the two of them. There's still a space where he was, which may as well be a gulf, but she could just reach out and touch Kit, if she was brave enough.

'He's a good guy,' says Haf.

'He is. He just has a lot of growing up to do.'

'Me too.'

Kit says nothing, but that's a response in and of itself. She *does* have a lot of growing up to do.

At least they've cleared one thing up. It's just . . . all the rest.

*Now or never*, she thinks.

'Kit—'

'No,' Kit says, looking down at the empty tumbler that she palms. 'I'm still . . . processing. All of this.'

For a moment, when Christopher left and apparently gave them his blessing, Haf had hoped the slate was wiped clean. Perhaps they'd reconcile? Kit would say nothing matters, and then they would kiss! It's silly, she realises. That's not what Kit would do, and it's not like this is a simple situation.

'Oh don't pull that face,' Kit groans, looking out the corner of her eye.

'What face?' Haf cries. 'I'm not making a face.'

'You look like a puppy that's just been kicked.'

'Why do you know what that looks like?'

'Figuratively.' Kit sighs, annoyed. 'Look, Christopher is my brother, my family. If I don't try to sort him out, he's going to blunder through life, fake dating away his problems, the big man-child.'

And now she turns to Haf, with a deep look of regret.

'And you? I hardly know you. And I always said I'd never be with someone who lied to me. I've had way too much of people cushioning the truth or avoiding what they mean so they don't "upset me and make me ill".' She uses air quotes, and Haf realises this is something someone has actually said to her. 'That matters to me. I understand that you were doing it for him, not out of maliciousness . . .'

'But?' Haf adds for her, and Kit smiles sadly.

'I have to work out if that's a deal-breaker for me, on top of everything else.'

A small hope flutters in her chest, like a moth in the dying of the light. Considering if this is a deal-breaker means Kit is thinking about whether there's a future for them. All she can do is wait.

Together, they watch the fire and finish their drinks. As the embers burn down, Kit's head lolls and Haf realises she's falling asleep. She takes the tumbler from her hand.

'Kit?' she calls in the voice you'd use for a sleepy child.

'I'm just napping. I'll wait here for Mum and Dad and then brave the stairs,' she mumbles, her voice muffled with sleep.

'Okay,' says Haf, taking a woollen blanket from the armchair and tucking it around Kit.

The grandfather clock in the dining room strikes twelve, and Haf wonders if either Calloway sibling made their Christmas wish in time.

She tries to ignore the pang in her chest as she turns off a few lights, locks the back door, and goes up the stairs.

As she reaches the landing, Esther and Otto clatter in through the front door. They laugh and dance, so completely in love with each other. From her pocket, Esther takes a sprig of mistletoe and holds it up between them. Beaming, Otto takes her into his arms and kisses her softly.

It's a movie kiss. His head bent down to her, still wearing their coats dappled with snow.

This is what she wants. The silliness, the lifetime of love. A family of their own.

And she wants it with Kit. If Kit can ever forgive her.

Upstairs, Christopher is fully tucked up in bed.

'Did it go okay?' he says, sitting up and flicking on the bedside light. He is wearing adorable green tartan flannel pyjamas that she hasn't seen before. 'Did you sort everything out?'

'Are you my wingman now?' she asks with affection. 'You did a pretty good job with that speech.'

'And?' he urges. 'What did she say?'

'She's . . . thinking.'

'Give her time.'

Haf nods. 'Please tell me about these pyjamas. You look so sweet I want to die.'

'There's a pair for you. Check under your pillow.'

He's right – she finds an identical pair to Christopher's, all wrapped up in a bright red bow with a tag that says, *With love from Santa.*

'Hope you didn't peek,' she says, sliding under the covers. After all they've been through, she hadn't even thought to be shy about changing in front of him. Being practically naked in front of Laurel probably helped.

'Course not. I'm a man of honour. A wingman of honour, perhaps.'

Haf curls up against him. 'You didn't have to do that, you know,' she whispers.

'I know. But I meant what I said. The way she looks at you . . . I don't think anyone has ever looked at me like that. It'll be all right.'

She groans softly. 'I hope you're right.'

He rolls over to face her and extends a pinkie finger towards her.

'Are we pinkie-promising again?' she asks. When he nods, she says, 'What to?'

'To another day, in this together.'

She wraps her little finger around his, and they both smile.

'Together,' she says.

# Chapter Eighteen

Haf wakes to the sound of her phone almost vibrating off the bedside table.

'Happy Christmaaaaaas!' Ambrose yells. On-screen, they are somehow already dressed, and accessorised with a Santa hat and an apron.

'Are you cooking already? What time is it?' Haf groans.

'Too early,' Christopher mutters.

'Is that Christopher in your bed? Hello, fake brother-in-law – I hope you're taking care of this absolute pigeon. Her survival is in your hands.'

Christopher rolls over, rubbing the sleep out of his eyes. 'Hello, Ambrose. Apologies, I didn't realise we were family now. I'm doing my best, just for you.'

'That's more like it. You look very dashing in those pyjamas,' they say with a purr, which sends Christopher under the duvet and out of view of the screen.

'Ambrose stop flirting with my fake boyfriend.'

'Oh boo to you too,' Ambrose says. 'Where's your Christmas spirit?'

'Mine normally doesn't wake up until after eight,' Christopher mutters from under the covers.

'So much for being an early riser,' Ambrose replies, which prompts a snort from Christopher.

'My Christmas spirit is entirely reliant on presents, croissants and something fizzy to drink, none of which I currently have,' sulks Haf.

'I don't think I can Deliveroo you any of that,' they say, taking a big swig of something decidedly fizzy in a flute.

'Oh, fuck off.'

'Very festive of you. Is that the Welsh for "Merry Christmas"?'

Haf mutters something very, very rude in Welsh that she once taught Ambrose, who starts giggling uncontrollably.

Once recovered, they shuffle the phone around, revealing the kitchen behind them.

'What are you doing exactly?'

'Got the goose in. I am on goose duty. Gooty,' they say with a laugh.

'This Christmas has had too many geese for my liking,' Haf mutters.

'Just think of it as revenge.'

'Who trusted you with that?'

'Listen, Haf, I am actually a *very* accomplished chef when someone gives me all the instructions, tells me what to do and also basically supervises me, I'll have you know. Mum and Popo have gone out for a power walk around the lake and apparently even I can be trusted with it for half an hour.'

'Or at least more than your cousins.'

'Potato potahto.'

'Maybe you should have less of the booze.'

'What would be the fun in that? How was the ball last night? I've had radio silence from you, apart from those pics. I was worried you were dead, or had fallen down the stairs or something.'

Behind her, Christopher groans.

'What did you do?' Ambrose says flatly, all jolliness gone.

'Why do you always presume *I* did something?' Haf whines.

Christopher lifts his head up and says, 'She kissed Kit.'

'*Shut your pretty mouth!*'

Shocked by the sudden outburst, Christopher complies.

'You snogged her? Ha ha ha ha. I mean, sorry, Christopher, but also—' They cackle.

'Yeah, but he was busy snogging Laurel, who knew all about us fake dating thanks to your Twitter.'

'OMG,' they say, as though it's a word. Their eyes light up. 'The drama! Tell me everything.'

Condensing the evening's top points takes less time than Haf expected it might. Throughout it all, Ambrose chops herbs with a very large knife, but their face runs through all the possible permutations of facial expressions.

'So now, what? You're waiting to see if she's going to decide to date you with all this baggage?' they say, waving the knife in the air.

'Did you just point at me?' Christopher asks.

'I meant just like her general aura, but yes, you too now, I guess. By the way, when your family finds out what's going on and disowns you, you can come stay with us. I love taking in waifs and strays. Especially when they're cute.'

'You know what? I like drunk Ambrose. This is nice.'

'For you maybe,' scoffs Haf. 'I'm just, I'm not doing anything. I'm just giving her space and time—'

'Yes, two things notoriously plentiful on Christmas Day.'

'It'll be fine. We've got this far. What else can life throw at us?'

'Has anyone told you about the concept of tempting fate?' groans Christopher.

'Doesn't really matter if fate throws anything more at you, though, does it? The bottom line is, who dates both siblings in a family? Not many people, I expect – bit of an awkward dinner-table situation. I doubt it'd be her thing from what you've said, never mind your parents, who you both seem so intent on impressing.'

There it is. The clanger of truth she'd been waiting for.

'Sorry,' says Ambrose, looking up into the camera. 'I just . . . I don't want you getting hurt.'

'I know,' she says softly.

'I'm going, but FaceTime me into the dinner conversation if things get spicy. Thank you,' and they disappear from the screen.

'Do they always just hang up suddenly?'

'Yeah, it's kind of their thing.'

Christopher stretches in the bed, then sits up, his long legs crossed. The whole movement is so childlike, more reminiscent of the boy she saw in the bookshelves, or in the hopeful glint in his eyes when he was making the gingerbread house.

'Is this a sign that we have to get up now?' she croaks. 'My lying face isn't ready.'

'Well, while you prepare yourself,' he says as he leans down and takes a very small parcel out of his side-table drawer, 'I got you something.'

'A present?'

There's no mood in the world that a present couldn't solve, at least for Haf, there isn't. Some might call that materialistic; she prefers easy to please. She's like Stella and Luna. They're all just easily pleased by a little treat. This is why Ambrose knows to always keep the lebkuchen tin stocked.

She holds out her hands, palms faced upwards, and he places the little box in the centre. It's wrapped in a tiny golden bow, which she pulls apart.

The box flips open, and inside is a ring.

Burnished gold antlers twist together, encrusted with tiny peachy pink stones. A tiny flower clusters in one bough, and on closer inspection Haf sees it's a four-leaf clover.

'Before you get worried, it's not *that* kind of ring.' He laughs. 'It's . . . a friendship ring.'

'A friendship ring? Oh, Christopher, you soft sausage.'

His cheeks and ears blush pink. 'It's a thing!'

'I'm sure it is, and it's also very adorable.'

'This has been an extremely weird time, and I don't think anyone as good as you would have gone along with such a silly plan.'

'Good? I think you mean "as ridiculous".'

'Close enough. But, I suppose, this is a kind of promise.'

'Aren't those for like deeply religious abstinent teens?'

'Oh God, I hope not. Did I get this wrong?'

'I'm just teasing you. What are you promising? Your soul? Your vast wealth? Your collection of fantasy novels from the early noughties? I do hope it's the latter.'

'Shush,' he scolds gently. 'I'm promising to be there for you, like you have been there for me.'

All her bravado and bluster melts.

'Oh, Christopher. There I was, all ready to take the piss out of you, and then you go ahead and say something so lovely that I just can't.'

Haf takes the ring from the box and slides it onto her fingers. It's not quite the right size for her middle finger, so slips it onto another. She admires it in the morning light.

'The antlers are for your daring rescue,' he says. 'And I read that clover means "I promise" in the language of flowers, so that seemed apt.'

This yanks something in her chest, and she's on the verge of crying with happiness. What a nice man. What a nice, very silly man.

'Christopher, you're actually killing me. The language of flowers? This ring might be the most lesbian thing in the world, and you're a straight man.'

'Mostly.'

'Mostly?' she says, her eyebrows practically falling off her face. 'Ohhh. This absolutely tracks.'

'How so?'

'The fake-dating, the falling in love with your sister, all the other nonsense. That's the combined force of two chaotic bisexuals.'

Thankfully, he laughs.

'Thank you for telling me,' she says, wrapping her arms around him and squeezing him against her. 'And for trusting me with . . . well, everything.'

She releases him and he takes a deep breath.

'Did I just smother you with my bosom or something?' she laughs.

'No, I just haven't told anyone that in a long time. It's kind of nice to be known, I suppose.'

'Eurgh, can't relate.' They both laugh.

'Shall we go make our entrance downstairs? Get some booze in you?'

'God, please,' she says, getting out of the bed. She takes a wrapped present from her rucksack and clutches it against her chest. 'You know, this is going to make my gift look a lot less cool now. You can have it downstairs in a little bit, so it doesn't look quite so shit.'

'I am positive it will not be shit.'

With his arms full of presents, Christopher follows her down the stairs. The house smells like freshly baked pastry and butter.

Luckily, it turns out that the Calloways are relaxed about pyjamas for Christmas breakfast and presents. It's way too cold for her to take off her pyjamas, and she hates waiting for the present opening, even if the one on her hand is the only one she's getting. She just loves the whole ceremony of it. Freddie's family always insisted on opening presents after Christmas dinner, which Haf had always thought must be some kind of human rights violation, or at least a very specific form of torture designed to make everyone miserable.

'Merry Christmas!' Esther cries, carrying a tray of baked pastries into the living room.

Under the tree is a large stack of neatly wrapped presents. She adds the one for Christopher.

In one corner of the couch sits Kit, curled up in thick blankets. Their eyes meet, just for a second.

'Merry Christmas, everyone,' says Christopher as Otto rushes in, energetically wielding a bottle opener and a huge bottle of Champagne. The real stuff.

'Let's get celebrating, shall we?' he says, and a loud pop fills the room. He fills up glasses laid out on his drinks trolley and starts passing them around.

Before she can tactfully sit down literally anywhere else, Otto ushers Haf onto the couch with a freshly topped-up glass, and she ends up wedged between the two Calloway siblings. This feels a bit too on the nose, even for her.

Determined to snaffle a few flecks of pastry, Stella and Luna bob around them, going from family member to family member. Eventually, Christopher picks up Luna and wedges her down on the couch between him and Haf, where she goes to sleep. Though, she wakes up briefly when Esther hands Haf a pain au chocolat on a tiny plate.

Unable to balance glass, dog petting and tiny plate, Haf tries to juggle things around until Kit intervenes, and helpfully places the pastry on the coffee table for her.

Once everyone has a drink, Otto swaps handing out Champagne for passing out presents, so that everyone – including, to her surprise, Haf – has one.

Rather than everyone taking turns opening one each, a slightly mortifying tradition imposed by her dad so he could get action shots of people opening gifts, the Calloways all dive in at once.

She wasn't expecting anything at all.

The gift box is wrapped in a bright red ribbon, and as she undoes the bow, the box falls open beautifully.

Inside is a very fancy-looking candle from a brand that she vaguely recognises from Laurel's bedroom. She pops open the cardboard and she's surrounded by the scent of figs. It's really, really good.

There's also a very thick pair of knitted blue and yellow socks from The White Stuff, a shop she thought only sold white things but apparently just sells pricy things.

'Thank you. This is so kind,' she says to the Calloways.

Esther gives her a warm wink. 'You're welcome, Haf. Merry Christmas.'

Next to her, Christopher is ripping into a parcel, and Haf realises it's the one from her. Luckily, the shop had been able to gift wrap it for her, else it would have been wrapped in a pillowcase.

His eyes shine as he lifts out a navy-blue knitted scarf with a tiny embroidered Paddington Bear on each end.

'When did you manage to get this?' he asks, wrapping it around his neck.

'I saw it when we were shopping. I suspect it might be for children, but I think everyone needs a Paddington Bear scarf.'

'Correct.'

'You like Paddington Bear?' Kit asks dryly.

'I've got a beating heart in my chest, haven't I?' Haf says with all seriousness.

Haf's phone buzzes, and on screen is a photo of her parents, already sun-kissed on the beach, drinking cocktails. Mum's message reads:

**Mum:** Merry Christmas, darling. Send us some piccies. Dad's already pissed x

She's pretty sure there isn't even a time difference between Madeira and the UK, which makes this even more impressive.

Ambrose has also sent a photo. They and their cousins in front of the tree posed like K-Pop idols.

'Looks like everyone is getting into the swing of things.' Christopher laughs.

Determined to dig into her pastries, Haf grabs her plate from the coffee table, and as she sits back, she brushes her arm against Kit's.

And now that she's leaned back and picking at a pastry, she could swear that Kit is touching her.

She is. Kit's arms are folded, but the hand closest to Haf is stroking her arm. An intentional, soft touch. A caress.

She doesn't know what to do, and so keeps stuffing her pastry into her face, but does give Kit a little glance to say hello.

Plate back on the table, Haf wraps her arms up in the folds of the dressing gown, and before she can realise what she's doing, she's wrapping her fingers around Kit's own. Kit squeezes back.

Her heart races and she's sure her face is blushing rose pink, but no one else seems to notice. It's like they're in their own bubble, unseen by everyone else.

Or at least she hopes so.

Does it mean something more? she wonders. Is this a sign of Kit thinking things through? Has she forgiven Haf for all the weird shit? Hopefully they can have a proper conversation soon, but until then, it'll have to be secret touches. It doesn't last long

– because how could it? – but it was enough. Her body aches when the touch ends.

More presents are passed around and unwrapped and shared and ogled. It's all so relaxed, a well-practised routine.

'We should get up and have a walk now before we get cooking,' Esther says to Otto, who slaps his thighs, startling the dogs.

They get to their feet, followed by Christopher, who gathers up the empty plates and takes them into the kitchen. Stella and Luna trot along after him, hopefully.

Grateful to be alone with Kit but too nervous to speak, Haf nervously fiddles with her ring.

'What's this?' Kit says, taking her hand to inspect the ring.

Every time Kit touches her, her skin feels alight. It's an addictive feeling.

'My present from Christopher,' she whispers.

'It's lovely. It suits you. Antlers for the patron saint of small mammals.' She smiles.

'Are we okay?' Haf asks, eyes darting to the door. She has no idea how long they have alone together, but she wants to know where she stands.

There's the longest pause in the history of the world, before Kit says, 'I'm not sure yet. Maybe.'

'Maybe?'

'Maybe, maybe,' she says, with a tiny smile.

'Okay.'

'Will you take these glasses through to the kitchen for me? I'm so stiff after last night,' she says, rolling her shoulders. 'I don't want to drop them.'

'And so you're trusting *me* with them?' Haf laughs, getting up to collect them. 'Tea? Painkillers?'

'You make the tea. I'll find the drugs,' Kit says, hauling herself to her feet, still blanket-wrapped.

All the glasses collected, Haf sets them down by the sink, where Christopher has started washing up, and fills the kettle.

At the kitchen island, Esther pours over a notebook, surrounded by several open cookbooks turned to well-thumbed and slightly spattered pages. The notebook shows a strict list of timings for dinner later. It reminds her of the layout of their gingerbread instructions – a kind of mood board that looks like chaos from far away, but is meticulously organised.

'Is there anything I can do to help?' she asks, flicking on the kettle. 'Caffeine for the walk?'

'No, thank you, dear. I'm all well on both fronts. Just double-checking the timings before we go out.'

'The offer is open for whenever you need a pair of not very competent hands.'

Esther chuckles throatily, and it makes Haf's heart swim to hear how close it is to Kit's own laugh. 'Perhaps it's best we keep you clear of the kitchen.'

'I think you're right. I'll stick to tea maid.'

'An important role,' says Esther, putting her pen down. 'Haf, I want to thank you. You've only just joined our family, but I'm very impressed with how hard you've been working to look after everyone. You saved the day at the fête – and me a significant amount of stress – and I heard you sorted out that Ratliff-Zouche boy and have been keeping an eye on Kit when she's not feeling well. We've both noticed.'

It all feels like unearned praise, and her mouth goes dry. What would Esther say if she knew all the rest of it?

Esther takes her hand, as if ready to say more, but as she does, a tiny flash of confusion crosses her face. She pushes up the sleeve of Haf's dressing gown and raises her hand up to see the ring.

With horror, Haf realises exactly what is going through Esther's mind.

'Is this—?' she begins, an enormous glittering smile spreading across her face.

Before she can protest or explain the ring, Esther has pulled her into a hug that knocks the wind out of her.

'Otto! Otto! Come quick! They're engaged!' Esther shouts.

From across the kitchen, Christopher looks up, his eyes wild. Christ, as he would say.

'Oh, what a joyous day!' Esther says, scuttling off to find Otto, still calling his name. Air rushes back into her lungs as Esther releases her.

At all the excitement and noise, Stella and Luna rush in, barking and yapping and jumping, quickly followed by Otto, who strides in with the air of Santa delivering presents. In his arms is an enormous and horrifyingly expensive-looking bottle of Champagne. Where do these people keep all this fancy fizz?

'Wait—' bleats Christopher, but his parents don't hear.

The bottle opens with a loud pop, and Esther's hands are full of clean glasses ready for toasting. At their feet, the dogs fight over who gets to play with the cork.

'My boy! I knew you could do it,' Otto bellows, clapping him hard on the back.

Her mouth hangs open, but realising she needs to look happy, she affects a distinctly *Wallace and Gromit* smile. A bit too much teeth, but hopefully it'll pass.

'A wedding! I can't believe we'll be having a wedding.' Esther laughs.

They look so happy, like Christopher and Haf have served them a Christmas miracle.

And all Haf can do is give Christopher the tiniest shrug. After all, is there a huge difference between fake dating and fake engagement? Probably, but hopefully not one so huge that it's going to make the next three days that much different from the chaos it already has been so far . . . right?

But oh God, Kit. What is Kit going to say?

As if on cue, she appears in the doorway.

'The news is out? Hurray!' Kit cries in the least convincing celebratory voice anyone has ever used in the history of unwanted, or possibly fake, engagements.

Hobbling over, still wrapped in her blanket, she pulls both Christopher and Haf into a hug, and says pointedly, 'What a brilliant, completely uncomplicated addition to our Christmas together!'

She releases them, and Haf wishes she could take it all back. This is a terrible idea.

'Let's have that toast, Dad,' Kit says, taking a very frothy glass of Champagne and knocking it back before they can actually toast.

'Steady on, girl, it's early still,' Otto laughs, raising his glass. 'To the happy couple.'

Haf breaks out in a ream of nervous, happy laughter and cheers her glass against his so that she can hurriedly bury her face in it.

'We should call your parents, Haf!' Esther says, which sends ice down Haf's back. 'What better time to meet them than at Christmas?'

'Oh, we can't. They're away,' Haf says.

'But they texted you already today, didn't they?'

'. . . Yes, they did,' begins Haf, looking around wildly for any excuse so she doesn't have to further the charade with two families. Them thinking Christopher is her boyfriend is bad enough. If they think they're engaged, she will never live it down when they're not.

*Come on, come on, think!*

'They don't really do phone calls on Christmas because . . .'

'It's not allowed,' Kit says smoothly, and Haf's heart is in her mouth, wondering what the fuck she is going on about.

'Oh? Why's that?'

'It's all part of that Christmas wellness retreat they're on, isn't it? Haf was telling me all about it last night. Sounds *so* fascinating,' Kit continues. The look she gives Haf is a challenge.

All Haf can do is play catch-up with her. 'Yes, that's right. They said they won't be able to use their phones, as they'll probably be—'

'In the ayahuasca ceremony, right?' Kit says with a sharp smile. Haf was going to say they were busy, but sure. Let's go for imbibing psychedelics.

'Yes, exactly. It's a very . . . long ceremony, and they don't like to be interrupted.'

It is slightly alarming how smoothly Kit can lie. And it is painfully obvious that she's enjoying this far, far too much.

'A pair of old hippies, are your lot?' Otto laughs. 'Or is it a bit more like a mid-life crisis, maybe?'

'There's definitely a crisis,' mutters Christopher, who is slightly green and looks like he's about to pass out from the stress of it all.

Visibly uncomfortable as she searches for the correct response, Esther says, 'I didn't realise Madeira was such a hub for . . . woo-woo.'

'Oh yes, they've been looking forward to it for ages.' Haf takes a big sip of Champagne.

'Why didn't you tell us before?' Otto asks.

'Yes, why not?' Kit adds sweetly.

'We didn't want to make a fuss,' Christopher says.

'You sneaky pair,' says Esther. 'It's a lovely surprise.'

'Yes, lovely!' Kit cries, a little too excitedly.

Esther looks at the neat little gold watch on her wrist, her Christmas present from Otto this year. 'Come on, time to get some air in our lungs. Walkies!'

Upon hearing the word, the dogs run straight to the front door, whining excitedly.

As Esther goes to leave, she leans over to Kit and says, with a gentle pat on the arm, 'Dear, do you maybe want to have a drink of water?'

Unsure what else to do, Haf finishes making tea for the three of them.

In the time it takes for Esther and Otto to dress and leave, the three of them say nothing. They stand clutching their mugs and awkwardly avoid looking at each other. When the front door slams, unable to hold back any more, Kit bursts into such large peals of laughter that she has to hold herself up against the wall.

'Are they really into all that?' Christopher asks Haf.

'Obviously not,' she huffs. 'Kit decided to go off-script.'

'Jesus Christ on a bike,' says Christopher, sagging against the counter. 'What a mess.'

'I can't believe you gave her *a ring* and didn't think that they would assume that's what was going on!' Kit says between wracks of laughter.

'It's a promise ring!'

'That's not a thing!'

'It doesn't even look like an engagement ring? It's got antlers.'

'They probably think you're being all *untraditional* because Haf is a weirdo.'

'Oi!' Haf says, breaking up the sibling bickering. 'I probably should have left it in the bedroom.'

'You think?!' Kit laughs, wiping her eyes.

'And what exactly did you think you were doing with that backstory?' Christopher huffs. 'You've made everything more complicated.'

'It was the first thing I could think of!' Kit protests, though Haf doesn't buy that.

'Well, my parents are hippies now. To be fair, English people always assume we're all myths and magic and sheep-shagging, so it probably was a good lie,' Haf admits, causing Kit to raise an eyebrow.

'I'm going to get dressed and warm up,' Kit says, taking the tea Haf made with her.

'She's on a weird one, all right.' Haf sighs. 'I suppose it's only fair she has a little fun at our expense.'

'We should probably go up and get dressed before they come back,' says Christopher. 'The last time I was in my pyjamas at lunchtime on Christmas, Dad berated me for being lazy.'

'Were you being lazy?' Haf asks as they walk up the stairs.

'I was *nine.*'

When Christopher disappears off for a shower, Haf tries not to shriek at the sting of the cold air against her bare skin. She throws on an oversized fluffy jumper woven with gold sparkles that she had saved for a nice celebration dinner over a leopard print shirt, tucked into a black denim miniskirt.

Really, after all this, she should wear the shagging-reindeer jumper, but she tucks that away, ready for the journey home.

Heading back downstairs, she passes the bathroom where Christopher, freshly pinked from the shower, appears in a haze of mist and peppercorn, towel wrapped around his waist. She wolf-whistles at him, sending him somehow pinker.

Downstairs in the kitchen, she decides to read over the cooking plans, anyway, in case she actually can be useful, before quickly running the mini hoover under the tree to pick up the loose needles, like she's seen Esther do. If she can't help make lunch, she can at least keep it tidy. Especially given Esther gave her so much praise about helping out. Anything to assuage her guilt about leading her on about basically everything.

A little while later, she spots Esther and Otto returning up the drive, muddy terriers in tow. Before they left, they'd set out a towel to dry the dogs off, so Haf grabs it, opens the front door and kneels in the porch ready to intercept muddy paws. Stella and Luna barrel in straight at the towel, burying their heads in it with such force that they almost knock her onto her bum. But after a momentary excitement, they calm down and diligently offer up a paw at a time to be dried off.

Warmed up and armed with a fresh cup of tea from Haf, Esther starts organising in the kitchen. On the counter is an enormous roll of meat.

'Lamb?' Haf asks.

'Venison,' Esther says, rooting through the fridge.

'Wow, I've never had that before.'

'It's very rich, but I'm sure you'll like it. The venison is Otto's domain.' She chuckles. 'What is it about men and huge hunks of meat?'

'Something primal, perhaps.' Haf laughs. 'Need me to do anything?'

'Actually, yes. I just sent him out to drop off a little Christmas something with the Howards. You wouldn't mind grabbing these bits from the pantry and garage?'

She rips off a piece of paper from the notebook in her hand and passes it to Haf.

'Sure, I'll go find it all,' Haf says.

It's a small list of things with instructions as to where one can find them in the garage, pantry and second freezer, as there are notes like *near the oil* and *underneath the ice cream, don't eat it*. She realises this might have been intended for Otto instead of her.

She vaguely remembers the other night when she and Kit dropped off things in the laundry room that there were a few other doors. That must be where she needs to go.

It's a strange little corridor that feels different to the rest of the house – a little too modern, perhaps. She pauses, working out which door to pick as she doesn't want to snoop, when one of the doors next to her opens inward.

Out comes a hand, and she's pulled inside, the door closed softly behind her.

Inside the tiny room, which appears to be a kind of odds-and-ends storage closet, is Kit.

'Hello?' Haf whispers. 'Are you helping me with my list?'

'Absolutely not.' She laughs. 'I'm hiding precisely so I don't get asked to do things.'

'What trouble are you making in here, then?'

'I was throwing my laundry in, but then heard you coming, so decided to scare you.' She flicks her hair, and with a wolfish smile, she says, 'You haven't seen me make trouble yet.'

While she would argue that the mystic mess in the kitchen was definitely Kit making trouble, Haf's heart catches in her chest. Because this feels like the old Kit. Bookshop Kit.

'Ominous,' she croaks. 'And you're even dressed like gender-swapped Loki at a Christmas party.'

She is desperately trying to ignore how good Kit looks in the velvet wrap dress. How her soft hair shimmers, and how good she smells.

'I was going more for Hera, seeing as green is my colour.'

*It is. It is*, Haf thinks, her mouth dry.

'So, you've brought me in to your secret hideout to what? Be nefarious? Aid and abet in your hiding? Is this now technically a game of sardines?'

With a finger against Haf's lips, Kit hushes her, and Haf is pretty sure, certain even, that this might be the end of her. 'Shh.' The command sends shivers down her spine.

'I'm shushed,' she whispers.

'I brought you in here because I realised there probably wasn't anywhere else I could do this without us getting caught.'

And before Haf can say anything else or spontaneously combust, Kit reaches up for her face and pulls her into a deep, soft kiss.

Kit's mouth is warm against her own. Haf breathes her in. The kiss tastes like the sweet berry flavour of Kit's lipstick, which is definitely smearing all over them both.

Through her horny fugue, her last brain cell bleats that this is a bad idea. They are crossing a boundary that can't be uncrossed.

She *should* stop. Anyone could walk in.

But she doesn't want to.

'Kit,' she whispers, and Kit's kisses her deeper, hungrier. Haf gives in to it. How can she not?

There is nothing in the world that can stop this kiss.

Chills run down her back as Kit clutches at her hair. A gasp escapes her lips.

'The door,' she whispers.

'It's locked,' Kit says, nuzzling into her neck and nipping at the soft skin with her teeth.

And with that little bite, everything else falls away.

Bottles clink as Kit presses her up against the shelves. For the first time, she is really aware of their height difference, as Kit seems to tower over her, an arm slung against the shelves over her head.

In her mind, she sees blankets clutched in fists, and Kit's dark hair spread out across a pillow.

The spark between them rages, licking at her wide-awake nerves. Her whole body feels on fire, and aching heat gathers between her legs. God, does Haf want her.

She wraps a thigh around Kit, drawing her hard against her body. Kit's sharp hips answer her own with a soft grind that makes her want to moan.

'Kit,' she whispers again.

'Shut up,' Kit replies softly through the kiss. 'Unless you want to stop?'

It's a purred question through their kisses, and obviously, Haf doesn't want to stop.

'No, I don't want to stop.'

With the hungriest look, Kit draws back so their kiss-bruised lips are moments apart.

'You have two options,' she purrs. 'Do you want to keep talking, or do you want me to fuck you?'

Kit's fingers glide into the soft crevasse where belly and hip meet, in which lies the elastic edge of her knickers.

Overcome, all Haf can do is press her lips together and nod enthusiastically.

She feels dizzy as Kit runs her hand up, over the curves of Haf's body, to the edge of her bra. They kiss deeper as Kit traces Haf's breast, and slowly, teasingly, she rubs a thumb over the nipple, and Haf moans right into Kit's mouth. Kit laps the sound up, like she could live off it alone.

And as Kit's hand slides back down slowly to her knickers, she bleats out a soft, 'Yes, Kit'.

Haf curses that she didn't wear prettier underwear, but all she packed were her most sensible belly-button covering M&S cotton pants. It doesn't seem to matter to Kit.

'Didn't I say no more talking?' Kit whispers. 'Although, I do like to hear you say my name.'

The heat between her legs is *unbearable*, and she rocks forward as Kit traces the edge of her underwear.

'Do you want?'

'Please,' Haf begs breathily, trying to keep her voice as quiet as possible, but she wants to scream with the agony of it all.

And with a gasp, she feels Kit's thumb slide right to the hottest point between her legs.

It's electricity and sparks and all the bright colours, and she has to press her face hard against Kit's sharp shoulders so that she doesn't just scream with the joy of it. It's so much. She aches for Kit to touch her everywhere, to be inside her, and then she is, and Haf could just die right at this moment, just be snuffed out in an instant for feeling way too much.

She comes quickly, thrown head first into orgasm from the tension and secrecy and Kit and everything else. Her body roils beneath Kit's.

Panting, she stares up at Kit, who runs a tongue over her bright white teeth.

Haf wants to kiss the smug smile right off her face.

And she does, dragging Kit's face back down to her hot mouth.

'My turn,' she whispers, both as much a question as a command.

She leans Kit down onto a – hopefully sturdy – shelf, kissing down from her mouth to her collarbone. The velvet dress has rucked up between them, and Haf reaches under to take her tights and underwear in her hands.

Kit moans a soft, 'Please,' as Haf pulls at the fabric teasingly, dragging it against Kit's hip.

'I thought you said no more talking.'

'That was to shut you up long enough so I could make you come,' she says.

'Well then,' she says and drops to her knees, rolling the tights down as she goes. Kit shivers as she plants a trail of kisses up the inside of her thigh, and her skin flushes with goosebumps, the soft hairs rising. As she goes higher, she takes her time, waiting between each kiss as Kit quivers under her touch.

'Is this okay?' she whispers, but before she can finish, Kit mutters something that sounds distinctly like, 'Yesshutup.'

The tiny moan of delight and relief she makes when Haf kisses her between her legs is the most delicious sound she has ever heard. Kit knots her hands in Haf's hair as she roils under her touch, and her knees shake in the most delightful way when she comes. Haf wants to do that to her again, and again, and forever.

Drunk with it all, Kit sinks to the floor to join Haf, peppering her with sweet kisses.

'Well. That was—'

'Fucking great,' moans Kit, still high on orgasm.

'Chaotic enough?'

'I don't think there's anything about this that isn't at least a bit chaotic.' She rolls her tights and underwear back up, smoothing her ruffled hair.

'We should probably get the things on that list, or Esther is going to come looking,' says Haf, wobbling to her feet and rescuing the list from its place of safety on a shelf. 'Do you need a hand getting up?'

Kit nods, and she lifts her up gently, pulling her into her arms. They would be face to face if Kit weren't so much taller than her.

Kit brushes lint off the bottom of her dress where clumps of what looked mostly like dog hair have clung on for dear life.

'I know you and my brother have some kind of extremely weird friendship, but maybe don't mention this to him,' she whispers.

Haf scoffs. 'I think there's a firm "Don't talk about sex" rule, anyway, never mind when it involves you.'

As Kit reaches for the bronzed lock, Haf says, 'I don't . . .' but the rest of the words die on her tongue.

'I can't promise it'll happen again, Haf,' Kit says softly, as if knowing exactly what Haf was thinking. 'It probably shouldn't have happened to start with.'

'Wait . . . what?'

'I'm still not ready to talk about it.'

'But you're ready to fuck?' Haf asks, her voice rising. 'Don't act like this was just blowing off steam.'

'It wasn't, but I can't ignore all the weird shit going on. Most of the time, I'm trying to decide whether I want to kick you or kiss you.'

'Fifty per cent is good odds, though I suppose you could do both.' It comes out sharper than she means it to be, and Kit fixes her with a hard stare.

'I'm serious, Haf. All this? As much as I can admit it could be great, eventually . . . the price of admission is high.'

'What are you talking about?' Her voice wavers, and she wishes it hadn't, but seriously, being dragged into a supply closet for sex seemed like a pretty definitive choice. But as Kit blinks furiously at her, she realises that she's got it wrong.

'Haf, I don't generally care what my parents think, but even this – me stealing my brother's girlfriend—'

'Fake girlfriend,' Haf mutters.

'—might be more fucking weirdness than I can handle. And bless him, but Christopher couldn't locate a spine on an anatomical model. He's never going to tell them it was all a lie, so that's the only scenario we as a couple would exist in. Is that how you want this to start? With everyone we know thinking you're a cheat and I'm fucking horrible?'

She wants to defend Christopher, but all that comes out is, 'Right, well, if you could let me know that you're still just thinking about it before you fuck me next time, that would be great.'

There's no more to say, and Kit ends the conversation by filling her arms with items from the list before bustling out of the cupboard into the garage. Haf follows silently, and Kit loads her arms with more ingredients, and then they're back in the kitchen, and Kit disappears down the hallway. It's just one huge blur.

She sets everything down on one of the clear counters, and Esther doesn't even comment on her prolonged absence, probably because she's surrounded by chopped and peeled vegetables in bowls of water ready to be used.

Haf excuses herself to the bathroom, and sits down on the closed lid, phone in her hand.

**Haf:** I did something stupid
**Ambrose:** hot and sexy stupid, or just plain stupid?
**Haf:** Both
**Ambrose:** please tell me you did not fuck that girl

Haf doesn't reply.

**Ambrose:** wow ok
**Ambrose:** was it at least good????
**Haf:** Way too good
**Haf:** Like bucket-list good
**Ambrose:** are you planning on expiring?

**Ambrose:** at least I can say you died doing what you loved, shagging someone you shouldn't

**Haf:** :(

**Ambrose:** that bad?

**Haf:** That bad

**Haf:** Christopher is going to kill me

**Ambrose:** no, he won't because he's a nice sweet person

**Ambrose:** i might though, for the good of the universe

**Ambrose:** the sheer chaos you've released over the last five days can't be good for, like, the karmic balance or whatever

**Ambrose:** a black hole opens every time you make a bad decision

**Ambrose:** anyway, isn't this what you wanted

**Ambrose:** maybe this is a good thing, even if it's a mess

**Haf:** You'd think.

**Haf:** Apparently it was more 'Merry Christmas, decision pending'.

**Ambrose:** noooo wtf

**Haf:** Yup

**Haf:** Uuugggggggggghhhhhhhhhhhh

**Haf:** I've got to go pretend that didn't happen

**Ambrose:** good luck

**Ambrose:** don't fuck anyone else in that house

**Ambrose:** it might make things somehow more awkward

# Chapter Nineteen

To her relief, the rest of the day goes by quickly in a blur of activities. Enough that she doesn't have to think about Kit.

Instead, she can fool herself into thinking everything is fine, playing pretend just as well as Kit does.

Everything Laurel had said about the Calloway competitiveness turns out to be an understatement, and doesn't stop at karaoke. The board games are brought out, and all four of them take it very, very seriously. While the evening's dinner cooks, the Calloways shuffle through a couple of games of Catan, followed by a furious game of Cheat, which sends a twinge of panic through Haf every time someone enthusiastically yells it. She's not even a cheater, not really. Christopher pretty much gave them his blessing after all, even though that probably didn't extend to shagging on the premises. But that old shitty lie about bisexuals being more likely to cheat, being untrustworthy, rattles around in her head in the quiet moments between turns.

The house is soon filled with the delicious smell of food, and Otto nips off a few times to check on his venison, which has been roasting slowly all afternoon.

Time flies past them, and soon they're all sitting at the dinner table. The roll of meat is carved up into slices, revealing a stuffed

core of wild berries and spices. There are mounds of roast potatoes, Parmesan-topped parsnips, bright little sprouts charred and
garnished with dashes of red chilli. She's suddenly ravenous, realising the endless nibbling of Christmas hasn't really filled her up.

Everyone raises a glass – this time she opts for a fancy soft
drink, just to be safe – and digs in.

After a little time, Esther taps her glass with a spoon.

'We've got an announcement of our own, haven't we, dear?'
Esther says pointedly to Otto.

'Oh yes! Quite.'

He turns to Christopher with a beaming smile. Realising it's
probably something to do with the wedding, her stomach sinks.
Under the table, she squeezes his hand.

'My boy, I'm so proud of you. You've worked so hard to get
where you are and you're really growing into the young man I
always expected you'd be.' He turns his gaze to Haf, a warm glow
of pride. 'And you've found yourself a wonderful partner to walk
this life with, and trust me when I say' – and now he takes Esther's
hand – 'that family is the most important thing. And so that is why
I've decided it's the time for your true inheritance.'

What on earth does he mean?

'True inheritance' doesn't sound like just money, which is what
she was realistically expecting for a potential future-wedding conversation. That's what rich parents do, right? Pay for stuff.

A very strange look shadows on Christopher's face, not quite
resignation. Maybe . . . fear?

Even Kit is softly frowning.

Something else is going on that she's missing.

'Dad—' begins Christopher, but Otto continues ahead.

'It's time for you to join the company. I want you to learn the
ropes and become my replacement. And then, it'll be yours.'

*Oh no.*

This is everything he didn't want. Everything this whole
fake-dating thing was set up to avoid. And it still happened.

After all of this . . . and maybe they even made it all worse with
the fake engagement. Her head swims.

Christopher looks green – like he's going to be sick.

'I . . . I . . .' he stammers.

'Look, he's overcome! Good news, isn't it? Father and son together, me teaching you the ropes.'

Christopher gasps like a fish out of water.

'Do you even want that, Christopher?' Kit nudges softly.

They can't make this decision for him; he must be brave enough to say it.

'Of course he does, Katharine,' Esther says. 'What a silly thing to say.'

'It's not silly. Look at him. Does he look happy to you?'

Kit's right – the green tinge has lessened a little, but he's flushed, and resolutely staring at the food on his plate.

'He's just surprised, aren't you, Christopher?' Otto says, beaming. 'He's been waiting for this his whole life.'

'I—'

That's all he says, to start with. He doesn't even look up from his plate, and under the table, Haf can feel his leg vibrating with anxiety. She places a hand on his thigh as if to say, 'I'm with you.'

'You just need to hand in your notice at work, and then we can organise a start date for you in the spring. You'll be free of the Ratliff-Zouches, at least,' he says with a booming laugh.

*Out of the pan and into the fire*, she thinks. Or out of one fire into a much bigger fire with more responsibility. A fire you have to keep burning.

'Of course, it'll come with a pay rise too.'

'And I know you love living in London, Christopher, but we just want to make it clear that if you want to move a little closer, you'd have grandparents to hand,' Esther says with a knowing smile that makes Haf feel so queasy.

This seems to be the last straw, because Christopher finally sits up straight, looks at his father and says, 'No.'

'No?' asks Otto, his smile warping in confusion.

'No. Thank you, Dad,' he says, slowly at first, building confidence with each word. 'But I can't accept the job offer.'

'Why not? You've earned it.'

'I just—'

'You just what, Christopher?' Esther asks, her eyebrows arched in bafflement.

'I just can't do it. I just . . .' He takes a deep breath. 'I need to take some time off work.'

'What's wrong, Christopher?' asks Esther, switching to motherly concern. 'Did something happen?'

'Over a long time, perhaps.'

Haf and Kit lock eyes over the table. Is he really going to tell them now?

'I'm burned out, and the job I already have is making me miserable, completely miserable. I can't go on working there. And I know that if I work for you, it'll be more of the same for me, and that's not because of you, Dad, or the business itself.' He steadies himself with a deep breath. 'It's me. It's just *me*. I'm not cut out for that world, or being in an office all the time. And I'm worried if I keep trying to squeeze myself into that box, into that mould of who you think I could be, then something in me is going to just break.'

Silence fills the table, only broken by Esther loudly saying, 'Oh.'

Otto seems to be vibrating with fury. 'You don't think everything I've built for you is good enough? Is that it, boy?' he barks so loudly that next to him, Kit, startled, drops her cutlery onto her plate with a clatter.

'No, Dad, it's not—'

'I've worked hard my whole life to build a life just for you and your sister, and you just what? Don't care?'

He's hurt, Haf realises. This was a gift of a secure life, a permanent financial blanket for their combined future and the future of their imaginary children. And Christopher has just turned around and said Otto's idea of what is good is *bad* for him.

Otto gets to his feet and paces, unsure what to do with himself.

'Dad, that's not what he's saying at all,' Kit says, getting to her feet and taking his large arm in her own, like Belle calming the Beast. 'Take a deep breath and sit back down. You need to listen to him.'

'What do you know about this?' Esther asks, rounding on Kit.

'I know that he's unhappy there. That's been obvious for ages.'

'It has not been obvious,' snaps Esther, affronted.

'Can we all just take a moment to remember that we should care about whether our family members are happy? That matters to us, doesn't it?'

Haf nods enthusiastically, but no one else replies and it is gutting.

'I just can't think about this right now,' Otto says, and he marches away from the table.

In the distance, a door slams, rattling the glass in the grandfather clock.

Without another word, Christopher gets up from the table and leaves the room.

Across the table, Kit returns to her seat.

'Well, that didn't go as planned,' says Esther, who begins gathering up the serving plates even though no one seems to be actually finished eating. 'You think he'd be thrilled that we just offered him a company.'

'Mum, come on,' says Kit, which is almost certainly the only time Kit hasn't called her Esther.

'Not now, Kit.'

'I know it's not what you both wanted, but maybe you both should listen to him when he says it's not what he wants. It's *his* life.'

'Kit, I don't want to hear it right now.'

'Well, you should. God knows this family needs to get better at being truthful with each other.'

Everyone seems to have lost their appetite, so Kit and Haf help Esther gather up the things from the table. Kit takes a platter in each hand and disappears to the kitchen.

'I'm sorry, Esther,' Haf says, hoping this apology covers a multitude of sins.

'See if you can talk some sense into him, will you? That is, provided it wasn't you who pushed him to this decision,' she snaps.

As much as she doesn't want to take it to heart, it hurts. She wants to stand up for him like Kit did, but anything she says is going to make this whole situation worse.

She gathers the plates still half-covered in food into her arms and follows Kit into the kitchen, where she stands filling the dishwasher.

'I can't believe he said it,' Haf whispers, scraping her plate into the food-waste caddy.

Stella and Luna sit on the kitchen rug, patiently awaiting any lunch scraps. *Someone deserves to be happy in this house*, she thinks, taking a bacon-wrapped mini sausage and throwing half to each dog. They gleefully snaffle it down and wag their tails in the hope of more.

'Me neither,' Kit replies, keeping her voice low. 'I'm glad he did, though.'

Their earlier conversation somehow feels less important now, and it feels like a weight of tension lifts between them. A temporary truce, perhaps. Kit encouraging Christopher warms Haf's heart a little. It's still bruised, but things feel relaxed again, at least for now.

'Christ, I'm glad they never asked me if I wanted to go work for them. I'd be driving back to London in a flash.' Kit laughs quietly.

'Should I go check on him?'

Kit shakes her head. 'Give him a bit of time. When he was a kid, he always needed some time alone just to, like, work through stuff in his head before he can talk about it. He knows you're proud of him.'

As she finishes her sentence, the voices in the dining room rise to a crescendo.

'Sounds like everyone needs to calm down.'

'Are you going in?'

'No,' scoffs Kit. 'I tried, but I think I'm just making it worse. He has to stand up to them. 'Come on, let's go watch some Christmas movies and hope they can drown that out. And you should keep out the way for now.'

'Why?'

'You don't think that line was all Esther will say to you, given the chance? They offered him the job because they think you two are about to settle down and pop out two point four kids.'

'Eurgh.'

'Precisely.'

None of the other Calloways join them, and so Kit and Haf sink into the couch, turning on a familiar Christmas film. Only Stella and Luna join them in the living room, curled up between them. Haf slightly regrets giving them those sausages when both of them start intermittently farting.

'How is it so spicy?' she whines, covering her mouth with her hand.

Even though the movie is one of her favourites, she can't hold her attention. Her mind keeps wandering to Christopher, wherever he is, to Kit at the other end of the couch and back, in an endless cycle of worry.

'Speaking of my brother,' says Kit, breaking her train of thought.

'I didn't say anything?' says Haf.

'You were thinking very loudly. Are *you* going to make a decision?'

'About what?'

'About your shitty, horrible job.'

'It's not that bad,' she says, a little defensively.

'Haf, I'm pretty sure that was a direct quote from you.'

'Oh.'

'Not going to follow in my brother's footsteps?' she asks softly. 'Maybe it won't be so bad if someone else is doing it too?'

'I'm pretty sure Christopher was on a living wage and probably has some savings to fall back on.'

'You're plucky. I'm sure you could find something new quickly. I really think you should quit,' she says. 'You'll spend so much of your life in a job. What's the point of doing something that makes you miserable?'

Haf sighs deeply. She really didn't want to talk about this at Christmas. 'I just feel like I'll have failed if I just quit. Like, what was the point of moving cities, and changing my whole life? What was it all for if I just leave?'.

'It's not failure. Not every job is perfect for every person. Stop being so hard on yourself.' She sighs. 'God, no one could pay me to be your age again.'

'Aren't you only like three years older than me?'

'Trust me. It makes the difference. You just have to think about what you actually want from life, you know?'

Haf's mind screams, *You, you, you!*

'If you're not bothered about a high-flying career, then why not find a job that does pays the bills and find your passions elsewhere?'

'You never know, I could be a corporate career girlboss just waiting to come out of my chaos chrysalis,' Haf says.

'Gross.' Kit laughs. 'But that doesn't sound like Haf Hughes.'

'You know what sounds more appealing? Swapping your house for the holidays to get away from your life,' she says, directing them back to the movie, even though the end credits are rolling. 'Jack Black should be the romantic lead more often.'

'Men aren't really my thing, but I get it,' Kit murmurs.

'His scene in *School of Rock* about being sexy and chubby and liking food sold it for me.'

It's still early, so they decide to do one more, picking the newest Christmas film where Vanessa Hudgens plays several versions of herself.

'You know, I like to think this film series takes place in the same universe as *Orphan Black*.'

'Isn't that the show about clones?'

'Yeah,' Haf reasons. 'They had Project Leda and Project Castor. Maybe this is Project Caster Sugar.'

Kit snorts. 'You're a dork.'

Somewhere in the middle of the film, they both fall asleep, only waking up as a loud, poppy Christmas song plays over the credits.

'Come on, we should go to bed,' sighs Haf, pushing herself up from the very comfortable couch. Both of them seem to freeze at the suggestion, before Haf stammers, 'In our separate beds.'

Exhausted from a very weird Christmas Day, they both giggle with nervous laughter.

At the bottom of the stairs, Kit sighs with weariness. 'This house is too damn tall.'

'Do you want a boost?' Haf asks, following her up, and just as Kit asks what that entails, she puts both her hands on Kit's bum and pushes.

'Don't.' Kit laughs. 'You're going to push me over.'

'Nope, come on. We can do this. I believe in us! You can make it,' Haf urges, and together they go up the two flights of stairs in tandem. Stella and Luna follow behind them.

'Goodnight,' they whisper, before disappearing into their respective rooms. The dogs follow Kit into hers.

It appears that Christopher has a truly magical talent to just sleep through any emotional distress, which is honestly admirable. He's snoring away, already in his flannel pyjamas, and even Haf clattering about as she gets undressed, flicking the lights on and off doesn't wake him up.

They'll talk in the morning.

They've got a lot to sort out. And maybe she can help him explain what he wants to do properly, without shouting, to both his parents.

Just as she's about to change into her pyjamas, she realises she's left her phone downstairs. Even if it's locked, with Ambrose texting her, it's too much of a risk to just leave it lying around.

She pads quietly down the stairs, cursing each step, and finds her phone wedged down the side of the couch.

From the hallway, she can see a light on, one they must have missed with all the stairs hijinks.

But when she goes to the dining room to turn it off, she finds Otto sitting in the corner, whisky in one hand, his head in the other.

'Oh, hi, sorry,' she says nervously, as he looks up to see her. 'I saw the light on and was worried I'd left one on and so came to turn it off.'

'Would you like one?' he asks, raising his glass slightly.

She knows Kit said not to intervene, but this seems like the only opportunity she's going to have. 'Sure,' she says.

He gets up and opens the sideboard, taking a new glass and filling it from a whisky bottle on the table.

'*Saluti*,' he says softly, clinking his glass against hers.

'*Saluti*,' she replies, taking a seat at the dining table next to him.

'I owe you an apology, Haf. I behaved monstrously in front of you earlier, and that's not the welcome to the family I'd have liked you to experience. Frankly, I'm a little embarrassed.'

'It was an emotional conversation,' she says. 'Did you and Christopher talk it out?'

He harrumphs. 'There was a lot of yelling and glaring, so no. Not yet. I'm not the most productive communicator, according to my wife.'

*Me neither*, thinks Haf.

'It must be difficult for you,' she says carefully. 'To hear how unhappy he is.'

'It is,' he whispers. 'It is. And I feel stupid for not realising. His happiness is the most important thing to me, and I've made him feel like it's tertiary.'

'Did you tell him that?'

He blushes a little. 'Foolishly, no. I was too busy suggesting he could do something different, trying to solve the problem, rather than listening to him. There's so many arms to it all – not just the luxury stays but the retirement homes and other aspects that I thought if I just kept talking to him about it, he'd say, "Aha, that's the one I want, really." I must accept that perhaps he needs something totally different.'

*Yes, like the baking*, she thinks. But she can't say it, because clearly Christopher hasn't admitted it either.

'Tell me about the retirement homes,' she says, changing tack a little. 'That seems like a very different operation from . . .'

'Fancy houses for people with too much money?' he says with a wry smile.

'You're the one who said it.' She laughs.

'Indeed. Well, the thing about getting older is that you unfortunately start contemplating your future when you're much, much older. When I was looking for assisted-living options for my parents as they got older, I realised there was a complete dearth of places with high standards.

'I know what you mean,' Haf says. 'Where I'm from is a big retirement area, but some of the places are . . .'

'A bit grim?'

'Yeah. When my granny was in one, I used to go in and read to the residents. That was pretty nice.'

'I can imagine you'd be good at that.'

'It was nice. One lady was super into raunchy historical romances, real bodice-ripper stuff. She said I was very good at the voices.'

Otto barks a laugh.

'So you decided to have your own ones?' she asks.

'Essentially, yes. I managed to acquire several estates, the houses of which were perfect once we'd refitted things, and the residents love walking the grounds and taking in nature. It's been growing steadily, and really it probably needs someone on the ground to run it properly, but that wasn't what I had in mind for Christopher – he's a polite boy, but not the most talkative of people.' He swirls his drink. 'Really, I suppose we need someone more like you who is willing to muck in.'

Haf finishes off the last of her whisky and tries not to wince as the peaty taste tickles her nose. 'Hah, I'm sure there's plenty of people willing to read a good bodice-ripper to an octogenarian.'

A huge yawn racks her body as she sets down her glass. 'That has properly finished me off. Thank you for the nightcap. I should get to sleep.'

'You're welcome. And Haf, thank you for talking to me. That was kind of you.'

She hangs in the doorway, turns back to him and says, 'Just talk to him. Listen to what he has to say. He just doesn't want to disappoint you. I know feelings aren't the easiest things to say, but lead with that.'

He gives her a warm smile and a nod as she leaves.

The whisky has warmed up her bones, and she practically glides back upstairs.

*Maybe this is a good sign that things will be okay,* she thinks as she sinks down into the covers.

Boxing Day is a new day.

# Chapter Twenty

When she wakes, Christopher is gone, but has left a note on his pillow.

*Gone to Laurel's to help take down the decorations. A good excuse to give me and Dad some space. Sorry for disappearing, thank you for yesterday. Be back after lunch, hopefully. C x*

*Bloody early risers*, she thinks.

She retrieves her phone from under the pillow and finds a message from her mum. Inside is a dodgy-looking link accompanied by, *Look what we got up to*, followed by a winky emoji. She hopes that it's not some kind of WhatsApp scam or something horribly raunchy, and clicks on it.

To her surprise, the Facebook app loads. She didn't think it was installed on this phone, as she's not been on there for so long.

Posted on the page of the hotel they must be staying at is a photo of her parents playing limbo very well, which is both alarming and impressive in equal measure. Her dad is almost horizontal under the beam, and behind him, Mum cheers.

She clicks out of the photo, but before she can navigate back to the message from her mum, she is presented with a new and entirely more devastating photo.

Freddie and Jennifer stand in front of the most enormous Christmas tree, dressed in matching but very tasteful Christmas jumpers. Her hand is extended towards the camera, and on one perfectly manicured finger is one hell of a rock.

They're engaged.

*Real* engaged, not fake engaged like she is.

As though no time has passed, she's right back in her old house, watching Jennifer walk right into the life she used to have. Remembering Freddie brushing her off like he'd never promised her a future, told her she was the love of his life. They had broken up, sure, but she had thought it was just while she got sorted in her new life. Clearly, he had moved on. He'd promised so many things to her when they were together, so many futures. But it was all a lie.

Maybe it was always a lie.

She doesn't even love him any more, but the hurt is still real.

Before she can think better of it, she opens the comments and scrolls through their mutual friends from uni, congratulating them both. That shouldn't feel like a betrayal, but it is. They know what he did to her. It stings.

Fuck everything.

No one ever says what they mean. It's all just empty words from them, and heartbreak for her.

Her heart aches like it's trying to claw its way out of her chest, and she launches her phone across the room, where it crunches hard against the wall.

And so, she curls up under the covers and cries until she can't cry any more.

Eventually, she gets dressed into yesterday's clothes, brushes a bit of make-up over her blotchy, just-bawled face, and heads to the kitchen in search of caffeine.

Downstairs, she finds Kit nursing a cup of coffee with a book open on the kitchen counter. She had kind of hoped Kit would have gone out too.

'Morning,' she croaks. The clock on the oven blinks eleven. 'Is that accurate?' she asks, pointing to it.

'Yep,' Kit nods, looking up from the pages. Her eyebrows furrow slightly as she takes Haf in. 'Are you all right?'

'Just didn't sleep great.'

'Welcome to the club,' says Kit slowly.

The dogs trot in from another room, ready for their morning pats. When she bends down to cuddle them, Luna hops up and gives her a little lick on the cheek as if to say 'I heard you went on your ex's Facebook – sorry about it.'

'Is everyone out?'

Kit holds up a bright yellow Post-it. 'I believe they've gone for a long walk.'

'What is it with your family and leaving notes?' Haf mutters. 'Christopher's gone to Laurel's.'

'Oh yeah, the decorations,' Kit says, wiping her face. 'It's the Howards' one concession. All the staff can go home once the dishwasher is full, and Christopher and I usually help with the decorations. It's a nice tradition. Laurel usually bullies us into going for a ride.'

'Not feeling it today?' Haf asks, as she pours herself a cup of coffee from a cafetière.

'No, and . . . erm, I should probably tell you that I told Laurel about everything.'

'You mean . . .'

'The adventures in the closet,' finishes Kit. 'Sorry, I just needed to talk to her and since she found out, she's been messaging me constantly about this . . . situation.'

'Oh God, there's two of them. I knew introducing her and Ambrose wasn't a good idea. I hope she won't tell Christopher.'

'No, no. And said she would look after Christopher on the condition that I, err, talked to you.' She shifts awkwardly in her seat.

'About?'

Kit gestures in the air in a way that Haf takes to mean everything.

Suddenly, the kitchen feels too small to contain all her feelings. 'Shall we take the dogs out?' Haf offers.

'Good plan,' says Kit. She decants the remains of her coffee into a thermos. 'Walkies!'

A soft layer of fresh snow has settled on top of everything. It's one of those perfect bright, sunny, cold days. The dogs lead her and Kit through the back garden to a gate that opens straight onto the fields. Stella and Luna slip through it as soon as there's a big enough gap for them, gambolling in the pure-white field.

Church bells ring in the distance, but otherwise there's little sound apart from the snuffling and panting of the dogs, who run back and forth as though they're herding Kit and Haf onwards. The air tastes cold and fresh.

From her pocket, Kit produces a ratty-looking ball and holds it out to Haf.

'Wow, for me? You shouldn't have.' Haf hops out of the way as Kit goes to whack her with her walking stick, sliding in the snow as she lands.

'Throw it for them, dickhead.' Kit laughs.

Stella vibrates with excitement at her feet. Haf has never been a good thrower, and when she releases the ball, it doesn't go very far. But the dogs, seemingly pleased to just be getting some attention, prance after it happily.

'Wow, that was almost as bad as my throwing, and when I do it, my shoulder pops out.'

'Don't be mean!' Haf laughs. 'I don't have a good excuse. I'm just rubbish. But . . .'

She reaches down to ball up some powder snow in her hands.

'I'll show you how rubbish at throwing I am.'

'Don't you dare! I'll whack you!'

'You can try, but I'm very quick.'

'This is unfair.' Kit laughs, ducking down as a snowball flies over her head.

Haf bends down to grab some more snow, and to her horror, Kit shoves a handful of snow down the back of her coat. Haf shrieks at the cold on her warm skin, and Kit scampers away, cackling.

'Aaaaah! I'm going to get you!'

Haf rushes up behind Kit and grabs her around the waist, pulling her tight against her body. Kit wriggles against her, laughing and squirming to get away, but she holds tight.

'I'm not letting you escape to cause more snow crimes!'

'You're the one threatening to throw things at me!'

Suddenly, Kit spins in Haf's grasp, and the sudden movement sends Haf off balance, her Doc Martens sliding on the old, icy snow underneath the powder layer, and both of them go crashing down.

'Oh my God, are you okay?' Haf asks Kit, who has landed completely on top of her. 'Was I a good crash mat, at least?'

'I'm fine.' She laughs. 'If I'm not, you can just carry me back.'

The shock of the fall fades and all that remains is the realisation that Kit is lying on top of her.

'I wouldn't bet on my noodle arms,' she says softly, trying to ignore how good it feels to have Kit's weight on her.

Frosted snowflakes glitter in Kit's hair, and her nose is blushed with the cold. She looks extremely cute, which is funny because "cute" is not a word that she usually thinks of when it comes to Kit. Striking, mildly terrifying, incredibly hot, sure. But in the snow, she looks undeniably adorable, and it makes Haf's heart ache. There's so much about this woman that she wants to know and learn. She wants to be the expert on all things Kit.

'Fashion a sledge and get the dogs to pull me back. I believe in you. Also, oh my God, your hands are freezing? Why aren't you wearing gloves?'

'Oh, guess I forgot to pack some,' Haf says nonchalantly. 'I always have cold fingers anyway.'

'Right,' says Kit slowly. She sits back, straddling her, and looks up at the tree above them. 'Hey, look. It's your favourite horrible plant.' She points at the bough above them where someone has tied a sprig of mistletoe with a tartan ribbon.

It's the most natural thing when Kit leans down to kiss her, like they've been fighting in the snow all their lives. The kiss is soft and warm and gentle, unlike their hungry kisses in the cupboard.

But sirens go off in Haf's brain, her thoughts leaping from Jennifer and Freddie, to the argument in the cupboard.

'Stop,' she says, pushing herself up to sitting.

Kit slides off her into the snow. 'Are you okay,? Haf? Talk to me.'

Hot tears prickle at her eyes, and she can't catch her breath. 'I can't. I can't.' She gasps, like a fish out of water. Melting snow seeps through her clothes, but still she feels too hot.

'You can't what?' Kit says, getting to her feet and holding out her hand to help Haf up.

She wants to yell, 'I can't just be okay with this when you're not. I can't just go along with you when you don't know how you feel. I can't be here right now, getting hurt again.'

But instead, what she does, is run.

At first, she hears Kit yelling behind her. It's a dick move to run off but she can't stop.

Haf slams into the house, leaving the back door wide open behind her, and stands over the kitchen sink, not sure if she's going to pass out, or be sick, or just get a drink of water. A few moments later, the dogs crash in after her, followed by the distant sound of a car driving away. Kit's, she presumes.

At least she's alone now, and can think. Not that she wants to do that either.

The dogs sniff her cautiously, and she sinks to the floor where they nose at her with wet, muddy faces.

*God, what a mess*, she thinks.

The dogs are soaked from the drying snow, so she gets up to grab the dog towel from the radiator, only for them to shoot through the house. The last thing she needs is Esther going completely spare about muddy feet.

'Girls, come here,' she yells, slipping out of her boots and rushing after them with the dog towel.

Luckily, they both stall long enough for her to dry them off before scampering off into the hallway. She mops up the floor with the towel, just to be safe, and follows the dogs through to the house. She needs to properly sit down for a minute.

The house is silent, apart from them.

But standing by the front door, hands clasped in front of her, is Esther.

There's a bag at her feet.

Haf's bag.

'Um, hi? Is everything okay? What's going on?'

Esther steps forward. 'I've decided that it's best you leave. All your things are packed, and if I've missed anything, we will forward it on to you after the holidays. I've called you a car to take you to the station. It'll be here in a few minutes.'

Haf blinks slowly, trying to process what Esther is telling her. 'I'm sorry, I don't understand. You want me to leave? Does Christopher know?'

'Yes, Haf, I want you to leave. And no, I haven't told him yet, but luckily, he was out with his father, which means he didn't see you and Katharine rolling about in the snow together.'

A stone plummets through Haf's body.

'It is bad enough that we are in the middle of a family disagreement, that up until now involved your future with my son,' she says, her voice as steady and coiled as a snake, ready to strike. Haf notes the past tense in her words. 'But the fact that you come into this house and seduce my daughter . . . Was it not enough?'

The rage ripples under Esther's skin, a fiercely protective mothering instinct. Lowering her voice to a hiss, she says, 'I will not have anyone hurting my children in this house. You must go.'

Panic swells in her chest, and she's so exhausted from everything that's happened over the last few days that all she says is, 'Okay.'

'Without a word to Christopher and Katharine.'

Haf nods, willing herself not to cry in front of Esther. She will not cry. She must not cry.

'Good.'

Gravel crackles outside, cutting through the heavy silence. Esther opens the front door for her as the car parks up.

As she leaves, Esther says, her voice low, 'You know, I really liked you, Haf. Or perhaps I just liked the person I thought you were. I'm disappointed it turned out this way.'

'Me too.'

'Get home safe,' and it's this care underneath everything else that threatens to break her.

Her resolve finally cracks as Stella and Luna follow her down the steps.

'Stay, girls,' she says, and they tilt their little heads in confusion, tails hanging low as they realise she's leaving.

The driver puts her bag in the boot and thankfully says nothing to her as she gets in. As the car drives away from the Calloway house, the tears finally fall.

# Chapter Twenty-One

The driver takes her to a station with a direct train back to London. She cries the whole way, and he deposits her in the snow with her bag, still sniffling.

It turns out that when she launched her phone across the room, it gained an ominous-looking crack across the screen protector and completely battered the daisy-print hard case. It's on, but the screen barely lights up, murky like oil on water. So much for using the train ticket app she diligently installed.

Refusing to subject anyone in the ticket office to her mildly hysterical demeanour, she buys a ticket from the machine, wincing at the price. The next train isn't for a good forty-five minutes, either.

A few people mill around, including a group of fashionable teenagers.

Typically, the Pumpkin Café on the platform is closed, a sign on the door saying they'll be back in half an hour. Enough time for her to get a coffee and some sympathy chocolate before she gets on the train.

'Hey, Siri,' she sniffles, hoping the microphone isn't broken. Magically, the little ding that says it's working sounds. 'Call Ambrose.'

Somehow, it does.

'Hey, stinker.'

She's about to reply, but just hearing Ambrose's voice makes her bursts into tears again.

'Wait, are you crying? Haf? What the fuck? Turn video on.'

'I can't,' she sobs. 'My phone is fucked.'

She sits down heavily on the bench in the station, wincing at the cold metal on her still snow-wet bum. If only Esther had given her time to change clothes before she threw her out.

'Oh, shit. What happened?'

Somehow, Haf manages to relay the whole mess in between heaving bouts of tears.

A packet of tissue appears in the air in front of her and she looks up to see one of the teenagers holding it out to her. She takes it and whispers a thank-you.

'I hope your day gets better,' they say, before scampering back to their friends.

'Are you being comforted by strangers?'

'Pretty much,' she says, balancing the phone between chin and shoulder as she blows her nose.

'What did you do to your phone, anyway?'

'Threw it against the wall because I saw Freddie and Jennifer's engagement announcement.'

'*No!*'

'Yeah.'

'Hang on a second.' It sounds like Ambrose moves rooms, followed by a very muffled conversation where Ambrose demands one of the teenagers in the house hands over their laptop.

'If you don't give me that laptop,' they hiss. 'I will send that girl you like all the videos I took of you doing karaoke. What's her name? Carmela? I bet she'd love to see your take on Celine Dion.'

'You wouldn't.'

There's a pause where presumably Ambrose is giving them a 'try me' look before the teenager relents.

'Hey, I'm back,' they say.

'Are you blackmailing your cousin for me?' Haf sniffs.

'Only a little. Look, by the time you get to Paddington, I should be able to get into London with all my stuff. Meet me at St Pancras so we can get some decent coffee, and then we can either come back here, or I'll take you home to York. Your choice. Does that sound . . . ? Oh, you're crying again.'

'In a good way,' Haf wails. 'Because I love you. Thank you. You don't have to do this.'

'I know, but I feel responsible. I should have locked you up or something. We could have avoided this whole mess.'

'Don't be silly, it's completely my fault.'

'Of course it is. I was just trying to be nice. But I did get a lot of enjoyment out of it, so I suppose I need to make up for all that.'

'It's okay. Look the café is opening up, I'm going to go warm up a minute. If my phone dies, meet me at the big Christmas tree.'

They hang up just as her phone makes an ominous noise that she's pretty sure means it's out of battery, and she wobbles to her feet. The teenagers, still looking on, concerned, give her a tiny thumbs up, which she returns, feeling very 'How do you do, my fellow kids?' about it.

The train arrives a few minutes late. No one else gets in the same carriage as her, which is probably for the best, as she radiates misery. Someone opened all the windows, so it's an absolute icebox. She huddles down in a corner of a four-person table seat, next to something that looks like it could be a radiator, though it doesn't seem to be churning out any heat.

'Welcome aboard, passengers, to this service direct to London Paddington. We've heard there's some disruption on the line up ahead, but hopefully that will be cleared by the time we get closer and you can all be on your way.'

She grips onto her rapidly cooling terrible coffee with both hands, hoping that the announcement is not a sign of worse things to come.

The train chugs slowly through the snowy white countryside, and she watches the countryside pass from her window.

Fresh snow falls from the sky as they pull into the next station, where a lot more people seem to get on. The driver announces that they're going to have to go at a reduced speed due to the snow.

'Fuck's sake,' she mutters.

Someone sits down opposite her, and to her surprise it's—

'Quiet Carriage Man,' she mumbles.

'Oh no.' He sighs. The stockinged Christmas jumper is gone, replaced with a tasteful cream Nordic one. 'I can move seats.'

'Don't go,' she says, her voice wobbling as fresh tears fall. 'I'm sorry I keep freaking you out. I'm very normal, really!'

He does not look remotely convinced by this, but nervously offers her a Costa Coffee napkin.

She takes it, and dabs at her eyes.

'Are you . . . all right?' he asks gently, and she blows her nose in response. 'I take it the fake dating didn't go so well.'

'You really heard all of that?' she sniffs.

'I really did.'

'Sorry about that. When I kept seeing you everywhere, I thought that you'd blow our cover or something.' She laughs ruefully.

'I'm allergic to drama, so you were safe with me,' he mutters.

'I did that all myself, though, so oh well!'

He winces.

'Sorry, I'll stop talking about my silly life. I don't even know your name.'

'Bryn,' he sighs, running his hand through his curly black hair.

'You're Welsh too?' she sobs, relieved to find some familiarity on this lonely train.

'A little bit.'

'I'm Haf.'

'Oh, trust me, I remember.'

Above them, the train driver announces that they're going to have to wait on the line while trains up ahead leave the next station.

'It's going to be a long journey.' Bryn sighs.

He's not wrong. The train stops and starts, and even when it is going, it's moving so slowly that it may as well not be.

Seeing her disaster of a dead phone, Bryn offers her his so she can text Ambrose a travel update. It's just a simple flip phone, taking her back to being a teenager.

'Your friend replied with just three train emojis and then an aubergine. What does that translate to in words?'

'I wish I knew. I just presume it means okay and try not to think too much about it.'

'What a bizarre little life you lead.' He sighs.

One of the conductors appears with the food and drinks trolley and in a generous display of Christmas spirit, the company has decided to allow them all a free bottle of water and a biscuit. Bryn buys them two watery teas.

'Thank you,' she says, clutching the cup to her.

'I wouldn't drink it,' he says, peering into the cup as the creamer swirls into it. 'It'll keep you warm, at least. And in return, seeing as we're stuck on a train and I was there for bits of it, you can tell me the whole story.'

Relieved to have someone to talk to, Haf starts telling the story. To her surprise, Bryn listens raptly, only interrupting occasionally to get her to explain some of the weirder points.

It turns out Bryn had also been visiting family, and is a second cousin of Laurel's, hence bumping into each other at the Howard party. She glosses over what happened in the closet; that seems too private to share.

Why is it that talking to a stranger about these things sometimes seems so much easier?

A while later, as the train finally inches past Reading station in the home stretch to London, Bryn gets really chatty.

'The thing I don't understand,' he says, 'is why you just didn't tell them it was all fake? Then you could have just dated the sister, right?'

'Her name is Kit, but I couldn't do that! Christopher wasn't even there to defend himself.'

'Who cares? You were getting thrown out! You think he would be upset you told everyone when the other option was you getting stuck on a train in a snow with a stranger?'

'You're not a stranger any more, Bryn,' she says, patting his hand.

'Don't try to sweet talk me out of getting a proper answer.'

Haf pouts, annoyed that it didn't work. 'I just wanted to protect him.'

'And in doing so, you ensured you didn't have to make a choice for yourself. Clever.'

'What do you mean?'

'Well, if you'd blown the cover, you could have professed your undying love for the sister.'

'If she even wants me,' she wails. 'Plus, look how well all my choices have gone for me so far? Wrong, horrible job that makes me feel like death. Fake dating a man I literally just met. Then falling in love with his sister,' she barks, counting her sins off on her fingers.

Copying her, he says, 'Right, city – you met your terrifying-emoji friend. As for the fake dating, you did that because you liked him, and now he's a good friend. And you fell in love! What's more wonderful than that? Being in love with someone is a choice you make every single day. That doesn't sound like a bad one to me.'

'I liked you better when I was scary to you.'

'Am I wrong? Am I wrong?' he says, opening his wide hands.

'Personally, I think I'm being more selfless than you make me sound.'

'Of course you do. If you're a martyr, then it's all worth it.'

Haf puts her head down on the table and groans.

'So, what? You're just going to run away and forget about it all?'

'No,' she mutters. 'I don't want to do that. But it's probably the only option.'

'Only if you're intent on being a coward. I watched you catch a gingerbread house in mid-air while chasing down a reindeer, and muscle a drunk man out of a fancy party. Those don't sound like actions of a coward, though.'

'Wow, you really pay attention.'

'Reluctantly, yes. I am observant to my core.'

Despite the train moving a little faster, it's still freezing in the carriage, and without the hot dishwater tea, the cold is getting to her. Haf waddles to the baggage rack and flips open her rucksack, which is packed alarmingly neatly. Her chest aches – if Esther was really unkind, she would have thrown everything in here. Instead, she took the time to fold everything up.

And at the top, there's something wrapped up in brown paper and tied in string.

She takes it, and another jumper, and heads back to her seat.

'What's that?' asks Bryn, as she wraps the jumper around her like a scarf. 'Did your fake mother-in-law give you a good-riddance present?'

'I'm not sure,' she mutters. 'And is that even a thing?'

'Just open it,' he urges, peering across the table.

She does, very carefully. The string unknots and the paper falls open, revealing a beautiful pair of gloves. They're just like the ones she had seen at the fête, but instead of snowflakes, it's little white reindeer.

Resting atop them is a small square of brown card. Written in cursive handwriting is a message:

*I'm in if you'll have me. Merry Christmas. Love K x*

'Oh my God,' she splutters. 'Oh my God, oh my God!'

Bryn grabs the card from her hands and reads it. 'Wait, when did she give this to you?'

'She didn't!' Haf shrieks, her mind racing. 'I must not have seen them, but, oh God, she even asked me about gloves when we were on the walk and I thought she was just laughing about my horrible cold hands. It's just like in the book! Oh no.'

'What?'

'I ran away!'

'Emotionally?'

'Literally! I literally ran away from her, and she said Laurel told her to talk to me about everything, and with these? Maybe she was going to tell me she wants to be with me, but *I ran away*!'

She grabs her battered and definitely dead phone and shakes it, willing it to somehow turn back on. 'I don't know her number, or even Christopher's number. Oh crap, I need to tell her.'

She looks up and smiles at Bryn.

'I'm going to do it. I'm going to tell her I love her.'

'Attagirl!'

She pockets the card and slips the gloves on. Her heart flutters in her chest, pounding out a rhythm of Kit. Kit. Kit.

The train driver announces that they're pulling into London, finally, and before long they're piling off the train together at Paddington station. Bryn kindly helps her with the enormous backpack.

Right behind him is the famous bronze statue of Paddington Bear.

'Where are you headed now?' Bryn asks as they reach the end of the platform.

'St Pancras. Ambrose is meeting me there. I think I'm going to get a cab so I don't knock someone out with this,' she says, lifting the backpack higher on her back.

'And then?'

'I don't know. I have to find a way to speak to her.'

'Good plan. I guess this is farewell,' says Bryn.

And to her surprise, he pulls her into a hug. 'Go get her.'

And with that, he's gone.

She rushes through Paddington station, and up to the taxi rank. The cabbie helps her launch the rucksack onto the back seat of the black cab, and she squeezes down next to it.

There's somehow even snowfall here, even though Christopher had told her it practically never snows in London. Some of it sticks on the roofs and tops of cars.

Haf leans her head against the window, hoping for one of those London montages where they drive past the London Eye and Big Ben, all the landmarks. Instead, they just trundle slowly down side roads, and soon they're at St Pancras and she's handing over an extortionate amount of money for the privilege.

She looks at the faces of everyone she walks past, looking for her.

Despite it being Boxing Day, St Pancras is quite busy. The decorations are all still up, of course, and even though the shops have added sale signs to the windows, she passes all the same displays.

The relief that she feels upon seeing Ambrose standing under the Christmas tree is overwhelming, and she immediately bursts into tears.

Ambrose opens their arms wide as she runs right into them, almost knocking them over with the force generated from her enormous backpack.

'Thank you,' she snuffles, crying all over Ambrose's nice clothes. 'Thank you for coming to get me.'

They release Haf from the hug so they can get a better look at her. 'Someone had to come rescue you from yourself,' they say, and Haf laugh-sobs.

'I think, somehow, I've fucked things up even more,' she says nervously. She holds up the gloves.

'Nice . . . gloves?'

'They're love-declaration gloves!'

'Is that a thing?'

'Like in *Carol*!' she splutters.

Ambrose pauses. 'Ohhh, okay, I'm pretty sure that's not the plot of the book, but I get it. Very good. Very gay.'

'I have to tell her. I have to tell her that I—'

Ambrose places their hands on her shoulders. 'Stop. First, coffee. Actually, something with no caffeine in it, you're positively vibrating as it is. Then you can explain what the heck is going on, and we can work out where we're going next.'

She opens her mouth to speak but Ambrose silences her with a curt 'shh' and drags her over to the takeaway counter of the little bistro where she and Christopher had lunch a few days ago. Ambrose orders a big coffee and a hot chocolate for Haf, as well as some sandwiches wrapped in paper to take with them.

'Are you and Laurel firm friends now?' asks Haf, while they wait.

Suddenly awkward, Ambrose flushes a little. 'She, err, proposed that we work together on a line.'

'What? That's sick! I'm so proud of you,' Haf says, hopping up and down with joy.

'Yeah, I think it will be cool. And we're going to look at designing collections that can be worn by different body types, so lots of pattern wizardry, but Laurel seems really invested in learning all that. Maybe we'll even make a unisex clothing line that isn't just beige sacks.'

'Woah, woah. Don't get too ambitious,' Haf laughs.

This is what she needed. Celebrating Ambrose's wins over coffee and thinking of the good things to come for them back home together.

They take their coffees and snacks and head to the concourse.

'It'll mean I have to come down to Oxlea a bit, you know,' Ambrose says gently. 'So I might not be around as much on the weekends.'

'And when you're at home, you'll be with Paco.'

'Well, I don't know about that,' they say casually, but their cheeks flush slightly. 'But, you know you could always come with me when I come down to Oxlea.'

'I don't think I'd be welcome.'

'I wouldn't be so sure of that if I were you,' says Ambrose, who points down the station concourse.

In the far distance are Kit, Laurel and Christopher, looking around, as if searching for something.

Laurel spots Ambrose and starts waving like she's trying to flag down a taxi.

Kit spins round to face them, and yells, '*Haf!*'

'Kit?' she whispers, and then shouts, '*Kit!*'

Before she realises what she's doing, she's running. Or, as her backpack is so huge and heavy, she trots and sways, dodging out of the way of people.

'Kit!'

And Kit speeds up, yelling at tourists and Londoners to just get out of her way. 'Haf! Fuck's sake, *move. Haf!*'

Not wanting to overtake either of them, though it would be admittedly easy to as neither of them are actually moving that quickly, Laurel and Christopher fall into step behind Kit, while Ambrose slinks along behind.

They meet in the middle, under the enormous Christmas tree. Kit and Haf stand a few metres apart, watching each other, too overcome to say anything else, suddenly incapable of moving any closer.

'What are you doing here?' Haf croaks.

Too excited to wait, Laurel squeezes Kit's shoulder and yells, 'We came on a mission to get you! It was jolly exciting. Hi, Ambrose!'

'Hi, Laurel!' they say, coming to stand beside Haf.

'Wait, did you tell them where I was going to be?' Haf lowers her voice so only Ambrose can hear. 'Is this an intervention? Am I being ambushed?'

'How dare you accuse me of something so iconic?' they say with a smile as Haf throws the giant backpack to the floor. 'And no, it's not an intervention, you goof.'

Christopher clearly can't sense the divide between them, he crosses it in seconds and pulls her into a hug.

'Just go talk to her,' Christopher says in her ear.

'I'm scared,' she whispers, worrying at her lip. 'What if I missed my chance?'

'Kit hasn't come all this way to palm you off and call you a dickhead.'

'She will probably call me a dickhead.'

'Okay, not *just* that. Look at me,' he commands softly, pulling back so he can look her in the eye. 'Nothing will make this sentence less strange for me to say, but go on, go tell my sister you love her.'

It appears Kit was getting a similar encouraging talk from Laurel. They both look up at the same time, eyes locking.

Suddenly, those few metres don't seem so insurmountable.

Time slows as Kit walks over to her slowly. In the emerald wool coat that Haf first saw her in, Kit looks beautiful. She looks exactly how she did only five days ago, when they first met in the bookshop opposite them. The only difference is the candy-cane walking stick, and the deep, deep certainty that Haf loves her.

'Kit,' she bleats. 'I'm so sorry.'

She reaches out for Kit, the gloves on her hands.

'I just got them. I promise, I didn't know you'd given me them, and I'm so sorry for, quite literally, running away, because that's not what I want and—'

'Haf,' Kit says, stopping her in her spiral. 'I get it. It wasn't . . . the most upfront communication of my life. I probably shouldn't have relied on a notecard.'

'Wait, how did you—?'

'Bryn texted me,' Ambrose pipes up. 'And I told her, because she was freaking out.'

'Have you all been conspiring?' Haf asks.

'Yes,' they chorus.

'Look, I should have just told you,' Kit says.

'That's what you were supposed to do, not have a snowball fight,' huffs Laurel behind them.

Kit rolls her eyes, but smiles. 'Let me do it now, okay?'

Haf nods silently and Kit takes a deep breath in.

'For days, I'd been trying to squash how I felt. My life is complicated, Haf – my job, my health, happiness. And I know it keeps me contained, and I keep my barriers up, but that's worked for me so far. And you bring so much chaos.' She laughs, her eyes sparkling. 'I mean you waded into a fucking duck pond to fight a goose, for fuck's sake. Who does that?'

'It was to rescue a reindeer,' Haf interrupts.

With a laugh, Kit continues, 'The thing is, all this mess, how ridiculous and silly you can be, and loyal to a fault way beyond logic . . . That all scares the shit out of me. But those are also the things I love about you.' Her dark eyes shine in the Christmas lights.

At this, Haf starts crying too, and she takes Kit's hand in her own.

She *loves* her.

'I know it's only been five days, which has to be some kind of U-Haul record.' Kit laughs softly. 'But somehow it feels like the most normal thing that happened this Christmas.' She pauses, and when she speaks again she's slower, more serious. 'You have so many decisions to make about your life – like quitting your horrible, fucking job – but I want to be one of your choices. But, just in case I've got this all wrong, and you really were going to just run away from it all, just let me down gently, okay?'

'I promise you, I wasn't running away from you. I mean, I *was*, but only to your house. I just needed to calm down, process some stuff. But, your mum was just so *furious*—'

'Haf,' Kit says, stilling her. 'I just need to know that I'm not foolish for literally running across the fucking country for you.'

'You're not!' she cries.

Christopher, Ambrose and Laurel huddle together beside them, watching with hopeful eyes.

'Go on,' she sees Christopher mouth from the corner of her eye.

Haf takes a deep breath and looks up at Kit, at the woman she loves. This brave, beautiful, smart woman with the foulest mouth in the world who just admitted that she loves her too.

'This has all been such a mess. I really didn't know that you'd made up your mind and chosen me. If I had, I would have jumped out the taxi.' They both laugh. 'I am a bit scared, you know? Over the last year, I feel like every choice I made has backfired on me, but that's because I was so caught up in the bad parts, and not dealing with my feelings about them . . . And that made me afraid of all the good things I already had, and the things I *could* have. You're right my life is a mess. I'm constantly grasping at straws and things feel really hard all the time, and I just don't know what I'm doing with myself. I don't have much to offer you. But when I look at you, I don't just see now. It was never just kisses in the snow, or the cupboard—'

At this, she hears Christopher mutter 'The cupboard?' which sets her and Kit giggling like drunk teenagers.

'I want forever for us. I want to grow into the person you deserve me to be. I love you, and I want that lifetime with you.'

'Then what are you waiting for?' Kit whispers, that ever-familiar smirk on her lips.

They kiss, and it's starlight and magic. That other universe where they can be together turned out to be this one, and a future opens up before them like a truth she can touch. A lifetime of dancing in the kitchen, of falling asleep together, of whatever they want it to be.

Their tears smear on each other's cheeks as they embrace, and between glorious kisses they laugh with relief. It's a moment plucked from her wildest dreams.

Huddled together arm in arm, Ambrose and Laurel bawl their eyes out.

'It's just—'

'So beautiful.'

'I'm so proud!'

'Me too!'

Around them, a chorus of cheers and applause starts up, echoing around the cavernous train station. 'All I Want for Christmas is You' sounds from one of the community pianos across the concourse, and Haf could swear the pianist is Bryn.

Christopher steps forward and pulls both of them into a hug.

'You two have some talking to do,' Kit whispers, slipping out of his embrace after a moment.

Haf sniffs hard and wipes her eyes. 'I'm sorry, Christopher. I feel like I ruined everything. We put so much effort into it, and I tanked it by being a horny goblin.'

They both laugh through thick tears.

'You might be a horny goblin, but you didn't *ruin* anything. You helped me so much. I never thought I'd tell my parents their hopes for me weren't what I wanted. You helped me be brave enough to do that. And I told them about all of this.'

'Oh no. How did they take it all?'

'They're a little . . . confused,' he begins.

'That's putting it lightly. Esther even swore.' Kit snorts. And in a perfect impression of her mother, she says, 'Bloody hell, Christopher, go bring that girl right back here this instant.'

'"I cannot believe you made me throw out a perfectly nice young woman on Boxing Day, Christopher,"' adds Christopher in a similarly flawless mimic. 'Honestly, I can't believe that we managed to fool anyone that we were romantically involved.'

'Hey, I'm a hot little piece. You *could* have been dating me,' Haf protests.

'Imagine what a mess that would have been,' Ambrose noisily agrees.

'Anyway, all I did was balls up a gingerbread house and cause a few scenes,' Haf says.

'While technically true, that's not all, and you know that. Maybe it was fate that had us meet, because we both needed to grow up a little, and to be brave. And you've done that. Your friendship, your confidence in me kept me going and pushed me towards choosing the life I really want,' he says, wiping the tears from her cheeks.

'Okay, that does sound like a bit more,' she says, glancing at Kit. 'Thank you for introducing me to the love of my life.'

'Gross!' Kit yells, wrapping her arms around Haf.

'I'm going to dine out on this for a long time,' he says.

'Who is that?' Kit asks, pointing to the man Laurel is talking to.

When Haf realises who it is, she laughs. 'It's the bookseller who tried to get me to leave my number for you.'

'Let's go say hi, then,' laughs Kit giddily, dragging her over.

As they approach hand in hand, the bookseller shrieks with glee. 'I knew it! You don't witness an emotionally charged moment over classic of lesbian literature every day. I *knew* you were destined to meet again. It's not every day you get to see the start of a great love story.'

'No, it's not.' Laurel beams.

'So what now?' Ambrose asks.

That question, which could feel so very big, doesn't feel quite so scary under the Christmas tree.

'Let's go home,' Christopher suggests.

'What? Back to Oxlea?' Haf asks nervously.

'Why not? I drove, so there's enough room for us all,' Laurel interjects. 'Except . . .'

She looks at the bookseller, who holds up his hands.

'Don't worry about me, I'm going back to work. Good luck with it all!' And with that, he rushes back to the shop.

'Well, that's one thing sorted. Ambrose, why don't you come as well? We can get started.'

'Why not, I'm already packed,' Ambrose says.

'All right then, sounds like everything is decided,' Haf says, trying to swallow her nerves.

'It'll be fine,' Kit and Christopher promise all at once, and she believes them.

Her heart is so full of warmth for these four people who she loves so deeply, and even though she's known three of them for barely any time at all, she knows they're friends for life. And the bookseller, he seems pretty all right too.

As they pass the piano, Bryn looks up and gives her a wink. So much for never seeing each other again.

The future looks bright, finally.

# Chapter Twenty-Two

It's a tight squeeze into Laurel's car – Haf, Ambrose and Kit in the back; Christopher up front so there's room for his long legs.

'God, this is going to be weird, isn't it?' Haf whispers as they pull out of London. 'This is like a textbook nightmare daughter-in-law situation for your parents.'

'I don't think anything remotely on par has been documented.' Ambrose yawns. 'Perhaps you'll be the first case study. The case of the fake-real fake-now-real daughter-in-not-law.'

Haf busies herself by drafting up a resignation letter on Kit's phone, and in a sudden act of bravery, logs into her email and sends it. That's another choice made. Kit beams with pride and kisses her on the cheek.

And even if she's scared or worried she's making a bad decision, it doesn't matter so much. Not when she has the love of this car-full of people to guide her along.

Up front, Laurel and Christopher giggle together, and she suddenly remembers, through all her own drama, that back at the Howard party she and Kit caught them kissing.

'Hang on a minute. Are you two getting back together?' she says, leaning through the gap of the front seats.

Laurel and Christopher smile at each other for a moment.

'Well, we had a good conversation about the fact we are really different people now,' begins Christopher, in the sort of tone a parent might use to explain complex stuff to their child.

'Exactly, and we're both following our passions now, which is really exciting. And we had a really honest conversation about how we might have accidentally pushed each other down paths we didn't want to go.'

'Replicating our parents.' He sighs.

'Typical, really!' Laurel does one of her adorable honk laughs.

'And you dumped Mark?' Haf prods.

'I dumped Mark!' she says, and everyone cheers. 'Wow, so everyone really hated him then?'

'Everyone,' they chorus.

'How did he take it?' asks Kit. 'I hope he cried.'

'He did,' says Laurel, trying to suppress a grin. 'Don't be mean. He's a person with feelings too.'

'Debatable.'

'Maybe we can be a bit sorry for him because he lost me, and I am excellent.'

'That is true,' adds Christopher, and the pair of them giggle together again.

'So you *are* back together?' Haf asks again.

Laurel glances at her through the wing mirror, and then the pair of them burst into laughter.

'Absolutely not,' she says.

'Oh,' she says, feeling a little silly.

'We agreed to just be friends,' she says. 'At least, we are right now.'

'We're not discounting anything, but that's not our priority, and we want to just be in each other's lives,' Christopher explains.

'Wow . . . this is, like, terrifyingly grown-up,' Haf murmurs.

'I know, I didn't know I had it in me.' Christopher laughs.

'And instead of dating, we're going to be like each other's, oh I don't know, coach . . . supporter, I guess? We're going to help each other with our new plans. Christopher has agreed to model for Ambrose and I, and he's going to use that big brain to help me with the accounts. And I'm going to help him find a school, and I said I'd help him set up a foodstagram.'

'I wish you wouldn't call it that, though.'

'What about cakestagram?'

'What about if I make things that aren't cake?'

'Bakestagram?' offers a sleepy Ambrose.

'The point is, Laurel's going to help me set up a professional social media thing.'

'And get you on television. You were born for your own baking show, or at least one of those fun competition ones.'

'We'll see.'

'Oh trust me, we *will* see. See you on the next season!'

They roll their eyes at each other and laugh, and there's just so much love between them that this feels like a happy ending all their own. One where they choose to be back in each other's lives, but in a new way to mark the new stage of their lives.

It's kind of gorgeous, really.

They stop off at a service station so everyone can use the bathroom and pick up some sugary sweet Christmas drinks from Starbucks. Haf finishes hers just as they get close to Oxlea and starts fiddling with the lid. Perhaps having a gigantic caffeinated sugary drink before an anxiety-inducing familial situation was not the right thing to do.

Kit reaches out and stills her hand, cupping it in hers. 'Hey, you okay? Bit nervous.'

'To say the least. It's going to be deeply weird, isn't it?'

'Oh, absolutely.'

'At least we've got the little fan club.' She laughs awkwardly.

'I think they're going to find that as weird as the rest of it, at least.'

When they pull up at the Calloway house, Otto and Esther stand waiting at the door.

'Come on in, everyone,' Otto beams as jolly as Santa and as though they'd just popped to the pub.

'Especially you, Haf,' adds Esther kindly as she approaches. 'And I suppose my silly children can come in too.'

In a flash, Stella and Luna appear at her feet, bouncing and whining and wiggling. Haf crouches down to pet them, but they dash around her, too excited for their little bodies to be still.

Eventually, she gets back to her feet because really, she can't avoid it any longer, even if she really, really wants to.

Christopher and Laurel follow Esther inside the house, and Otto, who still waits by the door, beckons her, Kit and Ambrose inside. Haf gulps down her nerves as she slips off her shoes in the hallway and follows everyone into the living room. Esther takes a seat in her usual armchair, but rather than taking his, Otto stands behind her.

Kit, Haf and Christopher squeeze onto the couch, while Laurel and Ambrose hang back by the Christmas tree, briefly distracted by baby photos.

It's weird to think that only five days ago she was in here choking on mulled wine and trying to impress them. And now? Where do you begin?

Luckily, Otto breaks the silence by clearing his throat. 'So! Haf, welcome back. I believe we owe you an apology.'

'No, honestly, you don't. No one is at fault here. Well, maybe Christopher and I for lying to everyone,' she says, trying to control the roil in her stomach. 'But, Esther, you only did what any parent would do in these . . . super weird circumstances.'

Clearly gathering her thoughts, Esther sits quietly, only reacting when Otto places a loving hand on her shoulder. Eventually, she looks up and takes a deep breath. 'Haf, before . . . everything happened, I told you that I deeply admired the way you went out of your way to help people. And I still feel that way, even if I think Christopher asked you to behave in a way that's . . . beyond comprehension.'

Even though this is mostly complimentary, Haf still wants to crawl up into a little ball and just vanish. Christopher seems to feel the same because he cringes.

'And even if I don't quite understand all of it, Christopher has made it very clear that you were doing it to help him. It would be wrong of me to snub you for something that I like about you, even if I don't quite understand it.'

'It wasn't just that,' she begins, and Kit elbows her sharply as if to say stop talking, but she doesn't. 'I just don't want you to think this was purely altruistic! I didn't want to spend Christmas alone . . .'

The words hang awkwardly in the air and Haf wishes she could take them back, grab them out of the air and stuff them back into her mouth.

'Loneliness drives us all to do strange things,' says Otto kindly.

'That's how we ended up on our first date,' Esther replies, and that breaks the tension. 'What I was upset about this morning was that I thought perhaps you'd lied to us about who you were. I'm not one to trust easily, as you might have guessed, and I reacted without thinking it through. And for that, I am sorry. Even if you say it's understandable, I still behaved unkindly and didn't give you an opportunity to explain yourself or speak to my children first.'

'Thank you, Esther. I'm sorry for hurting you,' Haf says.

Esther gives her a short nod. 'So, let me get this straight,' she says, her tone returned to classic pointed, slightly disbelieving Esther. 'You two were never together? And you two are now together. And you two aren't back together, but are friends again? And I'm terribly sorry, but I don't actually know who you are.'

'Oh, I'm Ambrose, the flatmate. I'm here for moral support,' they say. 'But yes, that sounds about right.'

'Naturally,' she says, a little bemused. 'It's like the end of a key party.'

'Oh God, Mother, why do you know what a key party is?' Kit shrieks.

'I'm not dead yet, Kit.'

'I wish I was.'

'It's all perfectly simple, if you ask me.' Otto laughs. 'Now, I'm not sure which bits we are celebrating or not celebrating, but I think perhaps we should, at the very least, have a toast to the most exciting Christmas we've had. What do you say, dear?'

'Yes, I think perhaps we should toast the official new member of our family,' she agrees. And after a pause, she adds, 'And Ambrose.'

To her relief, everything goes okay. With all the secrets out in the open, a weight has been lifted. They all settle around the fire, nibbling on canapés and drinking cocktails like it was a totally normal family gathering, and not the resolution of the weirdest Christmas in history. The dogs beg for corners of pastry and bits of cheese as they eat curled up in the living room.

When Haf clears up all the plates and tidies up the kitchen, Esther appears by her side and gives her a little arm squeeze of thanks. It's going to be a while before things become easy between them, but this feels like a good start.

With a little encouragement, Christopher talks about his plans for starting patisserie school and, to Haf's reliefs, both of his parents look extremely proud of him. Practically the moment he's finished speaking, Esther pulls up her calendar and books him to make cakes for several upcoming events. She even asks Laurel and Ambrose to design her some new outfits.

While they're chatting, Otto takes her aside and says, 'Now, I realise that this might seem like a poisoned chalice given everything else, but I do have a role in the care-home side of the business I need to fill that I think you would suit. I told you those estates come with large grounds, and honestly, I haven't known where to start on making sure we've got the best use of the habitat, never mind making it more accessible for the residents and perhaps even open to the public. I think you, with your combination of people skills and the on-hand knowledge, would be a great fit for that. And to be clear, I'm offering this with no expectations and not because you're my real and fake daughter-not-quite-in-law. It's because I think you'd be an asset to the business.'

'Thank you,' she says, a little overwhelmed at the offer. 'Let's talk about it after Christmas? I'd really like to know more.'

He gives her a clap on the back, which turns into a one-armed hug.

Later, she mistakenly says she can't quite believe they got away with it all, before Ambrose reminds her that she hasn't told her parents.

'Oops, well my phone is dead,' she sighs. 'Guess it will have to wait.'

'Don't worry, I have their number,' Ambrose says, starting a call before she can object. Luckily, they do help her explain everything to them – Christopher, the fake dating, the horrible job she just quit, and best of all, Kit. They are admittedly a bit confused, even more so when Esther enquires after the ayahuasca ceremony, which obviously did not happen, but seemed to accept it anyway.

As evening turns into night, Laurel and Ambrose decide to head off. Laurel had insisted that since Ambrose was already here, they get started on their plans and demanded they come stay with her. When they stand in the hallway putting on coats and shoes, Haf grabs them both and pulls them a huge hug.

'Thank you. Both of you,' she murmurs.

'You're welcome. This is the most fun I've had in ages,' laughs Laurel, whipping out the door into the icy night air.

'Enjoy the mansion,' Haf whispers to Ambrose.

'Oh, you bet I'm making her take me horse riding in the morning.' They lean over and kiss her on the forehead. 'Proud of you.'

This is the thing that tips her over to tears, and she grabs Ambrose for another quick hug before they leave. 'See you tomorrow,' she wobbles.

Next to disappear are Otto and Esther, who leave with a slightly drunk goodnight, and a gentle urge to not stay up too late.

Once they leave, Christopher stretches out in the armchair Otto usually occupies, his long legs resting on the coffee table, while Kit and Haf stretch out to fill the whole couch together. Stella and Luna snore by the fire, and everything feels right.

'Do we still have to share a bed now the truth is out?' asks Christopher with a smile.

'Oh, you're going to miss me teasing you.'

'You're only across the hall. I'm sure you could shout loud enough for me to hear.'

'Oi, oi,' laughs Haf, which makes both of the siblings groan.

'I'm never touching you again,' Kit jabs at her with a socked foot.

'That's fair. I'll sleep down here with the dogs.'

Luckily, it doesn't come to that, and a soon she is curled up in Kit's bed. Part of her can't quite believe that after all this, she's actually here.

She stretches out her tired body, thankful for the heated under-sheet blanket Kit has on her bed. Dressed in adorable button-up pyjamas, Kit climbs into bed, resting her head on Haf's chest. Lazily, Haf strokes her hair, and a mixture of the warm blanket, relief and sheer happiness drag her towards sleep.

There are so many things still to work out – where will she work? Will she move to London to be with Kit? Or will Kit move wherever she is and find a job at a different firm? But, for once, all that unknown doesn't feel scary. Not with Kit in her arms, and all the other people who love her in her life. It feels exciting, like there's a future out there just waiting for her to grab.

'I love you,' she whispers.

'I love you too,' Kit replies sleepily. 'Let's hope next Christmas is less eventful.'

'Oh, I don't know, I quite enjoyed some parts of it.' Haf smiles. 'Even if there's no fake dating, I'm sure we can think of some chaos.'

'Can it at least be minor chaos? Contained minor chaos,' murmurs Kit, her voice thick with sleep.

'For you, anything.'

The curtains aren't pulled completely across the window, and Haf can see a bright slither of moon in the dark velvet sky. As her eyes adjust, she spies stars.

'Hey,' she whispers. 'Did you even get to make your Christmas wish?'

'Of course I did,' Kit yawns.

'What did you wish for? Or would it jinx it? Or is that only if it hasn't happened yet?'

'That would be telling.' Kit nuzzles into her side. 'That's against the rules.'

'You haven't told me what the rules are.'

'Rule one: no telling. That's it. Hmm, I guess it's just one rule.'

'Was it about me?' Haf says, which turns into a squeak as Kit pokes her.

'You're not taking this very seriously,' Kit laughs, sitting up and clambering on top of her. 'But on this occasion, I suppose I can bend the rules slightly.'

Kit's hair falls over Haf's face, her eyes twinkling in the low light.

'You're my Christmas wish, Haf Hughes. You're always going to be my Christmas wish.'

'Not *just* for Christmas?'

'After all the chaos we went through to get here?' Kit says and leans down to give her the sweetest promise of a kiss. 'I'm never letting you go.'

# Author's Note

Hello! It's me, the actual author. Thanks for reading my book, or if you're like me and love to read the acknowledgements first, I hope you like it! Anyway, I just wanted to pop in to mention something.

While Haf is not me, a lot of her emotions at the beginning of the book was pulled from a specific time in my life where everything felt like constant chaos. And a very big part of that was because I didn't know I was autistic. I was diagnosed autistic as an adult as so many people are for myriad reasons, and while I was writing Haf, I realised that her autism probably would have been missed too.

Because she doesn't know, it's not said on the page, but she was written as an autistic person (who almost certainly has undiagnosed dyspraxia too). I try not to think about characters' lives after the book ends, but that's something I know she will find out, and a lot of stuff is going to make sense for her.

If she resonated with you, I'm glad.

All my love, Hux.

# Acknowledgements

Even though there's just my name on the cover, this book would truly not exist without the help, love and support of so many people.

First of all, thank you to my agent Abi Fellows for your encouragement and also the joyful live responses as you read the first full draft – I have screenshots of the messages saved for when I need a boost. Thank you for the book swaps, and everything else. And thanks to everyone at The Good Literary Agency for supporting me; it's an honour to be aligned with such amazing change-makers.

Thank you to my marvellous editor Bea Fitzgerald for choosing me and thus enabling me to enjoy Christmas all year round. I've never seen an editorial letter with so many excited capitals and exclamation points. Thank you for encouraging me to always turn the shenanigans dial up to 11.

Thank you to the team at Hodder Studio and Hodder Books for literally everything that makes a book happen. Laura Bartholomew, Rebecca Miller, Izzy Smith, Rachel Southey, Kay Gale and Ellie Wheeldon who all helped make this book fly. Thank you to Natalie Chen and Kerry Hyndman for the amazing cover.

Thank you to all the gorgeous people who make up the Honks, Queer Tears, Hogs, Peps, Snaccs, and alt for cheering me on always – I love all of you. The Honks and Snaccs get an extra thanks for helping me crowdsource Christmas things out of season. To 2022 Debut Chat 2: strap in, Patricia. Get off Goodreads.

Special thanks also go to Charlie for introducing me to Imagine Me & You, arguably one of the greatest f/f films of all, which definitely influenced this book; to Momo for the very useful playlists and to Elle Ha (plus Matzo and Catzo) for the sprints – you have seen every word count grow.

Extra thanks go to Lauren & Slice for coming over for a BBQ, and all the garden pandemic chats; to Tom for your unbridled enthusiasm over the last twenty-two years which extended to this romcom, and to Magoo and Facey for being the Ambroses in my life during my own chaos periods – you ensured I didn't get into half as many situations as Haf does.

Thank you to my family who have all been remarkably supportive about my writing career, especially my sister Julie. Your enthusiasm for my silly kissing books makes me very happy.

Apologies, as ever, to Nerys for ignoring you while I wrote this. Stella and Luna are absolutely based on you but as you can't read, you'll just have to take my word for it.

And finally, all my thanks go to Tim for listening to me talk about this book constantly. You make me a better writer by asking the right questions, and by showing me unconditional love every single day. Sorry our house is always full of books. There's no place I'd rather be than curled up with you.

# About The Author

Lizzie Huxley-Jones is an autistic author and editor based in London.

They are the editor of *Stim*, an anthology of autistic authors and artists, which was published by Unbound in April 2020 to coincide with World Autism Awareness Week. They are also the author of the children's biography *Sir David Attenborough: A Life Story* (2020) and a contributor to the anthology *Allies: Real Talk About Showing Up, Screwing Up, And Trying Again* (2021).

They tweet too much and enjoy taking breaks to walk their dog Nerys.

# Bookends

# When one book ends, another begins...

Bookends is a vibrant new reading community to help you ensure you're never without a good book.

You'll find exclusive previews of the brilliant new books from your favourite authors as well as exciting debuts and past classics. Read our blog, check out our recommendations for your reading group, enter great competitions and much more!

Visit our website to see which great books we're recommending this month.

Join the Bookends community:
# www.welcometobookends.co.uk

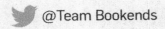 @Team Bookends   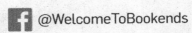 @WelcomeToBookends

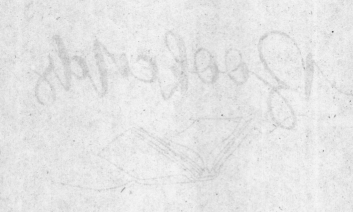